Blood on the Tracks

Edited and Introduced by Martin Edwards

P.O. Box 4410, Naperville, Illinois 60563-4410

(630) 961-3900

sourcebooks.com

Printed and bound in the United States of America.

POD

Contents

Introduction

Blood on the Tracks celebrates the classic railway mystery. Trains and rail travel have long provided evocative settings for tales of murder and mayhem, and succeeding generations of crime writers have made ingenious use of them.

The range of railway mystery stories is astonishingly diverse: from classic whodunits such as Agatha Christie's Murder on the Orient Express to those best-selling novels of psychological suspense, published more than sixty years apart, Patricia Highsmith's Strangers on a Train and Paula Hawkins' The Girl on the Train. And we can add to the eclectic mix a host of other titles, including Graham Greene's Stamboul Train, and John Godey's The Taking of Pelham One Two Three. All those books were adapted for film, while other memorable mystery movies set on trains include Alfred Hitchcock's The Lady Vanishes (based on Ethel Lina White's The Wheel Spins), Night Train to Munich (a film indebted to The Wheel Spins but enjoyable in its own right) and Transsiberian, a lively thriller released in 2008 and starring Woody Harrelson, Emily Mortimer, and Ben Kingsley.

A pleasing illustration of the unexpected links between trains and detective stories is supplied by 'Coronation Scot', composed by Vivian Ellis and named after the express train which ran on the L.M.S. Railway in the 1930s. The music became a popular, and somehow perfectly appropriate, theme tune for the long-running and incident-packed adventures broadcast in the BBC radio series Paul Temple.

What is it about train travel that makes it such a suitable background for a mystery? Part of the answer surely lies in the enclosed nature of life on board a train—the restrictions of space make for a wonderfully atmospheric environment in which tensions can rise rapidly between a small 'closed circle' of murder suspects or characters engaged (as in the enjoyable old film Sleeping Car to Trieste) in a deadly game of cat and mouse. Similarly, a train journey may provide a mobile equivalent of the 'locked room' scenario beloved of crime writers and readers alike, as several clever stories in this anthology demonstrate.

The immense potential of the train-based mystery was quickly recognised by nineteenth century writers. The most notable examples were Charles Dickens, one or two echoes of whose splendid tale of the supernatural 'The Signalman' can be found in stories in this book, and Arthur Conan Doyle, one of whose most entertaining non-Sherlockian puzzles features here. But there were several others, including L.T. Meade and Robert Eustace, one of whose 'impossible crime' stories featuring the 'ghost exposer' John Bell is included here.

John Oxenham's 'A Mystery of the Underground', originally serialised in Jerome K. Jerome's magazine To-Day in 1897, was a story about a serial killer on the Tube which is said to have caused such consternation amongst the travelling pub-lic that it led to a reduction in passenger numbers until the hysteria subsided. Modern readers can find it in the British Library anthology Capital Crimes. Underground railways are even more claustrophobic than their overground counterparts, and they have supplied backgrounds to stories as different in mood as Mavis Doriel Hay's Murder Underground, Cornell Woolrich's 'The Phantom of the Subway', and Michael Gilbert's 'A Case for Gourmets'.

The first specialist railway detective was Victor L. Whitechurch's Godfrey Page, a train enthusiast and amateur sleuth who appeared in a story published by Pearson's Weekly in 1903. Whitechurch, steeped in railway lore, and a regular contributor of articles to The Railway Magazine, subsequently created a rather more memorable railway detective in the vegetarian Thorpe Hazell, one of whose cases is included in this book.

As the years went by, writers of detective fiction increasingly set their mysteries on trains. An entertaining example is Death in the Tunnel, an ingenious novel by Miles Burton, which features his regular sleuth, Desmond Merrion. Burton is better known as John Rhode, whose vast output of novels include Tragedy on the Line, Dead on the Track, and Death on the Boat Train.

Like Murder Underground, Death in the Tunnel has been reprinted by the British Library, and so has J. Jefferson Farjeon's Mystery in White, a Christmas crime story which begins with a train journey coming to an abrupt end in a snowdrift. The most famous crime novel in which a train gets stuck in the snow remains Murder on the Orient Express; Agatha Christie wrote two other novels in which trains play such an important part as to earn a mention in the title, The Mystery of the Blue Train and 4.50 from Paddington. In a characteristically innovative touch, Christie has a plume of smoke from a passing train provide a significant clue to the solution of the puzzle in Taken at the Flood.

Freeman Wills Crofts, a railwayman who became a best-selling crime writer, regularly featured trains in his novels and short stories; one example, 'The Level Crossing', is included here. A strange coincidence arose in 1930, when Dorothy L. Sayers was working on a Lord Peter Wimsey novel, The Five Red Herrings. She wrote to her publisher, Victor Gollancz, that: 'The book, in which all the places are real and which turns on actual distances and real railway time-tables, is laid in exactly the same part of the country as Freeman Wills Crofts' new book, which also turns on real distances and time-tables.' The Crofts book to which she referred was Sir John Magill's Last Journey, and the pair discovered the similarities between their works-in-progress while corresponding with each other about something else. As Sayers said, 'The two plots are, of course, entirely different, and it doesn't really matter a pin.' She was right about that, but the incident is a reminder of the way in which, quite innocently, writers often chance upon similar concepts at much the same time.

In The Five Red Herrings, Sayers elaborated (with due acknowledgment) upon a plot device originated by J.J. Connington, who—like Sayers and Crofts—became a founder member of the Detection Club. In The Two Tickets Puzzle, Connington's Superintendent Ross investigates the murder of Oswald K. Preston, shot dead on the 10.35 from Horston. Connington was an exponent of the 'fair play' mystery that gave the reader every opportunity to compete with the fictional sleuth, and his US publishers emphasised that the book featured 'clever reasoning from the clues but no superhuman brain stuff'. Another Detection Club member, Milward Kennedy, found himself unable to resist poking gentle fun at his colleagues in Death to the Rescue, in which he refers to their 'tricky way with train tickets'.

Following the Second World War, railway mysteries in the traditional vein continued to appear; a notable example is Edmund Crispin's 'Beware of the Trains', included in the British Library anthology Miraculous Mysteries. This story, like 'The Problem of the Locked Caboose' by the prolific American Edward D. Hoch, illustrates how a railway setting can provide a superb background for an 'impossible crime' story. As late as 1967, Leo Bruce, a novelist more commonly associated with crime writing in the Golden Age tradition, published Death of a Commuter, a case investigated by his amateur sleuth Carolus Deene.

In an era of train cancellations, delays, and industrial action by drivers and guards, there is little scope for murder mysteries in which the culprits construct ingenious alibis reliant upon trains running to time. Unexpectedly, however, the railway detective has enjoyed a resurgence of popularity in the twenty-first century, thanks to two series with well-researched historical settings. Edward Marston's books set in the mid-nineteenth century and featuring Inspector Colbeck and Sergeant Leeming have won a devoted following, and the same is true of Andrew Martin's books about Jim Stringer. One feels sure that Victor L. Whitechurch would approve.

Recent years have seen a resurgence of interest in rail heritage in Britain, and preserved railways up and down the country enjoy a special place in the affections of the travelling public. The revival of interest in the Golden Age of Steam, like the renewed enthusiasm from long-forgotten books published during the Golden Age of Murder, owes something to nostalgia, and the parallels are emphasised by the reading public's enthusiasm for the cover artwork of the Crime Classics books, derived from vintage railway posters. But in each case, there is more to the renaissance than mere sentiment. A trip on, say the Severn Valley or Tal-y-Llyn Railways offers a highly enjoyable experience in its own right, and so do stories written by such fine authors as Anthony Berkeley, Christopher St John Sprigg, Anthony Rolls, and company.

Blood on the Tracks will, I hope, appeal both to train buffs and crime fans. Railway mysteries written over a span of more than half a century are presented in roughly chronological order, and the contributors include some of the most popular authors of their day, as well as less familiar names. I would like to express my thanks to Rob, Maria, and Abbie at the British Library for their support and hard work in bringing this book into being, and I hope that its contents will beguile even the most wearisome commute or long distance train journey.

Martin Edwards
www.martinedwardsbooks.com

The Man with the Watches

Arthur Conan Doyle

Arthur Conan Doyle was a seasoned traveller, and his love of train journeys is evident in several of his stories, including an excellent Sherlock Holmes tale, 'The Adventure of the Bruce-Partington Plans', and a non-series story, 'The Lost Special'; the latter is included in the British Library anthology Miraculous Mysteries.

This story was included in Doyle's collection Round the Fire (1908), but was first published in The Strand Magazine ten years earlier, at a time when Holmes had, as far as Doyle was concerned, been killed in a fatal encounter with Professor Moriarty at the Reichenbach Falls. Like 'The Lost Special', this is an example of the 'impossible crime' mystery, and it presents a puzzle that would tax Holmes himself. Doyle enjoys himself with a joke by presenting a solution to the riddle conceived by 'a well-known criminal investigator'—but is the un-named sleuth correct?

———

There are many who will still bear in mind the singular circumstances which, under the heading of the Rugby Mystery, filled many columns of the daily Press in the spring of the year 1892. Coming as it did at a period of exceptional dullness, it attracted perhaps rather more attention than it deserved, but it offered to the public that mixture of the whimsical and the tragic which is most stimulating to the popular imagination. Interest drooped, however, when, after weeks of fruitless investigation, it was found that no final explanation of the facts was forthcoming, and the tragedy seemed from that time to the present to have finally taken its place in the dark catalogue of inexplicable and unexpiated crimes. A recent communication (the authenticity of which appears to be above question) has, however, thrown some new and clear light upon the matter. Before laying it before the public it would be as well, perhaps, that I should refresh their memories as to the singular facts upon which this commentary is founded. These facts were briefly as follows:

At five o'clock on the evening of the 18th of March in the year already mentioned, a train left Euston Station for Manchester. It was a rainy, squally day, which grew wilder as it progressed, so it was by no means the weather in which anyone would travel who was not driven to do so by necessity. The train, however, is a favourite one among Manchester business men who are returning from town, for it does the journey in four hours and twenty minutes, with only three stoppages upon the way. In spite of the inclement evening it was, therefore, fairly well filled upon the occasion of which I speak. The guard of the train was a tried servant of the company—a man who had worked for twenty-two years without blemish or complaint. His name was John Palmer.

The station clock was upon the stroke of five, and the guard was about to give the customary signal to the engine-driver when he observed two belated passengers hurrying down the platform. The one was an exceptionally tall man, dressed in a long, black overcoat with astrakhan collar and cuffs. I have already said that the evening was an inclement one, and the tall traveller had the high, warm collar turned up to protect his throat against the bitter March wind. He appeared, as far as the guard could judge by so hurried an inspection, to be a man between fifty and sixty years of age, who had retained a good deal of the vigour and activity of his youth. In one hand he carried a brown leather Gladstone bag. His companion was a lady, tall and erect, walking with a vigorous step which outpaced the gentleman beside her. She wore a long, fawn-coloured dust-cloak, a black, close-fitting toque, and a dark veil which concealed the greater part of her face. The two might very well have passed as father and daughter. They walked swiftly down the line of carriages, glancing in at the windows, until the guard, John Palmer, overtook them.

'Now, then, sir, look sharp, the train is going,' said he.

'First-class,' the man answered.

The guard turned the handle of the nearest door. In the carriage which he had opened, there sat a small man with a cigar in his mouth. His appearance seems to have impressed itself upon the guard's memory, for he was prepared, afterwards, to describe or to identify him. He was a man of thirty-four or thirty-five years of age, dressed in some grey material, sharp-nosed, alert, with a ruddy, weather-beaten face, and a small, closely cropped, black beard. He glanced up as the door was opened. The tall man paused with his foot upon the step.

'This is a smoking compartment. The lady dislikes smoke,' said he, looking round at the guard.

'All right! Here you are, sir!' said John Palmer. He slammed the door of the smoking carriage, opened that of the next one, which was empty, and thrust the two travellers in. At the same moment he sounded his whistle and the wheels of the train began to move. The man with the cigar was at the window of his carriage, and said something to the guard as he rolled past him, but the words were lost in the bustle of the departure. Palmer stepped into the guard's van, as it came up to him, and thought no more of the incident.

Twelve minutes after its departure the train reached Willesden Junction, where it stopped for a very short interval. An examination of the tickets has made it certain that no one either joined or left it at this time, and no passenger was seen to alight upon the platform. At 5.14 the journey to Manchester was resumed, and Rugby was reached at 6.50, the express being five minutes late.

At Rugby the attention of the station officials was drawn to the fact that the door of one of the first-class carriages was open. An examination of that compartment, and of its neighbour, disclosed a remarkable state of affairs.

The smoking carriage in which the short, red-faced man with the black beard had been seen was now empty. Save for a half-smoked cigar, there was no trace whatever of its recent occupant. The door of this carriage was fastened. In the next compartment, to which attention had been originally drawn, there was no sign either of the gentleman with the astrakhan collar or of the young lady who accompanied him. All three passengers had disappeared. On the other hand, there was found upon the floor of this carriage—the one in which the tall traveller and the lady had been—a young man, fashionably dressed and of elegant appearance. He lay with his knees drawn up, and his head resting against the farther door, an elbow upon either seat. A bullet had penetrated his heart and his death must have been instantaneous. No one had seen such a man enter the train, and no railway ticket was found in his pocket, neither were there any markings upon his linen, nor papers nor personal property which might help to identify him. Who he was, whence he had come, and how he had met his end were each as great a mystery as what had occurred to the three people who had started an hour and a half before from Willesden in those two compartments.

I have said that there was no personal property which might help to identify him, but it is true that there was one peculiarity about this unknown young man which was much commented upon at the time. In his pockets were found no fewer than six valuable gold watches, three in the various pockets of his waistcoat, one in his ticket-pocket, one in his breast-pocket, and one small one set in a leather strap and fastened round his left wrist. The obvious explanation that the man was a pickpocket, and that this was his plunder, was discounted by the fact that all six were of American make and of a type which is rare in England. Three of them bore the mark of the Rochester Watchmaking Company; one was by Mason, of Elmira; one was unmarked; and the small one, which was highly jewelled and ornamented, was from Tiffany, of New York. The other contents of his pocket consisted of an ivory knife with a corkscrew by Rodgers, of Sheffield; a small, circular mirror, one inch in diameter; a re-admission slip to the Lyceum Theatre; a silver box full of vesta matches, and a brown leather cigar-case containing two cheroots—also two pounds fourteen shillings in money. It was clear, then, that whatever motives may have led to his death, robbery was not among them. As already mentioned, there were no markings upon the man's linen, which appeared to be new, and no tailor's name upon his coat. In appearance he was young, short, smooth-cheeked, and delicately featured. One of his front teeth was conspicuously stopped with gold.

On the discovery of the tragedy an examination was instantly made of the tickets of all passengers, and the number of the passengers themselves was counted. It was found that only three tickets were unaccounted for, corresponding to the three travellers who were missing. The express was then allowed to proceed, but a new guard was sent with it, and John Palmer was detained as a witness at Rugby. The carriage which included the two compartments in question was uncoupled and side-tracked. Then, on the arrival of Inspector Vane, of Scotland Yard, and of Mr Henderson, a detective in the service of the railway company, an exhaustive inquiry was made into all the circumstances.

That crime had been committed was certain. The bullet, which appeared to have come from a small pistol or revolver, had been fired from some little distance, as there was no scorching of the clothes. No weapon was found in the compartment (which finally disposed of the theory of suicide), nor was there any sign of the brown leather bag which the guard had seen in the hand of the tall gentleman. A lady's parasol was found upon the rack, but no other trace was to be seen of the travellers in either of the sections. Apart from the crime, the question of how or why three passengers (one of them a lady) could get out of the train, and one other get in during the unbroken run between Willesden and Rugby, was one which excited the utmost curiosity among the general public, and gave rise to much speculation in the London Press.

John Palmer, the guard, was able at the inquest to give some evidence which threw a little light upon the matter.

There was a spot between Tring and Cheddington, according to his statement, where, on account of some repairs to the line, the train had for a few minutes slowed down to a pace not exceeding eight or ten miles an hour. At that place it might be possible for a man, or even for an exceptionally active woman, to have left the train without serious injury. It was true that a gang of platelayers was there, and that they had seen nothing, but it was their custom to stand in the middle between the metals, and the open carriage door was upon the far side, so that it was conceivable that someone might have alighted unseen, as the darkness would by that time be drawing in. A steep embankment would instantly screen anyone who sprang out from the observation of the navvies.

The guard also deposed that there was a good deal of movement upon the platform at Willesden Junction, and that though it was certain that no one had either joined or left the train there, it was still quite possible that some of the passengers might have changed unseen from one compartment to another. It was by no means uncommon for a gentleman to finish his cigar in a smoking carriage and then to change to a clearer atmosphere. Supposing that the man with the black beard had done so at Willesden (and the half-smoked cigar upon the floor seemed to favour the supposition), he would naturally go into the nearest section, which would bring him into the company of the two other actors in this drama. Thus the first stage of the affair might be surmised without any great breach of probability. But what the second stage had been, or how the final one had been arrived at, neither the guard nor the experienced detective officers could suggest.

A careful examination of the line between Willesden and Rugby resulted in one discovery which might or might not have a bearing upon the tragedy. Near Tring, at the very place where the train slowed down, there was found at the bottom of the embankment a small pocket Testament, very shabby and worn. It was printed by the Bible Society of London, and bore an inscription: 'From John to Alice. Jan. 13th, 1856,' upon the flyleaf. Underneath was written: 'James, July 4th, 1859,' and beneath that again: 'Edward. Nov. 1st, 1869,' all the entries being in the same handwriting. This was the only clue, if it could be called a clue, which the police obtained, and the coroner's verdict of 'Murder by a person or persons unknown' was the unsatisfactory ending of a singular case. Advertisement, rewards, and inquiries proved equally fruitless, and nothing could be found which was solid enough to form the basis for a profitable investigation.

It would be a mistake, however, to suppose that no theories were formed to account for the facts. On the contrary, the Press, both in England and in America, teemed with suggestions and suppositions, most of which were obviously absurd. The fact that the watches were of American make, and some peculiarities in connection with the gold stopping of his front tooth, appeared to indicate that the deceased was a citizen of the United States, though his linen, clothes and boots were undoubtedly of British manufacture. It was surmised, by some, that he was concealed under the seat, and that, being discovered, he was for some reason, possibly because he had overheard their guilty secrets, put to death by his fellow-passengers. When coupled with generalities as to the ferocity and cunning of anarchical and other secret societies, this theory sounded as plausible as any.

The fact that he should be without a ticket would be consistent with the idea of concealment, and it was well known that women played a prominent part in the Nihilistic propaganda. On the other hand, it was clear, from the guard's statement, that the man must have been hidden there before the others arrived, and how unlikely the coincidence that conspirators should stray exactly into the very compartment in which a spy was already concealed! Besides, this explanation ignored the man in the smoking carriage, and gave no reason at all for his simultaneous disappearance. The police had little difficulty in showing that such a theory would not cover the facts, but they were unprepared in the absence of evidence to advance any alternative explanation.

There was a letter in the Daily Gazette, over the signature of a well-known criminal investigator, which gave rise to a considerable discussion at the time. He had formed a hypothesis which had at least ingenuity to recommend it, and I cannot do better than append it in his own words.

'Whatever may be the truth,' said he, 'it must depend upon some bizarre and rare combination of events, so we need have no hesitation in postulating such events in our explanation. In the absence of data we must abandon the analytic or scientific method of investigation, and must approach it in the synthetic fashion. In a word, instead of taking known events and deducing from them what has occurred, we must build up a fanciful explanation if it will only be consistent with known events. We can then test this explanation by any fresh facts which may arise. If they all fit into their places, the probability is that we are upon the right track, and with each fresh fact this probability increases in a geometrical progression until the evidence becomes final and convincing.

'Now, there is one most remarkable and suggestive fact which has not met with the attention which it deserves. There is a local train running through Harrow and King's Langley, which is timed in such a way that the express must have overtaken it at or about the period when it eased down its speed to eight miles an hour on account of the repairs of the line. The two trains would at that time be travelling in the same direction at a similar rate of speed and upon parallel lines. It is within every one's experience how, under such circumstances, the occupant of each carriage can see very plainly the passengers in the other carriages opposite to him. The lamps of the express had been lit at Willesden, so that each compartment was brightly illuminated, and most visible to an observer from outside.

'Now, the sequence of events as I reconstruct them would be after this fashion. This young man with the abnormal number of watches was alone in the carriage of the slow train. His ticket, with his papers and gloves and other things, was, we will suppose, on the seat beside him. He was probably an American, and also probably a man of weak intellect. The excessive wearing of jewellery is an early symptom in some forms of mania.

'As he sat watching the carriages of the express which were (on account of the state of the line) going at the same pace as himself, he suddenly saw some people in it whom he knew. We will suppose for the sake of our theory that these people were a woman whom he loved and a man whom he hated— and who in return hated him. The young man was excitable and impulsive. He opened the door of his carriage, stepped from the footboard of the local train to the footboard of the express, opened the other door, and made his way into the presence of these two people. The feat (on the supposition that the trains were going at the same pace) is by no means so perilous as it might appear.

'Having now got our young man, without his ticket, into the carriage in which the elder man and the young woman are travelling, it is not difficult to imagine that a violent scene ensued. It is possible that the pair were also Americans, which is the more probable as the man carried a weapon— an unusual thing in England. If our supposition of incipient mania is correct, the young man is likely to have assaulted the other. As the upshot of the quarrel the elder man shot the intruder, and then made his escape from the carriage, taking the young lady with him. We will suppose that all this happened very rapidly, and that the train was still going at so slow a pace that it was not difficult for them to leave it. A woman might leave a train going at eight miles an hour. As a matter of fact, we know that this woman did do so.

'And now we have to fit in the man in the smoking carriage. Presuming that we have, up to this point, reconstructed the tragedy correctly, we shall find nothing in this other man to cause us to reconsider our conclusions. According to my theory, this man saw the young fellow cross from one train to the other, saw him open the door, heard the pistol-shot, saw the two fugitives spring out on to the line, realised that murder had been done, and sprang out himself in pursuit. Why he has never been heard of since—whether he met his own death in the pursuit, or whether, as is more likely, he was made to realise that it was not a case for his interference—is a detail which we have at present no means of explaining. I acknowledge that there are some difficulties in the way. At first sight, it might seem improbable that at such a moment a murderer would burden himself in his flight with a brown leather bag. My answer is that he was well aware that if the bag were found his identity would be established. It was absolutely necessary for him to take it with him. My theory stands or falls upon one point, and I call upon the railway company to make strict inquiry as to whether a ticket was found unclaimed in the local train through Harrow and King's

Langley upon the 18th of March. If such a ticket were found my case is proved. If not, my theory may still be the correct one, for it is conceivable either that he travelled without a ticket or that his ticket was lost.'

To this elaborate and plausible hypothesis the answer of the police and of the company was, first, that no such ticket was found; secondly, that the slow train would never run parallel to the express; and, thirdly, that the local train had been stationary in King's Langley Station when the express, going at fifty miles an hour, had flashed past it. So perished the only satisfying explanation, and five years have elapsed without supplying a new one. Now, at last, there comes a statement which covers all the facts, and which must be regarded as authentic. It took the shape of a letter dated from New York, and addressed to the same criminal investigator whose theory I have quoted. It is given here in extenso, with the exception of the two opening paragraphs, which are personal in their nature:

'You'll excuse me if I'm not very free with names. There's less reason now than there was five years ago when mother was still living. But for all that, I had rather cover up our tracks all I can. But I owe you an explanation, for if your idea of it was wrong, it was a mighty ingenious one all the same. I'll have to go back a little so as you may understand all about it.

'My people came from Bucks, England, and emigrated to the States in the early fifties. They settled in Rochester, in the State of New York, where my father ran a large dry goods store. There were only two sons: myself, James, and my brother, Edward. I was ten years older than my brother, and after my father died I sort of took the place of a father to him, as an elder brother would. He was a bright, spirited boy, and just one of the most beautiful creatures that ever lived. But there was always a soft spot in him, and it was like mould in cheese, for it spread and spread, and nothing that you could do would stop it. Mother saw it just as clearly as I did, but she went on spoiling him all the same, for he had such a way with him that you could refuse him nothing. I did all I could to hold him in, and he hated me for my pains.

'At last he fairly got his head, and nothing that we could do would stop him. He got off into New York, and went rapidly from bad to worse. At first he was only fast, and then he was criminal; and then, at the end of a year or two, he was one of the most notorious young crooks in the city. He had formed a friendship with Sparrow MacCoy, who was at the head of his profession as a bunco-steerer, green goodsman, and general rascal. They took to card-sharping, and frequented some of the best hotels in New York. My brother was an excellent actor (he might have made an honest name for himself if he had chosen), and he would take the parts of a young Englishman of title, of a simple lad from the West, or of a college under-graduate, whichever suited Sparrow MacCoy's purpose. And then one day he dressed himself as a girl, and he carried it off so well, and made himself such a valuable decoy, that it was their favourite game afterwards. They had made it right with Tammany and with the police, so it seemed as if nothing could ever stop them, for those were in the days before the Lexow Commission, and if you only had a pull, you could do pretty nearly everything you wanted.

'And nothing would have stopped them if they had only stuck to cards and New York, but they must needs come up Rochester way, and forge a name upon a cheque. It was my brother that did it, though everyone knew that it was under the influence of Sparrow MacCoy. I bought up that cheque, and a pretty sum it cost me. Then I went to my brother, laid it before him on the table, and swore to him that I would prosecute if he did not clear out of the country. At first he simply laughed. I could not prosecute, he said, without breaking our mother's heart, and he knew that I would not do that. I made him understand, however, that our mother's heart was being broken in any case, and that I had set firm on the point that I would rather see him in Rochester gaol than in a New York hotel. So at last he gave in, and he made me a solemn promise that he would see Sparrow MacCoy no more, that he would go to Europe, and that he would turn his hand to any honest trade that I helped him to get. I took him down right away to an old family friend, Joe Willson, who is an exporter of American watches and clocks, and I got him to give Edward an agency in London, with a small salary and a 15 per cent commission on all business. His manner and appearance were so good that he won the old man over at once, and within a week he was sent off to London with a case full of samples.

'It seemed to me that this business of the cheque had really given my brother a fright, and that there was some chance of his settling down into an honest line of life. My mother had spoken with him, and what she said had touched him, for she had always been the best of mothers to him and he had been the great sorrow of her life. But I knew that this man Sparrow MacCoy had a great influence over Edward and my chance of keeping the lad straight lay in breaking the connection between them. I had a friend in the New York detective force, and through him I kept a watch upon MacCoy. When, within a fortnight of my brother's sailing, I heard that MacCoy had taken a berth in the Etruria, I was as certain as if he had told me that he was going over to England for the purpose of coaxing Edward back again into the ways that he had left. In an instant I had resolved to go also and to pit my influence against MacCoy's. I knew it was a losing fight, but I thought, and my mother thought, that it was my duty. We passed the last night together in prayer for my success, and she gave me her own Testament that my father had given her on the day of their marriage in the Old Country, so that I might always wear it next my heart.

'I was a fellow-traveller, on the steamship, with Sparrow MacCoy, and at least I had the satisfaction of spoiling his little game for the voyage. The very first night I went into the smoking-room, and found him at the head of a card-table, with half a dozen young fellows who were carrying their full purses and their empty skulls over to Europe. He was settling down for his harvest, and a rich one it would have been. But I soon changed all that.

'"Gentleman," said I, "are you aware whom you are playing with?"

'"What's that to you? You mind your own business!" said he, with an oath.

'"Who is it, anyway?" asked one of the dudes.

'"He's Sparrow MacCoy, the most notorious card-sharper in the States."

'Up he jumped with a bottle in his hand, but he remembered that he was under the flag of the effete Old Country, where law and order run, and Tammany has no pull. Gaol and the gallows wait for violence and murder, and there's no slipping out by the back door on board an ocean liner.

'"Prove your words, you—!" said he.'

'"I will!" said I. "If you will turn up your right shirt-sleeve to the shoulder, I will either prove my words or I will eat them."

'He turned white and said not a word. You see, I knew something of his ways, and I was aware that part of the mechanism which he and all such sharpers use consists of an elastic down the arm with a clip just above the wrist. It is by means of this clip that they withdraw from their hands the cards which they do not want, while they substitute other cards from another hiding-place. I reckoned on it being there, and it was. He cursed me, slunk out of the saloon, and was hardly seen again during the voyage. For once, at any rate, I got level with Mister Sparrow MacCoy.

'But he soon had his revenge upon me, for when it came to influencing my brother he outweighed me every time. Edward had kept himself straight in London for the first few weeks, and had done some business with his American watches, until this villain came across his path once more. I did my best, but the best was little enough. The next thing I heard there had been a scandal at one of the Northumberland Avenue hotels: a traveller had been fleeced of a large sum by two confederate card-sharpers, and the matter was in the hands of Scotland Yard. The first I learned of it was in the evening paper, and I was at once certain that my brother and MacCoy were back at their old games. I hurried at once to Edward's lodgings. They told me that he and a tall gentleman (whom I recognised as MacCoy) had gone off together, and that he had left the lodgings and taken his things with him. The landlady had heard them give several directions to the cabman, ending with Euston Station, and she had accidentally overheard the tall gentleman saying something about Manchester. She believed that that was their destination.

'A glance at the time-table showed me that the most likely train was at five, though there was another at 4.35 which they might have caught. I had only time to get the later one, but found no sign of them either at the depot or in the train. They must have gone on by the earlier one, so I determined to follow them to Manchester and search for them in the hotels there. One last appeal to my brother by all that he owed to my mother might even now be the salvation of him. My nerves were overstrung, and I lit a cigar to steady them. At that moment, just as the train was moving off, the door of my compartment was flung open, and there were MacCoy and my brother on the platform.

"They were both disguised, and with good reason, for they knew that the London police were after them. MacCoy had a great astrakhan collar drawn up, so that only his eyes and nose were showing. My brother was dressed like a woman, with a black veil half down his face, but of course it did not deceive me for an instant, nor would it have done so even if I had not known that he had often used such a dress before. I started up, and as I did so MacCoy recognised me. He said something, the conductor slammed the door, and they were shown into the next compartment. I tried to stop the train so as to follow them, but the wheels were already moving, and it was too late.

'When we stopped at Willesden, I instantly changed my carriage. It appears that I was not seen to do so, which is not surprising, as the station was crowded with people. MacCoy, of course, was expecting me, and he had spent the time between Euston and Willesden in saying all he could to harden my brother's heart and set him against me. That is what I fancy, for I had never found him so impossible to soften or to move. I tried this way and I tried that; I pictured his future in an English gaol; I described the sorrow of his mother when I came back with the news; I said everything to touch his heart, but all to no purpose. He sat there with a fixed sneer upon his handsome face, while every now and then Sparrow MacCoy would throw in a taunt at me, or some word of encouragement to hold my brother to his resolutions.

'"Why don't you run a Sunday-school?" he would say to me, and then, in the same breath: "He thinks you have no will of your own. He thinks you are just the baby brother and that he can lead you where he likes. He's only just finding out that you are a man as well as he."

'It was those words of his which set me talking bitterly. We had left Willesden, you understand, for all this took some time. My temper got the better of me, and for the first time in my life I let my brother see the rough side of me. Perhaps it would have been better had I done so earlier and more often.

'"A man!" said I. "Well, I'm glad to have your friend's assurance of it, for no one would suspect it to see you like a boarding-school missy. I don't suppose in all this country there is a more contemptible-looking creature than you are as you sit there with that Dolly pinafore upon you." He coloured up at that, for he was a vain man, and he winced from ridicule.

'"It's only a dust-cloak," said he, and he slipped it off. "One has to throw the coppers off one's scent, and I had no other way to do it." He took his toque off with the veil attached, and he put both it and the cloak into his brown bag. "Anyway, I don't need to wear it until the conductor comes round," said he.

'"Nor then, either," said I, and taking the bag I slung it with all my force out of the window. "Now," said I, "you'll never make a Mary Jane of yourself while I can help it. If nothing but that disguise stands between you and a gaol, then to gaol you shall go."

'That was the way to manage him. I felt my advantage at once. His supple nature was one which yielded to roughness far more readily than to entreaty. He flushed with shame, and his eyes filled with tears. But MacCoy saw my advantage also and was determined that I should not pursue it.

'"He's my pard, and you shall not bully him," he cried.

'"He's my brother, and you shall not ruin him," said I. "I believe a spell of prison is the very best way of keeping you apart, and you shall have it, or it will be no fault of mine."

'"Oh, you would squeal, would you?" he cried, and in an instant he whipped out his revolver. I sprang for his hand, but saw that I was too late and jumped aside. At the same instant he fired, and the bullet which would have struck me passed through the heart of my unfortunate brother.

'He dropped without a groan upon the floor of the compartment, and MacCoy and I, equally horrified, knelt at each side of him, trying to bring back some signs of life. MacCoy still held the loaded revolver in his hand, but his anger against me and my resentment towards him had both for the moment been swallowed up in this sudden tragedy. It was he who first realised the situation. The train was for some reason going very slowly at the moment, and he saw his opportunity for escape. In an instant he had the door open, but I was as quick as he, and jumping upon him the two of us fell off the footboard and rolled in each other's arms down a steep embankment. At the bottom I struck my head against a stone, and I remembered nothing more. When I came to myself I was lying among some low bushes, not far from the railroad track, and somebody was bathing my head with a wet handkerchief. It was Sparrow MacCoy.

'"I guess I couldn't leave you," said he. "I didn't want to have the blood of two of you on my hands in one day. You loved your brother, I've no doubt; but you didn't love him a cent more than I loved him, though you'll say that I took a queer way to show it. Anyhow, it seems a mighty empty world now that he is gone, and I don't care a continental whether you give me over to the hangman or not."

'He had turned his ankle in the fall, and there we sat, he with his useless foot, and I with my throbbing head, and we talked and talked until gradually my bitterness began to soften and to turn into something like sympathy. What was the use of revenging his death upon a man who was as much stricken by that death as I was? And then, as my wits gradually returned, I began to realise also that I could do nothing against MacCoy which would not recoil upon my mother and myself. How could we convict him without a full account of my brother's career being made public—the very thing which of all others we wished to avoid? It was really as much our interest as his to cover the matter up, and from being an avenger of crime I found myself changed to a conspirator against Justice. The place in which we found ourselves was one of those pheasant preserves which are so common in the Old Country, and as we groped our way through it I found myself consulting the slayer of my brother as to how far it would be possible to hush it up.

'I soon realised from what he said that unless there were some papers of which we knew nothing in my brother's pockets, there was really no possible means by which the police could identify him or learn how he had got there. His ticket was in MacCoy's pocket, and so was the ticket for some baggage which they had left at the depot. Like most Americans, he had found it cheaper and easier to buy an outfit in London than to bring one from New York, so that all his linen and clothes were new and unmarked. The bag, containing the dust-cloak, which I had thrown out of the window, may have fallen among some bramble patch where it is still concealed, or may have been carried off by some tramp, or may have come into the possession of the police, who kept the incident to themselves. Anyhow, I have seen nothing about it in the London papers. As to the watches, they were a selection from those which had been intrusted to him for business purposes. It may have been for the same business purposes that he was taking them to Manchester, but—well, it's too late to enter into that.

'I don't blame the police for being at fault. I don't see how it could have been otherwise. There was just one little clue that they might have followed up, but it was a small one. I mean that small, circular mirror which was found in my brother's pocket. It isn't a very common thing for a young man to carry about with him, is it? But a gambler might have told you what such a mirror may mean to a card-sharper. If you sit back a little from the table, and lay the mirror, face upwards, upon your lap, you can see, as you deal, every card that you give to your adversary. It is not hard to say whether you see a man or raise him when you know his cards as well as your own. It was as much a part of a sharper's outfit as the elastic clip upon Sparrow MacCoy's arm. Taking that, in connection with the recent frauds at the hotels, the police might have got hold of one end of the string.

'I don't think there is much more for me to explain. We got to a village called Amersham that night in the character of two gentlemen upon a walking tour, and afterwards we made our way quietly to London, whence MacCoy went on to Cairo, and I returned to New York. My mother died six months afterwards, and I am glad to say that to the day of her death she never knew what happened. She was always under the delusion that Edward was earning an honest living in London, and I never had the heart to tell her the truth. He never wrote; but, then, he never did write at any time, so that made no difference. His name was the last upon her lips.

'There's just one other thing that I have to ask you, sir, and I should take it as a kind return for all this explanation, if you could do it for me. You remember that Testament that was picked up. I always carried it in my inside pocket, and it must have come out in my fall. I value it very highly, for it was the family book with my birth and my brother's marked by my father in the beginning of it. I wish you would apply at the proper place and have it sent to me. It can be of no possible value to anyone else. If you address it to X, Bassano's Library, Broadway, New York, it is sure to come to hand.'

The Mystery of Felwyn Tunnel

L. T. Meade and Robert Eustace

L.T. Meade and Robert Eustace might seem, at first sight, to be unlikely literary collaborators, but their writing partnership enjoyed considerable success between 1898 and 1903. The Meade name concealed the identity of Elizabeth Thomasina Meade-Smith (1844–1914), an exceptionally prolific author who was best-known for books for young readers, but wrote in a range of genres, including historical, romantic, and crime fiction. She collaborated with Dr Clifford Halifax (in reality a doctor called Edgar Beaumont), who provided her with scientific know-how before joining forces with another pseudonymous medical man, Eustace, who performed a similar role. Eustace's real name was Eustace Robert Barton (1871–1943), and he later wrote with Edgar Jepson, most famously on a classic 'impossible crime' story, 'The Tea Leaf', and with Dorothy L. Sayers on *The Documents in the Case* (1930), her only detective novel in which Lord Peter Wimsey does not appear.

Meade and Eustace created two female arch-villains, Madame Kalouchy and Madame Sara; the latter, an exotic character whose skills included plastic surgery, chemistry, and impersonation, appeared in half a dozen stories gathered in *The Sorceress of the Strand* (1902). This story comes from *A Master of Mysteries* (1898), sometimes said to be the first collection of 'impossible crime' tales. The book chronicles the cases of John Bell, a wealthy sceptic and 'exposer of ghosts' who uses his scientific knowledge to make sense of 'queer events, enveloped at first in mystery, and apparently dark with portent, but, nevertheless, when grappled with in the true spirit of science, capable of explanation'.

———

I was making experiments of some interest at South Kensington, and hoped that I had perfected a small but not unimportant discovery, when, on returning home one evening in late October in the year 1893, I found a visiting card on my table. On it were inscribed the words, 'Mr Geoffrey Bainbridge.' This name was quite unknown to me, so I rang the bell and inquired of my servant who the visitor had been. He described him as a gentleman who wished to see me on most urgent business, and said further that Mr Bainbridge intended to call again later in the evening. It was with both curiosity and vexation that I awaited the return of the stranger. Urgent business with me generally meant a hurried rush to one part of the country or the other. I did not want to leave London just then; and when at half-past nine Mr Geoffrey Bainbridge was ushered into my room, I received him with a certain coldness which he could not fail to perceive. He was a tall, well-dressed, elderly man. He immediately plunged into the object of his visit.

'I hope you do not consider my unexpected presence an intrusion, Mr Bell,' he said. 'But I have heard of you from our mutual friends, the Greys of Uplands. You may remember once doing that family a great service.'

'I remember perfectly well,' I answered more cordially. 'Pray tell me what you want; I shall listen with attention.'

'I believe you are the one man in London who can help me,' he continued. 'I refer to a matter especially relating to your own particular study. I need hardly say that whatever you do will not be unrewarded.'

'That is neither here nor there,' I said; 'but before you go any further, allow me to ask one question. Do you want me to leave London at present?'

He raised his eyebrows in dismay.

'I certainly do,' he answered.

'Very well; pray proceed with your story.'

He looked at me with anxiety.

'In the first place,' he began, 'I must tell you that I am chairman of the Lytton Vale Railway Company in Wales, and that it is on an important matter connected with our line that I have come to consult you. When I explain to you the nature of the mystery, you will not wonder, I think, at my soliciting your aid.'

'I will give you my closest attention,' I answered; and then I added, impelled to say the latter words by a certain expression on his face, 'if I can see my way to assisting you I shall be ready to do so.'

'Pray accept my cordial thanks,' he replied. 'I have come up from my place at Felwyn today on purpose to consult you. It is in that neighbourhood that the affair has occurred. As it is essential that you should be in possession of the facts of the whole matter, I will go over things just as they happened.'

I bent forward and listened attentively.

'This day fortnight,' continued Mr Bainbridge, 'our quiet little village was horrified by the news that the signalman on duty at the mouth of the Felwyn Tunnel had been found dead under the most mysterious circumstances. The tunnel is at the end of a long cutting between Llanlys and Felwyn stations. It is about a mile long, and the signal-box is on the Felwyn side. The place is extremely lonely, being six miles from the village across the mountains. The name of the poor fellow who met his death in this mysterious fashion was David Pritchard. I have known him from a boy, and he was quite one of the steadiest and most trustworthy men on the line. On Tuesday evening he went on duty at six o'clock; on Wednesday morning the day-man who had come to relieve him was surprised not to find him in the box. It was just getting daylight, and the 6.30 local was coming down, so he pulled the signals and let her through. Then he went out, and, looking up the line towards the tunnel, saw Pritchard lying beside the line close to the mouth of the tunnel. Roberts, the day-man, ran up to him and found, to his horror, that he was quite dead. At first Roberts naturally supposed that he had been cut down by a train, as there was a wound at the back of the head; but he was not lying on the metals. Roberts ran back to the box and telegraphed through to Felwyn Station. The message was sent on to the village, and at half-past seven o'clock the police inspector came up to my house with the news. He and I, with the local doctor, went off at once to the tunnel. We found the dead man lying beside the metals a few yards away from the mouth of the tunnel, and the doctor immediately gave him a careful examination. There was a depressed fracture at the back of the skull, which must have caused his death; but how he came by it was not so clear. On examining the whole place most carefully, we saw, further, that there were marks on the rocks at the steep side of the embankment as if some one had tried to scramble up them. Why the poor fellow had attempted such a climb, God only knows. In doing so he must have slipped and fallen back on to the line, thus causing the fracture of the skull. In no case could he have gone up more than eight or ten feet, as the banks of the cutting run sheer up, almost perpendicularly, beyond that point for more than a hundred and fifty feet. There are some sharp boulders beside the line, and it was possible that he might have fallen on one of these and so sustained the injury. The affair must have occurred some time between 11.45 p.m. and 6 a.m., as the engine-driver of the express at 11.45 p.m. states that the line was signalled clear, and he also caught sight of Pritchard in his box as he passed.'

'This is deeply interesting,' I said; 'pray proceed.'

Bainbridge looked at me earnestly; he then continued:—

'The whole thing is shrouded in mystery. Why should Pritchard have left his box and gone down to the tunnel? Why, having done so, should he have made a wild attempt to scale the side of the cutting, an impossible feat at any time? Had danger threatened, the ordinary course of things would have been to run up the line towards the signal-box. These points are quite unexplained. Another curious fact is that death appears to have taken place just before the day-man came on duty, as the light at the mouth of the tunnel had been put out, and it was one of the night signalman's duties to do this as soon as daylight appeared; it is possible, therefore, that Pritchard went down to the tunnel for that purpose. Against this theory, however, and an objection that seems to nullify it, is the evidence of Dr Williams, who states that when he examined the body his opinion was that death had taken place some hours before. An inquest was held on the following day, but before it took place there was a new and most important development. I now come to what I consider the crucial point in the whole story.

'For a long time there had been a feud between Pritchard and another man of the name of Wynne, a platelayer on the line. The object of their quarrel was the blacksmith's daughter in the neighbouring village—a remarkably pretty girl and an arrant flirt. Both men were madly in love with her, and she played them off one against the other. The night but one before his death Pritchard and Wynne had met at the village inn, had quarrelled in the bar—Lucy, of course, being the subject of their difference. Wynne was heard to say (he was a man of powerful build and subject to fits of ungovernable rage) that he would have Pritchard's life. Pritchard swore a great oath that he would get Lucy on the following day to promise to marry him. This oath, it appears, he kept, and on his way to the signal-box on Tuesday evening met Wynne and triumphantly told him that Lucy had promised to be his wife. The men had a hand-to-hand fight on the spot, several people from the village being witnesses of it. They were separated with difficulty, each vowing vengeance on the other. Pritchard went off to his duty at the signal-box, and Wynne returned to the village to drown his sorrows at the public-house.

'Very late that same night Wynne was seen by a villager going in the direction of the tunnel. The man stopped him and questioned him. He explained that he had left some of his tools on the line and was on his way to fetch them. The villager noticed that he looked queer and excited but not wishing to pick a quarrel thought it best not to question him further. It has been proved that Wynne never returned home that night, but came back at an early hour on the following morning, looking dazed and stupid. He was arrested on suspicion, and at the inquest the verdict was against him.'

'Has he given any explanation of his own movements?' I asked.

'Yes; but nothing that can clear him. As a matter of fact, his tools were nowhere to be seen on the line, nor did he bring them home with him. His own story is that being considerably the worse for drink, he had fallen down in one of the fields and slept there till morning.'

'Things look black against him,' I said.

'They do; but listen, I have something more to add. Here comes a very queer feature in the affair. Lucy Ray, the girl who had caused the feud between Pritchard and Wynne, after hearing the news of Pritchard's death, completely lost her head, and ran frantically about the village declaring that Wynne was the man she really loved, and that she had only accepted Pritchard in a fit of rage with Wynne for not himself bringing matters to the point. The case looks very bad against Wynne, and yesterday the magistrate committed him for trial at the coming assizes. The unhappy Lucy Ray and the young man's parents are in a state bordering on distraction.'

'What is your own opinion with regard to Wynne's guilt?' I asked.

'Before God, Mr Bell, I believe the poor fellow is innocent, but the evidence against him is very strong. One of the favourite theories is that he went down to the tunnel and extinguished the light, knowing that this would bring Pritchard out of his box to see what was the matter, and that he then attacked him, striking the blow which fractured the skull.'

'Has any weapon been found about, with which he could have given such a blow?'

'No; nor has anything of the kind been discovered on Wynne's person; that fact is decidedly in his favour.'

'But what about the marks on the rocks?' I asked.

'It is possible that Wynne may have made them in order to divert suspicion by making people think that Pritchard must have fallen, and so killed himself. The holders of this theory base their belief on the absolute want of cause for Pritchard's trying to scale the rock. The whole thing is the most absolute enigma. Some of the country folk have declared that the tunnel is haunted (and there certainly has been such a rumour current among them for years). That Pritchard saw some apparition and in wild terror sought to escape from it by climbing the rocks, is another theory, but only the most imaginative hold it.'

'Well, it is a most extraordinary case,' I replied.

'Yes, Mr Bell, and I should like to get your opinion of it. Do you see your way to elucidate the mystery?'

'Not at present; but I shall be happy to investigate the matter to my utmost ability.'

'But you do not wish to leave London at present?'

'That is so; but a matter of such importance cannot be set aside. It appears, from what you say, that Wynne's life hangs more or less on my being able to clear away the mystery?'

'That is indeed the case. There ought not to be a single stone left unturned to get at the truth, for the sake of Wynne. Well, Mr Bell, what do you propose to do?'

'To see the place without delay,' I answered.

'That is right; when can you come?'

'Whenever you please.'

'Will you come down to Felwyn with me tomorrow? I shall

leave Paddington by the 7.10, and if you will be my guest I shall be only too pleased to put you up.'

'That arrangement will suit me admirably,' I replied. 'I will meet you by the train you mention, and the affair shall have my best attention.'

'Thank you,' he said, rising. He shook hands with me and took his leave.

The next day I met Bainbridge at Paddington Station, and we were soon flying westward in the luxurious private compartment that had been reserved for him. I could see by his abstracted manner and his long lapses of silence that the mysterious affair at Felwyn Tunnel was occupying all his thoughts.

It was two o'clock in the afternoon when the train slowed down at the little station of Felwyn. The station-master was at the door in an instant to receive us.

'I have some terribly bad news for you, sir,' he said, turning to Bainbridge as we alighted; 'and yet in one sense it is a relief, for it seems to clear Wynne.'

'What do you mean?' cried Bainbridge. 'Bad news? Speak out at once!'

'Well, sir, it is this: there has been another death at Felwyn signal-box. John Davidson, who was on duty last night, was found dead at an early hour this morning in the very same place where we found poor Pritchard.'

'Good God!' cried Bainbridge, starting back, 'what an awful thing! What, in the name of Heaven, does it mean, Mr Bell? This is too fearful. Thank goodness you have come down with us.'

'It is as black a business as I ever heard of, sir,' echoed the station-master; 'and what we are to do I don't know. Poor Davidson was found dead this morning, and there was neither mark nor sign of what killed him—that is the extraordinary part of it. There's a perfect panic abroad, and not a signalman on the line will take duty tonight. I was quite in despair and was afraid at one time that the line would have to be closed, but at last it occurred to me to wire to Lytton Vale, and they are sending down an inspector. I expect him by a special every moment. I believe this is he coming now,' added the station-master, looking up the line.

There was the sound of a whistle down the valley, and in a few moments a single engine shot into the station, and an official in uniform stepped on to the platform.

'Good-evening, sir,' he said, touching his cap to Bainbridge; 'I have just been sent down to inquire into this affair at the Felwyn Tunnel, and though it seems more of a matter for a Scotland Yard detective than one of ourselves, there was nothing for it but to come. All the same, Mr Bainbridge, I cannot say that I look forward to spending tonight alone at the place.'

'You wish for the services of a detective, but you shall have some one better,' said Bainbridge, turning towards me. 'This gentleman, Mr John Bell, is the man of all others for our business. I have just brought him down from London for the purpose.'

An expression of relief flitted across the inspector's face.

'I am very glad to see you, sir,' he said to me, 'and I hope you will be able to spend the night with me in the signal-box. I must say I don't much relish the idea of tackling the thing single-handed; but with your help, sir, I think we ought to get to the bottom of it somehow. I am afraid there is not a man on the line who will take duty until we do. So it is most important that the thing should be cleared and without delay.'

I readily assented to the inspector's proposition, and Bainbridge and I arranged that we should call for him at four o'clock at the village inn and drive him to the tunnel.

We then stepped into the waggonette which was waiting for us and drove to Bainbridge's house.

Mrs Bainbridge came out to meet us, and was full of the tragedy. Two pretty girls also ran to greet their father and to glance inquisitively at me. I could see that the entire family was in a state of much excitement.

'Lucy Ray has just left, Father,' said the elder of the girls. 'We had much trouble to soothe her; she is in a frantic state.'

'You have heard, Mr Bell, all about this dreadful mystery?' said Mrs Bainbridge as she led me towards the dining-room.

'Yes,' I answered; 'your husband has been good enough to give me every particular.'

'And you have really come here to help us?'

'I hope I may be able to discover the cause,' I answered.

'It certainly seems most extraordinary,' continued Mrs Bainbridge. 'My dear,' she continued, turning to her husband, 'you can easily imagine the state we were all in this morning when the news of the second death was brought to us.'

'For my part,' said Ella Bainbridge, 'I am sure that Felwyn Tunnel is haunted. The villagers have thought so for a long time, and this second death seems to prove it, does it not?' Here she looked anxiously at me.

'I can offer no opinion,' I replied, 'until I have sifted the matter thoroughly.'

'Come, Ella, don't worry Mr Bell,' said her father; 'if he is as hungry as I am, he must want his lunch.'

We then seated ourselves at the table and commenced the meal. Bainbridge, although he professed to be hungry, was in such a state of excitement that he could scarcely eat. Immediately after lunch he left me to the care of his family and went into the village.

'It is just like him,' said Mrs Bainbridge; 'he takes these sort of things to heart dreadfully. He is terribly upset about Lucy Ray, and also about the poor fellow Wynne. It is certainly a fearful tragedy from first to last.'

'Well, at any rate,' I said, 'this fresh death will upset the evidence against Wynne.'

'I hope so, and there is some satisfaction in the fact. Well, Mr Bell, I see you have finished lunch; will you come into the drawing-room?'

I followed her into a pleasant room overlooking the valley of the Lytton.

By-and-by Bainbridge returned, and soon afterwards the dog-cart came to the door. My host and I mounted, Bainbridge took the reins, and we started off at a brisk pace.

'Matters get worse and worse,' he said the moment we were alone. 'If you don't clear things up tonight, Bell, I say frankly that I cannot imagine what will happen.'

We entered the village, and as we rattled down the ill-paved streets I was greeted with curious glances on all sides. The people were standing about in groups, evidently talking about the tragedy and nothing else. Suddenly, as our trap bumped noisily over the paving-stones, a girl darted out of one of the houses and made frantic motions to Bainbridge to stop the horse. He pulled the mare nearly up on her haunches, and the girl came up to the side of the dog-cart.

'You have heard it?' she said, speaking eagerly and in a gasping voice. 'The death which occurred this morning will clear Stephen Wynne, won't it, Mr Bainbridge?—it will, you are sure, are you not?'

'It looks like it, Lucy, my poor girl,' he answered. 'But there, the whole thing is so terrible that I scarcely know what to think.'

She was a pretty girl with dark eyes, and under ordinary

circumstances must have had the vivacious expression of face and the brilliant complexion which so many of her country-women possess. But now her eyes were swollen with weeping and her complexion more or less disfigured by the agony she had gone through. She looked piteously at Bainbridge, her lips trembling. The next moment she burst into tears.

'Come away, Lucy,' said a woman who had followed her out of the cottage; 'Fie—for shame! Don't trouble the gentlemen; come back and stay quiet.'

'I can't, mother, I can't,' said the unfortunate girl. 'If they hang him, I'll go clean off my head. Oh, Mr Bainbridge, do say that the second death has cleared him!'

'I have every hope that it will do so, Lucy,' said Bainbridge, 'but now don't keep us, there's a good girl; go back into the house. This gentleman has come down from London on purpose to look into the whole matter. I may have good news for you in the morning.'

The girl raised her eyes to my face with a look of intense pleading. 'Oh, I have been cruel and a fool, and I deserve everything,' she gasped; 'but, sir, for the love of Heaven, try to clear him.'

I promised to do my best.

Bainbridge touched up the mare, she bounded forward, and Lucy disappeared into the cottage with her mother.

The next moment we drew up at the inn where the Inspector was waiting, and soon afterwards were bowling along between the high banks of the country lanes to the tunnel. It was a cold, still afternoon; the air was wonderfully keen, for a sharp frost had held the countryside in its grip for the last two days. The sun was just tipping the hills to westward when the trap pulled up at the top of the cutting. We hastily alighted, and the Inspector and I bade Bainbridge good-bye. He said that he only wished that he could stay with us for the night, assured us that little sleep would visit him, and that he would be back at the cutting at an early hour on the following morning; then the noise of his horse's feet was heard fainter and fainter as he drove back over the frost-bound roads. The Inspector and I ran along the little path to the wicket-gate in the fence, stamping our feet on the hard ground to restore circulation after our cold drive. The next moment we were looking down upon the scene of the mysterious deaths, and a weird and lonely place it looked. The tunnel was at one end of the rock cutting, the sides of which ran sheer down to the line for over a hundred and fifty feet. Above the tunnel's mouth the hills rose one upon the other. A more dreary place it would have been difficult to imagine. From a little clump of pines a delicate film of blue smoke rose straight up on the still air. This came from the chimney of the signal-box.

As we started to descend the precipitous path the Inspector sang out a cheery 'Hullo!' The man on duty in the box immediately answered. His voice echoed and reverberated down the cutting, and the next moment he appeared at the door of the box. He told us that he would be with us immediately; but we called back to him to stay where he was, and the next instant the Inspector and I entered the box.

'The first thing to do,' said Henderson the Inspector, 'is to send a message down the line to announce our arrival.'

This he did, and in a few moments a crawling goods train came panting up the cutting. After signalling her through we descended the wooden flight of steps which led from the box down to the line and walked along the metals towards the tunnel till we stood on the spot where poor Davidson had been found dead that morning. I examined the ground and all around it most carefully. Everything tallied exactly with the description I had received. There could be no possible way of approaching the spot except by going along the line, as the rocky sides of the cutting were inaccessible.

'It is a most extraordinary thing, sir,' said the signalman whom we had come to relieve. 'Davidson had neither mark nor sign on him—there he lay stone dead and cold, and not a bruise nowhere; but Pritchard had an awful wound at the back of the head. They said he got it by climbing the rocks—here, you can see the marks for yourself, sir. But now, is it likely that Pritchard would try to climb rocks like these, so steep as they are?'

'Certainly not,' I replied.

'Then how do you account for the wound, sir?' asked the man with an anxious face.

'I cannot tell you at present,' I answered.

'And you and Inspector Henderson are going to spend the night in the signal-box?'

'Yes.'

A horrified expression crept over the signalman's face.

'God preserve you both,' he said; 'I wouldn't do it—not for fifty pounds. It's not the first time I have heard tell that Felwyn Tunnel is haunted. But, there, I won't say any more about that. It's a black business and has given trouble enough. There's poor Wynne, the same thing as convicted of the murder of Pritchard; but now they say that Davidson's death will clear him. Davidson was as good a fellow as you would come across this side of the country; but for the matter of that, so was Pritchard. The whole thing is terrible—it upsets one, that it do, sir.'

'I don't wonder at your feelings,' I answered; 'but now, see here, I want to make a most careful examination of everything. One of the theories is that Wynne crept down this rocky side and fractured Pritchard's skull. I believe such a feat to be impossible. On examining these rocks I see that a man might climb up the side of the tunnel as far as from eight to ten feet, utilising the sharp projections of rock for the purpose; but it would be out of the question for any man to come down the cutting. No; the only way Wynne could have approached Pritchard was by the line itself. But, after all, the real thing to discover is this,' I continued: 'what killed Davidson? Whatever caused his death is, beyond doubt, equally responsible for Pritchard's. I am now going into the tunnel.'

Inspector Henderson went in with me. The place struck damp and chill. The walls were covered with green, evil-smelling fungi, and through the brickwork the moisture was oozing and had trickled down in long lines to the ground. Before us was nothing but dense darkness.

When we re-appeared the signalman was lighting the red lamp on the post, which stood about five feet from the ground just above the entrance to the tunnel.

'Is there plenty of oil?' asked the Inspector.

'Yes, sir, plenty,' replied the man. 'Is there anything more I can do for either of you gentlemen?' he asked, pausing, and evidently dying to be off.

'Nothing,' answered Henderson; 'I will wish you good-evening.'

'Good-evening to you both,' said the man. He made his way quickly up the path and was soon lost to sight.

Henderson and I then returned to the signal-box.

By this time it was nearly dark.

'How many trains pass in the night?' I asked of the Inspector.

'There's the 10.20 down express,' he said, 'it will pass here at about 10.40; then there's the 11.45 up, and then not another train till the 6.30 local tomorrow morning. We shan't have a very lively time,' he added.

I approached the fire and bent over it, holding out my hands to try and get some warmth into them.

'It will take a good deal to persuade me to go down to the tunnel, whatever I may see there,' said the man. 'I don't think, Mr Bell, I am a coward in any sense of the word, but there's something very uncanny about this place, right away from the rest of the world. I don't wonder one often hears of signalmen going mad in some of these lonely boxes. Have you any theory to account for these deaths, sir?'

'None at present,' I replied.

'This second death puts the idea of Pritchard being murdered quite out of court,' he continued.

'I am sure of it,' I answered.

'And so am I, and that's one comfort,' continued Henderson. 'That poor girl, Lucy Ray, although she was to be blamed for her conduct, is much to be pitied now; and as to poor Wynne himself, he protests his innocence through thick and thin. He was a wild fellow, but not the sort to take the life of a fellow-creature. I saw the doctor this afternoon while I was waiting for you at the inn, Mr Bell, and also the police sergeant. They both say they do not know what Davidson died of. There was not the least sign of violence on the body.'

'Well, I am as puzzled as the rest of you,' I said. 'I have one or two theories in my mind, but none of them will quite fit the situation.'

The night was piercingly cold, and, although there was not a breath of wind, the keen and frosty air penetrated into the lonely signal-box. We spoke little, and both of us were doubtless absorbed by our own thoughts and speculations. As to Henderson, he looked distinctly uncomfortable, and I cannot say that my own feelings were too pleasant. Never had I been given a tougher problem to solve, and never had I been so utterly at my wits' end for a solution.

Now and then the Inspector got up and went to the telegraph instrument, which intermittently clicked away in its box. As he did so he made some casual remark and then sat down again. After the 10.40 had gone through, there followed a period of silence which seemed almost oppressive. All at once the stillness was broken by the whirr of the electric bell, which sounded so sharply in our ears that we both started. Henderson rose.

'That's the 11.45 coming,' he said, and, going over to the three long levers, he pulled two of them down with a loud clang. The next moment, with a rush and a scream, the express tore down the cutting, the carriage lights streamed past in a rapid flash, the ground trembled, a few sparks from the engine whirled up into the darkness, and the train plunged into the tunnel.

'And now,' said Henderson, as he pushed back the levers, 'not another train till daylight. My word, it is cold!'

It was intensely so. I piled some more wood on the fire and, turning up the collar of my heavy ulster, sat down at one end of the bench and leant my back against the wall. Henderson did likewise; we were neither of us inclined to speak. As a rule, whenever I have any night work to do, I am never troubled with sleepiness, but on this occasion I felt unaccountably drowsy. I soon perceived that Henderson was in the same condition.

'Are you sleepy?' I asked of him.

'Dead with it, sir,' was his answer; 'but there's no fear, I won't drop off.'

I got up and went to the window of the box. I felt certain that if I sat still any longer I should be in a sound sleep. This would never do. Already it was becoming a matter of torture to keep my eyes open. I began to pace up and down; I opened the door of the box and went out on the little platform.

'What's the matter, sir?' inquired Henderson, jumping up with a start.

'I cannot keep awake,' I said.

'Nor can I,' he answered, 'and yet I have spent nights and nights of my life in signal-boxes and never was the least bit drowsy; perhaps it's the cold.'

'Perhaps it is,' I said; 'but I have been out on as freezing nights before, and—'

The man did not reply; he had sat down again; his head was nodding.

I was just about to go up to him and shake him, when it suddenly occurred to me that I might as well let him have his sleep out. I soon heard him snoring, and he presently fell forward in a heap on the floor. By dint of walking up and down, I managed to keep from dropping off myself, and in torture which I shall never be able to describe, the night wore itself away. At last, towards morning, I awoke Henderson.

'You have had a good nap,' I said; 'but never mind, I have been on guard and nothing has occurred.'

'Good God! Have I been asleep?' cried the man.

'Sound,' I answered.

'Well, I never felt anything like it,' he replied. 'Don't you find the air very close, sir?'

'No,' I said; 'it is as fresh as possible; it must be the cold.'

'I'll just go and have a look at the light at the tunnel,' said the man; 'it will rouse me.'

He went on to the little platform, whilst I bent over the fire and began to build it up. Presently he returned with a scared look on his face. I could see by the light of the oil lamp which hung on the wall that he was trembling.

'Mr Bell,' he said, 'I believe there is somebody or something down at the mouth of the tunnel now.' As he spoke he clutched me by the arm. 'Go and look,' he said; 'whoever it is, it has put out the light.'

'Put out the light?' I cried. 'Why, what's the time?'

Henderson pulled out his watch.

'Thank goodness, most of the night is gone,' he said; 'I didn't know it was so late, it is half-past five.'

'Then the local is not due for an hour yet?' I said.

'No; but who should put out the light?' cried Henderson.

I went to the door, flung it open, and looked out. The dim outline of the tunnel was just visible looming through the darkness, but the red light was out.

'What the dickens does it mean, sir?' gasped the Inspector. 'I know the lamp had plenty of oil in it. Can there be any one standing in front of it, do you think?'

We waited and watched for a few moments, but nothing stirred.

'Come along,' I said, 'let us go down together and see what it is.'

'I don't believe I can do it, sir; I really don't!'

'Nonsense,' I cried. 'I shall go down alone if you won't accompany me. Just hand me my stick, will you?'

'For God's sake, be careful, Mr Bell. Don't go down, whatever you do. I expect this is what happened before, and the poor fellows went down to see what it was and died there. There's some devilry at work, that's my belief.'

'That is as it may be,' I answered shortly; 'but we certainly shall not find out by stopping here. My business is to get to the bottom of this, and I am going to do it. That there is danger of some sort, I have very little doubt; but danger or not, I am going down.'

'If you'll be warned by me, sir, you'll just stay quietly here.'

'I must go down and see the matter out,' was my answer. 'Now listen to me, Henderson. I see that you are alarmed, and I don't wonder. Just stay quietly where you are and watch, but if I call come at once. Don't delay a single instant. Remember I am putting my life into your hands. If I call "Come," just come to me as quick as you can, for I may want help. Give me that lantern.'

He unhitched it from the wall, and taking it from him, I walked cautiously down the steps on to the line. I still felt curiously, unaccountably drowsy and heavy. I wondered at this, for the moment was such a critical one as to make almost any man wide awake. Holding the lamp high above my head, I walked rapidly along the line. I hardly knew what I expected to find. Cautiously along the metals I made my way, peering right and left until I was close to the fatal spot where the bodies had been found. An uncontrollable shudder passed over me. The next moment, to my horror, without the slightest warning, the light I was carrying went out, leaving me in total darkness. I started back, and stumbling against one of the loose boulders reeled against the wall and nearly fell. What was the matter with me? I could hardly stand. I felt giddy and faint, and a horrible sensation of great tightness seized me across the chest. A loud ringing noise sounded in my ears. Struggling madly for breath, and with the fear of impending death upon me, I turned and tried to run from a danger I could neither understand nor grapple with. But before I had taken two steps my legs gave way from under me, and uttering a loud cry I fell insensible to the ground.

———

Out of an oblivion which, for all I knew, might have lasted for moments or centuries, a dawning consciousness came to me. I knew that I was lying on hard ground; that I was absolutely incapable of realising, nor had I the slightest inclination to discover, where I was. All I wanted was to lie quite still and undisturbed. Presently I opened my eyes.

Some one was bending over me and looking into my face.

'Thank God, he is not dead,' I heard in whispered tones. Then, with a flash, memory returned to me.

'What has happened?' I asked.

'You may well ask that, sir,' said the Inspector gravely. 'It has been touch and go with you for the last quarter of an hour; and a near thing for me too.'

I sat up and looked around me. Daylight was just beginning to break, and I saw that we were at the bottom of the steps that led up to the signal-box. My teeth were chattering with the cold, and I was shivering like a man with ague.

'I am better now,' I said; 'just give me your hand.'

I took his arm, and, holding the rail with the other hand, staggered up into the box and sat down on the bench.

'Yes, it has been a near shave,' I said; 'and a big price to pay for solving a mystery.'

'Do you mean to say you know what it is?' asked Henderson eagerly.

'Yes,' I answered, 'I think I know now; but first tell me how long was I unconscious?'

'A good bit over half an hour, sir, I should think. As soon as I heard you call out I ran down as you told me, but before I got to you I nearly fainted. I never had such a horrible sensation in my life. I felt as weak as a baby, but I just managed to seize you by the arms and drag you along the line to the steps, and that was about all I could do.'

'Well, I owe you my life,' I said; 'just hand me that brandy flask, I shall be the better for some of its contents.'

I took a long pull. Just as I was laying the flask down Henderson started from my side.

'There,' he cried, 'the 6.30 is coming.' The electric bell at the instrument suddenly began to ring. 'Ought I to let her go through, sir?' he inquired.

'Certainly,' I answered. 'That is exactly what we want. Oh, she will be all right.'

'No danger to her, sir?'

'None, none; let her go through.'

He pulled the lever, and the next moment the train tore through the cutting.

'Now I think it will be safe to go down again,' I said. 'I believe I shall be able to get to the bottom of this business.'

Henderson stared at me aghast.

'Do you mean that you are going down again to the tunnel?' he gasped.

'Yes,' I said; 'give me those matches. You had better come too. I don't think there will be much danger now; and there is daylight, so we can see what we are about.'

The man was very loth to obey me, but at last I managed to persuade him. We went down the line, walking slowly, and at this moment we both felt our courage revived by a broad and cheerful ray of sunshine.

'We must advance cautiously,' I said, 'and be ready to run back at a moment's notice.'

'God knows, sir, I think we are running a great risk,' panted poor Henderson; 'and if that devil or whatever else it is should happen to be about—why, daylight or no daylight—'

'Nonsense! Man,' I interrupted; 'if we are careful, no harm will happen to us now. Ah! And here we are!' We had reached the spot where I had fallen. 'Just give me a match, Henderson.'

He did so, and I immediately lit the lamp. Opening the glass of the lamp, I held it close to the ground and passed it to and fro. Suddenly the flame went out.

'Don't you understand now?' I said, looking up at the Inspector.

'No, I don't, sir,' he replied with a bewildered expression.

Suddenly, before I could make an explanation, we both heard shouts from the top of the cutting, and looking up I saw Bainbridge hurrying down the path. He had come in the dog-cart to fetch us.

'Here's the mystery,' I cried as he rushed up to us, 'and a deadlier scheme of Dame Nature's to frighten and murder poor humanity I have never seen.'

As I spoke I lit the lamp again and held it just above a tiny fissure in the rock. It was at once extinguished.

'What is it?' said Bainbridge, panting with excitement.

'Something that nearly finished *me*,' I replied. 'Why, this is a natural escape of choke damp. Carbonic acid gas—the deadliest gas imaginable because it gives no warning of its presence and it has no smell. It must have collected here during the hours of the night when no train was passing, and gradually rising put out the signal light. The constant rushing of the trains through the cutting all day would temporarily disperse it.'

As I made this explanation Bainbridge stood like one electrified, while a curious expression of mingled relief and horror swept over Henderson's face.

'An escape of carbonic acid gas is not an uncommon phenomenon in volcanic districts,' I continued, 'as I take this to be; but it is odd what should have started it. It has sometimes been known to follow earthquake shocks, when there is a profound disturbance of the deep strata.'

'It is strange that you should have said that,' said Bainbridge, when he could find his voice.

'What do you mean?'

'Why, that about the earthquake. Don't you remember, Henderson,' he added, turning to the Inspector, 'we had felt a slight shock all over South Wales about three weeks back?'

'Then that, I think, explains it,' I said. 'It is evident that Pritchard really did climb the rocks in a frantic attempt to escape from the gas and fell back on to these boulders. The other man was cut down at once, before he had time to fly.'

'But what is to happen now?' asked Bainbridge. 'Will it go on for ever? How are we to stop it?'

'The fissure ought to be drenched with lime water, and then filled up; but all really depends on what is the size of the supply and also the depth. It is an extremely heavy gas, and would lie at the bottom of a cutting like water. I think there is more here just now than is good for us,' I added.

'But how,' continued Bainbridge, as we moved a few steps from the fatal spot, 'do you account for the interval between the first death and the second?'

'The escape must have been intermittent. If wind blew down the cutting, as probably was the case before this frost set in, it would keep the gas so diluted that its effects would not be noticed. There was enough down here this morning, before that train came through to poison an army. Indeed, if it had not been for Henderson's promptitude, there would have been another inquest—on myself.'

I then related my own experience.

'Well, this clears Wynne, without doubt,' said Bainbridge;

'but alas! For the two poor fellows who were victims. Bell, the Lytton Vale Railway Company owe you unlimited thanks; you have doubtless saved many lives, and also the Company, for the line must have been closed if you had not made your valuable discovery. But now come home with me to breakfast. We can discuss all those matters later on.

How He Cut His Stick

Matthias McDonnell Bodkin

The apparent demise of Sherlock Holmes in 'The Final Problem' in 1893 prompted a host of writers to try to replace the great detective in the affections of the public with sleuths of their own. Among them was Matthias McDonnell Bodkin (1850–1933), an Irish lawyer and author, who proceeded to create a whole family of detectives. He began with Paul Beck, 'the rule of thumb detective', whose adventures were first collected in 1898. Two years later, Bodkin published *Dora Myrl, Lady Detective*, comprising a dozen stories. Eventually, Paul married Dora, and the union produced Paul Junior, who inherited their taste for detection, and appeared in *Young Beck, a Chip Off the Old Block* (1911).

The *Spectator* was impressed by Dora Myrl, describing her as 'one of the most remarkable examples of new womanhood ever evolved in modern and ancient fiction'. The daughter of a professor, Dora studied medicine at Cambridge, drifting from job to job (as a telegraph girl, a telephone girl, and a journalist) before turning to crime-solving while acting as companion to an elderly woman who falls victim to a black-mailer. Dora's intelligence and flair for disguising herself make her an effective detective when she sets up her own agency. In this story, her ability as a cyclist also comes in handy.

————

He breathed freely at last as he lifted the small black Gladstone bag of stout calfskin, and set it carefully on the seat of the empty railway carriage close beside him.

He lifted the bag with a manifest effort. Yet he was a big powerfully built young fellow; handsome too in a way; with straw-coloured hair and moustache and a round face, placid, honest-looking but not too clever. His light blue eyes had an anxious, worried look. No wonder, poor chap! He was weighted with a heavy responsibility. That unobtrusive black bag held £5,000 in gold and notes which he—a junior clerk in the famous banking house of Gower and Grant—was taking from the head office in London to a branch two hundred miles down the line.

The older and more experienced clerk whose ordinary duty it was to convey the gold had been taken strangely and suddenly ill at the last moment.

'There's Jim Pollock,' said the bank manager, looking round for a substitute, 'he'll do. He is big enough to knock the head off anyone that interferes with him.'

So Jim Pollock had the heavy responsibility thrust upon him. The big fellow who would tackle any man in England in a football rush without a thought of fear was as nervous as a two-year-old child. All the way down to this point his watchful eyes and strong right hand had never left the bag for a moment. But here at the Eddiscombe Junction he had got locked in alone to a single first-class carriage, and there was a clear run of forty-seven miles to the next stoppage.

So with a sigh and shrug of relief, he threw away his anxiety, lay back on the soft seat, lit a pipe, drew a sporting paper from his pocket, and was speedily absorbed in the account of the Rugby International Championship match, for Jim himself was not without hopes of his 'cap' in the near future.

The train rattled out of the station and settled down to its smooth easy stride—a good fifty miles an hour through the open country.

Still absorbed in his paper he did not notice the gleam of two stealthy keen eyes that watched him from the dark shadow under the opposite seat. He did not see that long lithe wiry figure uncoil and creep out, silently as a snake, across the floor of the carriage.

He saw nothing and felt nothing till he felt two murderous hands clutching at his throat and a knee crushing his chest in.

Jim was strong, but before his sleeping strength had time to waken, he was down on his back on the carriage floor with a handkerchief soaked in chloroform jammed close to his mouth and nostrils.

He struggled desperately for a moment or so, half rose and almost flung off his clinging assailant. But even as he struggled the dreamy drug stole strength and sense away; he fell back heavily and lay like a log on the carriage floor.

The faithful fellow's last thought as his senses left him was 'The gold is gone.' It was his first thought as he awoke with dizzy pain and racked brain from the deathlike swoon. The train was still at full speed; the carriage doors were still locked; but the carriage empty and the bag was gone.

He searched despairingly in the racks, under the seats—all empty. Jim let the window down with a clash and bellowed.

The train began to slacken speed and rumble into the station. Half a dozen porters ran together—the station-master following more leisurely as beseemed his dignity. Speedily a crowd gathered round the door.

'I have been robbed,' Jim shouted, 'of a black bag with £5,000 in it!'

Then the superintendent pushed his way through the crowd. 'Where were you robbed, sir?' he said with a suspicious look at the dishevelled and excited Jim.

'Between this and Eddiscombe Junction.'

'Impossible, sir, there is no stoppage between this and Eddiscombe, and the carriage is empty.'

'I thought it was empty at Eddiscombe, but there must have been a man under the seat.'

'There is no man under the seat now,' retorted the superintendent curtly, 'you had better tell your story to the police. There is a detective on the platform.'

Jim told his story to the detective, who listened gravely and told him that he must consider himself in custody pending inquiries.

A telegram was sent to Eddiscombe, and it was found that communication had been stopped. This must have happened quite recently, for a telegram had gone through less than an hour before. The breakage was quickly located about nine miles outside Eddiscombe. Some of the wires had been pulled down halfway to the ground, and the insulators smashed to pieces on one of the poles. All round the place the ground was trampled with heavy footprints which passed through a couple of fields out on the high road and were lost. No other clue of any kind was forthcoming.

The next day but one, a card, with the name 'Sir Gregory Grant', was handed to Dora Myrl as she sat hard at work in the little drawing-room which she called her study. A portly, middle-aged, benevolent gentleman followed the card into the room.

'Miss Myrl?' he said, extending his hand, 'I have heard of you from my friend, Lord Millicent. I have come to entreat your assistance. I am the senior partner of the banking firm of Gower and Grant. You have heard of the railway robbery, I suppose?'

'I have heard all the paper had to tell me.'

'There is little more to tell. I have called on you personally, Miss Myrl, because, personally, I am deeply interested in the case. It is not so much the money though the amount is, of course, serious. But the honour of the bank is at stake. We have always prided ourselves on treating our clerks well, and heretofore we have reaped the reward. For nearly a century there has not been a single case of fraud or dishonesty amongst them. It is a proud record for our bank, and we should like to keep it unbroken if possible. Suspicion is heavy on young James Pollock. I want him punished, of course, if he is guilty, but I want him cleared if he is innocent. That's why I came to you.'

'The police think?'

'Oh, they think there can be no doubt about his guilt. They have their theory pat. No one was in the carriage—no one could leave it. Pollock threw out the bag to an accomplice along the line. They even pretend to find the mark in the ground where the heavy bag fell—a few hundred yards nearer to Eddiscombe than where the wires were pulled down.'

'What has been done?'

'They have arrested the lad and sent out the "Hue and Cry"

for a man with a very heavy calfskin bag—that's all. They are quite sure they have caught the principal thief anyway.'

'And you?'

'I will be frank with you, Miss Myrl. I have my doubts. The case *seems* conclusive. It is impossible that anybody could have got out of the train at full speed. But I have seen the lad, and I have my doubts.'

'Can I see him?'

'I would be very glad if you did.'

After five minutes' conversation with Jim Pollock, Dora drew Sir Gregory aside.

'I think I see my way,' she said, 'I will undertake the case on one condition.'

'Any fee that…'

'It's not the fee. I never talk of the fee till the case is over. I will undertake the case if you give me Mr Pollock to help me. Your instinct was right, Sir Gregory: the boy is innocent.'

There was much grumbling amongst the police when a *nolle prosequi* was entered on behalf of the bank, and James Pollock was discharged from custody, and it was plainly hinted the Crown would interpose.

Meanwhile Pollock was off by a morning train with Miss Dora Myrl, from London to Eddiscombe. He was brimming over with gratitude and devotion. Of course they talked of the robbery on the way down.

'The bag was very heavy, Mr Pollock?' Dora asked.

'I'd sooner carry it one mile than ten, Miss Myrl.'

'Yet you are pretty strong, I should think.'

She touched his protruding biceps professionally with her finger tips, and he coloured to the roots of his hair.

'Would you know the man that robbed you if you saw him again?' Dora asked.

'Not from Adam. He had his hands on my throat, the chloroform crammed into my mouth before I knew where I was. It was about nine or ten miles outside Eddiscombe. You believe there *was* a man—don't you, Miss Myrl? You are about the only person that does. I don't blame them, for how did the chap get out of the train going at the rate of sixty miles an hour—that's what fetches me, 'pon my word,' he concluded incoherently; 'if I was any other chap I'd believe myself guilty on the evidence. Can you tell me how the trick was done, Miss Myrl?'

'That's my secret for the present, Mr Pollock, but I may tell you this much, when we get to the pretty little town of Eddiscombe I will look out for a stranger with a crooked stick instead of a black bag.'

There were three hotels in Eddiscombe, but Mr Mark Brown and his sister were hard to please. They tried the three in succession, keeping their eyes about them for a stranger with a crooked stick, and spending their leisure time in exploring the town and country on a pair of capital bicycles, which they hired by the week.

As Miss Brown (alias Dora Myrl) was going down the stairs of the third hotel one sunshiny afternoon a week after their arrival, she met midway, face to face, a tall middle-aged man limping a little, a very little, and leaning on a stout oak stick, with a dark shiny varnish, and a crooked handle. She passed him without a second glance. But that evening she gossiped with the chambermaid, and learned that the stranger was a commercial traveller—Mr McCrowder—who had been staying some weeks at the hotel, with an occasional run up to London in the train, and run round the country on his bicycle, 'a nice, easily-pleased, pleasant-spoken gentleman,' the chambermaid added on her own account.

Next day Dora Myrl met the stranger again in the same place on the stairs. Was it her awkwardness or his? As she moved aside to let him pass, her little foot caught in the stick, jerked it from his hand, and sent it clattering down the stairs into the hall.

She ran swiftly down the stairs in pursuit, and carried it back with a pretty apology to the owner. But not before she had seen on the inside of the crook a deep notch, cutting through the varnish into the wood.

At dinner that day their table adjoined Mr McCrowder's. Halfway through the meal she asked Jim to tell her what the hour was, as her watch had stopped. It was a curious request, for she sat facing the clock, and he had to turn round to see it. But Jim turned obediently, and came face to face with Mr McCrowder, who started and stared at the sight of him as though he had seen a ghost. Jim stared back stolidly without a trace of recognition in his face, and Mr McCrowder, after a moment, resumed his dinner. Then Dora set, or seemed to set and wind, her watch, and so the curious little incident closed.

That evening Dora played a musical little jingle on the piano in their private sitting-room, touching the notes abstractedly and apparently deep in thought. Suddenly she closed the piano with a bang.

'Mr Pollock?'

'Well, Miss Myrl,' said Jim, who had been watching her with the patient, honest, stupid admiration of a big Newfoundland dog.

'We will take a ride together on our bicycles tomorrow. I cannot say what hour, but have them ready when I call for them.'

'Yes, Miss Myrl.'

'And bring a ball of stout twine in your pocket.'

'Yes, Miss Myrl.'

'By the way, have you a revolver?'

'Never had such a thing in my life.'

'Could you use it if you got it?'

'I hardly know the butt from the muzzle, but'—modestly—'I can fight a little bit with my fists if that's any use.'

'Not the least in this case. An ounce of lead can stop a fourteen-stone champion. Besides one six-shooter is enough, and I'm not too bad a shot.'

'You don't mean to say, Miss Myrl, that you…'

'I don't mean to say one word more at present, Mr Pollock, only have the bicycles ready when I want them and the twine.'

Next morning after an exceptionally early breakfast, Dora took her place with a book in her hand coiled up on a sofa in a bow-window of the empty drawing-room that looked out on the street. She kept one eye on her book and the other on the window from which the steps of the hotel were visible.

About half-past nine o'clock she saw Mr McCrowder go down the steps, not limping at all, but carrying his bicycle with a big canvas bicycle bag strapped to the handlebar.

In a moment she was down in the hall where the bicycles stood ready; in another she and Pollock were in the saddle sailing swiftly and smoothly along the street just as the tall figure of Mr McCrowder was vanishing round a distant corner.

'We have got to keep him in sight,' Dora whispered to her companion as they sped along, 'or rather I have got to keep him and you to keep me in sight. Now let me go to the front; hold as far back as you can without losing me, and the moment I wave a white handkerchief—scorch!'

Pollock nodded and fell back, and in this order—each about half a mile apart—the three riders swept out of the town into the open country.

The man in front was doing a strong steady twelve miles an hour, but the roads were good and Dora kept her distance without an effort, while Pollock held himself back. For a full hour this game of follow-my-leader was played without a change. Mr McCrowder had left the town at the opposite direction to the railway, but now he began to wheel round towards the line. Once he glanced behind and saw only a single girl cycling in the distance on the deserted road. The next time he saw no one, for Dora rode close to the inner curve.

They were now a mile or so from the place where the telegraph wires had been broken down, and Dora, who knew the lie of the land, felt sure their little bicycle trip was drawing to a close.

The road climbed a long easy winding slope thickly wooded on either side. The man in front put on a spurt; Dora answered it with another, and Pollock behind sprinted fiercely, lessening his distance from Dora. The leader crossed the top bend of the slope, turned a sharp curve, and went swiftly down a smooth decline, shaded by the interlacing branches of great trees.

Half a mile down at the bottom of the slope, he leaped suddenly from his bicycle with one quick glance back the way he had come. There was no one in view, for Dora held back at the turn. He ran his bicycle close into the wall on the left hand side where a deep trench hid it from the casual passers by; unstrapped the bag from the handlebar, and clambered over the wall with an agility that was surprising in one of his (apparent) age.

Dora was just round the corner in time to see him leap from the top of the wall into the thick wood. At once she drew out and waved her white handkerchief, then settled herself in the saddle and made her bicycle fly through the rush of a sudden wind, down the slope.

Pollock saw the signal; bent down over his handlebar and pedalled uphill like the piston rods of a steam engine.

The man's bicycle by the roadside was a finger post for Dora. She, in her turn, over-perched the wall as lightly as a bird. Gathering her tailor-made skirt tightly around her, she peered and listened intently. She could see nothing, but a little way in front a slight rustling of the branches caught her quick ears. Moving in the underwood, stealthily and silently as a rabbit, she caught a glimpse through the leaves of a dark grey tweed suit fifteen or twenty yards off. A few steps more and she had a clear view. The man was on his knees; he had drawn a black leather bag from a thick tangle of ferns at the foot of a great old beech tree, and was busy cramming a number of small canvas sacks into his bicycle bag.

Dora moved cautiously forward till she stood in a little opening, clear of the undergrowth, free to use her right arm.

'Good morning, Mr McCrowder!' she cried sharply.

The man started, and turned and saw a girl half a dozen yards off standing clear in the sunlight, with a mocking smile on her face.

His lips growled out a curse; his right hand left the bags and stole to his side pocket.

'Stop that!' The command came clear and sharp. 'Throw up your hands!'

He looked again. The sunlight glinted on the barrel of a revolver, pointed straight at his head, with a steady hand.

'Up with your hands, or I fire!' and his hands went up over his head. The next instant Jim Pollock came crashing through the underwood, like an elephant through the jungle. He stopped short with a cry of amazement.

'Steady!' came Dora's quiet voice; 'don't get in my line of fire. Round there to the left—that's the way. Take away his revolver. It is in his right-hand coat pocket. Now tie his hands!'

Jim Pollock did his work stolidly as directed. But while

he wound the strong cord round the wrists and arms of Mr McCrowder, he remembered the railway carriage and the strangling grip at his throat, and the chloroform, and the disgrace that followed, and if he strained the knots extra tight it's hard to blame him.

'Now,' said Dora, 'finish his packing,' and Jim crammed the remainder of the canvas sacks into the big bicycle bag.

'You don't mind the weight?'

He gave a delighted grin for answer, as he swung both bags in his hands.

'Get up!' said Dora to the thief, and he stumbled to his feet sulkily. 'Walk in front. I mean to take you back to Eddiscombe with me.'

When they got on the roadside Pollock strapped the bicycle bag to his own handlebar.

'May I trouble you, Mr Pollock, to unscrew one of the pedals of this gentleman's bicycle?' said Dora.

It was done in a twinkling. 'Now give him a lift up,' she said to Jim, 'he is going to ride back with one pedal.'

The abject thief held up his bound wrists imploringly.

'Oh, that's all right. I noticed you held the middle of your handlebar from choice coming out. You'll do it from necessity going back. We'll look after you. Don't whine; you've played a bold game and lost the odd trick, and you've got to pay up, that's all.'

There was a wild sensation in Eddiscombe when, in broad noon, the bank thief was brought in riding on a one-pedalled machine to the police barrack and handed into custody. Dora rode on through the cheering crowd to the hotel.

A wire brought Sir Gregory Grant down by the afternoon train, and the three dined together that night at his cost; the best dinner and wine the hotel could supply. Sir Gregory was brimming over with delight, like the bubbling champagne in his wine glass.

'Your health, Mr Pollock,' said the banker to the junior clerk. 'We will make up in the bank to you for the annoyance you have had. You shall fix your own fee, Miss Myrl—or, rather, I'll fix it for you if you allow me. Shall we say half the salvage? But I'm dying with curiosity to know how you managed to find the money and thief.'

'It was easy enough when you come to think of it, Sir Gregory. The man would have been a fool to tramp across the country with a black bag full of gold while the "Hue and Cry" was hot on him. His game was to hide it and lie low, and he did so. The sight of Mr Pollock at the hotel hurried him up as I hoped it would; that's the whole story.'

'Oh, that's not all. How did you find the man? How did the man get out of the train going at the rate of sixty miles an hour? But I suppose I'd best ask that question of Mr Pollock, who was there?'

'Don't ask me any questions, sir,' said Jim, with a look of profound admiration in Dora's direction. 'She played the game off her own bat. All I know is that the chap cut his stick after he had done for me. I cannot in the least tell how.'

'Will you have pity on my curiosity, Miss Myrl.'

'With pleasure, Sir Gregory. You must have noticed, as I did, that where the telegraph was broken down the line was embanked and the wires ran quite close to the railway carriage. It is easy for an active man to slip a crooked stick like this' (she held up Mr McCrowder's stick as she spoke) 'over the two or three of the wires and so swing himself into the air clear of the train. The acquired motion would carry him along the wires to the post and give him a chance of breaking down the insulators.'

'By Jove! You're right, Miss Myrl. It's quite simple when one comes to think of it. But, still, I don't understand how...'

'The friction of the wire,' Dora went on in the even tone of a lecturer, 'with a man's weight on it, would bite deep into the wood of the stick, like that!' Again she held out the crook of a dark thick oak stick for Sir Gregory to examine, and he peered at it through his gold spectacles.

'The moment I saw that notch,' Dora added quietly, 'I knew how Mr McCrowder had *"Cut his stick"*.

The Mysterious Death on the Underground Railway

Baroness Orczy

Baroness Orczy is today remembered principally as the creator of Sir Percy Blakeney, alias 'the Scarlet Pimpernel', but her contribution to crime fiction deserves to be remembered. Orczy (1865–1947), the daughter of a Hungarian musician, moved to England at the age of fourteen, and married an Englishman. She turned to writing as a means of supplementing the family income, and created three different detectives, including the title character in *Lady Molly of Scotland Yard* (1910) and the crafty lawyer Patrick Mulligan, whose cases are chronicled in *Skin O' My Tooth* (1928).

Orczy's principal sleuth was the Old Man in the Corner, who remains one of the most interesting and original examples of the 'armchair detective', even though his favourite seat in the corner of an A.B.C. teashop in London was scarcely an armchair. Rather than rushing around hunting for clues, he solves crimes by applying his intellect to puzzles recounted by the journalist Polly Burton. He first appeared in 1901 in 'The Fenchurch Street Mystery', and his case-book ultimately extended to three collections of stories. This story, which first appeared in the *Royal Magazine* in 1901, was televised in 1973 in the BBC TV series *The Rivals of Sherlock Holmes*. The cast included such notable actors as Judy Geeson (as Polly Burton), John Savident, Christopher Timothy, and Richard Beckinsale. In a classic example of the oddities of television adaptation, Alan Cooke's screenplay removed the Old Man in the Corner from the storyline, and Polly became the star of the show.

———

It was all very well for Mr Richard Frobisher (of the *London Mail*) to cut up rough about it. Polly did not altogether blame him.

She liked him all the better for that frank outburst of man-like ill-temper which, after all said and done, was only a very flattering form of masculine jealousy.

Moreover, Polly distinctly felt guilty about the whole thing. She had promised to meet Dickie—that is Mr Richard Frobisher—at two o'clock sharp outside the Palace Theatre, because she wanted to go to a Maud Allan matinée, and because he naturally wished to go with her.

But at two o'clock sharp she was still in Norfolk Street, Strand, inside an A.B.C. shop, sipping cold coffee opposite a grotesque old man who was fiddling with a bit of string.

How could she be expected to remember Maud Allan or the Palace Theatre, or Dickie himself for a matter of that? The man in the corner had begun to talk of that mysterious death on the Underground Railway, and Polly had lost count of time, of place, and circumstance.

She had gone to lunch quite early, for she was looking forward to the matinée at the Palace.

The old scarecrow was sitting in his accustomed place when she came into the A.B.C. shop, but he had made no remark all the time that the young girl was munching her scone and butter. She was just busy thinking how rude he was not even to have said 'Good morning', when an abrupt remark from him caused her to look up.

'Will you be good enough,' he said suddenly, 'to give me a description of the man who sat next to you just now, while you were having your cup of coffee and scone.'

Involuntarily Polly turned her head towards the distant door, through which a man in a light overcoat was even now quickly passing. That man had certainly sat at the next table to hers, when she first sat down to her coffee and scone; he had finished his luncheon—whatever it was—a moment ago, had paid at the desk and gone out. The incident did not appear to Polly as being of the slightest consequence.

Therefore she did not reply to the rude old man, but shrugged her shoulders, and called to the waitress to bring her bill.

'Do you know if he was tall or short, dark or fair?' continued the man in the corner, seemingly not the least disconcerted by the young girl's indifference. 'Can you tell me at all what he was like?'

'Of course I can,' rejoined Polly impatiently, 'but I don't see that my description of one of the customers of an A.B.C. shop can have the slightest importance.'

He was silent for a minute, while his nervous fingers fumbled about in his capacious pockets in search of the inevitable piece of string. When he had found this necessary 'adjunct to thought', he viewed the young girl again through his half-closed lids, and added maliciously:

'But supposing it were of paramount importance that you should give an accurate description of a man who sat next to you for half an hour today, how would you proceed?'

'I should say that he was of medium height—'

'Five foot eight, nine, or ten?' he interrupted quietly.

'How can one tell to an inch or two?' rejoined Polly crossly. 'He was between colours.'

'What's that?' he inquired blandly.

'Neither fair nor dark—his nose—'

'Well, what was his nose like? Will you sketch it?'

'I am not an artist. His nose was fairly straight—his eyes—'

'Were neither dark nor light—his hair had the same striking peculiarity—he was neither short nor tall—his nose was neither aquiline nor snub—' he recapitulated sarcastically.

'No,' she retorted; 'he was just ordinary looking.'

'Would you know him again—say tomorrow, and among a number of other men who were "neither tall nor short, dark nor fair, aquiline nor snub-nosed", etc.?'

'I don't know—I might—he was certainly not striking enough to be specially remembered.'

'Exactly,' he said, while he leant forward excitedly, for all the world like a Jack-in-the-box let loose. 'Precisely; and you are a journalist—call yourself one, at least—and it should be part of your business to notice and describe people. I don't mean only the wonderful personage with the clear Saxon features, the fine blue eyes, the noble brow and classic face, but the ordinary person—the person who represents ninety out of every hundred of his own kind—the average Englishman, say, of the middle classes, who is neither very tall nor very short, who wears a moustache which is neither fair nor dark, but which masks his mouth, and a top hat which hides the shape of his head and brow, a man, in fact, who dresses like hundreds of his fellow-creatures, moves like them, speaks like them, has no peculiarity.

'Try to describe *him*, to recognise him, say a week hence, among his other eighty-nine doubles; worse still, to swear his life away, if he happened to be implicated in some crime, wherein *your* recognition of him would place the halter round his neck.

'Try that, I say, and having utterly failed you will more readily understand how one of the greatest scoundrels unhung is still at large and why the mystery on the Underground Railway was never cleared up.

'I think it was the only time in my life that I was seriously tempted to give the police the benefit of my own views upon the matter. You see, though I admire the brute for his cleverness, I did not see that his being unpunished could possibly benefit anyone.

'In these days of tubes and motor traction of all kinds, the old-fashioned "best, cheapest, and quickest route to City and West End" is often deserted, and the good old Metropolitan Railway carriages cannot at any time be said to be over-crowded. Anyway, when that particular train steamed into Aldgate at about 4 p.m. on March 18th last, the first-class carriages were all but empty.

'The guard marched up and down the platform looking into all the carriages to see if anyone had left a halfpenny evening paper behind for him, and opening the door of one of the first-class compartments, he noticed a lady sitting in the further corner, with her head turned away towards the window, evidently oblivious of the fact that on this line Aldgate is the terminal station.

'"Where are you for, lady?" he said.

'The lady did not move, and the guard stepped into the

carriage, thinking that perhaps the lady was asleep. He touched her arm lightly and looked into her face. In his own poetic language, he was "struck all of a 'eap". In the glassy eyes, the ashen colour of the cheeks, the rigidity of the head, there was the unmistakable look of death.

'Hastily the guard, having carefully locked the carriage door, summoned a couple of porters, and sent one of them off to the police-station and the other in search of the station-master.

'Fortunately at this time of day the up platform is not very crowded, all the traffic tending westward in the afternoon. It was only when an inspector and two police constables, accompanied by a detective in plain clothes and a medical officer, appeared upon the scene, and stood round a first-class railway compartment, that a few idlers realised that something unusual had occurred, and crowded round, eager and curious.

'Thus it was that the later editions of the evening papers, under the sensational heading, "Mysterious Suicide on the Underground Railway", had already an account of the extraordinary event. The medical officer had very soon come to the decision that the guard had not been mistaken, and that life was indeed extinct.

'The lady was young, and must have been very pretty before the look of fright and horror had so terribly distorted her features. She was very elegantly dressed, and the more frivolous papers were able to give their feminine readers a detailed account of the unfortunate woman's gown, her shoes, hat, and gloves.

'It appears that one of the latter, the one on the right hand, was partly off, leaving the thumb and wrist bare. That hand held a small satchel, which the police opened, with a view to the possible identification of the deceased, but which was found to contain only a little loose silver, some smelling-salts, and a small empty bottle, which was handed over to the medical officer for purposes of analysis.

'It was the presence of that small bottle which had caused the report to circulate freely that the mysterious case on the Underground Railway was one of suicide. Certain it was that neither about the lady's person, nor in the appearance of the railway carriage, was there the slightest sign of struggle or even of resistance. Only the look in the poor woman's eyes spoke of sudden terror, of the rapid vision of an unexpected and violent death, which probably only lasted an infinitesimal fraction of a second, but which had left its indelible mark upon the face, otherwise so placid and so still.

'The body of the deceased was conveyed to the mortuary. So far, of course, not a soul had been able to identify her, or to throw the slightest light upon the mystery which hung around her death.

'Against that, quite a crowd of idlers—genuinely interested or not—obtained admission to view the body, on the pretext of having lost or mislaid a relative or a friend. At about 8.30 p.m. a young man, very well dressed, drove up to the station in a hansom, and sent in his card to the superintendent. It was Mr Hazeldene, shipping agent, of 11, Crown Lane, E.C., and No. 19, Addison Row, Kensington.

'The young man looked in a pitiable state of mental distress; his hand clutched nervously a copy of the *St James's Gazette*, which contained the fatal news. He said very little to the superintendent except that a person who was very dear to him had not returned home that evening.

'He had not felt really anxious until half an hour ago, when suddenly he thought of looking at his paper. The description of the deceased lady, though vague, had terribly alarmed him. He had jumped into a hansom, and now begged permission to view the body, in order that his worst fears might be allayed.

'You know what followed, of course,' continued the man in the corner, 'the grief of the young man was truly pitiable. In the woman lying there in a public mortuary before him, Mr Hazeldene had recognised his wife.

'I am waxing melodramatic,' said the man in the corner, who looked up at Polly with a mild and gentle smile, while his nervous fingers vainly endeavoured to add another knot on the scrappy bit of string with which he was continually playing, 'and I fear that the whole story savours of the penny novelette, but you must admit, and no doubt you remember, that it was an intensely pathetic and truly dramatic moment.

'The unfortunate young husband of the deceased lady was not much worried with questions that night. As a matter of fact, he was not in a fit condition to make any coherent statement. It was at the coroner's inquest on the following day that certain facts came to light, which for the time being seemed to clear up the mystery surrounding Mrs Hazeldene's death, only to plunge that same mystery, later on, into denser gloom than before.

'The first witness at the inquest was, of course, Mr Hazeldene himself. I think everyone's sympathy went out to the young man as he stood before the coroner and tried to throw what light he could upon the mystery. He was well-dressed, as he had been the day before, but he looked terribly ill and worried, and no doubt the fact that he had not shaved gave his face a careworn and neglected air.

'It appears that he and the deceased had been married some six years or so, and that they had always been happy in their married life. They had no children. Mrs Hazeldene seemed to enjoy the best of health till lately, when she had

had a slight attack of influenza, in which Dr Arthur Jones had attended her. The doctor was present at this moment, and would no doubt explain to the coroner and the jury whether he thought that Mrs Hazeldene had the slightest tendency to heart disease, which might have had a sudden and fatal ending.

'The coroner was, of course, very considerate to the bereaved husband. He tried by circumlocution to get at the point he wanted, namely, Mrs Hazeldene's mental condition lately. Mr Hazeldene seemed loath to talk about this. No doubt he had been warned as to the existence of the small bottle found in his wife's satchel.

'"It certainly did seem to me at times," he at last reluctantly admitted, "that my wife did not seem quite herself. She used to be very gay and bright, and lately I often saw her in the evening sitting, as if brooding over some matters, which evidently she did not care to communicate to me."

'Still the coroner insisted, and suggested the small bottle.

'"I know, I know," replied the young man, with a short, heavy sigh. "You mean—the question of suicide—I cannot understand it at all—it seems so sudden and so terrible—she certainly had seemed listless and troubled lately—but only at times—and yesterday morning, when I went to business, she appeared quite herself again, and I suggested that we should go to the opera in the evening. She was delighted, I know, and told me she would do some shopping, and pay a few calls in the afternoon."

'"Do you know at all where she intended to go when she got into the Underground Railway?"

'"Well, not with certainty. You see, she may have meant to get out at Baker Street, and go down to Bond Street to do her shopping. Then, again, she sometimes goes to a shop in

St Paul's Churchyard, in which case she would take a ticket to Aldersgate Street; but I cannot say."

'"Now, Mr Hazeldene," said the coroner at last very kindly, "will you try to tell me if there was anything in Mrs Hazeldene's life which you know of, and which might in some measure explain the cause of the distressed state of mind, which you yourself had noticed? Did there exist any financial difficulty which might have preyed upon Mrs Hazeldene's mind; was there any friend—to whose intercourse with Mrs Hazeldene— you—er—at any time took exception? In fact," added the coroner, as if thankful that he had got over an unpleasant moment, "can you give me the slightest indication which would tend to confirm the suspicion that the unfortunate lady, in a moment of mental anxiety or derangement, may have wished to take her own life?"

'There was silence in the court for a few moments. Mr Hazeldene seemed to everyone there present to be labouring under some terrible moral doubt. He looked very pale and wretched, and twice attempted to speak before he at last said in scarcely audible tones:

'"No; there were no financial difficulties of any sort. My wife had an independent fortune of her own—she had no extravagant tastes—"

'"Nor any friend you at any time objected to?" insisted the coroner.

'"Nor any friend, I—at any time objected to," stammered the unfortunate young man, evidently speaking with an effort.

'I was present at the inquest,' resumed the man in the corner, after he had drunk a glass of milk and ordered another, 'and I can assure you that the most obtuse person there plainly realised that Mr Hazeldene was telling a lie. It was pretty plain to the meanest intelligence that the unfortunate lady had not fallen into a state of morbid dejection for nothing, and that perhaps there existed a third person who could throw more light on her strange and sudden death than the unhappy, bereaved young widower.

'That the death was more mysterious even than it had at first appeared became very soon apparent. You read the case at the time, no doubt, and must remember the excitement in the public mind caused by the evidence of the two doctors. Dr Arthur Jones, the lady's usual medical man, who had attended her in a last very slight illness, and who had seen her in a professional capacity fairly recently, declared most emphatically that Mrs Hazeldene suffered from no organic complaint which could possibly have been the cause of sudden death. Moreover, he had assisted Mr Andrew Thornton, the district medical officer, in making a post mortem examination, and together they had come to the conclusion that death was due to the action of prussic acid, which had caused instantaneous failure of the heart, but how the drug had been administered neither he nor his colleague were at present able to state.

'"Do I understand, then, Dr Jones, that the deceased died, poisoned with prussic acid?"

'"Such is my opinion," replied the doctor.

'"Did the bottle found in her satchel contain prussic acid?"

'"It had contained some at one time, certainly."

'"In your opinion, then, the lady caused her own death by taking a dose of that drug?"

'"Pardon me, I never suggested such a thing: the lady died poisoned by the drug, but how the drug was administered we cannot say. By injection of some sort, certainly. The drug certainly was not swallowed; there was not a vestige of it in the stomach."

'"Yes," added the doctor in reply to another question from

the coroner, "death had probably followed the injection in this case almost immediately; say within a couple of minutes, or perhaps three. It was quite possible that the body would not have more than one quick and sudden convulsion, perhaps not that; death in such cases is absolutely sudden and crushing."

'I don't think that at the time anyone in the room realised how important the doctor's statement was, a statement, which, by the way, was confirmed in all its details by the district medical officer, who had conducted the post mortem. Mrs Hazeldene had died suddenly from an injection of prussic acid, administered no one knew how or when. She had been travelling in a first-class railway carriage in a busy time of the day. That young and elegant woman must have had singular nerve and coolness to go through the process of a self-inflicted injection of a deadly poison in the presence of perhaps two or three other persons.

'Mind you, when I say that no one there realised the importance of the doctor's statement at that moment, I am wrong; there were three persons, who fully understood at once the gravity of the situation, and the astounding development which the case was beginning to assume.

'Of course, I should have put myself out of the question,' added the weird old man, with that inimitable self-conceit peculiar to himself. 'I guessed then and there in a moment where the police were going wrong, and where they would go on going wrong until the mysterious death on the Underground Railway had sunk into oblivion, together with the other cases which they mismanage from time to time.

'I said there were three persons who understood the gravity of the two doctors' statements—the other two were, firstly, the detective who had originally examined the railway carriage, a young man of energy and plenty of misguided intelligence, the other was Mr Hazeldene.

'At this point the interesting element of the whole story was first introduced into the proceedings, and this was done through the humble channel of Emma Funnel, Mrs Hazeldene's maid, who, as far as was known then, was the last person who had seen the unfortunate lady alive and had spoken to her.

'"Mrs Hazeldene lunched at home," explained Emma, who was shy, and spoke almost in a whisper; "she seemed well and cheerful. She went out at about half-past three, and told me she was going to Spence's, in St Paul's Churchyard to try on her new tailor-made gown. Mrs Hazeldene had meant to go there in the morning, but was prevented as Mr Errington called."

'"Mr Errington?" asked the coroner casually. "Who is Mr Errington?"

'But this Emma found difficult to explain. Mr Errington was—Mr Errington, that's all.

'"Mr Errington was a friend of the family. He lived in a flat in the Albert Mansions. He very often came to Addison Row, and generally stayed late."

'Pressed still further with questions, Emma at last stated that latterly Mrs Hazeldene had been to the theatre several times with Mr Errington, and that on those nights the master looked very gloomy, and was very cross.

'Recalled, the young widower was strangely reticent. He gave forth his answers very grudgingly, and the coroner was evidently absolutely satisfied with himself at the marvellous way in which, after a quarter of an hour of firm yet very kind questionings, he had elicited from the witness what information he wanted.

'Mr Errington was a friend of his wife. He was a gentleman

of means, and seemed to have a great deal of time at his command. He himself did not particularly care about Mr Errington, but he certainly had never made any observations to his wife on the subject.

'"But who is Mr Errington?" repeated the coroner once more. "What does he do? What is his business or profession?"

'"He has no business or profession."

'"What is his occupation, then?"

'"He has no special occupation. He has ample private means. But he has a great and very absorbing hobby."

'"What is that?"

'"He spends all his time in chemical experiments, and is, I believe, as an amateur, a very distinguished toxicologist."

'Did you ever see Mr Errington, the gentleman so closely connected with the mysterious death on the Underground Railway?' asked the man in the corner as he placed one or two of his little snapshot photos before Miss Polly Burton.

'There he is, to the very life. Fairly good-looking, a pleasant face enough, but ordinary, absolutely ordinary.

'It was this absence of any peculiarity which very nearly, but not quite, placed the halter round Mr Errington's neck.

'But I am going too fast, and you will lose the thread. The public, of course, never heard how it actually came about that Mr Errington, the wealthy bachelor of Albert Mansions, of the Grosvenor, and other young dandies' clubs, one fine day found himself before the magistrates at Bow Street, charged with being concerned in the death of Mary Beatrice Hazeldene, late of No. 19, Addison Row.

'I can assure you both press and public were literally flabbergasted. You see, Mr Errington was a well-known and very popular member of a certain smart section of London society. He was a constant visitor at the opera, the race-course, the

Park, and the Carlton, he had a great many friends, and there was consequently quite a large attendance at the police court that morning. What had happened was this:

'After the very scrappy bits of evidence which came to light at the inquest, two gentlemen bethought themselves that perhaps they had some duty to perform towards the State and the public generally. Accordingly they had come forward offering to throw what light they could upon the mysterious affair on the Underground Railway.

'The police naturally felt that their information, such as it was, came rather late in the day, but as it proved of paramount importance, and the two gentlemen, moreover, were of undoubtedly good position in the world, they were thankful for what they could get, and acted accordingly; they accordingly brought Mr Errington up before the magistrate on a charge of murder.

'The accused looked pale and worried when I first caught sight of him in the court that day, which was not to be wondered at, considering the terrible position in which he found himself. He had been arrested at Marseilles, where he was preparing to start for Colombo.

'I don't think he realised how terrible his position was until later in the proceedings, when all the evidence relating to the arrest had been heard, and Emma Funnel had repeated her statement as to Mr Errington's call at 19, Addison Row, in the morning, and Mrs Hazeldene starting off for St Paul's Churchyard at 3.30 in the afternoon. Mr Hazeldene had nothing to add to the statements he had made at the coroner's inquest. He had last seen his wife alive on the morning of the fatal day. She had seemed very well and cheerful.

'I think everyone present understood that he was trying

to say as little as possible that could in any way couple his deceased wife's name with that of the accused.

'And yet, from the servant's evidence, it undoubtedly leaked out that Mrs Hazeldene, who was young, pretty, and evidently fond of admiration, had once or twice annoyed her husband by her somewhat open, yet perfectly innocent flirtation with Mr Errington.

'I think everyone was most agreeably impressed by the widower's moderate and dignified attitude. You will see his photo there, among this bundle. That is just how he appeared in court. In deep black, of course, but without any sign of ostentation in his mourning. He had allowed his beard to grow lately, and wore it closely cut in a point.

'After his evidence, the sensation of the day occurred. A tall, dark-haired man, with the word "City" written metaphorically all over him, had kissed the book, and was waiting to tell the truth, and nothing but the truth.

'He gave his name as Andrew Campbell, head of the firm of Campbell & Co., brokers, of Throgmorton Street.

'In the afternoon of March 18th Mr Campbell, travelling on the Underground Railway, had noticed a very pretty woman in the same carriage as himself. She had asked him if she was in the right train for Aldersgate. Mr Campbell replied in the affirmative, and then buried himself in the Stock Exchange quotations of his evening paper.

'At Gower Street, a gentleman in a tweed suit and bowler hat got into the carriage, and took a seat opposite the lady. She seemed very much astonished at seeing him, but Mr Campbell did not recollect the exact words she said.

'The two talked to one another a good deal, and certainly the lady appeared animated and cheerful. Witness took no notice of them; he was very much engrossed in some calculations, and finally got out at Farringdon Street. He noticed that the man in the tweed suit also got out close behind him, having shaken hands with the lady, and said in a pleasant way: "Au revoir! Don't be late tonight." Mr Campbell did not hear the lady's reply, and soon lost sight of the man in the crowd.

'Everyone was on tenter-hooks, and eagerly waiting for the palpitating moment when witness would describe and identify the man who last had seen and spoken to the unfortunate woman, within five minutes probably of her strange and unaccountable death.

'Personally I knew what was coming before the Scotch stockbroker spoke. I could have jotted down the graphic and lifelike description he would give of a probable murderer. It would have fitted equally well the man who sat and had luncheon at this table just now; it would certainly have described five out of every ten young Englishmen you know.

'The individual was of medium height, he wore a moustache which was not very fair nor yet very dark, his hair was between colours. He wore a bowler hat and a tweed suit—and—and—that was all—Mr Campbell might perhaps know him again, but then again, he might not—he was not paying much attention—the gentleman was sitting on the same side of the carriage as himself—and he had his hat on all the time. He himself was busy with his newspaper—yes—he might know him again—but he really could not say.

'Mr Andrew Campbell's evidence was not worth very much, you will say. No, it was not in itself, and would not have justified any arrest were it not for the additional statements made by Mr James Verner, manager of Messrs Rodney & Co., colour printers.

'Mr Verner is a personal friend of Mr Andrew Campbell, and it appears that at Farringdon Street, where he was waiting for his train, he saw Mr Campbell get out of a first-class railway carriage. Mr Verner spoke to him for a second, and then, just as the train was moving off, he stepped into the same compartment which had just been vacated by the stockbroker and the man in the tweed suit. He vaguely recollects a lady sitting in the opposite corner to his own, with her face turned away from him, apparently asleep, but he paid no special attention to her. He was like nearly all business men when they are travelling—engrossed in his paper. Presently a special quotation interested him; he wished to make a note of it, took out a pencil from his waistcoat pocket, and seeing a clean piece of paste-board on the floor, he picked it up, and scribbled on it the memorandum, which he wished to keep. He then slipped the card into his pocket-book.

'"It was only two or three days later," added Mr Verner in the midst of breathless silence, "that I had occasion to refer to these same notes again.

'"In the meanwhile the papers had been full of the mysterious death on the Underground Railway, and the names of those connected with it were pretty familiar to me. It was, therefore, with much astonishment that on looking at the paste-board which I had casually picked up in the railway carriage I saw the name on it, 'Frank Errington.'"

'There was no doubt that the sensation in court was almost unprecedented. Never since the days of the Fenchurch Street mystery, and the trial of Smethurst, had I seen so much excitement. Mind you, I was not excited—I knew by now every detail of that crime as if I had committed it myself. In fact, I could not have done it better, although I have been a student of crime for many years now. Many people there—his friends, mostly—believed that Errington was doomed. I think he thought so, too, for I could see that his face was terribly white, and he now and then passed his tongue over his lips, as if they were parched.

'You see he was in the awful dilemma—a perfectly natural one, by the way—of being absolutely incapable of proving an alibi. The crime—if crime there was—had been committed three weeks ago. A man about town like Mr Frank Errington might remember that he spent certain hours of a special afternoon at his club, or in the Park, but it is very doubtful in nine cases out of ten if he can find a friend who could positively swear as to having seen him there. No! No! Mr Errington was in a tight corner, and he knew it. You see, there were—besides the evidence—two or three circumstances which did not improve matters for him. His hobby in the direction of toxicology, to begin with. The police had found in his room every description of poisonous substances, including prussic acid.

'Then, again, that journey to Marseilles, the start for Colombo, was, though perfectly innocent, a very unfortunate one. Mr Errington had gone on an aimless voyage, but the public thought that he had fled, terrified at his own crime. Sir Arthur Inglewood, however, here again displayed his marvellous skill on behalf of his client by the masterly way in which he literally turned all the witnesses for the Crown inside out.

'Having first got Mr Andrew Campbell to state positively that in the accused he certainly did *not* recognise the man in the tweed suit, the eminent lawyer, after twenty minutes' cross-examination, had so completely upset the stockbroker's equanimity that it is very likely he would not have recognised his own office-boy.

'But through all his flurry and all his annoyance Mr Andrew Campbell remained very sure of one thing; namely, that the lady was alive and cheerful, and talking pleasantly with the man in the tweed suit up to the moment when the latter, having shaken hands with her, left her with a pleasant "Au revoir! Don't be late tonight." He had heard neither scream nor struggle, and in his opinion, if the individual in the tweed suit had administered a dose of poison to his companion, it must have been with her own knowledge and free will; and the lady in the train most emphatically neither looked nor spoke like a woman prepared for a sudden and violent death.

'Mr James Verner, against that, swore equally positively that he had stood in full view of the carriage door from the moment that Mr Campbell got out until he himself stepped into the compartment, that there was no one else in that carriage between Farringdon Street and Aldgate, and that the lady, to the best of his belief, had made no movement during the whole of that journey.

'No; Frank Errington was *not* committed for trial on the capital charge,' said the man in the corner with one of his sardonic smiles, 'thanks to the cleverness of Sir Arthur Inglewood, his lawyer. He absolutely denied his identity with the man in the tweed suit, and swore he had not seen Mrs Hazeldene since eleven o'clock in the morning of that fatal day. There was no proof that he had; moreover, according to Mr Campbell's opinion, the man in the tweed suit was in all probability not the murderer. Common sense would not admit that a woman could have a deadly poison injected into her without her knowledge, while chatting pleasantly to her murderer.

'Mr Errington lives abroad now. He is about to marry. I don't think any of his real friends for a moment believed that he committed the dastardly crime. The police think they know better. They do know this much, that it could not have been a case of suicide, that if the man who undoubtedly travelled with Mrs Hazeldene on that fatal afternoon had no crime upon his conscience he would long ago have come forward and thrown what light he could upon the mystery.

'As to who that man was, the police in their blindness have not the faintest doubt. Under the unshakable belief that Errington is guilty they have spent the last few months in unceasing labour to try and find further and stronger proofs of his guilt. But they won't find them, because there are none. There are no positive proofs against the actual murderer, for he was one of those clever blackguards who think of everything, foresee every eventuality, who know human nature well and can foretell exactly what evidence will be brought against them, and act accordingly.

'This blackguard from the first kept the figure, the personality, of Frank Errington before his mind. Frank Errington was the dust which the scoundrel threw metaphorically in the eyes of the police, and you must admit that he succeeded in blinding them—to the extent even of making them entirely forget the one simple little sentence, overheard by Mr Andrew Campbell, and which was, of course, the clue to the whole thing—the only slip the cunning rogue made—"Au revoir! Don't be late tonight." Mrs Hazeldene was going that night to the opera with her husband.

'You are astonished?' he added with a shrug of the shoulders, 'you do not see the tragedy yet, as I have seen it before me all along. The frivolous young wife, the flirtation with the friend?—all a blind, all pretence. I took the trouble which the police should have taken immediately, of finding out something about the finances of the Hazeldene ménage. Money is in nine cases out of ten the keynote to a crime.

'I found that the will of Mary Beatrice Hazeldene had been proved by the husband, her sole executor, the estate being sworn at £15,000. I found out, moreover, that Mr Edward Sholto Hazeldene was a poor shipper's clerk when he married the daughter of a wealthy builder in Kensington—and then I made note of the fact that the disconsolate widower had allowed his beard to grow since the death of his wife.

'There's no doubt that he was a clever rogue,' added the strange creature, leaning excitedly over the table, and peering into Polly's face. 'Do you know how that deadly poison was injected into the poor woman's system? By the simplest of all means, one known to every scoundrel in Southern Europe. A ring—yes! A ring, which has a tiny hollow needle capable of holding a sufficient quantity of prussic acid to have killed two persons instead of one. The man in the tweed suit shook hands with his fair companion—probably she hardly felt the prick, not sufficiently in any case to make her utter a scream. And, mind you, the scoundrel had every facility, through his friendship with Mr Errington, of procuring what poison he required, not to mention his friend's visiting card. We cannot gauge how many months ago he began to try and copy Frank Errington in his style of dress, the cut of his moustache, his general appearance, making the change probably so gradual, that no one in his own entourage would notice it. He selected for his model a man his own height and build, with the same coloured hair.'

'But there was the terrible risk of being identified by his fellow-traveller in the Underground,' suggested Polly.

'Yes, there certainly was that risk; he chose to take it, and he was wise. He reckoned that several days would in any case elapse before that person, who, by the way, was a business man absorbed in his newspaper, would actually see him again. The great secret of successful crime is to study human nature,' added the man in the corner, as he began looking for his hat and coat. 'Edward Hazeldene knew it well.'

'But the ring?'

'He may have bought that when he was on his honey-moon,' he suggested with a grim chuckle; 'the tragedy was not planned in a week, it may have taken years to mature. But you will own that there goes a frightful scoundrel unhung. I have left you his photograph as he was a year ago, and as he is now. You will see he has shaved his beard again, but also his moustache. I fancy he is a friend now of Mr Andrew Campbell.'

He left Miss Polly Burton wondering, not knowing what to believe.

And that is why she missed her appointment with Mr Richard Frobisher (of the *London Mail*) to go and see Maud Allan dance at the Palace Theatre that afternoon.

The Affair of the Corridor Express

Victor L. Whitechurch

Victor Lorenzo Whitechurch (1868–1933) was a clergyman who became such a successful crime writer that he was invited to become a founder member of the prestigious Detection Club, and contributed the opening chapter to the Club's round-robin novel *The Floating Admiral* (1931). In his later years, he concentrated increasingly on producing novels such as *The Crime at Diana's Pool* (1926) and *Murder at the College* (1932), but his most celebrated work features the railway detective Thorpe Hazell.

Introducing a reprinted edition of Whitechurch's *Thrilling Stories of the Railway* (1912) in 1977, Bryan Morgan said that the author was 'no mere Bradshaw-browser; he…[was] almost a practical railwayman. He knew how to scotch a point, what was the loading-gauge of the Great Northern, and how long an engine took to re-water…' Hazell was sharply differentiated from Sherlock Holmes, a health fanatic, book collector, and train enthusiast, who was regularly consulted by railway companies for advice about 'the bewildering task of altering their time-tables'.

Thorpe Hazell stood in his study in his London flat. On the opposite wall he had pinned a bit of paper, about an inch square, at the height of his eye, and was now going through the most extraordinary contortions.

With his eyes fixed on the paper he was craning his neck as far as it would reach and twisting his head about in all directions. This necessitated a fearful rolling of the eyes in order to keep them on the paper, and was supposed to be a means of strengthening the muscles of the eye for angular sight.

Presently there came a tap at the door.

'Come in!' cried Hazell, still whirling his head round.

'A gentleman wishes to see you at once, sir!' said the servant, handing him a card.

Hazell paused in his exercises, took it from the tray, and read:

'Mr F. W. Wingrave, M.A., B.Sc.'

'Oh, show him in,' said Hazell, rather impatiently, for he hated to be interrupted when he was doing his 'eye gymnastics.'

There entered a young man of about five-and-twenty, with a look of keen anxiety on his face.

'You are Mr Thorpe Hazell?' he asked.

'I am.'

'You will have seen my name on my card—I am one of the masters at Shillington School—I had heard your name, and they told me at the station that it might be well to consult you—I hope you don't mind—I know you're not an ordinary detective, but—'

'Sit down, Mr Wingrave,' said Hazell, interrupting his nervous flow of language. 'You look quite ill and tired.'

'I have just been through a very trying experience,' replied Wingrave, sinking into a seat. 'A boy I was in charge of has just mysteriously disappeared, and I want you to find him for me, and I want to ask your opinion. They say you know all about railways, but—'

'Now, look here, my dear sir, you just have some hot toast and water before you say another word. I conclude you want to consult me on some railway matter. I'll do what I can, but I won't hear you till you've had some refreshment. Perhaps you prefer whiskey—though I don't advise it.'

Wingrave, however, chose the whiskey, and Hazell poured him out some, adding soda-water.

'Thank you,' he said. 'I hope you'll be able to give me advice. I am afraid the poor boy must be killed; the whole thing is a mystery, and I—'

'Stop a bit, Mr Wingrave. I must ask you to tell me the story from the very beginning. That's the best way.'

'Quite right. The worry of it has made me incoherent, I fear. But I'll try and do what you propose. First of all, do you know the name of Carr-Mathers?'

'Yes, I think so. Very rich, is he not?'

'A millionaire. He has only one child, a boy of about ten, whose mother died at his birth. He is a small boy for his age, and idolised by his father. About three months ago this young Horace Carr-Mathers was sent to our school—Cragsbury House, just outside Shillington. It is not a very large school, but exceedingly select, and the headmaster, Dr Spring, is well known in high-class circles. I may tell you that we have the sons of some of the leading nobility preparing for the public schools. You will readily understand that in such an establishment as ours the most scrupulous care is exercised over the boys, not only as regards their moral and intellectual training, but also to guard against any outside influences.'

'Kidnapping, for example,' interposed Hazell.

'Exactly. There have been such cases known, and Dr Spring has a very high reputation to maintain. The slightest rumour against the school would go ill with him—and with all of us masters.

'Well, this morning the headmaster received a telegram about Horace Carr-Mathers, requesting that he should be sent up to town.'

'Do you know the exact wording?' asked Hazell.

'I have it with me,' replied Wingrave, drawing it from his pocket.

Hazell took it from him, and read as follows:

'Please grant Horace leave of absence for two days. Send him to London by 5.45 express from Shillington, in first-class carriage, giving guard instructions to look after him. We will meet train in town—Carr-Mathers.'

'Um,' grunted Hazell, as he handed it back. 'Well, he can afford telegrams.'

'Oh, he's always wiring about something or other,' replied Wingrave; 'he seldom writes a letter. Well, when the doctor received this he called me into his study.

'"I suppose I must let the boy go," he said, "but I'm not at all inclined to allow him to travel by himself. If anything should happen to him his father would hold us responsible as well as the railway company. So you had better take him up to town, Mr Wingrave."

'"Yes, sir."

'"You need do no more than deliver him to his father. If Mr Carr-Mathers is not at the terminus to meet him, take him with you in a cab to his house in Portland Place. You'll probably be able to catch the last train home, but, if not, you can get a bed at an hotel."

'"Very good, sir."

'So, shortly after half-past five, I found myself standing on the platform at Shillington, waiting for the London express.'

'Now, stop a moment,' interrupted Hazell, sipping a glass of filtered water which he had poured out for himself. 'I want to get a clear notion of this journey of yours from the beginning, for, I presume, you will shortly be telling me that something strange happened during it. Was there anything to be noticed before the train started?'

'Nothing at the time. But I remembered afterwards that two men seemed to be watching me rather closely when I took the tickets, and I heard one of them say "Confound," beneath his breath. But my suspicions were not aroused at the moment.'

'I see. If there is anything in this it was probably because he was disconcerted when he saw you were going to travel with the boy. Did these two men get into the train?'

'I'm coming to that. The train was in sharp to time, and we took our seats in a first-class compartment.'

'Please describe the exact position.'

'Our carriage was the third from the front. It was a corridor train, with access from carriage to carriage all the way through. Horace and myself were in a compartment alone. I had bought him some illustrated papers for the journey, and for some time he sat quietly enough, looking through them. After a bit he grew fidgety, as you know boys will.'

'Wait a minute. I want to know if the corridor of your carriage was on the left or on the right—supposing you to be seated facing the engine?'

'On the left.'

'Very well, go on.'

'The door leading into the corridor stood open. It was still daylight, but dusk was setting in fast—I should say it was about half-past six, or a little more. Horace had been looking out of the window on the right side of the train when I drew his attention to Rutherham Castle, which we were passing. It stands, as you know, on the left side of the line. In order to get a better view of it he went out into the corridor and stood there. I retained my seat on the right side of the compartment, glancing at him from time to time. He seemed interested in the corridor itself, looking about him, and once or twice shutting and opening the door of our compartment. I can see now that I ought to have kept a sharper eye on him, but I never dreamed that any accident could happen. I was reading a paper myself, and became rather interested in a paragraph. It may have been seven or eight minutes before I looked up. When I did so, Horace had disappeared.

'I didn't think anything of it at first, but only concluded that he had taken a walk along the corridor.'

'You don't know which way he went?' inquired Hazell.

'No. I couldn't say. I waited a minute or two, and then rose and looked out into the corridor. There was no one there. Still my suspicions were not aroused. It was possible that he had gone to the lavatory. So I sat down again, and waited. Then I began to get a little anxious, and determined to have a look for him. I walked to either end of the corridor and searched the lavatories, but they were both empty. Then I looked in all the other compartments of the carriage and asked their occupants if they had seen him go by, but none of them had noticed him.'

'Do you remember how these compartments were occupied?'

'Yes. In the first, which was reserved for ladies, there were five ladies. The next was a smoker with three gentlemen in it. Ours came next. Then, going towards the front of the train, were the two men I had noticed at Shillington; the last compartment had a gentleman and lady and their three children.'

'Ah! How about those two men—what were they doing?'

'One of them was reading a book, and the other appeared to be asleep.'

'Tell me. Was the door leading to the corridor from their compartment shut?'

'Yes, it was.'

'I was in a most terrible fright, and I went back to my compartment and pulled the electric communicator. In a few seconds the front guard came along the corridor and asked me what I wanted. I told him I had lost my charge. He suggested that the boy had walked through to another carriage, and I asked him if he would mind my making a thorough search of the train with him. To this he readily agreed. We went back to the first carriage and began to do so. We examined every compartment from end to end of the train; we looked under every seat, in spite of the protestations of some of the passengers; we searched all the lavatories—every corner of the train—and we found absolutely no trace of Horace Carr-Mathers. No one had seen the boy anywhere.'

'Had the train stopped?'

'Not for a second. It was going at full speed all the time. It only slowed down after we had finished the search—but it never quite stopped.'

'Ah! We'll come to that presently. I want to ask you some questions first. Was it still daylight?'

'Dusk, but quite light enough to see plainly—besides which, the train lamps were lit.'

'Exactly. Those two men, now, in the next compartment to yours—tell me precisely what happened when you visited them the second time with the guard.'

'They asked a lot of questions—like many of the other passengers—and seemed very surprised.'

'You looked underneath their seats?'

'Certainly.'

'On the luggage-racks? A small boy like that could be rolled up in a rug and put on the rack.'

'We examined every rack on the train.'

Thorpe Hazell lit a cigarette and smoked furiously, motioning to his companion to keep quiet. He was thinking out the situation. Suddenly he said:

'How about the window in those two men's compartment?'

'It was shut—I particularly noticed it.'

'You are quite sure you searched the whole of the train?'

'Absolutely certain; so was the guard.'

'Ah!' remarked Hazell. 'Even guards are mistaken sometimes. It—er—was only the inside of the train you searched, eh?'

'Of course.'

'Very well,' replied Hazell, 'now, before we go any further, I want to ask you this. Would it have been to anyone's interest to have murdered the boy?'

'I don't think so—from what I know. I don't see how it could be.'

'Very well. We will take it as a pure case of kidnapping, and presume that he is alive and well. This ought to console you to begin with.'

'Do you think you can help me?'

'I don't know yet. But go on and tell me all that happened.'

'Well, after we had searched the train I was at my wits'

end—and so was the guard. We both agreed, however, that nothing more could be done till we reached London. Somehow, my strongest suspicions concerning those two men were aroused, and I travelled in their compartment for the rest of the journey.'

'Oh! Did anything happen?'

'Nothing. They both wished me good-night, hoped I'd find the boy, got out, and drove off in a hansom.'

'And then?'

'I looked about for Mr Carr-Mathers, but he was nowhere to be seen. Then I saw an inspector and put the case before him. He promised to make inquiries and to have the line searched on the part where I missed Horace. I took a hansom to Portland Place, only to discover that Mr Carr-Mathers is on the Continent and not expected home for a week. Then I came on to you—the inspector had advised me to do so. And that's the whole story. It's a terrible thing for me, Mr Hazell. What do you think of it?'

'Well,' replied Hazell, 'of course it's very clear that there is a distinct plot. Someone sent that telegram, knowing Mr Carr-Mathers' proclivities. The object was to kidnap the boy. It sounds absurd to talk of brigands and ransoms in this country, but the thing is done over and over again for all that. It is obvious that the boy was expected to travel alone, and that the train was the place chosen for the kidnapping. Hence the elaborate directions. I think you were quite right in suspecting those two men, and it might have been better if you had followed them up without coming to me.'

'But they went off alone!'

'Exactly. It's my belief they had originally intended doing so after disposing of Horace, and that they carried out their original intentions.'

'But what became of the boy?—how did they—'

'Stop a bit, I'm not at all clear in my own mind. But you mentioned that while you were concluding your search with the guard, the train slackened speed?'

'Yes. It almost came to a stop—and then went very slowly for a minute or so. I asked the guard why, but I didn't understand his reply.'

'What was it?'

'He said it was a P.W. operation.'

Hazell laughed. 'P.W. stands for permanent way,' he explained, 'I know exactly what you mean now. There is a big job going on near Longmoor—they are raising the level of the line, and the up-trains are running on temporary rails. So they have to proceed very slowly. Now it was after this that you went back to the two men whom you suspected?'

'Yes.'

'Very well. Now let me think the thing over. Have some more whiskey? You might also like to glance at the contents of my book-case. If you know anything of first editions and bindings, they will interest you.'

Wingrave, it is to be feared, paid but small heed to the books, but watched Hazell anxiously as the latter smoked cigarette after cigarette, his brows knit in deep thought. After a bit he said slowly:

'You will understand that I am going to work upon the theory that the boy has been kidnapped and that the original intention has been carried out, in spite of the accident of your presence in the train. How the boy was disposed of meanwhile is what baffles me; but that is a detail—though it will be interesting to know how it was done. Now, I don't want to raise any false hopes, because I may very likely be wrong, but we are going to take action upon a very feasible assumption, and if I am at all correct, I hope to put you definitely on the track. Mind, I don't promise to do so, and, at best, I don't promise to do more than put you on a track. Let me see—it's just after nine. We have plenty of time. We'll drive first to Scotland Yard, for it will be as well to have a detective with us.'

He filled a flask with milk, put some plasmon biscuits and a banana into a sandwich case, and then ordered his servant to hail a cab.

An hour later, Hazell, Wingrave, and a man from Scotland Yard were closeted together in one of the private offices of the Mid-Eastern Railway with one of the chief officials of the line. The latter was listening attentively to Hazell.

'But I can't understand the boy not being anywhere in the train, Mr Hazell,' he said.

'I can—partly,' replied Hazell, 'but first let me see if my theory is correct.'

'By all means. There's a down-train in a few minutes. I'll go with you, for the matter is very interesting. Come along, gentlemen.'

He walked forward to the engine and gave a few instructions to the driver, and then they took their seats in the train. After a run of half an hour or so they passed a station.

'That's Longmoor,' said the official, 'now we shall soon be on the spot. It's about a mile down that the line is being raised.'

Hazell put his head out of the window. Presently an ominous red light showed itself. The train came almost to a stop, and then proceeded slowly, the man who had shown the red light changing it to green. They could see him as they passed, standing close to a little temporary hut. It was his duty to warn all approaching drivers, and for this purpose he was stationed some three hundred yards in front of the bit of line that was being operated upon. Very soon they were passing this bit. Naphtha lamps shed a weird light over a busy scene, for the work was being continued night and day. A score or so of sturdy navvies were shovelling and picking along the track.

Once more into the darkness. On the other side of the scene of operations, at the same distance, was another little hut, with a guardian for the up-train. Instead of increasing the speed in passing this hut, which would have been usual, the driver brought the train almost to a standstill. As he did so the four men got out of the carriage, jumping from the footboard to the ground. On went the train, leaving them on the left side of the down track, just opposite the little hut. They could see the man standing outside, his back partly turned to them. There was a fire in a brazier close by that dimly outlined his figure.

He started suddenly, as they crossed the line towards him.

'What are you doing here?' he cried. 'You've no business here—you're trespassing.'

He was a big, strong-looking man, and he backed a little towards his hut as he spoke.

'I am Mr Mills, the assistant-superintendent of the line,' replied the official, coming forward.

'Beg pardon, sir; but how was I to know that?' growled the man.

'Quite right. It's your duty to warn off strangers. How long have you been stationed here?'

'I came on at five o'clock; I'm regular nightwatchman, sir.'

'Ah! Pretty comfortable, eh?'

'Yes, thank you, sir,' replied the man, wondering why the question was asked, but thinking, not unnaturally, that the assistant-superintendent had come down with a party of engineers to supervise things.

'Got the hut to yourself?'

'Yes, sir.'

Without another word, Mr Mills walked to the door of the hut. The man, his face suddenly growing pale, moved, and stood with his back to it.

'It's—it's private, sir!' he growled.

Hazell laughed. 'All right, my man,' he said. 'I was right, I think—hullo!—look out! Don't let him go!'

For the man had made a quick rush forward. But the Scotland Yard officer and Hazell were on him in a moment, and a few seconds later the handcuffs clicked on his wrists. Then they flung the door open, and there, lying in the corner, gagged and bound, was Horace Carr-Mathers.

An exclamation of joy broke forth from Wingrave, as he opened his knife to cut the cords. But Hazell stopped him.

'Just half a moment,' he said. 'I want to see how they've tied him up.'

A peculiar method had been adopted in doing this. His wrists were fastened behind his back, a stout cord was round his body just under the armpits, and another cord above the knees. These were connected by a slack bit of rope.

'All right!' went on Hazell. 'Let's get the poor lad out of his troubles—there, that's better. How do you feel, my boy?'

'Awfully stiff!' said Horace. 'But I'm not hurt. I say, sir,' he continued to Wingrave, 'how did you know I was here? I am glad you've come.'

'The question is how did you get here?' replied Wingrave. 'Mr Hazell, here, seemed to know where you were, but it's a puzzle to me at present.'

'If you'd come half an hour later you wouldn't have found him,' growled the man who was handcuffed. 'I ain't so much to blame as them as employed me.'

'Oh, is that how the land lies?' exclaimed Hazell. 'I see. You shall tell us presently, my boy, how it happened. Meanwhile, Mr Mills, I think we can prepare a little trap—eh?'

In five minutes all was arranged. A couple of the navvies were brought up from the line, one stationed outside to guard against trains, and with certain other instructions, the other being inside the hut with the rest of them. A third navvy was also dispatched for the police.

'How are they coming?' asked Hazell of the handcuffed man.

'They were going to take a train down from London to Rockhampstead on the East-Northern, and drive over. It's about ten miles off.'

'Good! They ought soon to be here,' replied Hazell, as he munched some biscuits and washed them down with a draught of milk, after which he astonished them all by solemnly going through one of his 'digestive exercises.'

A little later they heard the sound of wheels on a road beside the line. Then the man on watch said, in gruff tones:

'The boy's inside!'

But they found more than the boy inside, and an hour later all three conspirators were safely lodged in Longmoor gaol.

'Oh, it was awfully nasty, I can tell you,' said Horace Carr-Mathers, as he explained matters afterwards. 'I went into the corridor, you know, and was looking about at things, when all of a sudden I felt my coat-collar grasped behind, and a hand was laid over my mouth. I tried to kick and shout, but it was no go. They got me into the compartment, stuffed a handkerchief into my mouth, and tied it in. It was just beastly. Then they bound me hand and foot, and opened the window on the right-hand side—opposite the corridor. I was in a funk, for I thought they were going to throw me out, but one of them told me to keep my pecker up, as they weren't going to hurt me. Then they let me down out of the window by that slack rope, and made it fast to the handle of the door outside. It was pretty bad. There was I, hanging from the door-handle in a sort of doubled-up position, my back resting on the foot-board of the carriage, and the train rushing along like mad. I felt sick and awful, and I had to shut my eyes. I seemed to hang there for ages.'

'I told you, you only examined the inside of the train,' said Thorpe Hazell to Wingrave. 'I had my suspicions that he was somewhere on the outside all the time, but I was puzzled to know where. It was a clever trick.'

'Well,' went on the boy, 'I heard the window open above me after a bit. I looked up and saw one of the men taking the rope off the handle. The train was just beginning to slow down. Then he hung out of the window, dangling me with one hand. It was horrible. I was hanging below the foot-board now. Then the train came almost to a stop, and someone caught me round the waist. I lost my senses for a minute or two, and then I found myself lying in the hut.'

'Well, Mr Hazell,' said the assistant-superintendent, 'you were perfectly right, and we all owe you a debt of gratitude.'

'Oh,' said Hazell, 'it was only a guess at the best. I presumed it was simply kidnapping, and the problem to be solved was how and where the boy was got off the train without injury. It was obvious that he had been disposed of before the train reached London. There was only one other inference. The man on duty was evidently the confederate, for, if not, his presence would have stopped the whole plan of action. I'm very glad to have been of any use. There are interesting points about the case, and it has been a pleasure to me to undertake it.'

A little while afterwards Mr Carr-Mathers himself called on Hazell to thank him.

'I should like,' he said, 'to express my deep gratitude substantially; but I understand you are not an ordinary detective. But is there any way in which I can serve you, Mr Hazell?'

'Yes—two ways.'

'Please name them.'

'I should be sorry for Mr Wingrave to get into trouble through this affair—or Dr Spring either.'

'I understand you, Mr Hazell. They were both to blame, in a way. But I will see that Dr Spring's reputation does not suffer and that Wingrave comes out of it harmlessly.'

'Thank you very much.'

'You said there was a second way in which I could serve you.'

'So there is. At Dunn's sale last month you were the purchaser of two first editions of "The New Bath Guide." If you cared to dispose of one, I—'

'Say no more, Mr Hazell. I shall be glad to give you one for your collection.'

Hazell stiffened.

'You misunderstand me!' he exclaimed icily. 'I was about to add that if you cared to dispose of a copy I would write you out a cheque.'

'Oh, certainly,' replied Mr Carr-Mathers with a smile, 'I shall be extremely pleased.'

Whereupon the transaction was concluded.

The Case of Oscar Brodski

R. Austin Freeman

Richard Austin Freeman (1862–1943) was, like Arthur Conan Doyle and Robert Eustace, a doctor who achieved greater fame as a crime writer than as a medical practitioner. He served with the Colonial Service in Africa, but contracted blackwater fever, and returned to England, where he turned to writing fiction as a means of supplementing a meagre income. Under the pen-name Clifford Ashdown, he wrote short stories in collaboration with J.J. Pitcairn, a medical officer at Holloway Prison, but it was not until he created Dr John Thorndyke, who first appeared in *The Red Thumb Mark* (1907), that he began to establish himself as a crime writer of distinction.

According to Freeman, 'The methods of even famous murderers are commonly crude and even foolish…I have met with but a single case which seemed to be worth using for fiction…And even this case was selected less for its ingenuity of plot than for the excellent opening that it offered for medico-legal investigation.' The case was that of *R. v Watson and wife* (Nottingham Assizes, 15th March 1867) and the story it inspired was this one, published in *The Singing Bone* in 1912. Even more noteworthy is the fact that 'The Case of Oscar Brodski' is widely regarded as the first example of the 'inverted' detective story where, as Freeman said, 'the usual conditions are reversed; the reader knows everything, the detective knows nothing, and the interest focuses on the unexpected significance of trivial circumstances'.

I. The Mechanism of Crime

A surprising amount of nonsense has been talked about conscience. On the one hand remorse (or the 'again-bite,' as certain scholars of ultra-Teutonic leanings would prefer to call it); on the other hand 'an easy conscience': these have been accepted as the determining factors of happiness or the reverse.

Of course there is an element of truth in the 'easy conscience' view, but it begs the whole question. A particularly hardy conscience may be quite easy under the most unfavourable conditions—conditions in which the more feeble conscience might be severely afflicted with the 'again-bite.' And, then, it seems to be the fact that some fortunate persons have no conscience at all; a negative gift that raises them above the mental vicissitudes of the common herd of humanity.

Now, Silas Hickler was a case in point. No one, looking into his cheerful, round face, beaming with benevolence and wreathed in perpetual smiles, would have imagined him to be a criminal. Least of all, his worthy, high-church housekeeper, who was a witness to his unvarying amiability, who constantly heard him carolling light-heartedly about the house and noted his appreciative zest at mealtimes.

Yet it is a fact that Silas earned his modest, though comfortable, income by the gentle art of burglary. A precarious trade and risky withal, yet not so very hazardous if pursued with judgment and moderation. And Silas was eminently a man of judgment. He worked invariably alone. He kept his own counsel. No confederate had he to turn King's Evidence at a pinch; no 'doxy' who might bounce off in a fit of temper to Scotland Yard. Nor was he greedy and thriftless, as most criminals are. His 'scoops' were few and far between, carefully planned, secretly executed, and the proceeds judiciously invested in 'weekly property.'

In early life Silas had been connected with the diamond industry, and he still did a little rather irregular dealing. In the trade he was suspected of transactions with IDBs, and one or two indiscreet dealers had gone so far as to whisper the ominous word 'fence.' But Silas smiled a benevolent smile and went his way. He knew what he knew, and his clients in Amsterdam were not inquisitive.

Such was Silas Hickler. As he strolled round his garden in the dusk of an October evening, he seemed the very type of modest, middle-class prosperity. He was dressed in the travelling suit that he wore on his little continental trips; his bag was packed and stood in readiness on the sitting-room sofa. A parcel of diamonds (purchased honestly, though without impertinent questions, at Southampton) was in the inside pocket of his waistcoat, and another more valuable parcel was stowed in a cavity in the heel of his right boot. In an hour and a half it would be time for him to set out to catch the boat train at the junction; meanwhile there was nothing to do but to stroll round the fading garden and consider how he should invest the proceeds of the impending deal. His housekeeper had gone over to Welham for the week's shopping, and would probably not be back until eleven o'clock. He was alone in the premises and just a trifle dull.

He was about to turn into the house when his ear caught the sound of footsteps on the unmade road that passed the end of the garden. He paused and listened. There was no other dwelling near, and the road led nowhere, fading away into the waste land beyond the house. Could this be a visitor? It seemed unlikely, for visitors were few at Silas Hickler's house. Meanwhile the footsteps continued to approach, ringing out with increasing loudness on the hard, stony path.

Silas strolled down to the gate, and, leaning on it, looked out with some curiosity. Presently a glow of light showed him the face of a man, apparently lighting his pipe; then a dim figure detached itself from the enveloping gloom, advanced towards him and halted opposite the garden. The stranger removed a cigarette from his mouth and, blowing out a cloud of smoke, asked—

'Can you tell me if this road will take me to Badsham Junction?'

'No,' replied Hickler, 'but there is a footpath farther on that leads to the station.'

'Footpath!' growled the stranger. 'I've had enough of footpaths. I came down from town to Catley intending to walk across to the junction. I started along the road, and then some fool directed me to a short cut, with the result that I have been blundering about in the dark for the last half-hour. My sight isn't very good, you know,' he added.

'What train do you want to catch?' asked Hickler.

'Seven fifty-eight,' was the reply.

'I am going to catch that train myself,' said Silas, 'but I shan't be starting for another hour. The station is only three-quarters of a mile from here. If you like to come in and take a rest, we can walk down together and then you'll be sure of not missing your way.'

'It's very good of you,' said the stranger, peering, with spectacled eyes, at the dark house, 'but—I think—'

'Might as well wait here as at the station,' said Silas in his genial way, holding the gate open, and the stranger, after a momentary hesitation, entered and, flinging away his cigarette, followed him to the door of the cottage.

The sitting-room was in darkness, save for the dull glow of the expiring fire, but, entering before his guest, Silas applied a match to the lamp that hung from the ceiling. As the flame leaped up, flooding the little interior with light, the two men regarded one another with mutual curiosity.

'Brodski, by Jingo!' was Hickler's silent commentary, as he looked at his guest. 'Doesn't know me, evidently—wouldn't, of course, after all these years and with his bad eyesight. Take a seat, sir,' he added aloud. 'Will you join me in a little refreshment to while away the time?'

Brodski murmured an indistinct acceptance, and, as his host turned to open a cupboard, he deposited his hat (a hard, grey felt) on a chair in a corner, placed his bag on the edge of the table, resting his umbrella against it, and sat down in a small arm-chair.

'Have a biscuit?' said Hickler, as he placed a whisky-bottle on the table together with a couple of his best star-pattern tumblers and a siphon.

'Thanks, I think I will,' said Brodski. 'The railway journey and all this confounded tramping about, you know—'

'Yes,' agreed Silas. 'Doesn't do to start with an empty

stomach. Hope you don't mind oat-cakes; I see they're the only biscuits I have.'

Brodski hastened to assure him that oat-cakes were his special and peculiar fancy; and in confirmation, having mixed himself a stiff jorum, he fell to upon the biscuits with evident gusto.

Brodski was a deliberate feeder, and at present appeared to be somewhat sharp set. His measured munching being unfavourable to conversation, most of the talking fell to Silas; and, for once, that genial transgressor found the task embarrassing. The natural thing would have been to discuss his guest's destination and perhaps the object of his journey; but this was precisely what Hickler avoided doing. For he knew both, and instinct told him to keep his knowledge to himself.

Brodski was a diamond merchant of considerable reputation, and in a large way of business. He bought stones principally in the rough, and of these he was a most excellent judge. His fancy was for stones of somewhat unusual size and value, and it was well known to be his custom, when he had accumulated a sufficient stock, to carry them himself to Amsterdam and supervise the cutting of the rough stones. Of this Hickler was aware, and he had no doubt that Brodski was now starting on one of his periodical excursions; that somewhere in the recesses of his rather shabby clothing was concealed a paper packet possibly worth several thousand pounds.

Brodski sat by the table munching monotonously and talking little. Hickler sat opposite him, talking nervously and rather wildly at times, and watching his guest with a growing fascination. Precious stones, and especially diamonds, were Hickler's speciality. 'Hard stuff'—silver plate—he avoided entirely; gold, excepting in the form of specie, he seldom touched; but stones, of which he could carry off a whole consignment in the heel of his boot and dispose of with absolute safety, formed the staple of his industry. And here was a man sitting opposite him with a parcel in his pocket containing the equivalent of a dozen of his most successful scoops, stones worth perhaps—Here he pulled himself up short and began to talk rapidly, though without much coherence. For, even as he talked, other words, formed subconsciously, seemed to insinuate themselves into the interstices of the sentences and to carry on a parallel train of thought.

'Gets chilly in the evenings now, doesn't it?' said Hickler.

'It does indeed,' Brodski agreed, and then resumed his slow munching, breathing audibly through his nose.

'Five thousand at least,' the subconscious train of thought resumed; 'probably six or seven, perhaps ten.' Silas fidgeted in his chair and endeavoured to concentrate his ideas on some topic of interest. He was growing disagreeably conscious of a new and unfamiliar state of mind.

'Do you take any interest in gardening?' he asked. Next to diamonds and weekly property, his besetting weakness was fuchsias.

Brodski chuckled sourly. 'Hatton Garden is the nearest approach—' He broke off suddenly, and then added, 'I am a Londoner, you know.'

The abrupt break in the sentence was not unnoticed by Silas, nor had he any difficulty in interpreting it. A man who carries untold wealth upon his person must needs be wary in his speech.

'Yes,' he answered absently, 'it's hardly a Londoner's hobby.' And then, half consciously, he began a rapid calculation. Put it at five thousand pounds. What would that represent in weekly property? His last set of houses had cost two hundred and fifty pounds apiece, and he had let them at ten shillings and six-pence a week. At that rate, five thousand pounds represented twenty houses at ten and sixpence a week—say ten pounds a week—one pound eight shillings a day—five hundred and twenty pounds a year—for life. It was a competency. Added to what he already had, it was wealth. With that income he could fling the tools of his trade into the river and live out the remainder of his life in comfort and security.

He glanced furtively at his guest across the table, and then looked away quickly as he felt stirring within him an impulse the nature of which he could not mistake. This must be put an end to. Crimes against the person he had always looked upon as sheer insanity. There was, it is true, that little affair of the Weybridge policeman, but that was unforeseen and unavoidable, and it was the constable's doing after all. And there was the old housekeeper at Epsom, too; but, of course, if the old idiot would shriek in that insane fashion—well, it was an accident, very regrettable, to be sure, and no one could be more sorry for the mishap than himself. But deliberate homicide!—robbery from the person! It was the act of a stark lunatic.

Of course, if he had happened to be that sort of person, here was the opportunity of a lifetime. The immense booty, the empty house, the solitary neighbourhood, away from the main road and from other habitations; the time, the dark-ness—but, of course, there was the body to be thought of; that was always the difficulty. What to do with the body— Here he caught the shriek of the up express, rounding the curve in the line that ran past the waste land at the back of the house. The sound started a new train of thought, and, as he followed it out, his eyes fixed themselves on the uncon-scious and taciturn Brodski, as he sat thoughtfully sipping his whisky. At length, averting his gaze with an effort, he rose suddenly from his chair and turned to look at the clock on the mantelpiece, spreading out his hands before the dying fire. A tumult of strange sensations warned him to leave the house. He shivered slightly, though he was rather hot than chilly, and, turning his head, looked at the door.

'Seems to be a confounded draught,' he said, with another slight shiver, 'did I shut the door properly, I wonder?' He strode across the room and, opening the door wide, looked out into the dark garden. A desire, sudden and urgent, had come over him to get out into the open air, to be on the road and have done with this madness that was knocking at the door of his brain.

'I wonder if it is worth while to start yet,' he said, with a yearning glance at the murky, starless sky.

Brodski roused himself and looked round. 'Is your clock right?' he asked.

Silas reluctantly admitted that it was.

'How long will it take us to walk to the station?' inquired Brodski.

'Oh, about twenty-five minutes to half-an-hour,' replied Silas unconsciously exaggerating the distance.

'Well,' said Brodski, 'we've got more than an hour yet, and it's more comfortable here than hanging about the station. I don't see the use of starting before we need.'

'No; of course not,' Silas agreed. A wave of strange emotion, half-regretful, half-triumphant, surged through his brain. For some moments he remained standing on the threshold; looking out dreamily into the night. Then he softly closed the door; and, seemingly without the exercise of his volition, the key turned noiselessly in the lock.

He returned to his chair and tried to open a conversation

with the taciturn Brodski, but the words came faltering and disjointed. He felt his face growing hot, his brain full and tense, and there was a faint, high-pitched singing in his ears. He was conscious of watching his guest with a new and fearful interest, and, by sheer force of will, turned away his eyes; only to find them a moment later involuntarily returning to fix the unconscious man with yet more horrible intensity. And ever through his mind walked, like a dreadful procession, the thoughts of what that other man—the man of blood and violence—would do in these circumstances. Detail by detail the hideous synthesis fitted together the parts of the imagined crime, and arranged them in due sequence until they formed a succession of events, rational, connected and coherent.

He rose uneasily from his chair, with his eyes still riveted upon his guest. He could not sit any longer opposite that man with his hidden store of precious gems. The impulse that he recognised with fear and wonder was growing more ungovernable from moment to moment. If he stayed it would presently overpower him, and then—He shrank with horror from the dreadful thought, but his fingers itched to handle the diamonds. For Silas was, after all, a criminal by nature and habit. He was a beast of prey. His livelihood had never been earned; it had been taken by stealth or, if necessary, by force. His instincts were predaceous, and the proximity of unguarded valuables suggested to him, as a logical consequence, their abstraction or seizure. His unwillingness to let these diamonds go away beyond his reach was fast becoming overwhelming.

But he would make one more effort to escape. He would keep out of Brodski's actual presence until the moment for starting came.

'If you'll excuse me,' he said, 'I will go and put on a

thicker pair of boots. After all this dry weather we may get a change, and damp feet are very uncomfortable when you are travelling.'

'Yes; dangerous too,' agreed Brodski.

Silas walked through into the adjoining kitchen, where, by the light of the little lamp that was burning there, he had seen his stout, country boots placed, cleaned and in readiness, and sat down upon a chair to make the change. He did not, of course, intend to wear the country boots, for the diamonds were concealed in those he had on. But he would make the change and then alter his mind; it would all help to pass the time. He took a deep breath. It was a relief, at any rate, to be out of that room. Perhaps, if he stayed away, the temptation would pass. Brodski would go on his way—he wished that he was going alone—and the danger would be over—at least—and the opportunity would have gone—the diamonds—

He looked up as he slowly unlaced his boot. From where he sat he could see Brodski sitting by the table with his back towards the kitchen door. He had finished eating now, and was composedly rolling a cigarette. Silas breathed heavily, and, slipping off his boot, sat for a while motionless, gazing steadily at the other man's back. Then he unlaced the other boot, still staring abstractedly at his unconscious guest, drew it off, and laid it very quietly on the floor.

Brodski calmly finished rolling his cigarette, licked the paper, put away his pouch, and, having dusted the crumbs of tobacco from his knees, began to search his pockets for a match. Suddenly, yielding to an uncontrollable impulse, Silas stood up and began stealthily to creep along the passage to the sitting-room. Not a sound came from his stockinged feet. Silently as a cat he stole forward, breathing softly with parted lips, until he stood at the threshold of the room. His face flushed duskily, his eyes, wide and staring, glittered in the lamplight, and the racing blood hummed in his ears.

Brodski struck a match—Silas noted that it was a wooden vesta—lighted his cigarette, blew out the match and flung it into the fender. Then he replaced the box in his pocket and commenced to smoke.

Slowly and without a sound Silas crept forward into the room, step by step, with catlike stealthiness, until he stood close behind Brodski's chair—so close that he had to turn his head that his breath might not stir the hair upon the other man's head. So, for half-a-minute, he stood motionless, like a symbolical statue of murder, glaring down with horrible, glittering eyes upon the unconscious diamond merchant, while his quick breath passed without a sound through his open mouth and his fingers writhed slowly like the tentacles of a giant hydra. And then, as noiselessly as ever, he backed away to the door, turned quickly and walked back into the kitchen.

He drew a deep breath. It had been a near thing. Brodski's life had hung upon a thread. For it had been so easy. Indeed, if he had happened, as he stood behind the man's chair, to have a weapon—a hammer, for instance, or even a stone—

He glanced round the kitchen and his eyes lighted on a bar that had been left by the workmen who had put up the new greenhouse. It was an odd piece cut off from a square, wrought-iron stanchion, and was about a foot long and perhaps three-quarters of an inch thick. Now, if he had had that in his hand a minute ago—

He picked the bar up, balanced it in his hand and swung it round his head. A formidable weapon this: silent, too. And it fitted the plan that had passed through his brain. Bah! He had better put the thing down.

But he did not. He stepped over to the door and looked

again at Brodski, sitting, as before, meditatively smoking, with his back towards the kitchen.

Suddenly a change came over Silas. His face flushed, the veins of his neck stood out and a sullen scowl settled on his face. He drew out his watch, glanced at it earnestly and replaced it. Then he strode swiftly but silently along the passage into the sitting-room.

A pace away from his victim's chair he halted and took deliberate aim. The bar swung aloft, but not without some faint rustle of movement, for Brodski looked round quickly even as the iron whistled through the air. The movement disturbed the murderer's aim, and the bar glanced off his victim's head, making only a trifling wound. Brodski sprang up with a tremulous, bleating cry, and clutched his assailant's arms with the tenacity of mortal terror.

Then began a terrible struggle as the two men, locked in a deadly embrace, swayed to and fro and trampled backwards and forwards. The chair was overturned, an empty glass swept from the table and, with Brodski's spectacles, crushed beneath stamping feet. And thrice that dreadful pitiful, bleating cry rang out into the night, filling Silas, despite his murderous frenzy, with terror lest some chance wayfarer should hear it. Gathering his great strength for a final effort, he forced his victim backwards on to the table and, snatching up a corner of the table-cloth, thrust it into his face and crammed it into his mouth as it opened to utter another shriek. And thus they remained for a full two minutes, almost motionless, like some dreadful group of tragic allegory. Then, when the last faint twitchings had died away, Silas relaxed his grasp and let the limp body slip softly on to the floor.

It was over. For good or for evil, the thing was done. Silas stood up, breathing heavily, and, as he wiped the sweat from

his face, he looked at the clock. The hands stood at one minute to seven. The whole thing had taken a little over three
minutes. He had nearly an hour in which to finish his task.
The goods train that entered into his scheme came by at
twenty minutes past, and it was only three hundred yards
to the line. Still, he must not waste time. He was now quite
composed, and only disturbed by the thought that Brodski's
cries might have been heard. If no one had heard them it was
all plain sailing.

He stooped, and, gently disengaging the table-cloth from
the dead man's teeth, began a careful search of his pockets.
He was not long finding what he sought, and, as he pinched
the paper packet and felt the little hard bodies grating on one
another inside, his faint regrets for what had happened were
swallowed up in self-congratulations.

He now set about his task with business-like briskness and
an attentive eye on the clock. A few large drops of blood had
fallen on the table-cloth, and there was a small bloody smear
on the carpet by the dead man's head. Silas fetched from the
kitchen some water, a nailbrush and a dry cloth, and, having
washed out the stains from the table-cover—not forgetting
the deal table-top underneath—and cleaned away the smear
from the carpet and rubbed the damp places dry, he slipped
a sheet of paper under the head of the corpse to prevent
further contamination. Then he set the table-cloth straight,
stood the chair upright, laid the broken spectacles on the
table and picked up the cigarette, which had been trodden
flat in the struggle, and flung it under the grate. Then there
was the broken glass, which he swept up into a dust-pan. Part
of it was the remains of the shattered tumbler, and the rest
the fragments of the broken spectacles. He turned it out on
to a sheet of paper and looked it over carefully, picking out

the larger recognisable pieces of the spectacle-glasses and putting them aside on a separate slip of paper, together with a sprinkling of the minute fragments. The remainder he shot back into the dust-pan and, having hurriedly put on his boots, carried it out to the rubbish-heap at the back of the house.

It was now time to start. Hastily cutting off a length of string from his string-box—for Silas was an orderly man and despised the oddments of string with which many people make shift—he tied it to the dead man's bag and umbrella and slung them from his shoulder. Then he folded up the paper of broken glass, and, slipping it and the spectacles into his pocket, picked up the body and threw it over his shoulder. Brodski was a small, spare man, weighing not more than nine stone; not a very formidable burden for a big, athletic man like Silas.

The night was intensely dark, and, when Silas looked out of the back gate over the waste land that stretched from his house to the railway, he could hardly see twenty yards ahead. After listening cautiously and hearing no sound, he went out, shut the gate swiftly behind him and set forth at a good pace, though carefully, over the broken ground. His progress was not as silent as he could have wished, for, though the scanty turf that covered the gravelly land was thick enough to deaden his footfalls, the swinging bag and umbrella made an irritating noise; indeed, his movements were more hampered by them than by the weightier burden.

The distance to the line was about three hundred yards. Ordinarily he would have walked it in from three to four minutes, but now, going cautiously with his burden and stopping now and again to listen, it took him just six minutes to reach the three-bar fence that separated the waste land from the railway. Arrived here he halted for a moment and once more listened attentively, peering into the darkness on all sides. Not a living creature was to be seen or heard in this desolate spot, but far away, the shriek of an engine's whistle warned him to hasten.

Lifting the corpse easily over the fence, he carried it a few yards farther to a point where the line curved sharply. Here he laid it face downwards, with the neck over the near rail. Drawing out his pocket-knife, he cut through the knot that fastened the umbrella to the string and also secured the bag; and when he had flung the bag and umbrella on the track beside the body, he carefully pocketed the string, excepting the little loop that had fallen to the ground when the knot was cut.

The quick snort and clanking rumble of an approaching goods train began now to be clearly audible. Rapidly, Silas drew from his pockets the battered spectacles and the packet of broken glass. The former he threw down by the dead man's head, and then, emptying the packet into his hand, sprinkled the fragments of glass around the spectacles.

He was none too soon. Already the quick, laboured puffing of the engine sounded close at hand. His impulse was to stay and watch; to witness the final catastrophe that should convert the murder into an accident or suicide. But it was hardly safe: it would be better that he should not be near lest he should not be able to get away without being seen. Hastily he climbed back over the fence and strode away across the rough fields, while the train came snorting and clattering towards the curve.

He had nearly reached his back gate when a sound from the line brought him to a sudden halt; it was a prolonged whistle accompanied by the groan of brakes and the loud clank of colliding trucks. The snorting of the engine had ceased and was replaced by the penetrating hiss of escaping steam.

The train had stopped!

For one brief moment Silas stood with bated breath and mouth agape like one petrified; then he strode forward quickly to the gate, and, letting himself in, silently slid the bolt. He was undeniably alarmed. What could have happened on the line? It was practically certain that the body had been seen; but what was happening now? And would they come to the house? He entered the kitchen, and having paused again to listen—for somebody might come and knock at the door at any moment—he walked through the sitting-room and looked round. All seemed in order there. There was the bar, though, lying where he had dropped it in the scuffle. He picked it up and held it under the lamp. There was no blood on it; only one or two hairs. Somewhat absently he wiped it with the table-cover, and then, running out through the kitchen into the back garden, dropped it over the wall into a bed of nettles. Not that there was anything incriminating in the bar, but, since he had used it as a weapon, it had somehow acquired a sinister aspect to his eye.

He now felt that it would be well to start for the station at once. It was not time yet, for it was barely twenty-five minutes past seven; but he did not wish to be found in the house if anyone should come. His soft hat was on the sofa with his bag, to which his umbrella was strapped. He put on the hat, caught up the bag and stepped over to the door; then he came back to turn down the lamp. And it was at this moment, when he stood with his hand raised to the burner, that his eye, travelling by chance into the dim corner of the room, lighted on Brodski's grey felt hat, reposing on the chair where the dead man had placed it when he entered the house.

Silas stood for a few moments as if petrified, with the chilly sweat of mortal fear standing in beads upon his forehead.

Another instant and he would have turned the lamp down and gone on his way; and then—He strode over to the chair, snatched up the hat and looked inside it. Yes, there was the name, 'Oscar Brodski,' written plainly on the lining. If he had gone away, leaving it to be discovered, he would have been lost; indeed, even now, if a search-party should come to the house, it was enough to send him to the gallows.

His limbs shook with horror at the thought, but in spite of his panic he did not lose his self-possession. Darting through into the kitchen, he grabbed up a handful of the dry brush-wood that was kept for lighting fires and carried it to the sitting-room grate where he thrust it on the extinct, but still hot, embers, and crumpling up the paper that he had placed under Brodski's head—on which paper he now noticed, for the first time, a minute bloody smear—he poked it in under the wood, and, striking a wax match, set light to it. As the wood flared up, he hacked at the hat with his pocket knife and threw the ragged strips into the blaze.

And all the while his heart was thumping and his hands a-tremble with the dread of discovery. The fragments of felt were far from inflammable, tending rather to fuse into cindery masses that smoked and smouldered, than to burn away into actual ash. Moreover, to his dismay, they emitted a powerful resinous stench mixed with the odour of burning hair, so that he had to open the kitchen window (since he dared not unlock the front door) to disperse the reek. And still, as he fed the fire with small cut fragments, he strained his ears to catch, above the crackling of the wood, the sound of the dreaded footsteps, the knock on the door that should be as the summons of fate.

The time, too, was speeding on. Twenty-one minutes to eight! In a few minutes more he must set out or he would miss the train. He dropped the dismembered hat-brim on the blazing wood and ran upstairs to open a window, since he must close that in the kitchen before he left. When he came back, the brim had already curled up into a black, clinkery mass that bubbled and hissed as the fat, pungent smoke rose from it sluggishly to the chimney.

Nineteen minutes to eight! It was time to start. He took up the poker and carefully beat the cinders into small particles, stirring them into the glowing embers of the wood and coal. There was nothing unusual in the appearance of the grate. It was his constant custom to burn letters and other discarded articles in the sitting-room fire: his housekeeper would notice nothing out of the common. Indeed, the cinders would probably be reduced to ashes before she returned. He had been careful to notice that there were no metallic fittings of any kind in the hat, which might have escaped burning.

Once more he picked up his bag, took a last look round, turned down the lamp and, unlocking the door, held it open for a few moments. Then he went out, locked the door, pocketed the key (of which his housekeeper had a duplicate) and set off at a brisk pace for the station.

He arrived in good time after all and, having taken his ticket, strolled through on to the platform. The train was not yet signalled, but there seemed to be an unusual stir in the place. The passengers were collected in a group at one end of the platform, and were all looking in one direction down the line; and, even as he walked towards them, with a certain tremulous, nauseating curiosity, two men emerged from the darkness and ascended the slope to the platform, carrying a stretcher covered with a tarpaulin. The passengers parted to let the bearers pass, turning fascinated eyes upon the shape that showed faintly through the rough pall; and, when the stretcher had been borne into the lamp-room, they fixed their attention upon a porter who followed carrying a hand-bag and an umbrella.

Suddenly one of the passengers started forward with an exclamation.

'Is that his umbrella?' he demanded.

'Yes, sir,' answered the porter, stopping and holding it out for the speaker's inspection.

'My God!' ejaculated the passenger; then, turning sharply to a tall man who stood close by, he said excitedly: 'That's Brodski's umbrella. I could swear to it. You remember Brodski?' The tall man nodded, and the passenger, turning once more to the porter, said: 'I identify that umbrella. It belongs to a gentleman named Brodski. If you look in his hat you will see his name written in it. He always writes his name in his hat.'

'We haven't found his hat yet,' said the porter; 'but here is the station-master coming up the line.' He awaited the arrival of his superior and then announced: 'This gentleman, sir, has identified the umbrella.'

'Oh,' said the station-master, 'you recognise the umbrella, sir, do you? Then perhaps you would step into the lamp-room and see if you can identify the body.'

The passenger recoiled with a look of alarm.

'Is it—is he—very much injured?' he asked tremulously.

'Well, yes,' was the reply. 'You see, the engine and six of the trucks went over him before they could stop the train. Took his head clean off, in fact.'

'Shocking! Shocking!' gasped the passenger. 'I think if you don't mind—I'd—I'd rather not. You don't think it's necessary, doctor, do you?'

'Yes, I do,' replied the tall man. 'Early identification may be of the first importance.'

'Then I suppose I must,' said the passenger.

Very reluctantly he allowed himself to be conducted by the station-master to the lamp-room, as the clang of the bell announced the approaching train. Silas Hickler followed and took his stand with the expectant crowd outside the closed door. In a few moments the passenger burst out, pale and awe-stricken, and rushed up to his tall friend. 'It is!' he exclaimed breathlessly. 'It's Brodski! Poor old Brodski! Horrible! Horrible! He was to have met me here and come on with me to Amsterdam.'

'Had he any—merchandise about him?' the tall man asked; and Silas strained his ears to catch the reply.

'He had some stones, no doubt, but I don't know what. His clerk will know, of course. By the way, doctor, could you watch the case for me? Just to be sure it was really an accident or—you know what. We were old friends, you know, fellow townsmen, too; we were both born in Warsaw. I'd like you to give an eye to the case.'

'Very well,' said the other. 'I will satisfy myself that—there is nothing more than appears and let you have a report. Will that do?'

'Thank you. It's excessively good of you, doctor. Ah! Here comes the train. I hope it won't inconvenience you to stay and see to this matter.'

'Not in the least,' replied the doctor. 'We are not due at Warmington until tomorrow afternoon, and I expect we can find out all that is necessary to know and still keep our appointment.'

Silas looked long and curiously at the tall, imposing man who was, as it were, taking his seat at the chess-board, to play against him for his life. A formidable antagonist he looked, with his keen, thoughtful face, so resolute and calm. As Silas stepped into his carriage he looked back at his opponent, and thinking with deep discomfort of Brodski's hat, he hoped that he had made no other oversight.

II. The Mechanism of Detection
(Related by Christopher Jervis, MD)

The singular circumstances that attended the death of Mr Oscar Brodski, the well-known diamond merchant of Hatton Garden, illustrated very forcibly the importance of one or two points in medico-legal practice which Thorndyke was accustomed to insist were not sufficiently appreciated. What those points were, I shall leave my friend and teacher to state at the proper place; and meanwhile, as the case is in the highest degree instructive, I shall record the incidents in the order of their occurrence.

The dusk of an October evening was closing in as Thorndyke and I, the sole occupants of a smoking compartment, found ourselves approaching the little station of Ludham; and, as the train slowed down, we peered out at the knot of country people who were waiting on the platform. Suddenly Thorndyke exclaimed in a tone of surprise: 'Why, that is surely Boscovitch!' And almost at the same moment a brisk, excitable little man darted at the door of our compartment and literally tumbled in.

'I hope I don't intrude on this learned conclave,' he said, shaking hands genially and banging his Gladstone with impulsive violence into the rack; 'but I saw your faces at the window, and naturally jumped at the chance of such pleasant companionship.'

'You are very flattering,' said Thorndyke; 'so flattering that you leave us nothing to say. But what in the name of fortune are you doing at—what's the name of the place?—Ludham?'

'My brother has a little place a mile or so from here, and I have been spending a couple of days with him,' Mr Boscovitch explained. 'I shall change at Badsham Junction and catch the boat train for Amsterdam. But whither are you two bound? I see you have your mysterious little green box up on the hat-rack, so I infer that you are on some romantic quest, eh? Going to unravel some dark and intricate crime?'

'No,' replied Thorndyke. 'We are bound for Warmington on a quite prosaic errand. I am instructed to watch the proceedings at an inquest there tomorrow on behalf of the Griffin Life Insurance Office, and we are travelling down tonight as it is rather a cross-country journey.'

'But why the box of magic?' asked Boscovitch, glancing up at the hat-rack.

'I never go away from home without it,' answered Thorndyke. 'One never knows what may turn up; the trouble of carrying it is small when set off against the comfort of having one's appliances at hand in case of an emergency.'

Boscovitch continued to stare up at the little square case covered with Willesden canvas. Presently he remarked: 'I often used to wonder what you had in it when you were down at Chelmsford in connection with that bank murder— what an amazing case that was, by the way, and didn't your methods of research astonish the police!' As he still looked up wistfully at the case, Thorndyke good-naturedly lifted it down and unlocked it. As a matter of fact he was rather proud of his 'portable laboratory,' and certainly it was a triumph of condensation, for, small as it was—only a foot square by four inches deep—it contained a fairly complete outfit for a preliminary investigation.

'Wonderful!' exclaimed Boscovitch, when the case lay open before him, displaying its rows of little reagent bottles, tiny test-tubes, diminutive spirit-lamp, dwarf microscope and assorted instruments on the same Lilliputian scale; 'it's like a doll's house—everything looks as if it was seen through the wrong end of a telescope. But are these tiny things really efficient? That microscope now—'

'Perfectly efficient at low and moderate magnifications,' said Thorndyke. 'It looks like a toy, but it isn't one; the lenses are the best that can be had. Of course, a full-sized instrument would be infinitely more convenient—but I shouldn't have it with me, and should have to make shift with a pocket-lens. And so with the rest of the under-sized appliances, they are the alternative to no appliances.'

Boscovitch pored over the case and its contents, fingering the instruments delicately and asking questions innumerable about their uses; indeed, his curiosity was but half appeased when, half-an-hour later, the train began to slow down.

'By Jove!' he exclaimed, starting up and seizing his bag. 'Here we are at the junction already. You change here too, don't you?'

'Yes,' replied Thorndyke. 'We take the branch train on to Warmington.'

As we stepped out on to the platform, we became aware that something unusual was happening or had happened. All the passengers and most of the porters and supernumeraries were gathered at one end of the station, and all were looking intently into the darkness down the line.

'Anything wrong?' asked Mr Boscovitch, addressing the station-inspector.

'Yes, sir,' the official replied; 'a man has been run over by the goods train about a mile down the line. The station-master has gone down with a stretcher to bring him in, and I expect that is his lantern that you see coming this way.'

As we stood watching the dancing light grow momentarily brighter, flashing fitful reflections from the burnished rails, a man came out of the booking-office and joined the group of onlookers. He attracted my attention, as I afterwards remembered, for two reasons: in the first place his round, jolly face was excessively pale and bore a strained and wild expression, and, in the second, though he stared into the darkness with eager curiosity, he asked no questions.

The swinging lantern continued to approach, and then suddenly two men came into sight bearing a stretcher covered with a tarpaulin, through which the shape of a human figure was dimly discernible. They ascended the slope to the platform and proceeded with their burden to the lamp-room, when the inquisitive gaze of the passengers was transferred to a porter who followed carrying a hand-bag and umbrella and to the station-master who brought up the rear with his lantern.

As the porter passed, Mr Boscovitch started forward with sudden excitement.

'Is that his umbrella?' he asked.

'Yes, sir,' answered the porter, stopping and holding it out for the speaker's inspection.

'My God!' ejaculated Boscovitch; then, turning sharply to Thorndyke, he exclaimed: 'That's Brodski's umbrella. I could swear to it. You remember Brodski?'

Thorndyke nodded, and Boscovitch, turning once more to the porter, said: 'I identify that umbrella. It belongs to a gentleman named Brodski. If you look in his hat, you will see his name written in it. He always writes his name in his hat.'

'We haven't found his hat yet,' said the porter; 'but here is the station-master.' He turned to his superior and announced: 'This gentleman, sir, has identified the umbrella.'

'Oh,' said the station-master, 'you recognise the umbrella,

sir, do you? Then perhaps you would step into the lamp room and see if you can identify the body.'

Mr Boscovitch recoiled with a look of alarm. 'Is it—is he—very much injured?' he asked nervously.

'Well, yes,' was the reply. 'You see, the engine and six of the trucks went over him before they could stop the train. Took his head clean off, in fact.'

'Shocking! Shocking!' gasped Boscovitch. 'I think—if you don't mind—I'd—I'd rather not. You don't think it necessary, doctor, do you?'

'Yes, I do,' replied Thorndyke. 'Early identification may be of the first importance.'

'Then I suppose I must,' said Boscovitch; and, with extreme reluctance, he followed the station-master to the lamp-room, as the loud ringing of the bell announced the approach of the boat train. His inspection must have been of the briefest, for, in a few moments, he burst out, pale and awe-stricken, and rushed up to Thorndyke.

'It is!' he exclaimed breathlessly. 'It's Brodski! Poor old Brodski! Horrible! Horrible! He was to have met me here and come on with me to Amsterdam.'

'Had he any—merchandise about him?' Thorndyke asked; and, as he spoke, the stranger whom I had previously noticed edged up closer as if to catch the reply.

'He had some stones, no doubt,' answered Boscovitch, 'but I don't know what they were. His clerk will know, of course. By the way, doctor, could you watch the case for me? Just to be sure it was really an accident or—you know what. We were old friends, you know, fellow townsmen, too; we were both born in Warsaw. I'd like you to give an eye to the case.'

'Very well,' said Thorndyke. 'I will satisfy myself that there is nothing more than appears; and let you have a report. Will that do?'

'Thank you,' said Boscovitch. 'It's excessively good of you, doctor. Ah, here comes the train. I hope it won't inconvenience you to stay and see to the matter.'

'Not in the least,' replied Thorndyke. 'We are not due at Warmington until tomorrow afternoon, and I expect we can find out all that is necessary to know and still keep our appointment.'

As Thorndyke spoke, the stranger, who had kept close to us with the evident purpose of hearing what was said, bestowed on him a very curious and attentive look; and it was only when the train had actually come to rest by the platform that he hurried away to find a compartment.

No sooner had the train left the station than Thorndyke sought out the station-master and informed him of the instructions that he had received from Boscovitch. 'Of course,' he added, in conclusion, 'we must not move in the matter until the police arrive. I suppose they have been informed?'

'Yes,' replied the station-master; 'I sent a message at once to the Chief Constable, and I expect him or an inspector at any moment. In fact, I think I will slip out to the approach and see if he is coming.' He evidently wished to have a word in private with the police officer before committing himself to any statement.

As the official departed, Thorndyke and I began to pace the now empty platform, and my friend, as was his wont when entering on a new inquiry, meditatively reviewed the features of the problem.

'In a case of this kind,' he remarked, 'we have to decide on one of three possible explanations: accident, suicide or homicide; and our decision will be determined by inferences from three sets of facts: first, the general facts of the case; second, the special data obtained by examination of the body, and, third, the special data obtained by examining the spot on which the body was found. Now the only general facts at present in our possession are that the deceased was a diamond merchant making a journey for a specific purpose and probably having on his person property of small bulk and great value. These facts are somewhat against the hypothesis of suicide and somewhat favourable to that of homicide. Facts relevant to the question of accident would be the existence or otherwise of a level crossing, a road or path leading to the line, an enclosing fence with or without a gate, and any other facts rendering probable or otherwise the accidental presence of the deceased at the spot where the body was found. As we do not possess these facts, it is desirable that we extend our knowledge.'

'Why not put a few discreet questions to the porter who brought in the bag and umbrella?' I suggested. 'He is at this moment in earnest conversation with the ticket collector and would, no doubt, be glad of a new listener.'

'An excellent suggestion, Jervis,' answered Thorndyke. 'Let us see what he has to tell us.' We approached the porter and found him, as I had anticipated, bursting to unburden himself of the tragic story.

'The way the thing happened, sir, was this,' he said, in answer to Thorndyke's question: 'There's a sharpish bend in the road just at that place, and the goods train was just rounding the curve when the driver suddenly caught sight of something lying across the rails. As the engine turned, the head-lights shone on it and then he saw it was a man. He shut off steam at once, blew his whistle, and put the brakes down hard, but, as you know, sir, a goods train takes some stopping;

before they could bring her up, the engine and half-a-dozen trucks had gone over the poor beggar.'

'Could the driver see how the man was lying?' Thorndyke asked.

'Yes, he could see him quite plain, because the head-lights were full on him. He was lying on his face with his neck over the near rail on the down side. His head was in the four-foot and his body by the side of the track. It looked as if he had laid himself out a-purpose.'

'Is there a level crossing thereabout?' asked Thorndyke.

'No, sir. No crossing, no road, no path, no nothing,' said the porter, ruthlessly sacrificing grammar to emphasis. 'He must have come across the fields and climbed over the fence to get on to the permanent way. Deliberate suicide is what it looks like.'

'How did you learn all this?' Thorndyke inquired.

'Why, the driver, you see, sir, when him and his mate had lifted the body off the track, went on to the next signal-box and sent in his report by telegram. The station-master told me all about it as we walked down the line.'

Thorndyke thanked the man for his information, and, as we strolled back towards the lamp-room, discussed the bearing of these new facts.

'Our friend is unquestionably right in one respect,' he said; 'this was not an accident. The man might, if he were near-sighted, deaf or stupid, have climbed over the fence and got knocked down by the train. But his position, lying across the rails, can only be explained by one of two hypotheses: either it was, as the porter says, deliberate suicide, or else the man was already dead or insensible. We must leave it at that until we have seen the body, that is, if the police will allow us to see it. But here comes the station-master and an officer with him. Let us hear what they have to say.'

The two officials had evidently made up their minds to decline any outside assistance. The divisional surgeon would make the necessary examination, and information could be obtained through the usual channels. The production of Thorndyke's card, however, somewhat altered the situation. The police inspector hummed and hawed irresolutely, with the card in his hand, but finally agreed to allow us to view the body, and we entered the lamp-room together, the station-master leading the way to turn up the gas.

The stretcher stood on the floor by one wall, its grim burden still hidden by the tarpaulin, and the hand-bag and umbrella lay on a large box, together with the battered frame of a pair of spectacles from which the glasses had fallen out.

'Were these spectacles found by the body?' Thorndyke inquired.

'Yes,' replied the station-master. 'They were close to the head and the glass was scattered about on the ballast.'

Thorndyke made a note in his pocket-book, and then, as the inspector removed the tarpaulin, he glanced down on the corpse, lying limply on the stretcher and looking grotesquely horrible with its displaced head and distorted limbs. For fully a minute he remained silently stooping over the uncanny object, on which the inspector was now throwing the light of a large lantern; then he stood up and said quietly to me: 'I think we can eliminate two out of the three hypotheses.'

The inspector looked at him quickly, and was about to ask a question, when his attention was diverted by the travelling-case which Thorndyke had laid on a shelf and now opened to abstract a couple of pairs of dissecting forceps.

'We've no authority to make a post-mortem, you know,' said the inspector.

'No, of course not,' said Thorndyke. 'I am merely going

to look into the mouth.' With one pair of forceps he turned back the lip and, having scrutinised its inner surface, closely examined the teeth.

'May I trouble you for your lens, Jervis?' he said; and, as I handed him my doublet ready opened, the inspector brought the lantern close to the dead face and leaned forward eagerly. In his usual systematic fashion, Thorndyke slowly passed the lens along the whole range of sharp, uneven teeth, and then, bringing it back to the centre, examined with more minuteness the upper incisors. At length, very delicately, he picked out with his forceps some minute object from between two of the upper front teeth and held it in the focus of the lens. Anticipating his next move, I took a labelled microscope-slide from the case and handed it to him together with a dissecting needle, and, as he transferred the object to the slide and spread it out with the needle, I set up the little microscope on the shelf.

'A drop of Farrant and a cover-glass, please, Jervis,' said Thorndyke.

I handed him the bottle, and, when he had let a drop of the mounting fluid fall gently on the object and put on the cover-slip, he placed the slide on the stage of the microscope and examined it attentively.

Happening to glance at the inspector, I observed on his countenance a faint grin, which he politely strove to suppress when he caught my eye.

'I was thinking, sir,' he said apologetically, 'that it's a bit off the track to be finding out what he had for dinner. He didn't die of unwholesome feeding.'

Thorndyke looked up with a smile. 'It doesn't do, Inspector, to assume that anything is off the track in an inquiry of this kind. Every fact must have some significance, you know.'

'I don't see any significance in the diet of a man who has had his head cut off,' the inspector rejoined defiantly.

'Don't you?' said Thorndyke. 'Is there no interest attaching to the last meal of a man who has met a violent death? These crumbs, for instance, that are scattered over the dead man's waistcoat. Can we learn nothing from them?'

'I don't see what you can learn,' was the dogged rejoinder.

Thorndyke picked off the crumbs, one by one, with his forceps, and, having deposited them on a slide, inspected them, first with the lens and then through the microscope.

'I learn,' said he, 'shortly before his death, the deceased partook of some kind of wholemeal biscuits, apparently composed partly of oatmeal.'

'I call that nothing,' said the inspector. 'The question that we have got to settle is not what refreshments had the deceased been taking, but what was the cause of his death: Did he commit suicide? Was he killed by accident? Or was there any foul play?'

'I beg your pardon,' said Thorndyke, 'the questions that remain to be settled are, who killed the deceased and with what motive? The others are already answered as far as I am concerned.'

The inspector stared in sheer amazement not unmixed with incredulity.

'You haven't been long coming to a conclusion, sir,' he said.

'No, it was a pretty obvious case of murder,' said Thorndyke. 'As to the motive, the deceased was a diamond merchant and is believed to have had a quantity of stones about his person. I should suggest that you search the body.'

The inspector gave vent to an exclamation of disgust. 'I see,' he said. 'It was just a guess on your part. The dead man was a diamond merchant and had valuable property about him; therefore he was murdered.' He drew himself up, and, regarding Thorndyke with stern reproach, added: 'But you must understand, sir, that this is a judicial inquiry, not a prize competition in a penny paper. And, as to searching the body, why, that is what I principally came for.' He ostentatiously turned his back on us and proceeded systematically to turn out the dead man's pockets, laying the articles, as he removed them, on the box by the side of the hand-bag and umbrella.

While he was thus occupied, Thorndyke looked over the body generally, paying special attention to the soles of the boots, which, to the inspector's undissembled amusement, he very thoroughly examined with the lens.

'I should have thought, sir, that his feet were large enough to be seen with the naked eye,' was his comment; 'but perhaps,' he added, with a sly glance at the station-master, 'you're a little near-sighted.'

Thorndyke chuckled good-humouredly, and, while the officer continued his search, he looked over the articles that had already been laid on the box. The purse and pocket-book he naturally left for the inspector to open, but the reading-glasses, pocket-knife and card-case and other small pocket articles were subjected to a searching scrutiny. The inspector watched him out of the corner of his eye with furtive amusement; saw him hold up the glasses to the light to estimate their refractive power, peer into the tobacco pouch, open the cigarette book and examine the watermark of the paper, and even inspect the contents of the silver match-box.

'What might you have expected to find in his tobacco pouch?' the officer asked, laying down a bunch of keys from the dead man's pocket.

'Tobacco,' Thorndyke replied stolidly; 'but I did not expect to find fine-cut Latakia. I don't remember ever having seen pure Latakia smoked in cigarettes.'

'You do take an interest in things, sir,' said the inspector, with a side glance at the stolid station-master.

'I do,' Thorndyke agreed; 'and I note that there are no diamonds among this collection.'

'No, and we don't know that he had any about him; but there's a gold watch and chain, a diamond scarf-pin, and a purse containing'—he opened it and tipped out its contents into his hand—'twelve pounds in gold. That doesn't look much like robbery, does it? What do you say to the murder theory now?'

'My opinion is unchanged,' said Thorndyke, 'and I should like to examine the spot where the body was found. Has the engine been inspected?' he added, addressing the station-master.

'I telegraphed to Bradfield to have it examined,' the official answered. 'The report has probably come in by now. I'd better see before we start down the line.'

We emerged from the lamp-room and, at the door, found the station-inspector waiting with a telegram. He handed it to the station-master, who read it aloud.

'The engine has been carefully examined by me. I find small smear of blood on near leading wheel and smaller one on next wheel following. No other marks.' He glanced questioningly at Thorndyke, who nodded and remarked: 'It will be interesting to see if the line tells the same tale.'

The station-master looked puzzled and was apparently about to ask for an explanation; but the inspector, who had carefully pocketed the dead man's property, was impatient to start and, accordingly, when Thorndyke had repacked his case and had, at his own request, been furnished with a lantern, we set off down the permanent way, Thorndyke carrying the light and I the indispensable green case.

'I am a little in the dark about this affair,' I said, when we had allowed the two officials to draw ahead out of earshot; 'you came to a conclusion remarkably quickly. What was it that so immediately determined the opinion of murder as against suicide?'

'It was a small matter but very conclusive,' replied Thorndyke. 'You noticed a small scalp-wound above the left temple? It was a glancing wound, and might easily have been made by the engine. But—the wound had bled; and it had bled for an appreciable time. There were two streams of blood from it, and in both the blood was firmly clotted and partially dried. But the man had been decapitated; and this wound if inflicted by the engine, must have been made after the decapitation, since it was on the side most distant from the engine as it approached. Now a decapitated head does not bleed. Therefore this wound was inflicted before the decapitation.

'But not only had the wound bled: the blood had trickled down in two streams at right angles to one another. First, in the order of time as shown by the appearance of the stream, it had trickled down the side of the face and dropped on the collar. The second stream ran from the wound to the back of the head. Now, you know, Jervis, there are no exceptions to the law of gravity. If the blood ran down the face towards the chin, the face must have been upright at the time; and if the blood trickled from the front to the back of the head, the head must have been horizontal and face upwards. But the man, when he was seen by the engine-driver, was lying *face downwards.* The only possible inference is that when the wound was inflicted, the man was in the upright position— standing or sitting; and that subsequently, and while he was still alive, he lay on his back for a sufficiently long time for the blood to have trickled to the back of his head.'

'I see. I was a duffer not to have reasoned this out for myself,' I remarked contritely.

'Quick observation and rapid inference come by practice,' replied Thorndyke. 'But, tell me, what did you notice about the face?'

'I thought there was a strong suggestion of asphyxia.'

'Undoubtedly,' said Thorndyke. 'It was the face of a suffocated man. You must have noticed, too, that the tongue was very distinctly swollen and that on the inside of the upper lip were deep indentations made by the teeth, as well as one or two slight wounds, obviously caused by heavy pressure on the mouth. And now observe how completely these facts and inferences agree with those from the scalp wound. If we knew that the deceased had received a blow on the head, had struggled with his assailant and been finally borne down and suffocated, we should look for precisely those signs which we have found.'

'By the way, what was it that you found wedged between the teeth? I did not get a chance to look through the microscope.'

'Ah!' said Thorndyke, 'there we not only get confirmation, but we carry our inferences a stage further. The object was a little tuft of some textile fabric. Under the microscope I found it to consist of several different fibres, differently dyed. The bulk of it consisted of wool fibres dyed crimson, but there were also cotton fibres dyed blue and a few which looked like jute, dyed yellow. It was obviously a parti-coloured fabric and might have been part of a woman's dress, though the presence of the jute is much more suggestive of a curtain or rug of inferior quality.'

'And its importance?'

'Is that, if it is not part of an article of clothing, then it must have come from an article of furniture, and furniture suggests a habitation.'

'That doesn't seem very conclusive,' I objected.

'It is not; but it is valuable corroboration.'

'Of what?'

'Of the suggestion offered by the soles of the dead man's boots. I examined them most minutely and could find no trace of sand, gravel or earth, in spite of the fact that he must have crossed fields and rough land to reach the place where he was found. What I did find was fine tobacco ash, a charred mark as if a cigar or cigarette had been trodden on, several crumbs of biscuit, and, on a projecting brad, some coloured fibres, apparently from a carpet. The manifest suggestion is that the man was killed in a house with a carpeted floor, and carried from thence to the railway.'

I was silent for some moments. Well as I knew Thorndyke, I was completely taken by surprise; a sensation, indeed, that I experienced anew every time that I accompanied him on one of his investigations. His marvellous power of co-ordinating apparently insignificant facts, of arranging them into an ordered sequence and making them tell a coherent story, was a phenomenon that I never got used to; every exhibition of it astonished me afresh.

'If your inferences are correct,' I said, 'the problem is practically solved. There must be abundant traces inside the house. The only question is, which house is it?'

'Quite so,' replied Thorndyke; 'that is the question, and a very difficult question it is. A glance at that interior would doubtless clear up the whole mystery. But how are we to get that glance? We cannot enter houses speculatively to see if they present traces of a murder. At present, our clue breaks off abruptly. The other end of it is in some unknown house, and, if we cannot join up the two ends, our problem remains unsolved. For the question is, you remember, Who killed Oscar Brodski?'

'Then what do you propose to do?' I asked.

'The next stage of the inquiry is to connect some particular house with this crime. To that end, I can only gather up all available facts and consider each in all its possible bearings. If I cannot establish any such connection, then the inquiry will have failed and we shall have to make a fresh start—say, at Amsterdam, if it turns out that Brodski really had diamonds on his person, as I have no doubt he had.'

Here our conversation was interrupted by our arrival at the spot where the body had been found. The station-master had halted, and he and the inspector were now examining the near rail by the light of their lanterns.

'There's remarkably little blood about,' said the former. 'I've seen a good many accidents of this kind and there has always been a lot of blood, both on the engine and on the road. It's very curious.'

Thorndyke glanced at the rail with but slight attention: that question had ceased to interest him. But the light of his lantern flashed on to the ground at the side of the track—a loose, gravelly soil mixed with fragments of chalk—and from thence to the soles of the inspector's boots, which were displayed as he knelt by the rail.

'You observe, Jervis?' he said in a low voice, and I nodded. The inspector's boot-soles were covered with adherent particles of gravel and conspicuously marked by the chalk on which he had trodden.

'You haven't found the hat, I suppose?' Thorndyke asked, stooping to pick up a short piece of string that lay on the ground at the side of the track.

'No,' replied the inspector, 'but it can't be far off. You seem to have found another clue, sir,' he added, with a grin, glancing at the piece of string.

'Who knows?' said Thorndyke. 'A short end of white twine with a green strand in it. It may tell us something later. At any rate we'll keep it,' and, taking from his pocket a small tin box containing, among other things, a number of seed envelopes, he slipped the string into one of the latter and scribbled a note in pencil on the outside. The inspector watched his proceedings with an indulgent smile, and then returned to his examination of the track, in which Thorndyke now joined.

'I suppose the poor chap was near-sighted,' the officer remarked, indicating the remains of the shattered spectacles; 'that might account for his having strayed on to the line.'

'Possibly,' said Thorndyke. He had already noticed the fragments scattered over a sleeper and the adjacent ballast, and now once more produced his 'collecting-box,' from which he took another seed envelope. 'Would you hand me a pair of forceps, Jervis,' he said; 'and perhaps you wouldn't mind taking a pair yourself and helping me to gather up these fragments.'

As I complied, the inspector looked up curiously.

'There isn't any doubt that these spectacles belonged to the deceased, is there?' he asked. 'He certainly wore spectacles, for I saw the mark on his nose.'

'Still, there is no harm in verifying the fact,' said Thorndyke, and he added to me in a lower tone, 'Pick up every particle you can find, Jervis. It may be most important.'

'I don't quite see how,' I said, groping amongst the shingle by the light of the lantern in search of the tiny splinters of glass.

'Don't you?' returned Thorndyke. 'Well, look at these fragments; some of them are a fair size, but many of these on the sleeper are mere grains. And consider their number. Obviously, the condition of the glass does not agree with the circumstances in which we find it. These are thick concave spectacle-lenses broken into a great number of minute fragments. Now how were they broken? Not merely by falling, evidently: such a lens, when it is dropped, breaks into a small number of large pieces. Nor were they broken by the wheel passing over them, for they would then have been reduced to fine powder, and that powder would have been visible on the rail, which it is not. The spectacle-frames, you may remember, presented the same incongruity: they were battered and damaged more than they would have been by falling, but not nearly so much as they would have been if the wheel had passed over them.'

'What do you suggest, then?' I asked.

'The appearances suggest that the spectacles had been trodden on. But, if the body was carried here, the probability is that the spectacles were carried here too, and that they were then already broken; for it is more likely that they were trodden on during the struggle than that the murderer trod on them after bringing them here. Hence the importance of picking up every fragment.'

'But why?' I inquired, rather foolishly I must admit.

'Because, if, when we have picked up every fragment that we can find, there still remains missing a larger portion of the lenses than we could reasonably expect, that would tend to support our hypothesis and we might find the missing remainder elsewhere. If, on the other hand, we find as much of the lenses as we could expect to find, we must conclude that they were broken on this spot.'

While we were conducting our search, the two officials were circling around with their lanterns in quest of the missing hat; and, when we had at length picked up the last fragment, and a careful search, even aided by a lens, failed to reveal any other, we could see their lanterns moving, like will-o'-the-wisps, some distance down the line.

'We may as well see what we have got before our friends come back,' said Thorndyke, glancing at the twinkling lights. 'Lay the case down on the grass by the fence; it will serve for a table.'

I did so, and Thorndyke, taking a letter from his pocket, opened it, spread it out flat on the case, securing it with a couple of heavy stones, although the night was quite calm. Then he tipped the contents of the seed envelope out on the paper, and, carefully spreading out the pieces of glass, looked at them for some moments in silence. And, as he looked, there stole over his face a very curious expression; with sudden eagerness he began picking out the larger fragments and laying them on two visiting-cards which he had taken from his card-case. Rapidly and with wonderful deftness he fitted the pieces together, and, as the reconstituted lenses began gradually to take shape on their cards I looked on with growing excitement, for something in my colleague's manner told me that we were on the verge of a discovery.

At length the two ovals of glass lay on their respective cards, complete save for one or two small gaps; and the little heap that remained consisted of fragments so minute as to render further reconstruction impossible. Then Thorndyke leaned back and laughed softly.

'This is certainly an unlooked-for result,' said he.

'What is?' I asked.

'Don't you see, my dear fellow? *There's too much glass.* We have almost completely built up the broken lenses, and the fragments that are left over are considerably more than are required to fill up the gaps.'

I looked at the little heap of small fragments and saw at once that it was as he had said. There was a surplus of small pieces.

'This is very extraordinary,' I said. 'What do you think can be the explanation?'

'The fragments will probably tell us,' he replied, 'if we ask them intelligently.'

He lifted the paper and the two cards carefully on to the ground, and, opening the case, took out the little microscope, to which he fitted the lowest-power objective and eye-piece—having a combined magnification of only ten diameters. Then he transferred the minute fragments of glass to a slide, and, having arranged the lantern as a microscope-lamp, commenced his examination.

'Ha!' he exclaimed presently. 'The plot thickens. There is too much glass and yet too little; that is to say, there are only one or two fragments here that belong to the spectacles; not nearly enough to complete the building up of the lenses. The remainder consists of a soft, uneven, moulded glass, easily distinguished from the clear, hard optical glass. These foreign fragments are all curved, as if they had formed part of a cylinder, and are, I should say, portions of a wineglass or tumbler.' He moved the slide once or twice, and then continued: 'We are in luck, Jervis. Here is a fragment with two little diverging lines etched on it, evidently the points of an eight-rayed star—and here is another with three points—the ends of three rays. This enables us to reconstruct the vessel perfectly. It was a clear, thin glass—probably a tumbler—decorated with scattered stars; I dare say you know the pattern. Sometimes there is an ornamented band in addition, but generally the stars form the only decoration. Have a look at the specimen.'

I had just applied my eye to the microscope when the station-master and the inspector came up. Our appearance, seated on the ground with the microscope between us, was too much for the police officer's gravity, and he laughed long and joyously.

'You must excuse me, gentlemen,' he said apologetically, 'but really, you know, to an old hand, like myself, it does look a little—well—you understand—I dare say a microscope is a very interesting and amusing thing, but it doesn't get you much forrader in a case like this, does it?'

'Perhaps not,' replied Thorndyke. 'By the way, where did you find the hat, after all?'

'We haven't found it,' the inspector replied, a little sheepishly.

'Then we must help you to continue the search,' said Thorndyke. 'If you will wait a few moments, we will come with you.' He poured a few drops of xylol balsam on the cards to fix the reconstituted lenses to their supports and then, packing them and the microscope in the case, announced that he was ready to start.

'Is there any village or hamlet near?' he asked the station-master.

'None nearer than Corfield. That is about half-a-mile from here.'

'And where is the nearest road?'

'There is a half-made road that runs past a house about three hundred yards from here. It belonged to a building estate that was never built. There is a footpath from it to the station.'

'Are there any other houses near?'

'No. That is the only house for half-a-mile round, and there is no other road near here.'

'Then the probability is that Brodski approached the railway from that direction, as he was found on that side of the permanent way.'

The inspector agreeing with this view, we all set off slowly towards the house, piloted by the station-master and searching the ground as we went. The waste land over which we passed was covered with patches of docks and nettles, through each of which the inspector kicked his way, searching with feet and lantern for the missing hat. A walk of three hundred yards brought us to a low wall enclosing a garden, beyond which we could see a small house; and here we halted while the inspector waded into a large bed of nettles beside the wall and kicked vigorously. Suddenly there came a clinking sound mingled with objurgations, and the inspector hopped out holding one foot and soliloquising profanely.

'I wonder what sort of a fool put a thing like that into a bed of nettles!' he exclaimed, stroking the injured foot. Thorndyke picked the object up and held it in the light of the lantern, displaying a piece of three-quarter inch rolled iron bar about a foot long. 'It doesn't seem to have been there very long,' he observed, examining it closely; 'there is hardly any rust on it.'

'It has been there long enough for me,' growled the inspector, 'and I'd like to bang it on the head of the blighter that put it there.'

Callously indifferent to the inspector's sufferings, Thorndyke continued calmly to examine the bar. At length, resting his lantern on the wall, he produced his pocket-lens, with which he resumed his investigation, a proceeding that so exasperated the inspector that that afflicted official limped off in dudgeon, followed by the station-master, and we heard him, presently, rapping at the front door of the house.

'Give me a slide, Jervis, with a drop of Farrant on it,' said Thorndyke. 'There are some fibres sticking to this bar.'

I prepared the slide, and, having handed it to him together with a cover-glass, a pair of forceps and a needle, set up the microscope on the wall.

'I'm sorry for the inspector,' Thorndyke remarked, with his eye applied to the little instrument, 'but that was a lucky kick for us. Just take a look at the specimen.'

I did so, and, having moved the slide about until I had seen the whole of the object, I gave my opinion. 'Red wool fibres, blue cotton fibres and some yellow, vegetable fibres that look like jute.'

'Yes,' said Thorndyke; 'the same combination of fibres as that which we found on the dead man's teeth and probably from the same source. This bar has probably been wiped on that very curtain or rug with which poor Brodski was stifled. We will place it on the wall for future reference, and meanwhile, by hook or by crook, we must get into that house. This is much too plain a hint to be disregarded.'

Hastily repacking the case, we hurried to the front of the house, where we found the two officials looking rather vaguely up the unmade road.

'There's a light in the house,' said the inspector, 'but there's no one at home. I have knocked a dozen times and got no answer. And I don't see what we are hanging about here for at all. The hat is probably close to where the body was found, and we shall find it in the morning.'

Thorndyke made no reply, but, entering the garden, stepped up the path, and having knocked gently at the door, stooped and listened attentively at the key-hole.

'I tell you there's no one in the house, sir,' said the inspector irritably; and, as Thorndyke continued to listen, he walked away, muttering angrily. As soon as he was gone, Thorndyke flashed his lantern over the door, the threshold, the path and the small flowerbeds; and, from one of the latter, I presently saw him stoop and pick something up.

'Here is a highly instructive object, Jervis,' he said, coming out to the gate, and displaying a cigarette of which only half-an-inch had been smoked.

'How instructive?' I asked. 'What do you learn from it?'

'Many things,' he replied. 'It has been lit and thrown away unsmoked; that indicates a sudden change of purpose. It was thrown away at the entrance to the house, almost certainly by someone entering it. That person was probably a stranger, or he would have taken it in with him. But he had not expected to enter the house, or he would not have lit it. These are the general suggestions; now as to the particular ones. The paper of the cigarette is of the kind known as the "Zig-Zag" brand; the very conspicuous water-mark is quite easy to see. Now Brodski's cigarette book was a "Zig-Zag" book—so called from the way in which the papers pull out. But let us see what the tobacco is like.' With a pin from his coat, he hooked out from the unburned end a wisp of dark, dirty brown tobacco, which he held out for my inspection.

'Fine-cut Latakia,' I pronounced, without hesitation.

'Very well,' said Thorndyke. 'Here is a cigarette made of an unusual tobacco similar to that in Brodski's pouch and wrapped in an unusual paper similar to those in Brodski's cigarette book. With due regard to the fourth rule of the syllogism, I suggest that this cigarette was made by Oscar Brodski. But, nevertheless, we will look for corroborative detail.'

'What is that?' I asked.

'You may have noticed that Brodski's match-box contained round wooden vestas—which are also rather unusual. As he must have lighted the cigarette within a few steps of the gate, we ought to be able to find the match with which he lighted it. Let us try up the road in the direction from which he would probably have approached.'

We walked very slowly up the road, searching the ground

with the lantern, and we had hardly gone a dozen paces when I espied a match lying on the rough path and eagerly picked it up. It was a round wooden vesta.

Thorndyke examined it with interest and having deposited it, with the cigarette, in his collecting-box, turned to retrace his steps. 'There is now, Jervis, no reasonable doubt that Brodski was murdered in that house. We have succeeded in connecting that house with the crime, and now we have got to force an entrance and join up the other clues.' We walked quickly back to the rear of the premises, where we found the inspector conversing disconsolately with the station-master.

'I think, sir,' said the former, 'we had better go back now; in fact, I don't see what we came here for, but—Here! I say, sir, you mustn't do that!' For Thorndyke, without a word of warning, had sprung up lightly and thrown one of his long legs over the wall.

'I can't allow you to enter private premises, sir,' continued the inspector; but Thorndyke quietly dropped down on the inside and turned to face the officer over the wall.

'Now, listen to me, Inspector,' said he. 'I have good reasons for believing that the dead man, Brodski, has been in this house—in fact, I am prepared to swear an information to that effect. But time is precious; we must follow the scent while it is hot. And I am not proposing to break into the house offhand. I merely wish to examine the dust-bin.'

'The dust-bin!' gasped the inspector. 'Well, you really are a most extraordinary gentleman! What do you expect to find in the dust-bin?'

'I am looking for a broken tumbler or wine-glass. It is a thin glass vessel decorated with a pattern of small, eight-pointed stars. It may be in the dust-bin or it may be inside the house.'

The inspector hesitated, but Thorndyke's confident manner had evidently impressed him.

'We can soon see what is in the dust-bin,' he said, 'though what in creation a broken tumbler has to do with the case is more than I can understand. However, here goes.' He sprang up on to the wall, and, as he dropped down into the garden, the station-master and I followed.

Thorndyke lingered a few moments by the gate examining the ground, while the two officials hurried up the path. Finding nothing of interest, however, he walked towards the house, looking keenly about him as he went; but we were hardly half-way up the path when we heard the voice of the inspector calling excitedly.

'Here you are, sir, this way,' he sang out, and, as we hurried forward, we suddenly came on the two officials standing over a small rubbish-heap and looking the picture of astonishment. The glare of their lanterns illuminated the heap, and showed us the scattered fragments of a thin glass, star-pattern tumbler.

'I can't imagine how you guessed it was here, sir,' said the inspector, with a new-born respect in his tone, 'nor what you're going to do with it now you have found it.'

'It is merely another link in the chain of evidence,' said Thorndyke, taking a pair of forceps from the case and stooping over the heap. 'Perhaps we shall find something else.' He picked up several small fragments of glass, looked at them closely and dropped them again. Suddenly his eye caught a small splinter at the base of the heap. Seizing it with the forceps, he held it close to his eye in the strong lamplight, and, taking out his lens, examined it with minute attention. 'Yes,' he said at length, 'this is what I was looking for. Let me have those two cards, Jervis.'

I produced the two visiting-cards with the reconstructed

lenses stuck to them, and, laying them on the lid of the case, threw the light of the lantern on them. Thorndyke looked at them intently for some time, and from them to the fragment that he held. Then, turning to the inspector, he said: 'You saw me pick up this splinter of glass?'

'Yes, sir,' replied the officer.

'And you saw where we found these spectacle-glasses and know whose they were?'

'Yes, sir. They are the dead man's spectacles, and you found them where the body had been.'

'Very well,' said Thorndyke, 'now observe'; and, as the two officials craned forward with parted lips, he laid the little splinter in a gap in one of the lenses and then gave it a gentle push forward, when it occupied the gap perfectly, joining edge to edge with the adjacent fragments and rendering that portion of the lens complete.

'My God!' exclaimed the inspector. 'How on earth did you know?'

'I must explain that later,' said Thorndyke. 'Meanwhile we had better have a look inside the house. I expect to find there a cigarette—or possibly a cigar—which has been trodden on, some wholemeal biscuits, possibly a wooden vesta, and perhaps even the missing hat.'

At the mention of the hat, the inspector stepped eagerly to the back door, but, finding it bolted, he tried the window. This also was securely fastened and, on Thorndyke's advice, we went round to the front door.

'This door is locked too,' said the inspector. 'I'm afraid we shall have to break in. It's a nuisance, though.'

'Have a look at the window,' suggested Thorndyke.

The officer did so, struggling vainly to undo the patent catch with his pocket-knife.

'It's no go,' he said, coming back to the door. 'We shall have to—' He broke off with an astonished stare, for the door stood open and Thorndyke was putting something in his pocket.

'Your friend doesn't waste much time—even in picking a lock,' he remarked to me, as we followed Thorndyke into the house; but his reflections were soon merged in a new surprise. Thorndyke had preceded us into a small sitting-room dimly lighted by a hanging lamp turned down low.

As we entered he turned up the light and glanced about the room. A whisky-bottle was on the table, with a siphon, a tumbler and a biscuit-box. Pointing to the latter, Thorndyke said to the inspector: 'See what is in that box.'

The inspector raised the lid and peeped in, the station-master peered over his shoulder, and then both stared at Thorndyke.

'How in the name of goodness did you know that there were wholemeal biscuits in the house, sir?' exclaimed the station-master.

'You'd be disappointed if I told you,' replied Thorndyke. 'But look at this.' He pointed to the hearth, where lay a flattened, half-smoked cigarette and a round wooden vesta. The inspector gazed at these objects in silent wonder, while, as to the station-master, he continued to stare at Thorndyke with what I can only describe as superstitious awe.

'You have the dead man's property with you, I believe?' said my colleague.

'Yes,' replied the inspector; 'I put the things in my pocket for safety.'

'Then,' said Thorndyke, picking up the flattened cigarette, 'let us have a look at his tobacco-pouch.'

As the officer produced and opened the pouch, Thorndyke neatly cut open the cigarette with his sharp pocket-knife. 'Now,' said he, 'what kind of tobacco is in the pouch?'

The inspector took out a pinch, looked at it and smelt it distastefully. 'It's one of those stinking tobaccos,' he said, 'that they put in mixtures—Latakia, I think.'

'And what is this?' asked Thorndyke, pointing to the open cigarette.

'Same stuff, undoubtedly,' replied the inspector.

'And now let us see his cigarette papers,' said Thorndyke.

The little book, or rather packet—for it consisted of separated papers—was produced from the officer's pocket and a sample paper abstracted. Thorndyke laid the half-burnt paper beside it, and the inspector having examined the two, held them up to the light.

'There isn't much chance of mistaking that "Zig-Zag" watermark,' he said. 'This cigarette was made by the deceased; there can't be the shadow of a doubt.'

'One more point,' said Thorndyke, laying the burnt wooden vesta on the table. 'You have his match-box?'

The inspector brought forth the little silver casket, opened it and compared the wooden vestas that it contained with the burnt end. Then he shut the box with a snap.

'You've proved it up to the hilt,' said he. 'If we could only find the hat, we should have a complete case.'

'I'm not sure that we haven't found the hat,' said Thorndyke. 'You notice that something besides coal has been burned in the grate.'

The inspector ran eagerly to the fire-place and began, with feverish hands, to pick out the remains of the extinct fire. 'The cinders are still warm,' he said, 'and they are certainly not all coal cinders. There has been wood burned here on top of the coal, and these little black lumps are neither coal nor wood. They may quite possibly be the remains of a burnt hat, but, lord! Who can tell? You can put together the pieces of broken spectacle-glasses, but you can't build up a hat out of a few cinders.' He held out a handful of little, black, spongy cinders and looked ruefully at Thorndyke, who took them from him and laid them out on a sheet of paper.

'We can't reconstitute the hat, certainly,' my friend agreed, 'but we may be able to ascertain the origin of these remains. They may not be cinders of a hat, after all.' He lit a wax match and, taking up one of the charred fragments, applied the flame to it. The cindery mass fused at once with a crackling, seething sound, emitting a dense smoke, and instantly the air became charged with a pungent, resinous odour mingled with the smell of burning animal matter.

'Smells like varnish,' the station-master remarked.

'Yes. Shellac,' said Thorndyke; 'so the first test gives a positive result. The next test will take more time.'

He opened the green case and took from it a little flask, fitted for Marsh's arsenic test, with a safety funnel and escape tube, a small folding tripod, a spirit lamp and a disc of asbestos to serve as a sand-bath. Dropping into the flask several of the cindery masses, selected after careful inspection, he filled it up with alcohol and placed it on the disc, which he rested on the tripod. Then he lighted the spirit lamp underneath and sat down to wait for the alcohol to boil.

'There is one little point that we may as well settle,' he said presently, as the bubbles began to rise in the flask. 'Give me a slide with a drop of Farrant on it, Jervis.'

I prepared the slide while Thorndyke, with a pair of forceps, picked out a tiny wisp from the table-cloth. 'I fancy we have seen this fabric before,' he remarked, as he laid the little pinch of fluff in the mounting fluid and slipped the slide on to the stage of the microscope. 'Yes,' he continued, looking into the eye-piece, 'here are our old acquaintances, the red wool fibres, the blue cotton and the yellow jute. We must label this at once or we may confuse it with the other specimens.'

'Have you any idea how the deceased met his death?' the inspector asked.

'Yes,' replied Thorndyke. 'I take it that the murderer enticed him into this room and gave him some refreshments. The murderer sat in the chair in which you are sitting, Brodski sat in that small arm-chair. Then I imagine the murderer attacked him with that iron bar that you found among the nettles, failed to kill him at the first stroke, struggled with him, and finally suffocated him with the table-cloth. By the way, there is just one more point. You recognise this piece of string?' He took from his collecting-box the little end of twine that had been picked up by the line. The inspector nodded. 'If you look behind you, you will see where it came from.'

The officer turned sharply and his eye lighted on a string-box on the mantelpiece. He lifted it down, and Thorndyke drew out from it a length of white twine with one green strand, which he compared with the piece in his hand. 'The green strand in it makes the identification fairly certain,' he said. 'Of course the string was used to secure the umbrella and hand-bag. He could not have carried them in his hand, encumbered as he was with the corpse. But I expect our other specimen is ready now.' He lifted the flask off the tripod, and, giving it a vigorous shake, examined the contents through his lens. The alcohol had now become dark-brown in colour, and was noticeably thicker and more syrupy in consistence.

'I think we have enough here for a rough test,' said he, selecting a pipette and a slide from the case. He dipped the former into the flask and, having sucked up a few drops of the alcohol from the bottom, held the pipette over the slide on which he allowed the contained fluid to drop.

Laying a cover-glass on the little pool of alcohol, he put the slide on the microscope stage and examined it attentively, while we watched him in expectant silence.

At length he looked up, and, addressing the inspector, asked: 'Do you know what felt hats are made of?'

'I can't say that I do, sir,' replied the officer.

'Well, the better quality hats are made of rabbits' and hares' wool—the soft under-fur, you know—cemented together with shellac. Now there is very little doubt that these cinders contain shellac, and with the microscope I find a number of small hairs of a rabbit. I have, therefore, little hesitation in saying that these cinders are the remains of a hard felt hat; and, as the hairs do not appear to be dyed, I should say it was a grey hat.'

At this moment our conclave was interrupted by hurried footsteps on the garden path and, as we turned with one accord, an elderly woman burst into the room.

She stood for a moment in mute astonishment, and then, looking from one to the other, demanded: 'Who are you? And what are you doing here?'

The inspector rose. 'I am a police officer, madam,' said he. 'I can't give you any further information just now, but, if you will excuse me asking, who are you?'

'I am Mr Hickler's housekeeper,' she replied.

'And Mr Hickler; are you expecting him home shortly?'

'No, I am not,' was the curt reply. 'Mr Hickler is away from home just now. He left this evening by the boat train.'

'For Amsterdam?' asked Thorndyke.

'I believe so, though I don't see what business it is of yours,' the housekeeper answered.

'I thought he might, perhaps, be a diamond broker or merchant,' said Thorndyke. 'A good many of them travel by that train.'

'So he is,' said the woman, 'at least, he has something to do with diamonds.'

'Ah. Well, we must be going, Jervis,' said Thorndyke, 'we have finished here, and we have to find an hotel or inn. Can I have a word with you, Inspector?'

The officer, now entirely humble and reverent, followed us out into the garden to receive Thorndyke's parting advice.

'You had better take possession of the house at once, and get rid of the housekeeper. Nothing must be removed. Preserve those cinders and see that the rubbish-heap is not disturbed, and, above all, don't have the room swept. The station-master or I will let them know at the police station, so that they can send an officer to relieve you.'

With a friendly 'good-night' we went on our way, guided by the station-master; and here our connection with the case came to an end. Hickler (whose Christian name turned out to be Silas) was, it is true, arrested as he stepped ashore from the steamer, and a packet of diamonds, subsequently identified as the property of Oscar Brodski, found upon his person. But he was never brought to trial, for on the return voyage he contrived to elude his guards for an instant as the ship was approaching the English coast, and it was not until three days later, when a handcuffed body was cast up on the lonely shore by Orfordness, that the authorities knew the fate of Silas Hickler.

'An appropriate and dramatic end to a singular and yet typical case,' said Thorndyke, as he put down the newspaper. 'I hope it has enlarged your knowledge, Jervis, and enabled you to form one or two useful corollaries.'

'I prefer to hear you sing the medico legal doxology,' I answered, turning upon him like the proverbial worm and grinning derisively (which the worm does not).

'I know you do,' he retorted, with mock gravity, 'and I lament your lack of mental initiative. However, the points that this case illustrates are these: First, the danger of delay; the vital importance of instant action before that frail and fleeting thing that we call a clue has time to evaporate. A delay of a few hours would have left us with hardly a single datum. Second, the necessity of pursuing the most trivial clue to an absolute finish, as illustrated by the spectacles. Third, the urgent need of a trained scientist to aid the police; and, last,' he concluded, with a smile, 'we learn never to go abroad without the invaluable green case.'

The Eighth Lamp

Roy Vickers

William Edward Vickers (1889–1965) wrote under the name Roy Vickers, as well as using a series of pseudonyms, including Sefton Kyle and David Durham. After briefly contemplating a career as a barrister, he turned to journalism and started writing fiction. So prolific did he become that his bibliography is a little uncertain, but it seems that his first published novel was *The Mystery of the Scented Death* (1921). He is best known for his stories about Scotland Yard's Department of Dead Ends, and he became a leading figure in the Crime Writers' Association after its formation by John Creasey in 1953.

On behalf of the CWA, Vickers edited the 1960 anthology *Some Like Them Dead*, and in his introduction, he discussed his views about the short crime story: 'a crime story has vitality when it presents a pattern of human behaviour—using the basic facts of crime and the police as a painter uses colours on a palette—to depict a fabular truth that is not concerned with the actuality of crime. The pattern should be based on a bright idea in a colourful setting and the technique of narration should not intrude on your attention.' This is one of his very earliest stories, dating from 1916.

————

With a muffled, metallic roar the twelve-forty-five, the last train on the Underground, lurched into Cheyne Road station. A small party of belated theatre-goers alighted; the sleepy guard blew his whistle, and the train rumbled on its way to the outlying suburbs.

A couple of minutes later, Signalman George Raoul emerged from the tunnel, swung himself on to the up-platform and switched off the nearest lamp. Simultaneously a door in the wall on the down-side opened and the stationmaster appeared.

'Nothing to report, Mr Jenkins,' said Raoul. He spoke in an ordinary speaking voice, but in the dead silence of the station his words carried easily across the rails—words that were totally untrue. He had something of considerable importance to report, but he knew that if he were to make that report he would probably be marked down as unfit for night duty, and he could not afford to risk that at present.

'All right, George. Good night.'

'G'night, Mr Jenkins.'

Raoul passed down the length of the up-platform, dousing each light as he came to the switch. Then he dropped on to the track, crossed, and made for the farthest switch on the down-platform.

Cheyne Road station was wholly underground—it was but an enlarged strip of tunnel—and the lighting regulations did not apply to it. There were eight lamps on each platform.

The snap of the switch echoed in the deserted station like the crack of a pistol. Raoul started. The silence that followed gripped him. Pulling himself together he hurried on to the second switch.

'Ugh!'

By the third lamp he stopped and shuddered as his eye fell upon a recruiting poster. In the gloom the colouring of the poster was lost—some crudity in the printing asserted itself—and the beckoning smile of a young soldier seemed like the mirthless grin of a death mask. And the death mask was just like—

'You're all right,' he assured himself aloud. 'It's the new station that's doing it.'

Yes, it was the new station that was doing it. But he would not grumble on that account. It was a bit of rare luck, being transferred from Baker Street—just when he was transferred. For all its familiarity, he could never have stood night-work at Baker Street—now.

Even after three weeks in the new signal-box he could never pass a Circle train without a faint shudder. The Circle trains had a morbid fascination for him. They passed you on the down-line. Half a dozen stations and they would be pulling up at Baker Street. Then on through the tunnel and, in about an hour, back they came past your box and still on the down-line. In the Circle trains his half-nurtured imagination saw something ruthless and inevitable—something vaguely connected with fate and eternity and things like that.

His mind had momentarily wandered so that he took the fourth switch unconsciously. As he made for the fifth, his nerve again faltered.

'Didn't ought to have taken on this extra work,' he seemed to shout into the dark mouth of the tunnel.

"Tain't worth it for three bob. It's the cleaner's job by rights.'

Yes, it was the cleaner's job by rights. But the cleaner was an old man, unreliable for night-work; and when the station-master had offered Raoul the job of 'clearing up last thing' for three shillings a week, he had jumped at it. The three shillings would make life perceptibly brighter for Jinny—her new life with him.

Between the fifth lamp and the sixth was the station-master's den. On a nail outside the door hung the keys with which Raoul would presently lock the ticket-barrier and the outer door of the booking-office.

He snatched the keys as he passed and then, as if to huma-nise the desolation, he broke into a piercing, tuneless whistle that carried him to the seventh lamp.

A trifling mechanical difficulty with the seventh switch was enough to check the whistling. For a moment he stood motionless in the silence—the silence that seemed to come out of the tunnel like a dank mist and envelop him. He mea-sured the distance to the switch of the eighth lamp. The switch of the eighth lamp was by the foot of the staircase. He need scarcely stop as he turned it—and then he would let himself take the staircase two, three, four steps at a time.

Click!

The eighth lamp was extinguished. From the ticket-office on the street level a single ray of light made blacker the dark-ness of the station. But Raoul, within a couple of feet of the staircase, waited, crouching.

His hand clutched the stair-rail and he twisted his body round so that he could look up the line. He could not see more than a few feet in front of him, but he could hear, distinct and unmistakable, the rumbling murmur of an approaching train.

All his instincts as a railway man told him that his senses were deceiving him. The twelve-forty-five was the last train down—and he and the stationmaster had together seen it through. There were a dozen reasons why it would be impossible for another train to run without previous notification to the signalling staff. And yet—the rumbling was growing momentarily louder. The air, driven through the tunnel before the advancing train, was blowing like a breeze upon his face.

Louder and louder grew the rumbling until it rose to the familiar roar. In another second he would see the lights.

But there were no lights. The train lurched and clattered through the station and was swallowed up in the down-side tunnel. There were no lights, but Raoul had seen that it was a Circle train.

For a nightmare eternity he seemed to be rushing with gigantic strides up an endless staircase—across a vast hall that had once been a ticket-office, and then:

'Hi! Where yer comin' to?'

The raucous indignation of the night constable, into whom he had cannoned, recalled him to sanity.

'Sorry, mate!' he panted. 'I didn't see you—as I come by.'

'Call that comin' by?' demanded the constable. 'Why, you was running like a house afire! What's going on down there, then?'

'Nothing,' retorted Raoul.

The constable, unsatisfied, walked through the ticket-office and peered over the barrier. The silence and the darkness gave him a hint.

'Bit lonesome down there, last thing, ain't it?' he suggested.

'Yes,' grunted Raoul, as he locked the barrier, 'somethin' chronic.'

'I know,' said the constable. He had not been on night duty for ten years without learning the meaning of nerves.

A short chat with the constable served to restore Raoul's balance, after which he locked up as usual and made his way to the tenement he shared with Jinny, resolving that this time he would report the occurrence to the stationmaster on the following day.

During their three weeks' occupation of the tenement Jinny had made a practice of waiting up to give him his supper. As he came in she was lying asleep, half-dressed, in the second-hand upholstered armchair that had been theirs for three weeks.

'Hullo, Jinny!' he called, with intentional loudness. He wanted to wake her up thoroughly so that she would chatter to him.

'Blessed if I hadn't dropped off!' she exclaimed by way of apology, as she hastily got up and busied herself with his cocoa.

'There's no need for you to wait up, you know, Jinny,' he said, as he seated himself at the table. 'Only I'm not denying as I'm glad to see you a bit before we turn in.

'Funny thing 'appened tonight,' he went on. 'After I'd seen the twelve-forty-five through and Mr Jenkins 'ad gone and I'd nearly finished turnin' off the lights—'

He told the whole story jovially, jauntily, as if it were a rather good joke. He attained a certain vividness of expression which only became blurred at that part which dealt with his own sensations after the passing of the train.

The woman was wide awake before he had finished. All her

life she had indirectly depended on the Underground railway, and knew its workings almost as well as the signalman himself.

"Arf a mo', George!' she said, as he finished. 'How did it get past the signal if you was out of your box?'

'That's what beats me!' exclaimed George Raoul, thumping the table as if herein lay the very cream of the joke.

She looked at him with the dawning suspicion that he had been drinking; but as she looked she knew that he had not.

'What sort o' train was it?' she asked; keeping her eyes fixed on his.

For a moment he did not reply. His gaze dwelt on his cocoa as he answered:

'Circle train.'

Jinny made no reply, and the subject was dropped.

An hour later neither of them was asleep.

'Jinny,' said Raoul, 'what yer thinkin' about?'

'Nothing,' she retorted, and her voice came sulkily through the darkness.

'Go on. Out with it!'

'All right! 'Ave it your own way, an' don't blame me. I was wonderin' what Pete was doin' now—this minute.'

'Pete!' echoed Raoul, through teeth that chattered, though he tried to clench them. 'You've no call to wonder about 'im—not after the way he served you, his lawful, wedded wife.'

'I didn't mean to,' she defended herself; 'only you tellin' me about that train—and 'im being a Circle driver—set me off.'

'You've no call to think about 'im,' repeated Raoul doggedly. 'You can lay he ain't thinkin' about you—'e's thinkin' about the woman he left you for.'

There was a moment's silence, and then:

'P'r'aps—and p'r'aps not,' replied Jinny.

On the following morning Raoul decided that he would still say nothing to the stationmaster about the train that had followed the twelve-forty-five.

The position was by no means an easy one. He knew that his nerves would not stand the strain of turning out the lights on the platform—not yet awhile, anyhow. On the other hand, he dared not throw up his job. During the last three weeks he had seen something of Jinny's nature; and although his animal love for her had in no way abated, he had a pretty shrewd suspicion that she would not face even temporary destitution with him.

After much deliberation, he hit on a comparatively neat compromise. As he left home to go on duty he approached an elderly loafer leaning against the wall of a public-house near the station.

'Suppose you don't want a tanner a night for five minutes' work as a child could do?' he suggested.

'All accordin' to what the work is,' answered the loafer.

'Turnin' off the lights mostly,' said Raoul. 'Anyway, if you want the job 'ang about 'ere'—indicating the station—'at twelve-forty-five sharp until you see the stationmaster come off. Then 'op into the station. You'll find me on the platform.

'I'm doing this on me own,' he added. 'My missis likes me to be 'ome early, and it's worth a tanner a night for a bit of 'elp. See?'

The loss of the extra three shillings a week, Raoul decided, could safely be ascribed to an act of war economy on the part of the railway company. Better lose three bob a week than have to chuck up your job, he reasoned.

The services of the loafer proved a wise investment. Raoul

showed him where to find the switches. On the first night he explained it all over and over again, glancing from time to time towards the tunnel, thereby extracting full value for his sixpence.

The explanation finished, and while three lamps remained burning, he left the loafer for a suddenly remembered duty on the ticket-office level. Thence, in a comfortable circle of light, he presently called:

'Turn off them last three lights, mate, and come up.'

The loafer sluggishly obeyed, and then shambled up the staircase to receive the most easily earned sixpence of his life.

'Same time tomorrer night if you're on,' said Raoul.

'I'm on right enough,' replied the loafer.

That formula was repeated every night for some half-a-dozen nights. Then came a night on which the loafer failed to appear.

For five minutes Raoul waited. He went up to the street level and looked round. The station was deserted—there was not even a constable on point duty.

When the loafer's defection became obvious, Raoul's first thought was to leave the lights burning and go straight home. Reflection showed that this would mean the sack—which in turn would mean the probable loss of Jinny—the loss of that for which the very agonies he was now enduring had been incurred.

Besides, there was another thought that drove him back into the station. Somehow or other he would be compelled to explain why he had left the lights burning—why he had been afraid to return to the station. They would ask questions. And God knew where those questions might lead!

The up-platform presented no terrors. On the down-platform—in the moment of utter darkness when the eighth lamp was extinguished—he knew that his fear would reach its zenith. And precisely at that moment the distant rumbling in the tunnel began—the driven air, like a breeze, played about his temples.

He could not prevent his eyes from staring in the direction of the tunnel. He tried to move backwards up the staircase, but all power of voluntary action had left him.

The train seemed to slacken speed as it rolled into the station. As it came towards him, slowly and more slowly, his eyes were glued to a faint luminosity in the driver's window—a luminosity that gathered shape as it came nearer and nearer.

'Pete!' he gasped—and with that conscious effort of the muscles his brain regained control of his body and he rushed up the stairs, uncertain whether the train had stopped—knowing that if it came again it would stop and wait for him.

Jinny was awake and moving about the room when he returned. She glanced at his drawn face and knew what had happened.

'Seen it again?' she asked.

'Wot if I have?' he demanded.

'Nothing,' she retorted.

She waited while he ate his supper in silence.

'George,' she said, as he put down his cup for the last time.

'Well?'

'Suppose we knew for certain as Pete was *dead*'—she paused, but did not know enough to look at his mouth, and his eyes were turned from her—'why, then we—we could get spliced proper, couldn't we?'

Still avoiding her gaze he nodded.

'Suppose,' she said, leaning across the table until her elbows touched his, 'suppose we was to go about the banns tomorrer?'

Then did Raoul look up and meet the woman's gaze. In her

eye there was nothing of accusation. But there was nothing of doubt.

'Right-o!' he said.

On the following morning they went together to the parish church and, being recommended thence to the vicarage, explained their needs. They learnt that they would have to wait for three Sundays before they could be married.

He was gloomy and depressed as they left the vicarage.

'Three weeks'll soon pass,' she said, as if to console him.

'Aye,' he grunted.

'An' you'll feel a lot better when it's done,' she added.

To this he made no reply, and she did not labour the point. Indeed, it was the last veiled allusion she ever made to the subject.

On his way to the station he came across the loafer in the usual place outside the public-house. The man shambled towards him ready with an excuse, but Raoul cut him short.

'Shan't be wantin' you no more,' he said gruffly, and thereby burnt his boats behind him.

During the hours that passed between his going on duty in the early afternoon and his leaving the box after the passing of the twelve-forty-five, he did not once repent having dispensed with the services of the loafer. True, his mind dwelt almost continuously on the ordeal before him. But Jinny had unconsciously given him a weapon when she had told him he would feel better when *it* was done.

That night, as he doused the eighth lamp, he turned and faced the tunnel.

'I'm actin' square by 'er now, ain't I?' he shouted.

Then, for all the furious beating of his heart, he walked at a leisurely pace up the staircase, and so, completing his duties, into the street.

On the next night it was easier, and, with each night that brought his marriage nearer, his confidence grew. His nerve would falter sometimes, but always he managed to ascend the staircase one step at a time. Jinny was a secret tower of strength to him—so that all went reasonably well with him until, by the merest accident, the tower of strength crumbled.

Three Sundays had passed since their visit to the vicarage when the accident happened. The accident took the form of his meeting Mabel Owen as he was returning home from duty.

He had known Mabel in the Baker Street days before he had known Jinny—a fact of which Jinny was well aware. Mabel was returning from some unmentioned errand in the West End when she ran into him and exclaimed:

'Blessed if it ain't George Raoul! 'Ow goes it, George? Seems ages since we met, don't it! An' what might you be doin' in these parts?'

'I work over 'ere now,' explained Raoul. 'Cheyne Road. 'Ow goes it with you?'

Then, because he had no wish to appear churlish to a girl with whom he had once walked out, he invited her to an adjacent coffee stall.

He arrived at the tenement barely half an hour later than usual. But that half-hour was more than enough for Jinny.

'You're late, George,' she said, as he came in.

'Sorry, Jinny,' he replied. 'Couldn't help myself. Met a friend as I was comin' off. Had to say a civil word to 'er.'

'*'Er!*' repeated Jinny.

'Mabel Owen,' he said—and his clumsy effort to say it casually fanned her suspicion.

'Oh!' shrilled Jinny. 'So you keep me waitin' while you go gallivantin' about with that dressed up bit o' damaged goods!'

'You've no right to say that of Mabel,' protested Raoul.

'No right!' she echoed. 'Oh no! I've no right to say that of 'er, me livin' with you with no weddin'-ring as you've given me. No better than 'er, I'm not. And don't you let me forget it neither, George Raoul!'

'Stow that, Jinny!' he commanded, with rising anger. 'Ain't we fixed it up to get spliced proper day after tomorrer?'

The glint in his eye, partly of anger but partly also of fear, restrained her from further outburst and drove her indignation inwards so that she sulked.

She was still sulking on the following day, compelling him to eat his midday meal in gloomy silence, wherefore he left home for work sooner than was necessary.

He was in the signal-box before he recognised that the secret tower of strength had crumbled as a result of the accident of his meeting with Mabel Owen. Jinny had shown him a side of her nature that had been conspicuously absent in the earlier stages of his infatuation. And now his life was to become irrevocably linked with hers.

With the first taste of the bitterness of his sin came remorse; and with remorse came, with renewed strength, the terror which he had partly beaten back.

The terror began to grip him even before the stationmaster had left. In the signal-box he had formed the plan of telling the stationmaster that he could not turn out the lights that night—that he must hurry to the bedside of a dying child—any lie would do provided it saved him for that night.

Tomorrow night he would be married to Jinny. He would have made what reparation lay in his power and would feel the safer.

'Good night, George.'

'G'night, Mr Jenkins.'

The stationmaster hung the keys on the nail outside his den and walked off. Raoul would have called after him, but checked himself. The stationmaster would not believe that lie about the dying child. His face would betray his terror—his terror of the tunnel. The stationmaster would ask him why he was afraid of the tunnel, and—*God knew where those questions would lead!*

'Funny, it's worse'n ever tonight!' he said, as he finished the lights on the up-platform—for he was not analytical and did not wholly understand why the secret tower of strength had crumbled. He only knew that he did not want to marry Jinny on the following day. He only saw his sin in gaining possession of her—in the way that he had gained possession of her—in its naked hideousness.

The odd fatalism of his class prevented him from shirking the lights on the down-platform. What has to be will be. The same fatalism drove him ultimately to dousing the eighth lamp and turning, like a doomed rat, to face the already rumbling horror of the tunnel.

More slowly than before, as if it knew that he must wait for it, the train came on. Then in his ears sounded the familiar grinding of the brakes.

The train had stopped in the station. The faint luminosity in the driver's window grinned its welcome. Then it beckoned.

'I'm comin', Pete.'

From the corner by the staircase, where he had been crouching, he moved across the platform and boarded the train.

Dawn, breaking over the serried roofs of Chelsea, found Jinny sitting wide-eyed before the untouched meal she had prepared hours ago for Raoul.

As if the first faint streaks of light ended her vigil she dropped her face on her arms and burst into tears.

'Fool that I was! Why couldn't I 'ave 'eld me jore about Mabel Owen till we was spliced proper? And now he's left me, and Pete—'

The passion of weeping rose to its height, spent itself, and left her in another mood.

''E needn't think 'e can get away as easy as all that,' she muttered savagely. 'If I'm a fool, he's a worse one—as 'e'll soon find to 'is cost.'

At eight o'clock she washed herself and donned her black dress. Thus arrayed as a respectable woman of the working-class she made her way to the nearest police-station and asked for the Inspector.

'I'm Mrs Pete Comber,' she explained. 'My husband used to be a driver on the Underground. Circle train, he druv.'

'Well?' said the Inspector.

She did not hesitate in her confession. She had weighed the cost of her revenge, and did not shrink from paying it.

'A man called George Raoul used to lodge with us—a signaller, 'e was, and worked at Baker Street. Me and 'im got friendly, if you understand, only I wouldn't 'ave nothing to do with him while I was livin' with my 'usband, not being that sort.

''Bout a couple of months ago George come to me and says, "Jinny," he says, "you won't see Pete no more," he says. "Why not?" I says. "Chucked up his job and everythink," he says; "met him when we was bein' paid," he says, "an' he asked me to tell you quite friendly like," he says.'

'Look here,' interrupted the Inspector, 'we can't have anything to do with all this.'

'You wait,' replied Jinny, scarcely noticing the interruption. 'As soon as George told me, I was that wild with my 'usbin that I let George take me off—me that had always been a respectable woman. Never entered my 'ead as he wasn't tellin' the truth. Next day George was turned on to Cheyne Road an' we come to live up 'ere.

'Well, first he begun tellin' me as he'd bin seein' things on the Underground. That started me thinkin'. I can put two an' two together, same as anyone else, an' I started takin' notice of what he was talking about in 'is sleep. And I tell you as sure as I stand here, George Raoul killed my 'usbin, and I dessay 'e's put 'im in one of the old holes in the Baker Street tunnel wot they used to use for storin' the tools.'

The Inspector began to take notes and to ask a number of questions. Of one thing only was he sure—that the woman before him was giving a genuine expression of opinion.

'And now George has left you, I suppose, and that's why you've come along to us?' he suggested.

'He has left me,' replied the woman. 'But I only found all this out properly night before last, an' I couldn't be sure. I'd have come along 'ere any'ow.'

The Inspector guessed that the last statement was a lie. But unless the man, when they caught him, definitely implicated the woman he knew that the Crown would not prosecute her.

'All right,' he said. 'We'll find George for you. Leave your address and call here tomorrow.'

The Inspector, after instructing a plain-clothes man to

shadow Jinny to her home, went to interview the Cheyne Road stationmaster.

On the following morning, when Jinny called at the police-station, she was asked to examine a suit of clothing, a pocket-knife, and a greasy case containing a number of small personal papers and other belongings.

'Yes, they're Pete's right enough, pore dear!' she exclaimed, and then burst into a flood of maudlin tears.

The Inspector waited unmoved. He believed not at all in the genuineness of Jinny's grief; but convention had its claims, and he said nothing until the storm of tears had subsided.

'Now, Mrs Comber,' he said presently, 'I want you to dry your face and come along o' me.'

'It's all right,' he added. 'Nothing's going to happen to you.'

He took her for some distance in a taxi-cab to a low, vault-like building near the river. There, after parley with the local officials, he led her to an inner room.

'Steady now,' he warned her. 'We're going to show you a dead body.'

Someone removed a cloth, and at the same moment the Inspector demanded:

'Who's that?'

'George Raoul!' gasped Jinny.

As the Inspector, taking her by the arm, led her from the room a question forced itself to her lips.

'You—you ain't 'ung him already?'

'No,' replied the Inspector, with a grim laugh, 'we ain't 'ung him. Wasn't needed. We found your husband in that disused hole, same as you said—and we found George Raoul along-side him—like that. Heart failure, the doctor says. Funny thing! As far as I can make out, he must have been skeered or something and run all the way through the tunnel from

Cheyne Road to Baker Street where he done it. Must have been the running as did for his heart.'

That, at any rate, was the explanation based on the findings of the Coroner's Court.

The Knight's Cross
Signal Problem

Ernest Bramah

Ernest Bramah's first book, *English Farming and Why I Turned It Up*, was published in 1894, and was inspired by the principle 'write what you know': at the age of seventeen he had become a farmer, but it proved an unhappy career choice. Bramah, who came from Manchester, and whose real name was Ernest Brammah Smith, dabbled in journalism, and took a job as secretary to Jerome K. Jerome, before becoming a full-time writer. His humorous stories about the Chinese rogue Kai Lung enjoyed considerable popularity in their day, but it is his detective fiction that has stood the test of time.

The success of his mysteries is due in part to his smoothly professional writing, but mainly to his creation in 1914 of a memorable sleuth. Max Carrados is by no means the only blind detective in fiction, but he is probably the most highly regarded. In his history of the genre, *Bloody Murder* (1972), Julian Symons said that Carrados and his friend, the discredited solicitor turned inquiry agent Louis Carlyle, 'make an agreeable variation on the Holmes-Watson relationship, with Carlyle more sophisticated and more distinctively characterised than most assistants, and Carrados insistent on the value of having "no blundering, self-confident eyes to be hoodwinked".'

'Louis,' exclaimed Mr Carrados, with the air of genial gaiety that Carlyle had found so incongruous to his conception of a blind man, 'you have a mystery somewhere about you! I know it by your step.'

Nearly a month had passed since the incident of the false Dionysius had led to the two men meeting. It was now December. Whatever Mr Carlyle's step might indicate to the inner eye it betokened to the casual observer the manner of a crisp, alert, self-possessed man of business. Carlyle, in truth, betrayed nothing of the pessimism and despondency that had marked him on the earlier occasion.

'You have only yourself to thank that it is a very poor one,' he retorted. 'If you hadn't held me to a hasty promise—'

'To give me an option on the next case that baffled you, no matter what it was—'

'Just so. The consequence is that you get a very unsatisfactory affair that has no special interest to an amateur and is only baffling because it is—well—'

'Well, baffling?'

'Exactly, Max. Your would-be jest has discovered the proverbial truth. I need hardly tell you that it is only the insoluble that is finally baffling and this is very probably insoluble. You remember the awful smash on the Central and Suburban at Knight's Cross Station a few weeks ago?'

'Yes,' replied Carrados, with interest. 'I read the whole ghastly details at the time.'

'You read?' exclaimed his friend suspiciously.

'I still use the familiar phrases,' explained Carrados, with a smile. 'As a matter of fact, my secretary reads to me. I mark what I want to hear and when he comes at ten o'clock we clear off the morning papers in no time.'

'And how do you know what to mark?' demanded Mr Carlyle cunningly.

Carrados's right hand, lying idly on the table, moved to a newspaper near. He ran his finger along a column heading, his eyes still turned towards his visitor.

'"The Money Market. Continued from page 2. British Railways,"' he announced.

'Extraordinary,' murmured Carlyle.

'Not very,' said Carrados. 'If someone dipped a stick in treacle and wrote "Rats" across a marble slab you would probably be able to distinguish what was there, blindfold.'

'Probably,' admitted Mr Carlyle. 'At all events we will not test the experiment.'

'The difference to you of treacle on a marble background is scarcely greater than that of printers' ink on newspaper to me. But anything smaller than pica I do not read with comfort, and below long primer I cannot read at all. Hence the secretary. Now the accident, Louis.'

'The accident: well, you remember all about that. An ordinary Central and Suburban passenger train, non-stop at Knight's Cross, ran past the signal and crashed into a crowded electric train that was just beginning to move out. It was like sending a garden roller down a row of handlights. Two carriages of the electric train were flattened out of existence; the next two were broken up. For the first time on an English railway there was a good stand-up smash between a heavy steam-engine and a train of light cars, and it was "bad for the coo."'

'Twenty-seven killed, forty something injured, eight died since,' commented Carrados.

'That was bad for the Co.,' said Carlyle. 'Well, the main fact was plain enough. The heavy train was in the wrong. But was the engine-driver responsible? He claimed, and he claimed vehemently from the first and he never varied one iota, that he had a "clear" signal—that is to say, the green light, it being dark. The signalman concerned was equally dogged that he never pulled off the signal—that it was at "danger" when the accident happened and that it had been for five minutes before. Obviously, they could not both be right.'

'Why, Louis?' asked Mr Carrados smoothly.

'The signal must either have been up or down—red or green.'

'Did you ever notice the signals on the Great Northern Railway, Louis?'

'Not particularly. Why?'

'One winterly day, about the year when you and I were concerned in being born, the engine-driver of a Scotch express received the "clear" from a signal near a little Huntingdon station called Abbots Ripton. He went on and crashed into a goods train and into the thick of the smash a down express mowed its way. Thirteen killed and the usual tale of injured. He was positive that the signal gave him a "clear"; the signalman was equally confident that he had never pulled it off the "danger." Both were right, and yet the signal was in working order. As I said, it was a winterly day; it had been snowing hard and the snow froze and accumulated on the upper edge of the signal arm until its weight bore it down.

That is a fact that no fiction writer dare have invented, but to this day every signal on the Great Northern pivots from the centre of the arm instead of from the end, in memory of that snowstorm.'

'That came out at the inquest, I presume?' said Mr Carlyle. 'We have had the Board of Trade inquiry and the inquest here and no explanation is forthcoming. Everything was in perfect order. It rests between the word of the signalman and the word of the engine-driver—not a jot of direct evidence either way. Which is right?'

'That is what you are going to find out, Louis?' suggested Carrados.

'It is what I am being paid for finding out,' admitted Mr Carlyle frankly. 'But so far we are just where the inquest left it, and, between ourselves, I candidly can't see an inch in front of my face in the matter.'

'Nor can I,' said the blind man, with a rather wry smile. 'Never mind. The engine-driver is your client, of course?'

'Yes,' admitted Carlyle. 'But how the deuce did you know?'

'Let us say that your sympathies are enlisted on his behalf. The jury were inclined to exonerate the signalman, weren't they? What has the company done with your man?'

'Both are suspended. Hutchins, the driver, hears that he may probably be given charge of a lavatory at one of the stations. He is a decent, bluff, short-spoken old chap, with his heart in his work. Just now you'll find him at his worst—bitter and suspicious. The thought of swabbing down a lavatory and taking pennies all day is poisoning him.'

'Naturally. Well, there we have honest Hutchins: taciturn, a little touchy perhaps, grown grey in the service of the company, and manifesting quite a bulldog-like devotion to his favourite 538.'

'Why, that actually was the number of his engine—how do you know it?' demanded Carlyle sharply.

'It was mentioned two or three times at the inquest, Louis,' replied Carrados mildly.

'And you remembered—with no reason to?'

'You can generally trust a blind man's memory, especially if he has taken the trouble to develop it.'

'Then you will remember that Hutchins did not make a very good impression at the time. He was surly and irritable under the ordeal. I want you to see the case from all sides.'

'He called the signalman—Mead—a "lying young dog," across the room, I believe. Now, Mead, what is he like? You have seen him, of course?'

'Yes. He does not impress me favourably. He is glib, ingratiating, and distinctly "greasy." He has a ready answer for everything almost before the question is out of your mouth. He has thought of everything.'

'And now you are going to tell me something, Louis,' said Carrados encouragingly.

Mr Carlyle laughed a little to cover an involuntary movement of surprise.

'There is a suggestive line that was not touched at the inquiries,' he admitted. 'Hutchins has been a saving man all his life, and he has received good wages. Among his class he is regarded as wealthy. I daresay that he has five hundred pounds in the bank. He is a widower with one daughter, a very nice-mannered girl of about twenty. Mead is a young man, and he and the girl are sweethearts—have been informally engaged for some time. But old Hutchins would not hear of it; he seems to have taken a dislike to the signalman from the first and latterly he had forbidden him to come to his house or his daughter to speak to him.'

'Excellent, Louis,' cried Carrados in great delight. 'We shall clear your man in a blaze of red and green lights yet and hang the glib, "greasy" signalman from his own signal-post.'

'It is a significant fact, seriously?'

'It is absolutely convincing.'

'It may have been a slip, a mental lapse on Mead's part which he discovered the moment it was too late, and then, being too cowardly to admit his fault, and having so much at stake, he took care to make detection impossible. It may have been that, but my idea is rather that probably it was neither quite pure accident nor pure design. I can imagine Mead meanly pluming himself over the fact that the life of this man who stands in his way, and whom he must cordially dislike, lies in his power. I can imagine the idea becoming an obsession as he dwells on it. A dozen times with his hand on the lever he lets his mind explore the possibilities of a moment's defection. Then one day he pulls the signal off in sheer bravado—and hastily puts it at danger again. He may have done it once or he may have done it oftener before he was caught in a fatal moment of irresolution. The chances are about even that the engine-driver would be killed. In any case he would be disgraced, for it is easier on the face of it to believe that a man might run past a danger signal in absentmindedness, without noticing it, than that a man should pull off a signal and replace it without being conscious of his actions.'

'The fireman was killed. Does your theory involve the certainty of the fireman being killed, Louis?'

'No,' said Carlyle. 'The fireman is a difficulty, but looking at it from Mead's point of view—whether he has been guilty of an error or a crime—it resolves itself into this: First, the fireman may be killed. Second, he may not notice the signal at all. Third, in any case he will loyally corroborate his driver and the good old jury will discount that.'

Carrados smoked thoughtfully, his open, sightless eyes merely appearing to be set in a tranquil gaze across the room.

'It would not be an improbable explanation,' he said presently. 'Ninety-nine men out of a hundred would say: "People do not do these things." But you and I, who have in our different ways studied criminology, know that they sometimes do, or else there would be no curious crimes. What have you done on that line?'

To anyone who could see, Mr Carlyle's expression conveyed an answer.

'You are behind the scenes, Max. What was there for me to do? Still I must do something for my money. Well, I have had a very close inquiry made confidentially among the men. There might be a whisper of one of them knowing more than had come out—a man restrained by friendship, or enmity, or even grade jealousy. Nothing came of that. Then there was the remote chance that some private person had noticed the signal without attaching any importance to it then, one who would be able to identify it still by something associated with the time. I went over the line myself. Opposite the signal the line on one side is shut in by a high blank wall; on the other side are houses, but coming below the butt-end of a scullery the signal does not happen to be visible from any road or from any window.'

'My poor Louis!' said Carrados, in friendly ridicule. 'You were at the end of your tether?'

'I was,' admitted Carlyle. 'And now that you know the sort of job it is I don't suppose that you are keen on wasting your time over it.'

'That would hardly be fair, would it?' said Carrados reasonably. 'No, Louis, I will take over your honest old driver, and your greasy young signalman, and your fatal signal that cannot be seen from anywhere.'

'But it is an important point for you to remember, Max, that although the signal cannot be seen from the box, if the mechanism had gone wrong, or anyone tampered with the arm, the automatic indicator would at once have told Mead that the green light was showing. Oh, I have gone very thoroughly into the technical points, I assure you.'

'I must do so too,' commented Mr Carrados gravely.

'For that matter, if there is anything you want to know, I dare say that I can tell you,' suggested his visitor. 'It might save your time.'

'True,' acquiesced Carrados. 'I should like to know whether anyone belonging to the houses that bound the line there came of age or got married on the twenty-sixth of November.'

Mr Carlyle looked across curiously at his host.

'I really do not know, Max,' he replied, in his crisp, precise way. 'What on earth has that got to do with it, may I inquire?'

'The only explanation of the Pont St Lin swing-bridge disaster of '75 was the reflection of a green bengal light on a cottage window.'

Mr Carlyle smiled his indulgence privately.

'My dear chap, you mustn't let your retentive memory of obscure happenings run away with you,' he remarked wisely. 'In nine cases out of ten the obvious explanation is the true one. The difficulty, as here, lies in proving it. Now, you would like to see these men?'

'I expect so; in any case, I will see Hutchins first.'

'Both live in Holloway. Shall I ask Hutchins to come here to see you—say tomorrow? He is doing nothing.'

'No,' replied Carrados. 'Tomorrow I must call on my brokers and my time may be filled up.'

'Quite right; you mustn't neglect your own affairs for this—experiment,' assented Carlyle.

'Besides, I should prefer to drop in on Hutchins at his own home. Now, Louis, enough of the honest old man for one night. I have a lovely thing by Eumenes that I want to show you. Today is—Tuesday. Come to dinner on Sunday and pour the vials of your ridicule on my want of success.'

'That's an amiable way of putting it,' replied Carlyle. 'All right, I will.'

Two hours later Carrados was again in his study, apparently, for a wonder, sitting idle. Sometimes he smiled to himself, and once or twice he laughed a little, but for the most part his pleasant, impassive face reflected no emotion, and he sat with his useless eyes tranquilly fixed on an unseen distance. It was a fantastic caprice of the man to mock his sightlessness by a parade of light, and under the soft brilliance of a dozen electric brackets the room was as bright as day. At length he stood up and rang the bell.

'I suppose Mr Greatorex isn't still here by any chance, Parkinson?' he asked, referring to his secretary.

'I think not, sir, but I will ascertain,' replied the man.

'Never mind. Go to his room and bring me the last two files of *The Times*. Now'—when he returned—'turn to the earliest you have there. The date?'

'November the second.'

'That will do. Find the Money Market; it will be in the Supplement. Now look down the columns until you come to British Railways.'

'I have it, sir.'

'Central and Suburban. Read the closing price and the change.'

'Central and Suburban Ordinary, 66-1/2-67-1/2, fall 1/8. Preferred Ordinary, 81-81-1/2, no change. Deferred Ordinary, 27-1/2-27-3/4, fall 1/4. That is all, sir.'

'Now take a paper about a week on. Read the Deferred only.'

'27-27-1/4, no change.'

'Another week.'

'29-1/2-30, rise 5/8.'

'Another.'

'31-1/2-32-1/2, rise 1.'

'Very good. Now on Tuesday the twenty-seventh November.'

'31-7/8-32-3/4, rise 1/2.'

'Yes. The next day.'

'24-1/2-23-1/2, fall 9.'

'Quite so, Parkinson. There had been an accident, you see.'

'Yes, sir. Very unpleasant accident. Jane knows a person whose sister's young man has a cousin who had his arm torn off in it—torn off at the socket, she says, sir. It seems to bring it home to one, sir.'

'That is all. Stay—in the paper you have, look down the first money column and see if there is any reference to the Central and Suburban.'

'Yes, sir. "City and Suburbans, which after their late depression on the projected extension of the motor bus service, had been steadily creeping up on the abandonment of the scheme, and as a result of their own excellent traffic returns, suffered a heavy slump through the lamentable accident of Thursday night. The Deferred in particular at one time fell eleven points as it was felt that the possible dividend, with which rumour has of late been busy, was now out of the question."'

'Yes; that is all. Now you can take the papers back. And let it be a warning to you, Parkinson, not to invest your savings in speculative railway deferreds.'

'Yes, sir. Thank you, sir, I will endeavour to remember.' He lingered for a moment as he shook the file of papers level. 'I may say, sir, that I have my eye on a small block of cottage property at Acton. But even cottage property scarcely seems safe from legislative depredation now, sir.'

The next day Mr Carrados called on his brokers in the city. It is to be presumed that he got through his private business quicker than he expected, for after leaving Austin Friars he continued his journey to Holloway, where he found Hutchins at home and sitting morosely before his kitchen fire. Rightly assuming that his luxuriant car would involve him in a certain amount of public attention in Klondyke Street, the blind man dismissed it some distance from the house, and walked the rest of the way, guided by the almost imperceptible touch of Parkinson's arm.

'Here is a gentleman to see you, father,' explained Miss Hutchins, who had come to the door. She divined the relative positions of the two visitors at a glance.

'Then why don't you take him into the parlour?' grumbled the ex-driver. His face was a testimonial of hard work and general sobriety, but at the moment one might hazard from his voice and manner that he had been drinking earlier in the day.

'I don't think that the gentleman would be impressed by the difference between our parlour and our kitchen,' replied the girl quaintly, 'and it is warmer here.'

'What's the matter with the parlour now?' demanded her father sourly. 'It was good enough for your mother and me. It used to be good enough for you.'

'There is nothing the matter with it, nor with the kitchen either.' She turned impassively to the two who had followed her along the narrow passage. 'Will you go in, sir?'

'I don't want to see no gentleman,' cried Hutchins noisily. 'Unless'—his manner suddenly changed to one of pitiable anxiety—'unless you're from the Company, sir, to—to—'

'No; I have come on Mr Carlyle's behalf,' replied Carrados, walking to a chair as though he moved by a kind of instinct.

Hutchins laughed his wry contempt.

'Mr Carlyle!' he reiterated; 'Mr Carlyle! Fat lot of good he's been. Why don't he *do* something for his money?'

'He has,' replied Carrados, with imperturbable good-humour; 'he has sent me. Now, I want to ask you a few questions.'

'A few questions!' roared the irate man. 'Why, blast it, I have done nothing else but answer questions for a month. I didn't pay Mr Carlyle to ask me questions; I can get enough of that for nixes. Why don't you go and ask Mr Herbert Ananias Mead your few questions—then you might find out something.'

There was a slight movement by the door and Carrados knew that the girl had quietly left the room.

'You saw that, sir?' demanded the father, diverted to a new line of bitterness. 'You saw that girl—my own daughter, that I've worked for all her life?'

'No,' replied Carrados.

'The girl that's just gone out—she's my daughter,' explained Hutchins.

'I know, but I did not see her. I see nothing. I am blind.'

'Blind!' exclaimed the old fellow, sitting up in startled wonderment. 'You mean it, sir? You walk all right and you look at me as if you saw me. You're kidding surely.'

'No,' smiled Carrados. 'It's quite right.'

'Then it's a funny business, sir—you what are blind expecting to find something that those with their eyes couldn't,' ruminated Hutchins sagely.

'There are things that you can't see with your eyes, Hutchins.'

'Perhaps you are right, sir. Well, what is it you want to know?'

'Light a cigar first,' said the blind man, holding out his case and waiting until the various sounds told him that his host was smoking contentedly. 'The train you were driving at the time of the accident was the six-twenty-seven from Notcliff. It stopped everywhere until it reached Lambeth Bridge, the chief London station of your line. There it became something of an express, and leaving Lambeth Bridge at seven-eleven, should not stop again until it fetched Swanstead on Thames, eleven miles out, at seven-thirty-four. Then it stopped on and off from Swanstead to Ingerfield, the terminus of that branch, which it reached at eight-five.'

Hutchins nodded, and then, remembering, said: 'That's right, sir.'

'That was your business all day—running between Notcliff and Ingerfield?'

'Yes, sir. Three journeys up and three down mostly.'

'With the same stops on all the down journeys?'

'No. The seven-eleven is the only one that does a run from the Bridge to Swanstead. You see, it is just on the close of the evening rush, as they call it. A good many late business gentlemen living at Swanstead use the seven-eleven regular. The other journeys we stop at every station to Lambeth Bridge, and then here and there beyond.'

'There are, of course, other trains doing exactly the same journey—a service, in fact?'

'Yes, sir. About six.'

'And do any of those— say, during the rush—do any of those run non-stop from Lambeth to Swanstead?'

Hutchins reflected a moment. All the choler and restlessness had melted out of the man's face. He was again the excellent artisan, slow but capable and self-reliant.

'That I couldn't definitely say, sir. Very few short-distance trains pass the junction, but some of those may. A guide would show us in a minute but I haven't got one.'

'Never mind. You said at the inquest that it was no uncommon thing for you to be pulled up at the "stop" signal east of Knight's Cross Station. How often would that happen—only with the seven-eleven, mind.'

'Perhaps three times a week; perhaps twice.'

'The accident was on a Thursday. Have you noticed that you were pulled up oftener on a Thursday than on any other day?'

A smile crossed the driver's face at the question.

'You don't happen to live at Swanstead yourself, sir?' he asked in reply.

'No,' admitted Carrados. 'Why?'

'Well, sir, we were *always* pulled up on Thursday; practically always, you may say. It got to be quite a saying among those who used the train regular; they used to look out for it.'

Carrados's sightless eyes had the one quality of concealing emotion supremely. 'Oh,' he commented softly, 'always; and it was quite a saying, was it? And *why* was it always so on Thursday?'

'It had to do with the early closing, I'm told. The suburban traffic was a bit different. By rights we ought to have been set back two minutes for that day, but I suppose it wasn't thought worth while to alter us in the time-table, so we most always had to wait outside Three Deep tunnel for a west-bound electric to make good.'

'You were prepared for it then?'

'Yes, sir, I was,' said Hutchins, reddening at some recollection, 'and very down about it was one of the jury over that. But, mayhap once in three months, I did get through even on a Thursday, and it's not for me to question whether things are right or wrong just because they are not what I may expect. The signals are my orders, sir—stop! Go on! And it's for me to obey, as you would a general on the field of battle. What would happen otherwise! It was nonsense what they said about going cautious; and the man who started it was a barber who didn't know the difference between a "distance" and a "stop" signal down to the minute they gave their verdict. My orders, sir, given me by that signal, was "Go right ahead and keep to your running time!"'

Carrados nodded a soothing assent. 'That is all, I think,' he remarked.

'All!' exclaimed Hutchins in surprise. 'Why, sir, you can't have got much idea of it yet.'

'Quite enough. And I know it isn't pleasant for you to be taken along the same ground over and over again.'

The man moved awkwardly in his chair and pulled nervously at his grizzled beard.

'You mustn't take any notice of what I said just now, sir,' he apologised. 'You somehow make me feel that something may come of it; but I've been badgered about and accused and cross-examined from one to another of them these weeks till it's fairly made me bitter against everything. And now they talk of putting me in a lavatory—me that has been with the company for five and forty years and on the foot-plate thirty-two—a man suspected of running past a danger signal.'

'You have had a rough time, Hutchins; you will have to exercise your patience a little longer yet,' said Carrados sympathetically.

'You think something may come of it, sir? You think you will be able to clear me? Believe me, sir, if you could give me something to look forward to it might save me from—' He pulled himself up and shook his head sorrowfully. 'I've been near it,' he added simply.

Carrados reflected and took his resolution.

'Today is Wednesday. I think you may hope to hear something from your general manager towards the middle of next week.'

'Good God, sir! You really mean that?'

'In the interval, show your good sense by behaving reasonably. Keep civilly to yourself and don't talk. Above all'—he nodded towards a quart jug that stood on the table between them, an incident that filled the simple-minded engineer with boundless wonder when he recalled it afterwards—'above all, leave that alone.'

Hutchins snatched up the vessel and brought it crashing down on the hearthstone, his face shining with a set resolution.

'I've done with it, sir. It was the bitterness and despair that drove me to that. Now I can do without it.'

The door was hastily opened and Miss Hutchins looked anxiously from her father to the visitors and back again.

'Oh, whatever is the matter?' she exclaimed. 'I heard a great crash.'

'This gentleman is going to clear me, Meg, my dear,' blurted out the old man irrepressibly. 'And I've done with the drink for ever.'

'Hutchins! Hutchins!' said Carrados warningly.

'My daughter, sir; you wouldn't have her not know?' pleaded Hutchins, rather crest-fallen. 'It won't go any further.'

Carrados laughed quietly to himself as he felt Margaret Hutchins's startled and questioning eyes attempting to read his mind. He shook hands with the engine-driver without further comment, however, and walked out into the commonplace little street under Parkinson's unobtrusive guidance.

'Very nice of Miss Hutchins to go into half-mourning, Parkinson,' he remarked as they went along. 'Thoughtful, and yet not ostentatious.'

'Yes, sir,' agreed Parkinson, who had long ceased to wonder at his master's perceptions.

"The Romans, Parkinson, had a saying to the effect that gold carries no smell. That is a pity sometimes. What jewellery did Miss Hutchins wear?'

'Very little, sir. A plain gold brooch representing a merry-thought—the merry-thought of a sparrow, I should say, sir. The only other article was a smooth-backed gun-metal watch, suspended from a gun-metal bow.'

'Nothing showy or expensive, eh?'

'Oh dear no, sir. Quite appropriate for a young person of her position.'

'Just what I should have expected.' He slackened his pace. 'We are passing a hoarding, are we not?'

'Yes, sir.'

'We will stand here a moment. Read me the letterpress of the poster before us.'

'This "Oxo" one, sir?'

'Yes.'

'"Oxo," sir.'

Carrados was convulsed with silent laughter. Parkinson had infinitely more dignity and conceded merely a tolerant recognition of the ludicrous.

'That was a bad shot, Parkinson,' remarked his master when he could speak. 'We will try another.'

For three minutes, with scrupulous conscientiousness on the part of the reader and every appearance of keen interest on the part of the hearer, there were set forth the particulars of a sale by auction of superfluous timber and builders' material.

'That will do,' said Carrados, when the last detail had been reached. 'We can be seen from the door of No. 107 still?'

'Yes, sir.'

'No indication of anyone coming to us from there?'

'No, sir.'

Carrados walked thoughtfully on again. In the Holloway Road they rejoined the waiting motor car. 'Lambeth Bridge Station,' was the order the driver received.

From the station the car was sent on home and Parkinson was instructed to take two first-class singles for Richmond, which could be reached by changing at Stafford Road. The 'evening rush' had not yet commenced and they had no difficulty in finding an empty carriage when the train came in.

Parkinson was kept busy that journey describing what he saw at various points between Lambeth Bridge and Knight's Cross. For a quarter of a mile Carrados's demands on the eyes and the memory of his remarkable servant were wide and incessant. Then his questions ceased. They had passed the 'stop' signal, east of Knight's Cross Station.

The following afternoon they made the return journey as far as Knight's Cross. This time, however, the surroundings failed to interest Carrados. 'We are going to look at some rooms,' was the information he offered on the subject, and an imperturbable 'Yes, sir' had been the extent of Parkinson's comment on the unusual proceeding. After leaving the station they turned sharply along a road that ran parallel with the line, a dull thoroughfare of substantial, elderly houses that were beginning to sink into decrepitude. Here and there a corner residence displayed the brass plate of a professional occupant, but for the most part they were given up to the various branches of second-rate apartment letting.

'The third house after the one with the flagstaff,' said Carrados.

Parkinson rang the bell, which was answered by a young servant, who took an early opportunity of assuring them that she was not tidy as it was rather early in the afternoon. She informed Carrados, in reply to his inquiry, that Miss Chubb was at home, and showed them into a melancholy little sitting-room to await her appearance.

'I shall be "almost" blind here, Parkinson,' remarked Carrados, walking about the room. 'It saves explanation.'

'Very good, sir,' replied Parkinson.

Five minutes later, an interval suggesting that Miss Chubb also found it rather early in the afternoon, Carrados was arranging to take rooms for his attendant and himself for the short time that he would be in London, seeing an oculist.

'One bedroom, mine, must face north,' he stipulated. 'It has to do with the light.'

Miss Chubb replied that she quite understood. Some gentlemen, she added, had their requirements, others their fancies. She endeavoured to suit all. The bedroom she had in view from the first *did* face north. She would not have known, only the last gentleman, curiously enough, had made the same request.

'A sufferer like myself?' inquired Carrados affably.

Miss Chubb did not think so. In his case she regarded it merely as a fancy. He had said that he could not sleep on any other side. She had had to turn out of her own room to accommodate him, but if one kept an apartment-house one had to be adaptable; and Mr Ghoosh was certainly very liberal in his ideas.

'Ghoosh? An Indian gentleman, I presume?' hazarded Carrados.

It appeared that Mr Ghoosh was an Indian. Miss Chubb confided that at first she had been rather perturbed at the idea of taking in 'a black man,' as she confessed to regarding him. She reiterated, however, that Mr Ghoosh proved to be 'quite the gentleman.' Five minutes of affability put Carrados in full possession of Mr Ghoosh's manner of life and movements—the dates of his arrival and departure, his solitariness and his daily habits.

'This would be the best bedroom,' said Miss Chubb.

It was a fair-sized room on the first floor. The window looked out on to the roof of an outbuilding; beyond, the deep cutting of the railway line. Opposite stood the dead wall that Mr Carlyle had spoken of.

Carrados 'looked' round the room with the discriminating glance that sometimes proved so embarrassing to those who knew him.

'I have to take a little daily exercise,' he remarked, walking to the window and running his hand up the woodwork. 'You will not mind my fixing a "developer" here, Miss Chubb—a few small screws?'

Miss Chubb thought not. Then she was sure not. Finally she ridiculed the idea of minding with scorn.

'If there is width enough,' mused Carrados, spanning the upright critically. 'Do you happen to have a wooden foot-rule convenient?'

'Well, to be sure!' exclaimed Miss Chubb, opening a rapid succession of drawers until she produced the required article. 'When we did out this room after Mr Ghoosh, there was this very ruler among the things that he hadn't thought worth taking. This is what you require, sir?'

'Yes,' replied Carrados, accepting it, 'I think this is exactly what I require.' It was a common new white-wood rule, such as one might buy at any small stationer's for a penny. He carelessly took off the width of the upright, reading the figures with a touch; and then continued to run a finger-tip delicately up and down the edges of the instrument.

'Four and seven-eighths,' was his unspoken conclusion.

'I hope it will do, sir.'

'Admirably,' replied Carrados. 'But I haven't reached the end of my requirements yet, Miss Chubb.'

'No, sir?' said the landlady, feeling that it would be a pleasure to oblige so agreeable a gentleman, 'what else might there be?'

'Although I can see very little I like to have a light, but not any kind of light. Gas I cannot do with. Do you think that you would be able to find me an oil lamp?'

'Certainly, sir. I got out a very nice brass lamp that I have specially for Mr Ghoosh. He read a good deal of an evening, and he preferred a lamp.'

'That is very convenient. I suppose it is large enough to burn for a whole evening?'

'Yes, indeed. And very particular he was always to have it filled every day.'

'A lamp without oil is not very useful,' smiled Carrados, following her towards another room, and absentmindedly slipping the foot-rule into his pocket.

Whatever Parkinson thought of the arrangement of going into second-rate apartments in an obscure street it is to be inferred that his devotion to his master was sufficient to overcome his private emotions as a self-respecting 'man.' At all events, as they were approaching the station he asked, and without a trace of feeling, whether there were any orders for him with reference to the proposed migration.

'None, Parkinson,' replied his master. 'We must be satisfied with our present quarters.'

'I beg your pardon, sir,' said Parkinson, with some constraint. 'I understood that you had taken the rooms for a week certain.'

'I am afraid that Miss Chubb will be under the same impression. Unforeseen circumstances will prevent our going, however. Mr Greatorex must write tomorrow, enclosing a cheque, with my regrets, and adding a penny for this ruler which I seem to have brought away with me. It, at least, is something for the money.'

Parkinson may be excused for not attempting to understand the course of events.

'Here is your train coming in, sir,' he merely said.

'We will let it go and wait for another. Is there a signal at either end of the platform?'

'Yes, sir; at the further end.'

'Let us walk towards it. Are there any of the porters or officials about here?'

'No, sir; none.'

'Take this ruler. I want you to go up the steps—there are steps up the signal, by the way?'

'Yes, sir.'

'I want you to measure the glass of the lamp. Do not go up any higher than is necessary, but if you have to stretch be careful not to mark on the measurement with your nail, although the impulse is a natural one. That has been done already.'

Parkinson looked apprehensively around and about. Fortunately the part was a dark and unfrequented spot, and everyone else was moving towards the exit at the other end of the platform. Fortunately, also, the signal was not a high one.

'As near as I can judge on the rounded surface, the glass is four and seven-eighths across,' reported Parkinson.

'Thank you,' replied Carrados, returning the measure to his pocket, 'four and seven-eighths is quite near enough. Now we will take the next train back.'

Sunday evening came, and with it Mr Carlyle to The Turrets at the appointed hour. He brought to the situation a mind poised for any eventuality and a trenchant eye. As the time went on and the impenetrable Carrados made no allusion to the case, Carlyle's manner inclined to a waggish commiseration of his host's position. Actually, he said little, but the crisp precision of his voice when the path lay open to a remark of any significance left little to be said.

It was not until they had finished dinner and returned to the library that Carrados gave the slightest hint of anything unusual being in the air. His first indication of coming events was to remove the key from the outside to the inside of the door.

'What are you doing, Max?' demanded Mr Carlyle, his curiosity overcoming the indirect attitude.

'You have been very entertaining, Louis,' replied his friend, 'but Parkinson should be back very soon now and it is as well to be prepared. Do you happen to carry a revolver?'

'Not when I come to dine with you, Max,' replied Carlyle, with all the aplomb he could muster. 'Is it usual?'

Carrados smiled affectionately at his guest's agile recovery and touched the secret spring of a drawer in an antique bureau by his side. The little hidden receptacle shot smoothly out, disclosing a pair of dull-blued pistols.

'Tonight, at all events, it might be prudent,' he replied, handing one to Carlyle and putting the other into his own pocket. 'Our man may be here at any minute, and we do not know in what temper he will come.'

'Our man!' exclaimed Carlyle, craning forward in excitement. 'Max! You don't mean to say that you have got Mead to admit it?'

'No one has admitted it,' said Carrados. 'And it is not Mead.'

'Not Mead...Do you mean that Hutchins—?'

'Neither Mead nor Hutchins. The man who tampered with the signal—for Hutchins was right and a green light *was* exhibited—is a young Indian from Bengal. His name is Drishna and he lives at Swanstead.'

Mr Carlyle stared at his friend between sheer surprise and blank incredulity.

'You really mean this, Carrados?' he said.

'My fatal reputation for humour!' smiled Carrados. 'If I am wrong, Louis, the next hour will expose it.'

'But why—why—why? The colossal villainy, the unparalleled audacity!' Mr Carlyle lost himself among incredulous superlatives and could only stare.

'Chiefly to get himself out of a disastrous speculation,' replied Carrados, answering the question. 'If there was another motive—or at least an incentive—which I suspect, doubtless we shall hear of it.'

'All the same, Max, I don't think that you have treated me quite fairly,' protested Carlyle, getting over his first surprise and passing to a sense of injury. 'Here we are and I know nothing, absolutely nothing, of the whole affair.'

'We both have our ideas of pleasantry, Louis,' replied Carrados genially. 'But I dare say you are right and perhaps there is still time to atone.' In the fewest possible words he outlined the course of his investigations. 'And now you know all that is to be known until Drishna arrives.'

'But will he come?' questioned Carlyle doubtfully. 'He may be suspicious.'

'Yes, he will be suspicious.'

'Then he will not come.'

'On the contrary, Louis, he will come because my letter will make him suspicious. He *is* coming; otherwise Parkinson would have telephoned me at once and we should have had to take other measures.'

'What did you say, Max?' asked Carlyle curiously.

'I wrote that I was anxious to discuss an Indo-Scythian inscription with him and sent my car in the hope that he would be able to oblige me.'

'But is he interested in Indo-Scythian inscriptions?'

'I haven't the faintest idea,' admitted Carrados, and Mr Carlyle was throwing up his hands in despair when the sound of a motor car wheels softly kissing the gravel surface of the drive outside brought him to his feet.

'By gad, you are right, Max!' he exclaimed, peeping through the curtains. 'There is a man inside.'

'Mr Drishna,' announced Parkinson, a minute later.

The visitor came into the room with leisurely self-possession that might have been real or a desperate assumption. He was a slightly built young man of about twenty-five, with black hair and eyes, a small, carefully trained moustache, and a dark olive skin. His physiognomy was not displeasing, but his expression had a harsh and supercilious tinge. In attire he erred towards the immaculately spruce.

'Mr Carrados?' he said inquiringly.

Carrados, who had risen, bowed slightly without offering his hand.

'This gentleman,' he said, indicating his friend, 'is Mr Carlyle, the celebrated private detective.'

The Indian shot a very sharp glance at the object of this description. Then he sat down.

'You wrote me a letter, Mr Carrados,' he remarked, in English that scarcely betrayed any foreign origin, 'a rather curious letter, I may say. You asked me about an ancient inscription. I know nothing of antiquities; but I thought, as you had sent, that it would be more courteous if I came and explained this to you.'

'That was the object of my letter,' replied Carrados.

'You wished to see me?' said Drishna, unable to stand the ordeal of the silence that Carrados imposed after his remark.

'When you left Miss Chubb's house you left a ruler behind.' One lay on the desk by Carrados and he took it up as he spoke.

'I don't understand what you are talking about,' said Drishna guardedly. 'You are making some mistake.'

'The ruler was marked at four and seven-eighths inches— the measure of the glass of the signal lamp outside.'

The unfortunate young man was unable to repress a start. His face lost its healthy tone. Then, with a sudden impulse, he made a step forward and snatched the object from Carrados's hand.

'If it is mine I have a right to it,' he exclaimed, snapping the ruler in two and throwing it on to the back of the blazing fire. 'It is nothing.'

'Pardon me, I did not say that the one you have so impetuously disposed of was yours. As a matter of fact, it was mine. Yours is—elsewhere.'

'Wherever it is you have no right to it if it is mine,' panted Drishna, with rising excitement. 'You are a thief, Mr Carrados. I will not stay any longer here.'

He jumped up and turned towards the door. Carlyle made a step forward, but the precaution was unnecessary.

'One moment, Mr Drishna,' interposed Carrados, in his smoothest tones. 'It is a pity, after you have come so far, to leave without hearing of my investigations in the neighbourhood of Shaftesbury Avenue.'

Drishna sat down again.

'As you like,' he muttered. 'It does not interest me.'

'I wanted to obtain a lamp of a certain pattern,' continued Carrados. 'It seemed to me that the simplest explanation would be to say that I wanted it for a motor car. Naturally I went to Long Acre. At the first shop I said: "Wasn't it here that a friend of mine, an Indian gentleman, recently had a lamp made with a green glass that was nearly five inches across?" No, it was not there, but they could make me one. At the next shop the same; at the third, and fourth, and so on. Finally my persistence was rewarded. I found the place where the lamp had been made, and at the cost of ordering another I obtained all the details I wanted. It was news to them, the shopman informed me, that in some parts of India green was the danger colour and therefore tail lamps had to show a green light. The incident made some impression on him, and he would be able to identify their customer—who paid in advance and gave no address—among a thousand of his countrymen. Do I succeed in interesting you, Mr Drishna?'

'Do you?' replied Drishna, with a languid yawn. 'Do I look interested?'

'You must make allowance for my unfortunate blindness,' apologised Carrados, with grim irony.

'Blindness!' exclaimed Drishna, dropping his affectation of unconcern as though electrified by the word, 'do you mean—really blind—that you do not see me?'

'Alas, no,' admitted Carrados.

The Indian withdrew his right hand from his coat pocket and, with a tragic gesture, flung a heavy revolver down on the table between them.

'I have had you covered all the time, Mr Carrados, and if I had wished to go and you or your friend had raised a hand to stop me, it would have been at the peril of your lives,' he said, in a voice of melancholy triumph. 'But what is the use of defying fate, and who successfully evades his destiny? A month ago I went to see one of our people who reads the future and sought to know the course of certain events. "You need fear no human eye," was the message given to me. Then she added: "But when the sightless sees the unseen, make your peace with Yama." And I thought she spoke of the Great Hereafter!'

'This amounts to an admission of your guilt,' exclaimed Mr Carlyle practically.

'I bow to the decree of fate,' replied Drishna. 'And it is fitting to the universal irony of existence that a blind man should be the instrument. I don't imagine, Mr Carlyle,' he added maliciously, 'that you, with your eyes, would ever have brought that result about.'

'You are a very cold-blooded young scoundrel, sir!' retorted Mr Carlyle. 'Good heavens! Do you realise that you are responsible for the death of scores of innocent men and women?'

'Do *you* realise, Mr Carlyle, that you and your Government and your soldiers are responsible for the death of thousands of innocent men and women in my country every day? If England was occupied by the Germans who quartered an army and an administration with their wives and their families and all their expensive paraphernalia on the unfortunate country until the whole nation was reduced to the verge of famine, and the appointment of every new official meant the callous death sentence on a thousand men and women to pay his salary, then if you went to Berlin and wrecked a train you would be hailed a patriot. What Boadicea did and—and Samson, so have I. If they were heroes, so am I.'

'Well, upon my word!' cried the highly scandalised Carlyle, 'what next! Boadicea was a—er—semi-legendary person, whom we may possibly admire at a distance. Personally, I do not profess to express an opinion. But Samson, I would remind you, is a Biblical character. Samson was mocked as an enemy. You, I do not doubt, have been entertained as a friend.'

'And haven't I been mocked and despised and sneered at every day of my life here by your supercilious, superior, empty-headed men?' flashed back Drishna, his eyes leaping into malignity and his voice trembling with sudden passion. 'Oh! How I hated them as I passed them in the street and recognised by a thousand petty insults their lordly English contempt for me as an inferior being—a nigger. How I longed with Caligula that a nation had a single neck that I might destroy it at one blow. I loathe you in your complacent hypocrisy, Mr Carlyle, despise and utterly abominate you from an eminence of superiority that you can never even understand.'

'I think we are getting rather away from the point, Mr Drishna,' interposed Carrados, with the impartiality of a judge. 'Unless I am misinformed, you are not so ungallant as to include everyone you have met here in your execration?'

'Ah, no,' admitted Drishna, descending into a quite ingenuous frankness. 'Much as I hate your men I love your women. How is it possible that a nation should be so divided—its men so dull-witted and offensive, its women so quick, sympathetic and capable of appreciating?'

'But a little expensive, too, at times?' suggested Carrados.

Drishna sighed heavily.

'Yes; it is incredible. It is the generosity of their large nature. My allowance, though what most of you would call noble, has proved quite inadequate. I was compelled to borrow money and the interest became overwhelming. Bankruptcy was impracticable because I should have then been recalled by my people, and much as I detest England a certain reason made the thought of leaving it unbearable.'

'Connected with the Arcady Theatre?'

'You know? Well, do not let us introduce the lady's name. In order to restore myself I speculated on the Stock Exchange. My credit was good through my father's position and the standing of the firm to which I am attached. I heard on reliable authority, and very early, that the Central and Suburban, and the Deferred especially, was safe to fall heavily, through a motor bus amalgamation that was then a secret. I opened a bear account and sold largely. The shares fell, but only fractionally, and I waited. Then, unfortunately, they began to go up. Adverse forces were at work and rumours were put about. I could not stand the settlement, and in order to carry over an account I was literally compelled to deal temporarily with some securities that were not technically my own property.'

'Embezzlement, sir,' commented Mr Carlyle icily. 'But what is embezzlement on the top of wholesale murder!'

'That is what it is called. In my case, however, it was only to be temporary. Unfortunately, the rise continued. Then, at the height of my despair, I chanced to be returning to Swanstead rather earlier than usual one evening, and the train was stopped at a certain signal to let another pass. There was conversation in the carriage and I learned certain details. One said that there would be an accident some day, and so forth. In a flash—as by an inspiration—I saw how the circumstance might be turned to account. A bad accident and the shares would certainly fall and my position would be retrieved. I think Mr Carrados has somehow learned the rest.'

'Max,' said Mr Carlyle, with emotion, 'is there any reason why you should not send your man for a police officer and have this monster arrested on his own confession without further delay?'

'Pray do so, Mr Carrados,' acquiesced Drishna. 'I shall

certainly be hanged, but the speech I shall prepare will ring from one end of India to the other; my memory will be venerated as that of a martyr; and the emancipation of my motherland will be hastened by my sacrifice.'

'In other words,' commented Carrados, 'there will be disturbances at half-a-dozen disaffected places, a few unfortunate police will be clubbed to death, and possibly worse things may happen. That does not suit us, Mr Drishna.'

'And how do you propose to prevent it?' asked Drishna, with cool assurance.

'It is very unpleasant being hanged on a dark winter morning; very cold, very friendless, very inhuman. The long trial, the solitude and the confinement, the thoughts of the long sleepless night before, the hangman and the pinioning and the noosing of the rope, are apt to prey on the imagination. Only a very stupid man can take hanging easily.'

'What do you want me to do instead, Mr Carrados?' asked Drishna shrewdly.

Carrados's hand closed on the weapon that still lay on the table between them. Without a word he pushed it across.

'I see,' commented Drishna, with a short laugh and a gleaming eye. 'Shoot myself and hush it up to suit your purpose. Withhold my message to save the exposures of a trial, and keep the flame from the torch of insurrectionary freedom.'

'Also,' interposed Carrados mildly, 'to save your worthy people a good deal of shame, and to save the lady who is nameless the unpleasant necessity of relinquishing the house and the income which you have just settled on her. She certainly would not then venerate your memory.'

'What is that?'

'The transaction which you carried through was based on a felony and could not be upheld. The firm you dealt with will go to the courts, and the money, being directly traceable, will be held forfeit as no good consideration passed.'

'Max!' cried Mr Carlyle hotly, 'you are not going to let this scoundrel cheat the gallows after all?'

'The best use you can make of the gallows is to cheat it, Louis,' replied Carrados. 'Have you ever reflected what human beings will think of us a hundred years hence?'

'Oh, of course I'm not really in favour of hanging,' admitted Mr Carlyle.

'Nobody really is. But we go on hanging. Mr Drishna is a dangerous animal who for the sake of pacific animals must cease to exist. Let his barbarous exploit pass into oblivion with him. The disadvantages of spreading it broadcast immeasurably outweigh the benefits.'

'I have considered,' announced Drishna. 'I will do as you wish.'

'Very well,' said Carrados. 'Here is some plain notepaper. You had better write a letter to someone saying that the financial difficulties in which you are involved make life unbearable.'

'But there are no financial difficulties—now.'

'That does not matter in the least. It will be put down to an hallucination and taken as showing the state of your mind.'

'But what guarantee have we that he will not escape?' whispered Mr Carlyle.

'He cannot escape,' replied Carrados tranquilly. 'His identity is too clear.'

'I have no intention of trying to escape,' put in Drishna, as he wrote. 'You hardly imagine that I have not considered this eventuality, do you?'

'All the same,' murmured the ex-lawyer, 'I should like to

have a jury behind me. It is one thing to execute a man morally; it is another to do it almost literally.'

'Is that all right?' asked Drishna, passing across the letter he had written.

Carrados smiled at this tribute to his perception.

'Quite excellent,' he replied courteously. 'There is a train at nine-forty. Will that suit you?'

Drishna nodded and stood up. Mr Carlyle had a very uneasy feeling that he ought to do something but could not suggest to himself what.

The next moment he heard his friend heartily thanking the visitor for the assistance he had been in the matter of the Indo-Scythian inscription, as they walked across the hall together. Then a door closed.

'I believe that there is something positively uncanny about Max at times,' murmured the perturbed gentleman to himself.

The Unsolved Puzzle of the Man with No Face

Dorothy L. Sayers

Dorothy Leigh Sayers (1893–1957) was one of the leading lights among detective novelists during the Golden Age of Murder between the two world wars. She introduced Lord Peter Wimsey in her first novel, *Whose Body?* (1923), and became an articulate advocate for the well-written detective story both in essays and in her reviews for the *Sunday Times*, now collected in *Taking Detective Stories Seriously* (2017). *The Documents in the Case* (1930) was an ambitious attempt at the epistolary detective novel pioneered by Wilkie Collins. In writing the book, she collaborated with L.T. Meade's former writing partner, Robert Eustace; in *Dorothy L. Sayers: Her Life and Soul* (1993), Barbara Reynolds includes a fascinating and in-depth account of how the pair worked together on the story. It proved, however, to be an experiment they never repeated.

The scope afforded by the novel was particularly well suited to Sayers' literary talents and ambitions, but several of her short stories are pleasing and original. This story, which was included in *Lord Peter Views the Body* (1928), is one of the most intriguing of them.

———

'And what would *you* say, sir,' said the stout man, 'to this here business of the bloke what's been found down on the beach at East Felpham?'

The rush of travellers after the Bank Holiday had caused an overflow of third-class passengers into the firsts, and the stout man was anxious to seem at ease in his surroundings. The youngish gentleman whom he addressed had obviously paid full fare for a seclusion which he was fated to forgo. He took the matter amiably enough, however, and replied in a courteous tone:

'I'm afraid I haven't read more than the headlines. Murdered, I suppose, wasn't he?'

'It's murder, right enough,' said the stout man, with relish. 'Cut about he was, something shocking.'

'More like as if a wild beast had done it,' chimed in the thin, elderly man opposite. 'No face at all he hadn't got, by what my paper says. It'll be one of these maniacs, I shouldn't be surprised, what goes about killing children.'

'I wish you wouldn't talk about such things,' said his wife, with a shudder. 'I lays awake at nights thinking what might 'appen to Lizzie's girls, till my head feels regular in a fever, and I has such a sinking in my inside I has to get up and eat biscuits. They didn't ought to put such dreadful things in the papers.'

'It's better they should, ma'am,' said the stout man, 'then we're warned, so to speak, and can take our measures accordingly. Now, from what I can make out, this unfortunate gentleman had gone bathing all by himself in a lonely spot. Now, quite apart from cramps, as is a thing that might 'appen to the best of us, that's a very foolish thing to do.'

'Just what I'm always telling my husband,' said the young wife. The young husband frowned and fidgeted. 'Well, dear, it really isn't safe, and you with your heart not strong—' Her hand sought his under the newspaper. He drew away, self-consciously, saying: 'That'll do, Kitty.'

'The way I look at it is this,' pursued the stout man. 'Here we've been and had a war, what has left 'undreds o' men in what you might call a state of unstable ekilibrium. They've seen all their friends blown up or shot to pieces. They've been through five years of 'orrors and bloodshed, and it's given 'em what you might call a twist in the mind towards 'orrors. They may seem to forget it and go along as peaceable as anybody to all outward appearance, but it's all artificial, if you get my meaning. Then, one day something 'appens to upset them— they 'as words with the wife, or the weather's extra hot, as it is today—and something goes pop inside their brains and makes raving monsters of them. It's all in the books. I do a good bit of reading myself of an evening, being a bachelor without encumbrances.'

'That's all very true,' said a prim little man, looking up from his magazine, 'very true indeed—too true. But do you think it applies in the present case? I've studied the literature of crime a good deal—I may say I make it my hobby—and it's my opinion there's more in this than meets the eye. If you will compare this murder with some of the most mysterious crimes of late years—crimes which, mind you, have never been solved, and, in my opinion, never will be—what do you find?' He paused and looked round. 'You will find many features in common with this case. But especially you will find that the face—and the face only, mark you—has been disfigured, as though to prevent recognition. As though to blot out the victim's personality from the world. And you will find that, in spite of the most thorough investigation, the criminal is never discovered. Now what does all that point to? To Organisation. Organisation. To an immensely powerful influence at work behind the scenes. In this very magazine that I'm reading now—' he tapped the page impressively—'there's an account—not a faked-up story, but an account extracted from the annals of the police—of the organisation of one of these secret societies, which mark down men against whom they bear a grudge, and destroy them. And, when they do this, they disfigure their faces with the mark of the Secret Society, and they cover up the track of the assassin so completely—having money and resources at their disposal—that nobody is ever able to get at them.'

'I've read of such things, of course,' admitted the stout man, 'but I thought as they mostly belonged to the medeevial days. They had a thing like that in Italy once. What did they call it now? A Gomorrah, was it? Are there any Gomorrahs nowadays?'

'You spoke a true word, sir, when you said Italy,' replied the prim man. 'The Italian mind is made for intrigue. There's the Fascisti. That's come to the surface now, of course, but it started by being a secret society. And, if you were to look below the surface, you would be amazed at the way in which that country is honeycombed with hidden organisations of all sorts. Don't you agree with me, sir?' he added, addressing the first-class passenger.

'Ah!' said the stout man, 'no doubt this gentleman has been in Italy and knows all about it. Should you say this murder was the work of a Gomorrah, sir?'

'I hope not, I'm sure,' said the first-class passenger. 'I mean, it rather destroys the interest, don't you think? I like a nice, quiet, domestic murder myself, with the millionaire found dead in the library. The minute I open a detective story and find a Camorra in it, my interest seems to dry up and turn to dust and ashes—a sort of Sodom and Camorra, as you might say.'

'I agree with you there,' said the young husband, 'from what you might call the artistic standpoint. But in this particular case I think there may be something to be said for this gentleman's point of view.'

'Well,' admitted the first-class passenger, 'not having read the details—'

'The details are clear enough,' said the prim man. 'This poor creature was found lying dead on the beach at East Felpham early this morning, with his face cut about in the most dreadful manner. He had nothing on him but his bathing-dress—'

'Stop a minute. Who was he, to begin with?'

'They haven't identified him yet. His clothes had been taken—'

'That looks more like robbery, doesn't it?' suggested Kitty.

'If it was just robbery,' retorted the prim man, 'why should his face have been cut up in that way? No—the clothes were taken away, as I said, to prevent identification. That's what these societies always try to do.'

'Was he stabbed?' demanded the first-class passenger.

'No,' said the stout man. 'He wasn't. He was strangled.'

'Not a characteristically Italian method of killing,' observed the first-class passenger.

'No more it is,' said the stout man. The prim man seemed a little disconcerted.

'And if he went down there to bathe,' said the thin, elderly man, 'how did he get there? Surely somebody must have missed him before now, if he was staying at Felpham. It's a busy spot for visitors in the holiday season.'

'No,' said the stout man, 'not East Felpham. You're thinking of West Felpham, where the yacht-club is. East Felpham is one of the loneliest spots on the coast. There's no house near except a little pub all by itself at the end of a long road, and after that you have to go through three fields to get to the sea. There's no real road, only a cart-track, but you can take a car through. I've been there.'

'He came in a car,' said the prim man. 'They found the track of the wheels. But it had been driven away again.'

'It looks as though the two men had come there together,' suggested Kitty.

'I think they did,' said the prim man. 'The victim was probably gagged and bound and taken along in the car to the place, and then he was taken out and strangled and—'

'But why should they have troubled to put on his bathing-dress?' said the first-class passenger.

'Because,' said the prim man, 'as I said, they didn't want to leave any clothes to reveal his identity.'

'Quite; but why not leave him naked? A bathing-dress seems to indicate an almost excessive regard for decorum, under the circumstances.'

'Yes, yes,' said the stout man impatiently, 'but you 'aven't read the paper carefully. The two men couldn't have come there in company, and for why? There was only one set of footprints found, and they belonged to the murdered man.'

He looked round triumphantly.

'Only one set of footprints, eh?' said the first-class passenger quickly. 'This looks interesting. Are you sure?'

'It says so in the paper. A single set of footprints, it says, made by bare feet, which by a careful comparison 'ave been shown to be those of the murdered man, lead from the position occupied by the car to the place where the body was found. What do you make of that?'

'Why,' said the first-class passenger, 'that tells one quite a lot, don't you know. It gives one a sort of a bird's-eye view of the place, and it tells one the time of the murder, besides castin' quite a good bit of light on the character and circumstances of the murderer—or murderers.'

'How do you make that out, sir?' demanded the elderly man.

'Well, to begin with—though I've never been near the place, there is obviously a sandy beach from which one can bathe.'

'That's right,' said the stout man.

'There is also, I fancy, in the neighbourhood, a spur of rock running out into the sea, quite possibly with a handy diving-pool. It must run out pretty far; at any rate, one can bathe there before it is high water on the beach.'

'I don't know how you know that, sir, but it's a fact. There's rocks and a bathing-pool, exactly as you describe, about a hundred yards farther along. Many's the time I've had a dip off the end of them.'

'And the rocks run right back inland, where they are covered with short grass.'

'That's right.'

'The murder took place shortly before high tide, I fancy, and the body lay just about at high-tide mark.'

'Why so?'

'Well, you say there were footsteps leading right up to the body. That means that the water hadn't been up beyond the body. But there were no other marks. Therefore the murderer's footprints must have been washed away by the tide. The only explanation is that the two men were standing together just below the tide-mark. The murderer came up out of the sea. He attacked the other man—maybe he forced him back a little on his own tracks—and there he killed him. Then the water came up and washed out any marks the murderer may have left. One can imagine him squatting there, wondering if the sea was going to come up high enough.'

'Ow!' said Kitty, 'you make me creep all over.'

'Now, as to these marks on the face,' pursued the first-class passenger. 'The murderer, according to the idea I get of the thing, was already in the sea when the victim came along. You see the idea?'

'I get you,' said the stout man. 'You think as he went in off them rocks what we was speaking of, and came up through the water, and that's why there weren't no footprints.'

'Exactly. And since the water is deep round those rocks, as you say, he was presumably in a bathing-dress too.'

'Looks like it.'

'Quite so. Well, now—what was the face-slashing done with? People don't usually take knives out with them when they go for a morning dip.'

'That's a puzzle,' said the stout man.

'Not altogether. Let's say, either the murderer had a knife with him or he had not. If he had—'

'If he had,' put in the prim man eagerly, 'he must have laid wait for the deceased on purpose. And, to my mind, that bears out my idea of a deep and cunning plot.'

'Yes. But, if he was waiting there with the knife, why didn't he stab the man and have done with it? Why strangle him, when he had a perfectly good weapon there to hand? No—I think he came unprovided, and, when he saw his enemy there, he made for him with his hands in the characteristic British way.'

'But the slashing?'

'Well, I think that when he had got his man down, dead before him, he was filled with a pretty grim sort of fury and wanted to do more damage. He caught up something that was lying near him on the sand—it might be a bit of old iron, or even one of those sharp shells you sometimes see about, or a bit of glass—and he went for him with that in a desperate rage of jealousy or hatred.'

'Dreadful, dreadful!' said the elderly woman.

'Of course, one can only guess in the dark, not having seen the wounds. It's quite possible that the murderer dropped his knife in the struggle, and had to do the actual killing with his hands, picking the knife up afterwards. If the wounds were clean knife-wounds, that is probably what happened, and the murder was premeditated. But if they were rough, jagged gashes, made by an impromptu weapon, then I should say it was a chance encounter, and that the murderer was either mad or—'

'Or?'

'Or had suddenly come upon somebody whom he hated very much.'

'What do you think happened afterwards?'

'That's pretty clear. The murderer, having waited, as I said, to see that all his footprints were cleaned up by the tide, waded or swam back to the rock where he had left his clothes, taking the weapon with him. The sea would wash away any blood from his bathing-dress or body. He then climbed out upon the rocks, walked, with bare feet, so as to leave no tracks on any seaweed or anything, to the short grass of the shore, dressed, went along to the murdered man's car, and drove it away.'

'Why did he do that?'

'Yes, why? He may have wanted to get somewhere in a hurry. Or he may have been afraid that if the murdered man were identified too soon it would cast suspicion on him. Or it may have been a mixture of motives. The point is, where did he come from? How did he come to be bathing at that remote spot, early in the morning? He didn't get there by car, or there would be a second car to be accounted for. He may have been camping near the spot; but it would have taken him a long time to strike camp and pack all his belongings into the car, and he might have been seen. I am rather inclined to think he had bicycled there, and that he hoisted the bicycle into the back of the car, and took it away with him.'

'But in that case, why take the car?'

'Because he had been down at East Felpham longer than he expected, and he was afraid of being late. Either he had to get back to breakfast at some house, where his absence would be noticed, or else he lived some distance off, and had only just time enough for the journey home. I think, though, he had to be back to breakfast.'

'Why?'

'Because, if it was merely a question of making up time on the road, all he had to do was to put himself and his bicycle on the train for part of the way. No; I fancy he was staying in a smallish hotel somewhere. Not a large hotel, because there nobody would notice whether he came in or not. And not, I think, in lodgings, or somebody would have mentioned before now that they had had a lodger who went bathing at East Felpham. Either he lives in the neighbourhood, in which case he should be easy to trace, or was staying with friends who have an interest in concealing his movements. Or else—which I think is more likely—he was in a smallish hotel, where he would be missed from the breakfast-table, but where his favourite bathing-place was not a matter of common knowledge.'

'That seems feasible,' said the stout man.

'In any case,' went on the first-class passenger, 'he must have been staying within easy bicycling distance of East Felpham, so it shouldn't be too hard to trace him. And then there is the car.'

'Yes. Where is the car, on your theory?' demanded the prim man, who obviously still had hankerings after the Camorra theory.

'In a garage, waiting to be called for,' said the first-class passenger promptly.

'Where?' persisted the prim man.

'Oh, somewhere on the other side of wherever it was the murderer was staying. If you have a particular reason for not wanting it to be known that you were in a certain place at a specified time, it's not a bad idea to come back from the opposite direction. I rather think I should look for the car at West Felpham, and the hotel in the nearest town on the main road beyond where the two roads to East and West Felpham join. When you've found the car, you've found the name of the victim, naturally. As for the murderer, you will have to look for an active man, a good swimmer, and ardent cyclist—probably not very well off, since he cannot afford to have a car—who has been taking a holiday in the neighbourhood of the Felphams, and who has a good reason for disliking the victim, whoever he may be.'

'Well, I never,' said the elderly woman admiringly. 'How beautiful you do put it all together. Like Sherlock Holmes, I do declare.'

'It's a very pretty theory,' said the prim man, 'but, all the same, you'll find it's a secret society. Mark my words. Dear me! We're just running in. Only twenty minutes late. I call that very good for holiday time. Will you excuse me? My bag is just under your feet.'

There was an eighth person in the compartment, who had remained throughout the conversation apparently buried in a newspaper. As the passengers decanted themselves upon the platform, this man touched the first-class passenger upon the arm.

'Excuse me, sir,' he said. 'That was a very interesting suggestion of yours. My name is Winterbottom, and I am investigating this case. Do you mind giving me your name? I might wish to communicate with you later on.'

'Certainly,' said the first-class passenger. 'Always delighted to have a finger in any pie, don't you know. Here is my card. Look me up any time you like.'

Detective-Inspector Winterbottom took the card, and read the name:

Lord Peter Wimsey
110a Piccadilly.

The *Evening Views* vendor outside Piccadilly Tube Station arranged his placard with some care. It looked very well, he thought.

MAN WITH
NO FACE
IDENTIFIED

It was, in his opinion, considerably more striking than that displayed by a rival organ, which announced, unimaginatively:

BEACH MURDER
VICTIM
IDENTIFIED

A youngish gentleman in a grey suit who emerged at that moment from the Criterion Bar appeared to think so too, for he exchanged a copper for the *Evening Views,* and at once plunged into its perusal with such concentrated interest that he bumped into a hurried man outside the station, and had to apologise.

The *Evening Views,* grateful to murderer and victim alike for providing so useful a sensation in the dead days after the Bank Holiday, had torn Messrs. Negretti & Zambra's rocketing thermometrical statistics from the 'banner' position which they had occupied in the lunch edition, and substituted:

FACELESS VICTIM OF
BEACH OUTRAGE IDENTIFIED
•••

MURDER OF PROMINENT PUBLICITY ARTIST
•••

POLICE CLUES

The body of a middle-aged man who was discovered, attired only in a bathing costume, and with his face horribly disfigured by some jagged instrument, on the beach at East Felpham last Monday morning, has been identified as that of Mr Coreggio Plant, studio manager of Messrs. Crichton, Ltd., the well-known publicity experts of Holborn.

Mr Plant, who was forty-five years of age and a bachelor, was spending his annual holiday in making a motoring tour along the West Coast. He had no companion with him, and had left no address for the forwarding of letters, so that, without the smart work of Detective-Inspector Winterbottom of the Westshire Police, his disappearance might not in the ordinary way have been noticed until he became due to return to his place of business in three weeks' time. The murderer had no doubt counted on this, and had removed the motor-car, containing the belongings of his victim, in the hope of covering up all traces of this dastardly outrage so as to gain time for escape.

A rigorous search for the missing car, however, eventuated in its discovery in a garage at West Felpham, where it had been left for decarbonization and repairs to the magneto. Mr Spiller, the garage proprietor, himself saw the man who left the car, and has furnished a description of him to the police. He is said to be a small, dark man of foreign appearance. The police hold a clue to his identity, and an arrest is confidently expected in the near future.

Mr Plant was for fifteen years in the employment of Messrs. Crichton, being appointed Studio Manager in the latter years of the war. He was greatly liked by all his colleagues, and his skill in the lay-out and designing of advertisements did much to justify the truth of Messrs. Crichton's well-known slogan: 'Crichton's for Admirable Advertising.'

The funeral of the victim will take place tomorrow at Golders Green Cemetery.

(Pictures on Back Page.)

Lord Peter Wimsey turned to the back page. The portrait of the victim did not detain him long; it was one of those characterless studio photographs which establish nothing except that the sitter has a tolerable set of features. He noted that Mr Plant had been thin rather than fat, commercial in appearance rather than artistic, and that the photographer had chosen to show him serious rather than smiling. A picture of East Felpham beach, marked with a cross where the body was found, seemed to arouse in him rather more than a casual interest. He studied it intently for some time, making little surprised noises. There was no obvious reason why he should have been surprised, for the photograph bore out in every detail the deductions he had made in the train. There was the curved line of sand, with a long spur of rock stretching out behind it into deep water, and running back till it mingled with the short, dry turf. Nevertheless, he looked at it for several minutes with close attention before folding the newspaper and hailing a taxi; and when he was in the taxi he unfolded the paper and looked at it again.

———

'Your lordship having been kind enough,' said Inspector Winterbottom, emptying his glass rather too rapidly for true connoisseurship, 'to suggest I should look you up in Town, I made so bold to give you a call in passing. Thank you, I won't say no. Well, as you've seen in the papers by now, we found that car, all right.'

Wimsey expressed his gratification at this result.

'And very much obliged I was to your lordship for the hint,' went on the Inspector generously, 'not but what I wouldn't say but I should have come to the same conclusion myself, given a little more time. And, what's more, we're on the track of the man.'

'I see he's supposed to be foreign-looking. Don't say he's going to turn out to be a Camorrist, after all!'

'No, my lord.' The Inspector winked. 'Our friend in the corner had got his magazine stories a bit on the brain, if you

ask me. And *you* were a bit out, too, my lord, with your bicy-
clist idea.'

'Was I? That's a blow.'

'Well, my lord, these here theories *sound* all right, but
half the time they're too fine-spun altogether. Go for the
facts—that's our motto in the Force—facts and motive, and
you won't go far wrong.'

'Oh, you've discovered the motive, then?'

The Inspector winked again.

'There's not many motives for doing a man in,' said he.
'Women or money—or women *and* money—it mostly comes
down to one or the other. This fellow Plant went in for being
a bit of a lad, you see. He kept a little cottage down Felpham
way, with a nice little skirt to furnish it and keep the love-nest
warm for him—see?'

'Oh! I thought he was doing a motor tour.'

'Motor tour your foot!' said the Inspector, with more
energy than politeness. 'That's what the old (epithet) told
'em at the office. Handy reason, don't you see, for leaving no
address behind him. No, no. There was a lady in it all right.
I've seen her. A very taking piece, too, if you like 'em skinny,
which I don't. I prefer 'em better upholstered, myself.'

'That chair is really more comfortable with a cushion,' put
in Wimsey, with anxious solicitude. 'Allow me.'

'Thanks, my lord, thanks. I'm doing very well. It seems
that this woman—by the way, we're speaking in confidence,
you understand. I don't want this to go further till I've got
my man under lock and key.'

Wimsey promised discretion.

'That's all right, my lord, that's all right. I know I can rely
on you. Well, the long and the short is, this young woman
had another fancy man—a sort of an Italiano, whom she'd

chucked for Plant, and this same dago got wind of the business, and came down to East Felpham on the Sunday night looking for her. He's one of these professional partners in a Palais de Dance up Cricklewood way, and that's where the girl comes from, too. I suppose she thought Plant was a cut above him. Anyway, down he comes, and busts in upon them Sunday night when they were having a bit of supper—and that's when the row started.'

'Didn't you know about this cottage and the goings-on there?'

'Well, you know, there's such a lot of these week-enders nowadays. We can't keep tabs on all of them, so long as they behave themselves and don't make a disturbance. The woman's been there—so they tell me—since last June, with him coming down Saturday to Monday; but it's a lonely spot, and the constable didn't take much notice. He came in the evenings, so there wasn't anybody much to recognise him, except the old girl who did the slops and things, and she's half-blind. And of course, when they found him, he hadn't any face to recognise. It'd be thought he'd just gone off in the ordinary way. I dare say the dago fellow reckoned on that. As I was saying, there was a big row, and the dago was kicked out. He must have lain in wait for Plant down by the bathing-place, and done him in.'

'By strangling?'

'Well, he *was* strangled.'

'Was his face cut up with a knife, then?'

'Well, no—I don't think it was a knife. More like a broken bottle, I should say, if you ask me. There's plenty of them come in with the tide.'

'But then we're brought back to our old problem. If this Italian was lying in wait to murder Plant, why didn't he take a weapon with him, instead of trusting to the chance of his hands and a broken bottle?'

The Inspector shook his head.

'Flighty,' he said. 'All these foreigners are flighty. No headpiece. But there's our man, and there's our motive, plain as a pikestaff. You don't want more.'

'And where is the Italian fellow now?'

'Run away. That's pretty good proof of guilt in itself. But we'll have him before long. That's what I've come to Town about. He can't get out of the country. I've had an all-stations call sent out to stop him. The dance-hall people were able to supply us with a photo and a good description. I'm expecting a report in now any minute. In fact, I'd best be getting along. Thank you very much for your hospitality, my lord.'

'The pleasure is mine,' said Wimsey, ringing the bell to have the visitor shown out. 'I have enjoyed our little chat immensely.'

———

Sauntering into the Falstaff at twelve o'clock the following morning, Wimsey, as he had expected, found Salcombe Hardy supporting his rather plump contours against the bar. The reporter greeted his arrival with a heartiness amounting almost to enthusiasm, and called for two large Scotches immediately. When the usual skirmish as to who should pay had been honourably settled by the prompt disposal of the drinks and the standing of two more, Wimsey pulled from his pocket the copy of last night's *Evening Views*.

'I wish you'd ask the people over at your place to get hold of a decent print of this for me,' he said, indicating the picture of East Felpham beach.

Salcombe Hardy gazed limpid inquiry at him from eyes

like drowned violets.

'See here, you old sleuth,' he said, 'does this mean you've got a theory about the thing? I'm wanting a story badly. Must keep up the excitement, you know. The police don't seem to have got any further since last night.'

'No; I'm interested in this from another point of view altogether. I did have a theory—of sorts—but it seems it's all wrong. Bally old Homer nodding, I suppose. But I'd like a copy of the thing.'

'I'll get Warren to get you one when we come back. I'm just taking him down with me to Crichton's. We're going to have a look at a picture. I say, I wish you'd come, too. Tell me what to say about the damned thing.'

'Good God! I don't know anything about commercial art.'

''Tisn't commercial art. It's supposed to be a portrait of this blighter Plant. Done by one of the chaps in his studio or something. Kid who told me about it says it's clever. I don't know. Don't suppose she knows, either. You go in for being artistic, don't you?'

'I wish you wouldn't use such filthy expressions, Sally. Artistic! Who is this girl?'

'Typist in the copy department.'

'Oh, Sally!'

'Nothing of that sort. I've never met her. Name's Gladys Twitterton. I'm sure that's beastly enough to put anybody off. Rang us up last night and told us there was a bloke there who'd done old Plant in oils, and was it any use to us? Drummer thought it might be worth looking into. Make a change from that everlasting syndicated photograph.'

'I see. If you haven't got an exclusive story, an exclusive picture's better than nothing. The girl seems to have her wits about her. Friend of the artist's?'

'No—said he'd probably be frightfully annoyed at her

having told me. But I can wangle that. Only I wish you'd come and have a look at it. Tell me whether I ought to say it's an unknown masterpiece or merely a striking likeness.'

'How the devil can I say if it's a striking likeness of a bloke I've never seen?'

'I'll say it's that, in any case. But I want to know if it's well painted.'

'Curse it, Sally, what's it matter whether it is or not? I've got other things to do. Who's the artist, by the way? Anybody one's ever heard of?'

'Dunno. I've got the name here somewhere.' Sally rooted in his hip-pocket, and produced a mass of dirty correspondence, its angles blunted by constant attrition. 'Some comic name like Buggle or Snagtooth—wait a bit—here it is. Crowder. Thomas Crowder. I knew it was something out of the way.'

'Singularly like Buggle or Snagtooth. All right, Sally. I'll make a martyr of myself. Lead me to it.'

'We'll have another quick one. Here's Warren. This is Lord Peter Wimsey. This is on me.'

'On me,' corrected the photographer, a jaded young man with a disillusioned manner. 'Three large White Labels, please. Well, here's all the best. Are you fit, Sally? Because we'd better make tracks. I've got to be up at Golders Green by two for the funeral.'

Mr Crowder of Crichton's appeared to have had the news broken to him already by Miss Twitterton, for he received the embassy in a spirit of gloomy acquiescence.

'The directors won't like it,' he said, 'but they've had to put up with such a lot that I suppose one irregularity more or less won't give 'em apoplexy.' He had a small, anxious, yellow face like a monkey. Wimsey put him down as being in the late thirties. He noticed his fine, capable hands, one of which was disfigured by a strip of sticking-plaster.

'Damaged yourself?' said Wimsey pleasantly, as they made their way upstairs to the studio. 'Mustn't make a practice of that, what? An artist's hands are his livelihood—except, of course for Armless Wonders and people of that kind! Awkward job, painting with your toes.'

'Oh, it's nothing much,' said Crowder, 'but it's best to keep the paint out of surface scratches. There's such a thing as lead-poisoning. Well, here's this dud portrait, such as it is. I don't mind telling you that it didn't please the sitter. In fact, he wouldn't have it at any price.'

'Not flattering enough?' asked Hardy.

'As you say.' The painter pulled out a four by three canvas from its hiding-place behind a stack of poster cartoons, and heaved it up on to the easel.

'Oh!' said Hardy, a little surprised. Not that there was any reason for surprise as far as the painting itself was concerned. It was a straightforward handling enough; the skill and originality of the brushwork being of the kind that interests the painter without shocking the ignorant.

'Oh!' said Hardy. 'Was he really like that?'

He moved closer to the canvas, peering into it as he might have peered into the face of the living man, hoping to get something out of him. Under this microscopic scrutiny, the portrait, as is the way of portraits, dislimned, and became no more than a conglomeration of painted spots and streaks. He made the discovery that, to the painter's eye, the human face is full of green and purple patches.

He moved back again, and altered the form of his question: 'So that's what he was like, was he?'

He pulled out the photograph of Plant from his pocket, and compared it with the portrait. The portrait seemed to sneer at his surprise.

'Of course, they touch these things up at these fashionable photographers,' he said. 'Anyway, that's not my business. This thing will make a jolly good eye-catcher, don't you think so, Wimsey? Wonder if they'd give us a two-column spread on the front page? Well, Warren, you'd better get down to it.'

The photographer, bleakly unmoved by artistic or journalistic considerations, took silent charge of the canvas, mentally resolving it into a question of pan-chromatic plates and coloured screens. Crowder gave him a hand in shifting the easel into a better light. Two or three people from other departments, passing through the studio on their lawful occasions, stopped, and lingered in the neighbourhood of the disturbance, as though it were a street accident. A melancholy, grey-haired man, temporary head of the studio, *vice* Coreggio Plant, deceased, took Crowder aside, with a muttered apology, to give him some instructions about adapting a whole quad to an eleven-inch treble. Hardy turned to Lord Peter.

'It's damned ugly,' he said. 'Is it good?'

'Brilliant,' said Wimsey. 'You can go all out. Say what you like about it.'

'Oh, splendid! Could we discover one of our neglected British masters?'

'Yes; why not? You'll probably make the man the fashion, and ruin him as an artist, but that's his pigeon.'

'But, I say—do you think it's a good likeness? He's made him look a most sinister sort of fellow. After all, Plant thought it was so bad he wouldn't have it.'

'The more fool he. Ever heard of the portrait of a certain statesman that was so revealing of his inner emptiness that he hurriedly bought it up and hid it to prevent people like you from getting hold of it?'

Crowder came back.

'I say,' said Wimsey, 'whom does that picture belong to? You? Or the heirs of the deceased, or what?'

'I suppose it's back on my hands,' said the painter. 'Plant—well, he more or less commissioned it, you see, but—'

'How more or less?'

'Well, he kept on hinting, don't you know, that he would like me to do him, and, as he was my boss, I thought I'd better. No price actually mentioned. When he saw it, he didn't like it, and told me to alter it.'

'But you didn't.'

'Oh—well, I put it aside, and said I'd see what I could do with it. I thought he'd perhaps forget about it.'

'I see. Then presumably it's yours to dispose of.'

'I should think so. Why?'

'You have a very individual technique, haven't you?' pursued Wimsey. 'Do you exhibit much?'

'Here and there. I've never had a show in London.'

'I fancy I once saw a couple of small seascapes of yours somewhere. Manchester, was it? Or Liverpool? I wasn't sure of your name, but I recognised the technique immediately.'

'I dare say. I did send a few things to Manchester about two years ago.'

'Yes—I felt sure I couldn't be mistaken. I want to buy the portrait. Here's my card, by the way. I'm not a journalist; I collect things.'

Crowder looked from the card to Wimsey, and from Wimsey to the card a little reluctantly.

'If you want to exhibit it, of course,' said Lord Peter, 'I should be delighted to leave it with you as long as you liked.'

'Oh, it's not that,' said Crowder. 'The fact is, I'm not

altogether keen on the thing. I should like to—that is to say, it's not really finished.'

'My dear man, it's a bally masterpiece.'

'Oh, the painting's all right. But it's not altogether satisfactory as a likeness.'

'What the devil does the likeness matter? I don't know what the late Plant looked like, and I don't care. As I look at the thing it's a damn' fine bit of brushwork, and if you tinker about with it you'll spoil it. You know that as well as I do. What's biting you? It isn't the price, is it? You know I shan't boggle about that. I can afford my modest pleasures, even in these thin and piping times. You don't want me to have it? Come, now—what's the real reason?'

'There's no reason at all why you shouldn't have it if you really want it, I suppose,' said the painter, still a little sullenly. 'If it's really the painting that interests you.'

'What do you suppose it is? The notoriety? I can have all I want of *that* commodity, you know, for the asking—or even without asking. Well, anyhow, think it over, and when you've decided, send me a line and name your price.'

Crowder nodded without speaking, and the photographer having by this time finished his job, the party took their leave.

As they left the building, they became involved in the stream of Crichton's staff going out to lunch. A girl, who seemed to have been loitering in a semi-intentional way in the lower hall, caught them as the lift descended.

'Are you the *Evening Views* people? Did you get your picture all right?'

'Miss Twitterton?' said Hardy interrogatively. 'Yes, rather—thank you so much for giving us the tip. You'll see it on the front page this evening.'

'Oh, that's splendid! I'm frightfully thrilled. It has made an excitement here—all this business. Do they know anything yet about who murdered Mr Plant? Or am I being horribly indiscreet?'

'We're expecting news of an arrest any minute now,' said Hardy. 'As a matter of fact, I shall have to buzz back to the office as fast as I can to sit with one ear glued to the telephone. You will excuse me, won't you? And, look here—will you let me come round another day, when things aren't so busy, and take you out to lunch?'

'Of course. I should love to.' Miss Twitterton giggled. 'I do so want to hear about all the murder cases.'

'Then here's the man to tell you about them, Miss Twitterton,' said Hardy, with mischief in his eye. 'Allow me to introduce Lord Peter Wimsey.'

Miss Twitterton offered her hand in an ecstasy of excitement which almost robbed her of speech.

'How do you do?' said Wimsey. 'As this blighter is in such a hurry to get back to his gossip-shop, what do you say to having a spot of lunch with me?'

'Well, really—' began Miss Twitterton.

'He's all right,' said Hardy; 'he won't lure you into any gilded dens of infamy. If you look at him you will see he has a kind, innocent face.'

'I'm sure I never thought of such a thing,' said Miss Twitterton. 'But, you know—really—I've only got my old things on. It's no good wearing anything decent in this dusty old place.'

'Oh, nonsense!' said Wimsey. 'You couldn't possibly look nicer. It isn't the frock that matters—it's the person who wears it. *That's* all right, then. See you later, Sally! Taxi! Where shall we go? What time do you have to be back, by the way?'

'Two o'clock,' said Miss Twitterton regretfully.

'Then we'll make the Savoy do,' said Wimsey; 'it's

reasonably handy.'

Miss Twitterton hopped into the waiting taxi with a little squeak of agitation.

'Did you see Mr Crichton?' she said. 'He went by just as we were talking. However, I dare say he doesn't really know me by sight. I hope not—or he'll think I'm getting too grand to need a salary.' She rooted in her handbag. 'I'm sure my face is getting all shiny with excitement. What a silly taxi. It hasn't got a mirror—and I've bust mine.'

Wimsey solemnly produced a small looking-glass from his pocket.

'How wonderfully competent of you!' exclaimed Miss Twitterton. 'I'm afraid, Lord Peter, you are used to taking girls about.'

'Moderately so,' said Wimsey. He did not think it necessary to mention that the last time he had used that mirror it had been to examine the back teeth of a murdered man.

'Of course,' said Miss Twitterton, 'they had to say he was popular with his colleagues. Haven't you noticed that murdered people are always well dressed and popular?'

'They have to be,' said Wimsey. 'It makes it more mysterious and pathetic. Just as girls who disappear are always bright and home-loving, and have no men friends.'

'Silly, isn't it?' said Miss Twitterton, with her mouth full of roast duck and green peas. 'I should think everybody was only too glad to get rid of Plant—nasty, rude creature. So mean, too, always taking credit for other people's work. All those poor things in the studio, with all the spirit squashed out of them. I always say, Lord Peter, you can tell if a head of a department's fitted for his job by noticing the atmosphere of the place as you go into it. Take the copy-room, now. We're all as cheerful and friendly as you like, though I must say the language that goes on there is something awful, but these writing fellows are like that, and they don't mean anything by it. But then, Mr Ormerod is a real gentleman—that's our copy-chief, you know—and he makes them all take an interest in the work, for all they grumble about the cheese-bills and the department store bilge they have to turn out. But it's quite different in the studio. A sort of dead-and-alive feeling about it, if you understand what I mean. We girls notice things like that more than some of the high-up people think. Of course, I'm very sensitive to these feelings—almost psychic, I've been told.'

Lord Peter said there was nobody like a woman for sizing up character at a glance. Women, he thought, were remarkably intuitive.

'That's a fact,' said Miss Twitterton. 'I've often said, if I could have a few frank words with Mr Crichton, I could tell him a thing or two. There are wheels within wheels beneath the surface of a place like this that these brass-hats have no idea of.'

Lord Peter said he felt sure of it.

'The way Mr Plant treated people he thought were beneath him,' went on Miss Twitterton, 'I'm sure it was enough to make your blood boil. I'm sure, if Mr Ormerod sent me with a message to him, I was glad to get out of the room again. Humiliating, it was, the way he'd speak to you. I don't care if he's dead or not; being dead doesn't make a person's past behaviour any better, Lord Peter. It wasn't so much the rude things he said. There's Mr Birkett, for example; *he's* rude enough, but nobody minds him. He's just like a big, blundering puppy—rather a lamb, really. It was Mr Plant's nasty sneering way we all hated so. And he was always running people down.'

'How about this portrait?' asked Wimsey. 'Was it like him at all?'

'It was a lot too like him,' said Miss Twitterton emphatically. 'That's why he hated it so. He didn't like Crowder, either. But, of course, he knew he could paint, and he made him do it because he thought he'd be getting a valuable thing cheap. And Crowder couldn't very well refuse or Plant would have got him sacked.'

'I shouldn't have thought that would have mattered much to a man of Crowder's ability.'

'Poor Mr Crowder! I don't think he's ever had much luck. Good artists don't always seem able to sell their pictures. And I know he wanted to get married—otherwise he'd never have taken up this commercial work. He's told me a good bit about himself. I don't know why—but I'm one of the people men seem to tell things to.'

Lord Peter filled Miss Twitterton's glass.

'Oh, please! No, really! Not a drop more! I'm talking a lot too much as it is. I don't know what Mr Ormerod will say when I go in to take his letters. I shall be writing down all kinds of funny things. Ooh! I really must be getting back. Just look at the time!'

'It's not really late. Have a black coffee—just as a corrective.' Wimsey smiled. 'You haven't been talking at all too much. I've enjoyed your picture of office life enormously. You have a very vivid way of putting things, you know. I see now why Mr Plant was not altogether a popular character.'

'Not in the office, anyway—whatever he may have been elsewhere,' said Miss Twitterton darkly.

'Oh?'

'Oh, he was a one!' said Miss Twitterton. 'He certainly was a one. Some friends of mine met him one evening up in the West End, and they came back with some nice stories. It was quite a joke in the office—old Plant and his rosebuds, you know. Mr Cowley—he's *the* Cowley, you know, who rides in the motor-cycle races—he always said he knew what to think of Mr Plant and his motor tours. That time Mr Plant pretended he'd gone touring in Wales, Mr Cowley was asking him about the roads, and he didn't know a thing about them. Because Mr Cowley really had been touring there, and he knew quite well Mr Plant hadn't been where he said he had; and, as a matter of fact, Mr Cowley knew he'd been staying the whole time in a hotel at Aberystwyth, in very attractive company.'

Miss Twitterton finished her coffee, and slapped the cup down defiantly.

'And now I really *must* run away or I shall be most dreadfully late. And thank you ever so much.'

———

'Hullo!' said Inspector Winterbottom, 'you've bought that portrait, then?'

'Yes,' said Wimsey. 'It's a fine bit of work.' He gazed thoughtfully at the canvas. 'Sit down, Inspector; I want to tell you a story.'

'And I want to tell *you* a story,' replied the Inspector.

'Let's have yours first,' said Wimsey, with an air of flattering eagerness.

'No, no, my lord. You take precedence. Go ahead.'

He snuggled down with a chuckle into his arm-chair.

'Well,' said Wimsey. 'Mine's a sort of a fairy-story. And,

mind you, I haven't verified it.'

'Go ahead, my lord, go ahead.'

'Once upon a time—' said Wimsey sighing.

'That's the good old-fashioned way to begin a fairy-story,' said Inspector Winterbottom.

'Once upon a time,' repeated Wimsey, 'there was a painter. He was a good painter, but the bad fairy of Financial Success had not been asked to his christening—what?'

'That's often the way with painters,' agreed the Inspector.

'So he had to take up a job as a commercial artist, because nobody would buy his pictures and, like so many people in fairy-tales, he wanted to marry a goose-girl.'

'There's many people want to do the same,' said the Inspector.

'The head of his department,' went on Wimsey, 'was a man with a mean, sneering soul. He wasn't even really good at his job, but he had been pushed into authority during the war, when better men went to the Front. Mind you, I'm rather sorry for the man. He suffered from an inferiority complex'—the Inspector snorted—'and he thought the only way to keep his end up was to keep other people's end down. So he became a little tin tyrant and a bully. He took all the credit for the work of the men under his charge, and he sneered and harassed them till they got inferiority complexes even worse than his own.'

'I've known that sort,' said the Inspector, 'and the marvel to me is how they get away with it.'

'Just so,' said Wimsey. 'Well, I dare say this man would have gone on getting away with it all right if he hadn't thought of getting this painter to paint his portrait.'

'Damn' silly thing to do,' said the Inspector. 'It was only making the painter fellow conceited with himself.'

'True. But, you see, this tin tyrant person had a fascinating female in tow, and he wanted the portrait for the lady. He thought that, by making the painter do it, he would get a good portrait at starvation price. But unhappily he'd forgotten that, however much an artist will put up with in the ordinary way, he is bound to be sincere with his art. That's the one thing a genuine artist won't muck about with.'

'I dare say,' said the Inspector. 'I don't know much about artists.'

'Well, you can take it from me. So the painter painted the portrait as he saw it, and he put the man's whole creeping, sneering, paltry soul on the canvas for everybody to see.'

Inspector Winterbottom stared at the portrait, and the portrait sneered back at him.

'It's not what you'd call a flattering picture, certainly,' he admitted.

'Now, when a painter paints a portrait of anybody,' went on Wimsey, 'that person's face is never the same to him again. It's like—what shall I say? Well, it's like the way a gunner, say, looks at a landscape where he happens to be posted. He doesn't see it as a landscape. He doesn't see it as a thing of magic beauty, full of sweeping lines and lovely colour. He sees it as so much cover, so many landmarks to aim by, so many gun-emplacements. And when the war is over and he goes back to it, he will still see it as cover and landmarks and gun-emplacements. It isn't a landscape any more. It's a war map.'

'I know that,' said Inspector Winterbottom. 'I was a gunner myself.'

'A painter gets just the same feeling of deadly familiarity with every line of a face he's once painted,' pursued Wimsey. 'And, if it's a face he hates, he hates it with a new and more irritable hatred. It's like a defective barrel-organ, everlastingly grinding out the same old maddening tune, and making the same damned awful wrong note every time the barrel goes round.'

'Lord, how you can talk!' ejaculated the Inspector.

'That was the way the painter felt about this man's hateful face. All day and every day he had to see it. He couldn't get away because he was tied to his job, you see.'

'He ought to have cut loose,' said the Inspector. 'It's no good going on like that, trying to work with uncongenial people.'

'Well, anyway, he said to himself, he could escape for a bit during his holidays. There was a beautiful little quiet spot he knew on the West Coast where nobody ever came. He'd been there before and painted it. Oh, by the way, that reminds me—I've got another picture to show you.'

He went to a bureau and extracted a small panel in oils from a drawer.

'I saw that two years ago at a show in Manchester, and I happened to remember the name of the dealer who bought it.'

Inspector Winterbottom gaped at the panel.

'But that's East Felpham!' he exclaimed.

'Yes. It's only signed T.C., but the technique is rather unmistakable, don't you think?'

The Inspector knew little about technique, but initials he understood. He looked from the portrait to the panel, and back at Lord Peter.

'The painter—'

'Crowder?'

'If it's all the same to you, I'd rather go on calling him the painter. He packed up his traps on his push-bike carrier, and took his tormented nerves down to this beloved and secret spot for a quiet week-end. He stayed at a quiet little hotel in the neighbourhood, and each morning he cycled off to this lovely little beach to bathe. He never told anybody at the hotel where he went, because it was *his* place, and he didn't want other people to find it out.'

Inspector Winterbottom set the panel down on the table and helped himself to whisky.

'One morning—it happened to be the Monday morning'—Wimsey's voice became slower and more reluctant—'he went down as usual. The tide was not yet fully in, but he ran out over the rocks to where he knew there was a deep bathing pool. He plunged in and swam about, and let the small noise of his jangling troubles be swallowed up in the innumerable laughter of the sea.'

'Eh?'

'κυμάτων ἀνήριθμον γέλασμα—quotation from the classics. Some people say it means the dimpled surface of the waves in the sunlight—but how could Prometheus, bound upon his rock, have seen it? Surely it was the chuckle of the incoming tide among the stones that came up to his ears on the lonely peak where the vulture fretted at his heart. I remember arguing about it with old Philpotts in class, and getting rapped over the knuckles for contradicting him. I didn't know at the time that he was engaged in producing a translation on his own account, or doubtless I should have contradicted him more rudely, and been told to take my trousers down. Dear old Philpotts!'

'I don't know anything about that,' said the Inspector.

'I beg your pardon. Shocking way I have of wandering. The painter—well, he swam round the end of the rocks, for the tide was nearly in by that time; and, as he came up from the sea he saw a man standing on the beach—that beloved beach, remember, which he thought was his own sacred haven of peace. He came wading towards it, cursing the Bank Holiday rabble who must needs swarm about everywhere with their cigarette-packets and their Kodaks and their gramophones—and then he saw that it was a face he knew. He knew every hated line in it, on that clear, sunny morning. And, early as it was, the heat was coming up over the sea like a haze.'

'It was a hot week-end,' said the Inspector.

'And then the man hailed him, in his smug, mincing voice. "Hullo!" he said, "you here? How did you find my little bathing-place?" And that was too much for the painter. He felt as if his last sanctuary had been invaded. He leapt at the lean throat—it's rather a stringy one, you may notice, with a prominent Adam's apple—an irritating throat. The water chuckled round their feet as they swayed to and fro. He felt his thumbs sink into the flesh he had painted. He saw, and laughed to see, the hateful familiarity of the features change and swell into an unrecognisable purple. He watched the sunken eyes bulge out, and the thin mouth distort itself as the blackened tongue thrust through it—I am not unnerving you, I hope?'

The Inspector laughed.

'Not a bit. It's wonderful, the way you describe things. You ought to write a book.'

> 'I sing but as the throstle sings,
> Amid the branches dwelling,'

replied his lordship negligently, and went on without further comment.

'The painter throttled him. He flung him back on the sand. He looked at him, and his heart crowed within him. He stretched out his hand, and found a broken bottle, with a good jagged edge. He went to work with a will, stamping and tearing away every trace of the face he knew and loathed. He blotted it out, and destroyed it utterly.

'He sat beside the thing he had made. He began to be frightened. They had staggered back beyond the edge of the water, and there were the marks of his feet on the sand. He had blood on his face and on his bathing-suit, and he had cut his hand with the bottle. But the blessed sea was still coming in. He watched it pass over the bloodstains and the footprints, and wipe the story of his madness away. He remembered that this man had gone from his place, leaving no address behind him. He went back, step by step, into the water, and as it came up to his breast, he saw the red stains smoke away like a faint mist in the brown-blueness of the tide. He went—wading and swimming and plunging his face and arms deep in the water, looking back from time to time to see what he had left behind him. I think that when he got back to the point and drew himself out, clean and cool, upon the rocks, he remembered that he ought to have taken the body back with him, and let the tide carry it away, but it was too late. He was clean, and he could not bear to go back for the thing. Besides, he was late, and they would wonder at the hotel if he was not back in time for breakfast. He ran lightly over the bare rocks and the grass that showed no footprint. He dressed himself, taking care to leave no trace of his presence. He took the car, which would have told a story. He put his bicycle in the back seat, under the rugs, and he went—but you know as well as I do where he went.'

Lord Peter got up with an impatient movement, and went over to the picture, rubbing his thumb meditatively over the texture of the painting.

'You may say, if he hated the face so much, why didn't he

destroy the picture? He couldn't. It was the best thing he'd
ever done. He took a hundred guineas for it. It was cheap at
a hundred guineas. But then—I think he was afraid to refuse
me. My name is rather well known. It was a sort of blackmail,
I suppose. But I wanted that picture.'

Inspector Winterbottom laughed again.

'Did you take any steps, my lord, to find out if Crowder
has really been staying at East Felpham?'

'No.' Wimsey swung round abruptly. 'I have taken no steps
at all. That's your business. I have told you the story, and, on
my soul, I'd rather have stood by and said nothing.'

'You needn't worry.' The Inspector laughed for the third
time. 'It's a good story, my lord, and you told it well. But
you're right when you say it's a fairy-story. We've found this
Italian fellow—Francesco, he called himself, and he's the
man, all right.'

'How do you know? Has he confessed?'

'Practically. He's dead. Killed himself. He left a letter to
the woman, begging for forgiveness, and saying that when
he saw her with Plant he felt murder come into his heart. "I
have revenged myself," he says, "on him who dared to love
you." I suppose he got the wind up when he saw we were after
him—I wish these newspapers wouldn't be always putting
these criminals on their guard—so he did away with himself
to cheat the gallows. I may say it's been a disappointment to
me.'

'It must have been,' said Wimsey. 'Very unsatisfactory, of
course. But I'm glad my story turned out to be only a fairy-
tale, after all. You're not going?'

'Got to get back to my duty,' said the Inspector, heaving
himself to his feet. 'Very pleased to have met you, my lord.
And I mean what I say—you ought to take to literature.'

Wimsey remained after he had gone, still looking at the portrait.

'"What is Truth?" said jesting Pilate. No wonder, since it is so completely unbelievable...I could prove it...if I liked... but the man had a villainous face, and there are few good painters in the world.'

The Railway Carriage

F. Tennyson Jesse

Wynifriede Margaret Tennyson Jesse (1888–1958) inverted her first name, and called herself Friniwyd (or 'Fryn' for short), and wrote both fiction and non-fiction as F. Tennyson Jesse. Her first story about Solange Fontaine, 'Mademoiselle Lamont of the Mantles', appeared in the *Metropolitan Magazine* in 1918. In her foreword to *The Solange Stories* (1931), Jesse explained that she created a female sleuth because she thought this would be commercially beneficial, and that since 'I myself have occasionally had...a sudden warning of the nerves', she 'built up a woman detective with a "feeling" that told her of evil'.

'The Railway Carriage' was Solange's final recorded case, first published in the *Strand* in 1931, shortly after *The Solange Stories* appeared. Introducing *The Compleat Adventures of Solange Fontaine* (2014), Douglas Greene described the story as one of her finest, and Solange as 'one of the most convincing occult sleuths in the literature'. The story also reflects Jesse's abiding interest in 'true crime'. Her *Murder and its Motives* (1924) displays her insight into the psychology of crime, and she also edited volumes of *Notable British Trials*. Even her most famous novel, *A Pin to See the Peep-Show* (1934), is effectively a fictionalisation of the Thompson-Bywaters case. That book reflects her thought-provoking approach to murder cases and capital punishment; so does 'The Railway Carriage'.

Solange Fontaine nearly missed the train that Monday morning. She had been staying at Merchester for the weekend, with that old Colonel Evelyn, whose son she had been the means of saving from the gallows, and the old gentleman had kept on talking, with the pathetic garrulity of age, till the cab-driver had warned her that there was a bare five minutes to get to the station. Luckily, Solange had only a small suitcase, and she ran across the platform to the nearest carriage, wrenched open the door, and jumped in as the cabman flung the case in after her. She handed him his half-crown through the window as the train began to move.

At first, Solange, like anyone who has ever just caught a train at the last moment, leaned back, breathed thankfully, and took no notice of her surroundings. Then, also like everyone else, she looked round with a little smile of self-congratulation on her lips, ready to share with any strangers present that fraction of intimacy which such a happening strikes, like a spark, from one's fellow men.

It was a third-class carriage, with hard seats and varnished wooden doors. Its only other occupant was a woman who was sitting in the far corner. Apparently she had noticed neither

Solange's abrupt entry nor her smile. She was an elderly woman, dressed in shabby black, she had no luggage, and she was sitting with her hands—the knotted veiny hands of a working woman—folded together in her lap. She was staring out of the window, and her lips were moving a little, as though she were talking to herself soundlessly.

Solange's smile died a natural death; she looked at herself in the little mirror from her handbag to make sure her hurry had not disturbed the set of her plain little helmet-hat. All was well; she was her usual clear, fine-drawn self, save for an unwonted flush on her pale cheeks, and one loose feather of fair hair that lay against her temple. She tucked it back and put the mirror in her bag again. Her cigarette-case caught her eye as she did so; she took it out, then hesitated, and glanced at the silent woman.

'Do you mind if I smoke?' asked Solange.

The woman drew her eyes away from their blind staring as though by a physical wrench, and looked at her. Something in that gaze struck unpleasantly on Solange's senses, but, as the woman did not seem to have understood her, she repeated her question.

'Eh? Oh, naow. It don't make no matter.'

The woman had a slight Cockney accent, but a surprisingly soft voice for one of her hard, almost wooden appearance. Solange thanked her and took out a cigarette, only to discover that she had no matches and that, as usual, her lighter wouldn't work. She glanced again at the woman, who had reverted to her occupation of staring out of the window. No good asking her for a light. She would just have to wait till someone else got in; the train was due to stop at the junction in another couple of minutes.

The platform was crowded, for it was market day at a

neighbouring town, and it seemed that every farmer in the countryside was going in by this train. The carriage in which Solange was, however, being at the tail-end of the train, only one man came towards it and got in. He was a small, insignificant-looking man, with a big grey felt hat pulled right over his ears, and he carried a black bag.

He glanced sharply from Solange to the woman in black as he opened the carriage door and seemed satisfied by what he saw. Before he took his seat he stood for a moment, his bag in his hand, as though uncertain what to do with it. He glanced up at the rack, and even made a movement towards it, then sat down opposite Solange and stowed the bag away between his feet, under the seat. The whistle blew, the guard waved his flag, and the train started off again through the hot, summer countryside.

Solange took out a cigarette and leaned towards him with a smile.

'Will you be so kind as to let me have a match?' she asked. The little man started. He, like the woman in black, seemed oddly abstracted. He stared at her, and then repeated: 'A match? Oh, yes.' He also had an accent, but it was a North-country one, Solange noted. He almost said: 'A match. Oh, yez…' Solange began to feel a little impatient. Was the world peopled by the half-dead this fine morning?

He brought out his matchbox pretty smartly, however, and struck a light for her. His gallantry might be a little clumsy, but his movements were noticeably deft and economical, so much so that Solange was struck by the contrast between his stubby fingers and their neat precision of action.

Her cigarette alight, she leaned back, and the little man relapsed into a sort of surly abstraction. The elderly woman continued to stare out of the window at the bleached fields and the dark trees, and the rhythmic movements of the hay-makers. The train gathered speed and roared and rattled through the lovely domestic landscape, a landscape with no touch of savagery or wild beauty, but which held in its contented folds the pastoral activities of men for generations past.

It was a run of ten minutes to the next stop—the village before the market town—after which the train would suddenly become converted into an express and pursue its quickened and uninterrupted way to London.

To Solange, in spite of the lovely country, and of the inoffensiveness of her fellow-travellers, that ten minutes seemed like one of those curious spaces when time, as we know it, ceases, and an endless period, like a breath held beyond human endurance, is the only measure. Why this should be so, she could not have told. She only knew that she would have given a great deal to be out of that little third-class carriage, to be in a modern corridor train, to be—this, above all—away from her travelling companions. Inoffensive…? Obviously… then what was wrong—and when had it begun?

The silent wooden woman had struck her with a sense of oddness, but not with any feeling of something definitely wrong. The commonplace little man, with his shaven cheeks and his deft, stubby fingers, had seemed unusual in a way that was not altogether good, but no message of evil such as had so often told her of harm, had knocked upon her senses when he entered the carriage. Yet it was only since he and the old woman had been in it together that she had felt this spiritual unease. Something was wrong between these two human beings—and yet they apparently did not know each other. Neither even knew that the other was in some queer way inimical, each was self-absorbed to the exclusion of the other, the woman in her strange daze of thought that was like a stupor, the man in some stony sort of regret. Sorry—that was the word for him, thought Solange, sorry but stubborn. He wasn't unhappy as the woman was unhappy, only ill at ease, as an animal is ill at ease when it is driven up the road to the slaughter-house.

Solange was glad when the train drew up at a little wayside station. This time their carriage was invaded by four or five men, for the front of the train was already full. Solange felt a curious sense of relief at this influx of other human beings. At least she would not be penned in with the two strange, lost people who had sat silently on the seat opposite her, one at each end, for the last ten minutes. There was only another quarter of an hour to go before the market town was reached, and then, doubtless, everybody would get out and she would have the carriage to herself for the rest of the run to London.

A big red-faced farmer, with side-whiskers, sat beside Solange, and pulled out his pipe, glanced at her, and saw she was smoking herself. She smiled at him, and he grinned back and proceeded to light up.

'That's good, Missis,' he said. 'I don't like to get the ladies' hair full of smoke, but it's hard luck on a man not to have his pipe.'

A thin, dried-up man, who was sitting opposite to the farmer, nodded several times as he proceeded to pack his own pipe with peculiarly evil-looking tobacco.

'That's so,' he agreed. 'I wonder if they let that poor young devil have a last smoke this morning.'

'Sure they did,' said the farmer, authoritatively, 'they always let 'em do what they like. He could 'ave 'ad a bottle of champagne if he'd fancied it.'

'No!' said the other man, in admiring disbelief. 'Is that so?'

'That is so,' asseverated the farmer.

'Well, now, I thought,' said a third man, 'that all they was allowed was an ordinary sort of breakfast—a good one, mind you, eggs and bacon, and anything like that.'

'I heard they was given nothing but brandy in the way of a pick-me-up,' said the thin man, rather encouraged by this contradiction of the farmer on the part of the third man.

'Anything they likes,' repeated the farmer, stubbornly, 'everyone knows that.'

'Suppose they wanted poison, eh?' asked the thin man. 'Something that would do it nice and quick without having to stand on the trap and have their necks broken. Don't tell me they'd give 'em poison.'

The farmer was rather staggered by this novel suggestion. 'Perhaps not poison,' he said, 'but champagne I don't doubt.'

Solange guessed of what they must be speaking. There must have been an execution that morning. She refrained from saying that bromide and four ounces of brandy was the official assuagement for the last agony. The execution must have been at Merchester, and it was not remarkable that she heard nothing of it, for she had been staying with Colonel Evelyn, and such subjects were never mentioned in his house since that dreadful night, which might have been young Charles Evelyn's last. That was why the servants had watched the old Colonel so anxiously and why the local paper had not been forthcoming...The Colonel had been very childish since his son's narrow escape, and it was easy to delude him in little practical matters.

'I don't believe,' said a fourth man, of the black-coat class, perhaps some lawyer's clerk travelling to his work at the market town, 'that they ought ever to have hanged him. It was a cruel shame, that's what it was. After all, it was only circumstantial evidence.'

'That's as good as any other evidence, and better,' said the farmer, stoutly: 'the only other evidence is what folks tells you they've seen, and we have it on the authority of the Bible that all men are liars. Give me circumstances every time, I says, they can't lie nearly as well as a man can.'

'And a man can't lie near as well as a woman,' said the clerk, with a little snigger.

'That's true enough,' said both the other men in chorus.

It suddenly struck Solange as odd that only the newcomers were talking. The little man with the black bag and the woman in the corner were still silent.

'Well,' said the farmer, 'I met young Jackson once or twice, and he seemed to me a decent young fellow enough, not the sort of chap you'd expect to go and cut a man's throat behind his back, as you might say.'

'He did it all right,' said the clerk, 'that's plain enough.'

'They were both after the same woman, weren't they? And t'other man got her. You don't need to look much further than that. There's motive enough for you. Must ha' been fools.'

'Come now,' said the farmer, 'that's not very polite, with ladies present.' He glanced at the silent woman in the corner, but she seemed to have heard nothing. She was no longer staring out of the window, her eyes were closed, and her hands were tightly folded together in her lap, and he looked away from her to Solange.

'I only came over from France on Friday,' she said, 'so I'm afraid I'm very ignorant. Has something—been happening?' She didn't like to say: 'Has there been an execution?' so strongly were the memories of that dreadful morning in Merchester Jail implanted in her consciousness.

'Something happening!' said the farmer, 'I should say so. Why, all Merchester has talked of nothing else for weeks and weeks. A young fellow called Jackson, Timothy Jackson, who served in Jordan's, the corn chandler's at Merchester, was walking out with a young woman who was already tokened a bit above her station—to a young lawyer. Smart fellow, young Ted Emery. My lawyer he was, at least his father's my lawyer,' added the farmer, importantly, 'and one night in a dark lane young Jackson has a row with him and cuts his throat. He was hanged this morning, young Jackson was, in Merchester Jail. People were pretty sorry round about. Tim Jackson was a good fellow, though he was a Londoner. Had to live in the country for his health. He was delicate-looking, white as a girl, but handsome enough if it hadn't been for one of them birthmarks on one cheek. Shaped like a bat's wing, it were, and my old missus allers said it fair gave her a turn to look at. But he was handsome, in spite of it, and this girl took a fancy to him. But he was no match for young Emery, who was one of those smart young fellows who think no end of themselves, and had a motor-bike and a sidecar to take his girl in and all that sort of thing. She was pretty bitter against Tim Jackson at the trial. If you ask me, she had only been amusing herself and would rather have got Emery than young Jackson. Now she's got neither, and serve her right, too.'

'Aye, that's right enough,' said the man opposite him.

Solange remembered having read something about the case in the Continental *Daily Mail* three weeks earlier. Only a short paragraph, for it had been an ordinary enough crime of jealousy. The judge had made some scathing remarks as to the method of the murder. It was 'un-English' to cut a man's throat. It would have been more English, and consequently better, if he had killed his adversary with a blow of a club, or his fist. Jackson, being a rather weedy town-product, had been unable to do this essentially English thing, and had resorted, in a moment of passion, to a razor. There had been a struggle, he hadn't crept up to the other man from behind, but undoubtedly in the course of the struggle he had cut his throat from behind, getting his arm round his neck and pulling the heavier man back towards him.

'I hear he confessed,' said the clerk, importantly, 'they were saying that at our Merchester office this morning, so I was told. It's my day at Winborough, you know, but they rang me up and told me just before I left home.'

The whole carriage, still with the exception of the little man with the black bag and the elderly woman, was agog at this piece of news.

'Confessed, did he?' said the farmer. 'Oh well, that'll put everybody's mind at rest. It's something to know justice has been done.'

'Justice?' said the man opposite, bitterly. 'Do you call it right to hang a decent young fellow because a woman had been driving him crazy? And if it comes to that, I'm not so keen on this capital punishment business. What right have we got to take life, I should like to know? I can tell you this, I'd sooner meet a young fellow like Timothy Jackson than meet the man who hanged him. There's a fellow I shouldn't like to shake by the hand. That's a dirty trade.'

'Dirty enough,' agreed the farmer, soberly.

The rhythm of the train began to slacken. Winborough was

reached, and the carriage was emptied, but Solange saw, with a little feeling of dismay, that her original companions were continuing with her to London. She suddenly felt she couldn't bear this strange atmosphere of which she was conscious as surrounding them, and she got up to see if she couldn't change her carriage, but she had left it till too late. For the fourth time since the brief half-hour when she had jumped into the carriage at Merchester, she heard the guard blow his whistle, and the rhythm of the train began to beat upon her senses once more. Now there was no getting away from her strange, dumb companions for an hour and a half. She had to stay with them whether she would or no. It was really an outrage, she thought to herself, that such a thing as a non-corridor train should still exist. This wasn't even a very good train of the old-fashioned type. It ran very bumpily. Perhaps, thought Solange, all the rolling-stock on this line was very old. Then in a flash she realised that something had gone wrong. The train was bumping in a curious fashion, its rattle changed to a roar, a crashing sound broke through the rapidly accelerating conglomeration of other noises, and then the whole world seemed to go mad. The coach reared up, attacked the coach in front like a mad beast, rocked, lurched sideways, and at last came to a standstill, like a leaning tower, poised on its rear end. Solange and her two companions were spilled like rubbish from a shoot, against the door and windows at the bottom end, splintered glass all about them, and the black bag hit Solange full upon the temple...

———

Why did this voice persist in waking her up? She didn't want to wake up, she only wanted to stay in this dark world where she felt numb and sleepy. She tried hard not to listen to the voice, but it went on and on. *Wake up, wake up, wake up*...the words beat over and over upon her brain, would let her have no rest. Reluctantly at last she allowed her mind to pay attention. The voice sounded more clearly now, *Wake up, wake up, you must wake up.* The darkness of the world began to be shot with flashes and gleams of light even before she opened her eyes. *Wake up, wake up*...

She opened her eyes and slowly realised where she was and what had happened.

'You're all right,' the voice went on, 'but you must get out.' The voice seemed to come from above her head, and rather surprised to find she could move, Solange looked up. She saw the head of a young man, dark against the blinding square of light made by the window of the carriage which was right up above her head. The young man looked down at her as though she were at the bottom of a well, and he were peering in over the rim. She stirred and felt herself cautiously. Yes...she was intact, she could waggle all her fingers and toes, her back was not broken, she could feel pain where a sharp angle of splintered coachwork stuck into one thigh. She looked about her, still dazed by the shock and her senses confused by the shouts and wails of terrified human beings that came to her ears. The elderly woman was either unconscious or dead, she was lying crumpled up, her eyes shut, and a thin skein of blood, where a splinter of glass had caught her, lying across her face like a ravelling of red worsted. The commonplace little man was doubled up, his head sunk sideways on his shoulder, his eyes closed and his face very pale. His hat had been knocked off, and Solange saw with a shock of irrational surprise, that, save where it was grey at the sides, his hair was a bright red. It was one of those stupid and irrelevant details that strike the mind at such moments of stress.

Solange looked up. There was the face of the young man still peering in from the top of that strange well into which the railway carriage had become changed as though by magic.

'Can't you help us out?' she called.

He shook his head. She saw the dark weaving motion of it against the clear square blue of sky.

'You must wake him up,' he called down to her. 'Shake him, wake him up.'

Solange managed to stagger to her feet, pushing aside bits of broken wood that hemmed her in. She looked doubtfully at the little man crumpled up at her feet. She hardly liked to shake him, and yet she couldn't climb up the tower that was the up-ended railway carriage without his help. She put her hand on to his shoulder and spoke urgently.

'Are you hurt? Oh, do try and do something. We've got to get out. We've got to get the old woman out. Wake up. Wake up,' and she did actually begin to shake him, as one shakes someone who is having a bad dream. Slowly, the commonplace little light eyes opened and looked at her unintelligently. Then the man moaned a little, and put up one hand to his head.

'You're all right, you really are,' said Solange, urgently. 'Do see if you can climb up. There's someone up there who will help you if you only can.' She glanced up and the young man above her met her gaze.

'Make him hurry up,' he said, 'there's a fire. Listen.' And Solange, with a pang of pure fear that she never forgot, realised that the crackling sound which she had thought came entirely from breaking woodwork, was really made by the burning of the next coach, perhaps even by the burning of one end of the coach she was in.

'There was petrol in the van,' said the young man, 'and the guard was smoking.'

The little red-haired man now began to feel himself all over, as Solange herself had done.

'I'm a'reet, Miss,' he said, a little unsteadily, 'I'll climb oop and hold down my hand to you.'

He looked round him and saw the woman still lying crumpled up, unconscious, and a worried look came across his face. However, he wasted no words, and began laboriously by the aid of the splintered luggage rack to try and pull himself up to the gaping window above his head. Solange saw, to her disgust, that the young man had gone. She managed to climb on the wreck of the seat, and exerting all her force, gave the little man a leg-up. With a mighty effort he pulled himself through the jagged frame of glass above his head and levered himself out into the air. For one awful moment Solange thought that perhaps he, too, was going to desert her, but he wriggled himself round on the up-ended side of the carriage, and looking down at her, held a hand that was cut and bleeding down towards her.

'Get a grip o' that,' he said.

'I can't,' said Solange. 'I can't leave the old woman. We must get her out somehow.'

The head of the young man came back now, and she saw it behind red-head's shoulder.

'You want a rope,' said the young man, 'make a rope fast round her. Oh, hurry up.'

Solange looked frantically round the shattered compartment. There was not so much as a luggage strap round the little man's black bag, and none round her suitcase. 'Can't you get a rope?' she called up to the little man, 'ask someone for a rope.'

Then the red-headed man spoke, slightly hesitating, in spite of that dreadful crackling that was coming nearer and nearer.

'Ma bag, Miss,' he said, 'ma bag. Tha'll find a rope there.'

Solange seized the little black bag, and struggled with the lock.

'Don't pull it,' called the little man, 'slide it. That's reet.'

The bag gaped open, and Solange saw a rather crumpled nightshirt and a shabby sponge bag.

'Look underneath,' called down the little man.

She plunged in her hand and to her intense thankfulness her fingers met a good, strong rope, that filled up with its coils the whole of the bottom of the bag, as a serpent might have done. She pulled it out. It was amazingly strong, smooth, and flexible. The next moment she saw that it had a running noose at one end that passed through a brass ring. Her mind became very clear and cold. She handled the thing without any distaste. She even thought how convenient the running noose would be.

'Be quick,' urged the young man, who was still peering in behind the flaming red head of that apparently commonplace little man. 'Get her out before she sees what it is.'

Solange worked the noose down over the limp form of the elderly woman, pulled her arms through it so that they hung out helplessly each side, and then flung the free end of the rope upwards. The little man with the red head caught hold of it, and began to pull. Solange heaved with all her strength upon the dead weight of the old lady. She was a very frail old lady, it appeared, now that Solange had her hands upon her, but she was heavy, nevertheless, with the weight of her unconsciousness.

'Be careful. Try not to cut her face any worse,' Solange called up.

The little man seemed amazingly strong as well as deft with his hands. He groaned and sweated, but he pulled the woman up till her head and shoulders were through the window untouched by the jagged frame of glass. Then he clutched her under the arms and pulled her right through the opening.

'Wait a moment, lass,' he called down to Solange. 'I'll have thee out in a jiffy.'

He disappeared, and Solange felt terrifyingly alone. The heat seemed suffocating, the crackling was nearer, and through the roar of escaping steam and the roar of the flames she could still hear faint thin cries from further down the train. She was never so thankful to see anyone in her life as she was to see the red head of the public executioner appear once more above her. He lowered the rope down to her, and she fitted it round her waist and, taking a good purchase with her hands, kicked her way up the carriage and was in her turn pulled out into safety. The air was fresh and sweet, for the smoke was being blown away in the opposite direction, and for a moment Solange felt, as she stood swaying a little upon the grass at the side of the track, that it was good merely to be alive. Then she looked about her. The train was piled on itself in the most fantastic fashion. The engine lay upon its side. The accident had happened at a level crossing, and already there were motor-cars going backwards and forwards, and people busy at work.

'I reckon they're all out now,' said the little red-headed man, wiping his wet brow with the back of his hand. 'Eh, that was a near thing, lass!'

It dawned on Solange that he was still holding one end of the rope, which was round her waist, as if she were a heifer being led to market, and she suddenly realised, emotionally, as well as with her mind, what it was that had saved her. She began to tear at it with her fingers, feeling as near to hysteria as she had ever felt in her calm, well-ordered life.

'I'll tak' it off, lass,' said the little man, apologetically. 'I was sorry about it. I didn't want you to see it, but there weren't no other way.'

While he was talking, he began to ease the rope from about her waist.

'That's why I didn't get in at Merchester. You see, with my red hair, I'm what you might call noticeable like. They drove me from t'jail t'next station.'

He had got the rope off her by now, and was coiling it round his own waist, under his coat. 'Government property nowadays,' he explained as he did so. 'I mun use this again next week.'

'Did the young man help you?' asked Solange. 'Was he helping you with us? It must have been dreadfully heavy work otherwise.'

The little red-headed man stared at her.

'What young man?' he asked.

'The young man who looked in at the carriage window and woke me up. He told me to wake you up. The young man who told us we must have a rope.'

'I'll get one o' they cars to take 'e home, lass,' said the red-headed little man, with a rather worried expression on his face. 'Tha'll be wanting a lay down.'

'But did he?' persisted Solange.

'There weren't no young man that I ever saw or heard of, nowt but you waking me and telling me to get out and get rope. You saved my life, lass. I'd ha burned...' and he pointed to the railway carriage which was now a roaring furnace, the flames were pale almost to invisibility in the bright sunlight, but their heat reached Solange where she stood.

'Well, there was a young man,' said Solange, wondering whether red-head had been too confused to notice him, 'and, what's more, it was the young man who woke me up. It was he saved the lot of us.'

She looked about her and saw the elderly woman lying in the grass some twenty yards away where the little man had dragged her. The young man was kneeling beside her, his head bent down to hers. The woman's eyes were open, and she was looking up into his face with a smile upon her own. She opened her mouth as though to speak but the young man very gently laid his fingers, long, delicate, over-white fingers, against her lips. A little crowd of people, among them two men bearing a stretcher, were approaching the woman. The young man bent a little lower over her, then raised his head and looked across at Solange. She could see his face clearly now in the bright sunlight, it was no longer shadowed as it had been when he was peering down into the railway carriage, and with a pang, half of incredulity, half of pure terror, she saw that he had a port-wine stain, shaped like a bat's wing, lying over one cheek beneath the eye. The stretcher-bearers and their assistants closed in about the woman and began to lift her. Solange ran towards them. She seemed to have lost the young man in the little crowd of people, but she motioned the stretcher-bearers to stay still for a moment, and thinking she might be some relation or friend, they did so.

'Did you see him?' asked Solange, bending over the woman. 'Did you see him?'

The woman smiled at her: 'I saw him,' she said; 'he must have escaped after all. You won't tell anyone, will you?'

'No, no,' said Solange, 'I won't tell anyone.'

'He said it was all right,' said the woman, feebly. 'He said I should meet him this evening. He was always a good boy, was my Tim, though I knew he was marked for misfortune from the moment I first set eyes on that bat's wing on his poor face, but he was always good to his mother. "Don't worry, mother," he's just told me, "it's all right. I'll see you this evening!"'

She closed her eyes and seemed to drift into unconsciousness.

'Where are you taking her?' asked Solange.

'Cottage Hospital, Miss,' said one of the stretcher-bearers. 'It isn't far. Just down the road,' and they set off, carrying their burden carefully over the uneven ground.

The little red-headed man, who had stayed behind to fasten his coat completely over the rope, now came up to Solange.

'I wish I could get a hat,' he complained. He was evidently worried about his conspicuous hair.

'I don't think anybody will notice,' said Solange; 'they've got other things to think about now, you see.'

He jerked his red head towards the disappearing stretcher. 'Who was t'owd lady?' he asked. 'Did tha know her?'

'She was the mother of the young man who saved us,' said Solange.

———

It was most unreasonable, she concluded later, that she had refused to share the offer of a car up to town with the little red-headed man. After all, he had, under instruction, saved her life, and there were souls evidently capable of resentment and crime but capable also of forgiveness. There was no reason why she shouldn't like to stay with the red-headed man whom Tim Jackson had saved from a death by fire. Nevertheless, Solange was glad to have seen the last of him, and glad also that Mrs Jackson died that evening in the local hospital, without knowing what it was that had been passed over her head and fastened about her body.

Mystery of the Slip-Coach

Sapper

Herman Cyril McNeile (1888–1937) was a soldier before becoming a best-selling thriller writer. He adopted the pen-name Sapper as a hat-tip to the Royal Engineers, in which he had served with distinction during the First World War, being awarded the Military Cross. In 1920, he created Captain Hugh 'Bulldog' Drummond, 'a demobilised officer who found peace dull' whose principal adversary is the master-criminal Carl Peterson. The Drummond stories became bestsellers, and in 1929, Ronald Coleman, who played the lead in the film *Bulldog Drummond*, was nominated for an Academy Award. The *New York Times* called it 'the happiest and most enjoyable entertainment of its kind that has so far reached the screen', but after Sapper's death from cancer, his reputation faded.

Sapper was not a sophisticated writer, but he knew how to tell a story, and this knack is on display in several of his tales featuring Ronald Standish, who appeared in short story collections and also in three of the Bulldog Drummond books.

This story comes from *Ronald Standish* (1933), in which he is presented as a charismatic Great Detective of the type so popular at that time: 'A born player of games, wealthy, and distinctly good-looking...With the official police he was on excellent terms, which was not to be wondered at in view of the fact that on many occasions he had put them on the right track.' In this tale, Standish makes one of those pleasingly enigmatic remarks beloved of Great Detectives, urging the hapless Inspector Grantham to 'consider in all its aspects the extraordinary phenomenon of the raw egg'. Sure enough, therein lies the clue to the solution of the mystery.

'Well, I'll be danged. She's signalled through, and yet she's stopping, though she's late already. Be there summat up?'

The stationmaster of Marley Junction scratched his head, and stared at the oncoming express which was now slowing down rapidly.

'Isn't she supposed to stop?' Ronald Standish asked.

'No, sir; she ain't. There be a slip coach for here, but main part goes through.'

Rows of heads were already protruding from carriage windows as the train came to a standstill, and the guard got out.

'What's the matter, Joe?' demanded the stationmaster.

'Murder's the matter,' was the unexpected answer; and with a lift of his eyebrows Ronald turned to the other member of our little party.

'You seem to be having a busy time of it, Inspector,' he said, and with an expression of relief the two railway officials turned round.

'Are you the police, sir?' cried the guard.

'I'm Inspector Grantham of Scotland Yard,' answered the other. 'What's that you say? Murder!'

'Yes, sir. And I'll be pleased if you can come this way, for we're a lot behind time. He's in the slip coach.'

We followed him to the rear of the train, paying no attention to the excited comments of the passengers, several of whom had got out on the platform. And as we got to the back carriage an irascible-looking, elderly man, who might have been a retired colonel, an old clergyman and his wife, and a young man of perhaps thirty, with a worried expression on his face, descended.

The Inspector paused for a moment.

'This coach is separate from the rest of the train, I take it?' he said. 'There's no connecting corridor?'

'That's so, sir,' said the guard, 'as you can see. No one can pass farther than my van, which is just in front of it.'

'Then get the coach uncoupled. And all passengers, please, who were in this coach must wait.'

He entered, and we followed him along the corridor of the carriage. The stationmaster had gone off to give the necessary orders; the guard accompanied us.

'Everything is as it was found, sir,' he said. 'After the train was stopped I travelled in this coach myself.'

'Why did the train stop? I thought this was fast to Downwater?'

'Communication cord was pulled, sir, by the reverend gentleman.'

The Inspector nodded.

'We'll go into that later,' he said. 'Where's the body?'

For answer, the guard opened the door of the centre compartment. On the seat by the opposite window was sprawling the body of a man. One hand hung limply downwards, and on the cushion and the carpet lay an ominous red pool. A glance was sufficient to show that he was dead, and that the cause of death was a wound in the head. The window was shut; his suit-case littered up the rack; and in the opposite corner to the body a pair of wash-leather gloves was lying on the seat.

Suddenly Ronald gave a whistle.

'Good Lord!' he cried, 'it's old Samuel Goldberg, the bookmaker.'

'You know him?' said the Inspector.

'I've betted with him from time to time,' Ronald answered. 'But all in due course, for you'll have to do something about this train, Grantham. Why not let it go on with a relief guard and run this coach into a siding.'

The Inspector nodded, and a few moments later the express was speeding on her way, whilst the slip coach, with us still on board, was shunted off the main line.

'Yes—I knew him, Grantham,' said Ronald. 'He was a book-maker and quite a decent fellow. Great Scott! What's that mess?'

He was studying the woodwork of the door with a puzzled expression.

'Why—it's the remains of a raw egg! Here are bits of the shell on the carpet. And there's the place it hit the door. What an extraordinary thing to find in a railway carriage. Did you notice it, guard, when you came in?'

'Can't say as 'ow I did, sir. I was so worried and bemused that I didn't think of little things like that. When I sees there was nothing to be done for the poor gentleman I just shut the door again and started the train off after telling the driver to stop her here.'

'And you shut the window, too?'

'No, sir. The window was shut already. Both the window and the door was shut when I got here.'

'I think we'd better start our investigation, Mr Standish,' said the Inspector. 'We can come back again later to the body. Pull down the blinds'—he turned to the stationmaster—'and lock the carriage up. No one is to enter it.'

We found the other occupants of the coach pacing about the platform. The young man had joined up with the clergyman and his wife; the irascible military man was fuming visibly.

'I hope you'll hurry this business as much as possible,' he cried irritably. 'I'm judging hounds this afternoon, and I shall be late. I may say that I knew nothing about it till the train was stopped.'

'Quite, sir, quite,' said the Inspector soothingly. 'But in view of the fact that a man has been found dead in circumstances which preclude natural causes, you will appreciate that I must make inquiries. Now, sir,' he turned to the clergyman, 'I understand that it was you who pulled the communication cord and stopped the train. Presumably, therefore, it was you who first discovered the body. Will you tell me all you know? First—your name, please.'

'I am the Reverend John Stocker,' said the old man, 'of the parish of Meston, not far from here. And really I fear I can tell you but little of this terrible affair. I was reading in my carriage—'

'Which compartment did you occupy, Mr Stocker?'

'Let me see—which was it, my love?' he asked his wife.

'The third-class one—two away,' she answered promptly.

'Please proceed,' said the Inspector, making a note.

'It so chanced,' continued the clergyman, 'that I happened to glance out of the window at a passing train. It was travelling in the same direction as ourselves, at about the same speed, on the next line. I watched it idly, as we very slowly overtook it, when suddenly, to my amazement, I saw some people in the train beckoning to me. They were shouting and pointing, and though, of course, I could not hear what they said, it seemed to me by their agitation that something must be wrong, and that whatever that something was, it was in our train. So I got up and walked along the corridor to find, to my horror, the body of that unfortunate man.'

'What did you do then?' said the Inspector.

'I pulled the communication cord.'

'Did you go into the carriage?'

'No, I did not. The door was shut, and the sight had unnerved me.'

'And what happened then?'

'This gentleman'—he indicated the hound judge—'came out from his compartment at the other end of the carriage, and I called to him. He came at once, and I showed him what had happened. By that time, of course, the train was slowing up.'

'Quite correct,' barked the other. 'I went—'

'One moment, sir, if you please,' said the Inspector. 'Your name?'

'Blackton—Major Blackton. Late of the Gunners.'

'Now, sir. When you saw the dead man what did you do?'

'Opened the door, and went in to make certain, though, when you've seen as many men shot through the head as I have, it was obvious to me at first sight that he was beyond aid.'

'Did you shut the window?'

'No, sir, I did not. The window was already shut. I noticed it particularly, because I remember thinking to myself what an extraordinary thing it was that a man should be travelling with both door and window shut on a hot day like this.'

The Inspector nodded thoughtfully.

'Any more you'd like to say, sir?'

'Naturally, my first thought,' continued Major Blackton, 'was that it was a case of suicide.'

'Why naturally?'

'Damme, man. I hadn't shot the feller, and it wasn't likely the padre had, and at that time I thought we were the only people in the coach. However, when I found no sign of any weapon on the floor or the seat I realised it couldn't be suicide. That wound caused instantaneous death, or I'm no judge of such matters, so that by no human possibility could he have got rid of the gun.'

Once again the Inspector nodded.

'You said, sir,' he remarked after a pause, 'that at that time you thought you were the only people on the coach. When did you find you weren't?'

'Just before the train stopped, when that young man joined us in the corridor. And it seems to me that he might be able to tell you something, because he'd been talking to the dead man.'

'How do you know that?'

'Because he said so. "Good God!" he said, "what's happened? I was only talking to him ten minutes ago." Then he had another look and said: "What on earth has he done that for?" And by that time the train had stopped and the guard took charge.'

He glanced at his watch.

'That's positively all I can tell you, Inspector, so with your permission I'll get away.'

'Sorry, sir,' said the Inspector quietly, 'but at the present juncture that is quite impossible. You don't seem to realise,' he continued a little sternly, 'that a man has, so far as we know, just been murdered under conditions that render it imperative that the other occupants of the coach should place themselves unreservedly at the disposal of the police. Other points may arise over which I shall want to see you later. And now, before I interrogate the other gentleman, there is one further question. Did either of you two gentlemen hear the sound of a shot?'

'I certainly didn't,' said Major Blackton, 'but then I was at the far end of the coach.'

'I didn't, either.' The clergyman glanced at his wife. 'Did you, my love?'

She shook her head decidedly.

'I heard nothing,' she said. 'Nothing at all.'

'Thank you, madam.' He beckoned to the young man. 'Now, sir, will you tell me what you know of this affair? First—your name.'

'Carter—Harry Carter.'

'Did you know the dead man?'

'I did,' said Carter quietly.

'What was his name?'

'Samuel Goldberg.'

'Had you spoken to him since leaving London?'

'I had a long talk with him. That's what made it so amazing, because he seemed his usual self when I left his compartment.'

The Inspector consulted his notebook.

'You said to Major Blackton: "What on earth has he done that for?" or words to that effect. What did you mean by that remark?'

Carter stared at him.

'Just what I said. I couldn't make out why he should commit suicide.'

'Why should you assume it was suicide?'

Carter stared at him even harder.

'What else could it have been? Unless it was an accident.'

'It was neither suicide nor an accident, Mr Carter. Goldberg was murdered.'

'Murdered? But who by?'

'That is what we are endeavouring to find out. Now, Mr Carter, am I to understand that you didn't hear Major Blackton and the guard talking in the corridor after the train started again and saying it was murder?'

'I did not, and for a very good reason. I returned almost at once to my own compartment to try and think out how this very unexpected development was going to affect me.'

The Inspector stopped writing and glanced at Standish. Then he looked steadily at Carter.

'Mr Carter,' he said gravely, 'it is my duty to say one thing to you. We are investigating a case of murder, and everything points to the fact that the murderer was one of the people who travelled from London in that slip coach. You need not tell me anything that might, in certain eventualities, incriminate you.'

Carter stared at him in amazement.

'Good God!' he burst out at length, 'you aren't suggesting that I had anything to do with it?'

'I am suggesting nothing,' answered the Inspector shortly. 'I am merely pointing out your possible future position. And having done so I will now ask you in what way Goldberg's death could affect you? You need not answer if you don't wish to.'

'But, of course, I wish to. I've got nothing to hide. I owed him money, and I was wondering whether his suicide—as I then thought it was—would wipe out this debt.'

'Had your discussion with him previously concerned this debt?'

'It had,' said Carter.

'Was it an acrimonious interview?' asked the Inspector mildly.

'Well, when you ask your bookie not to press for payment and he cuts up rough, it's not very pleasant.'

'And it terminated some ten minutes before you found that Goldberg had, as you thought, committed suicide?'

'That's right.'

'May I ask how much was the sum involved?'

'A thousand pounds.'

Inspector Grantham tapped his teeth with his pencil.

'One final question, Mr Carter. Did you know that Goldberg was going to travel by this train?'

'I hadn't an idea of it until I found him in the same coach.'

The inspector rose and closed his notebook with a snap.

'That is all for the present,' he said, and then, for the first time, Ronald spoke.

'I should like to ask you two or three other questions, Mr Carter. When you had your interview with Goldberg, did you sit by the door?'

'I did—in the opposite corner to him. By Jove! Now I come to think of it, I've left my gloves there!'

'Was the window open?'

Carter thought for a moment.

'It was: wide.'

'And the door?'

'Shut.'

'Now, Mr Carter, I want you to think carefully. Did he throw a raw egg at you?'

Carter stared at Ronald with a look of utter amazement, which changed to an angry flush.

'Are you trying to be funny? Because, if so, it seems to me neither the time nor the place. A raw egg? Why the devil should he throw one at me?'

'Exactly,' said Ronald. 'Why the devil should he? Well, Grantham, what do you propose to do now?'

The Inspector, who had frowned slightly at Ronald's last question, again took charge.

'I'm afraid I must request you three gentlemen, and you, too, madam, to remain here for a little while yet. I know, sir, I know about your hound show, but this is even more important. Guard—come with me. And you too, Mr Standish—if you care to.'

We returned to the slip coach and the guard unlocked the door. Then, leaving him on the platform, we entered the carriage.

'What do you make of it, Mr Standish?' said the Inspector.

'At the moment, Grantham, remarkably little,' said Ronald. 'There are one or two very strange features about the case. Have you come to any conclusion yourself?'

'Only to the obvious one that Goldberg was murdered by someone who was in this coach. Further than that I would not care to go, though it would be idle to deny that of the four occupants the most likely is Carter. Of course, it is possible that there was someone else in the carriage who escaped when the train stopped, but there are two grave difficulties to put up against that theory. First, it was the clergyman who pulled the communication cord. Surely, the murderer would have done it himself. And even if he didn't, but had seized on this unlooked-for chance of escaping, he would have been bound to be seen by people in the train. I mean, one knows that when a train stops unexpectedly everyone's head goes out of the window.'

'And what about the egg?' remarked Ronald thoughtfully.

'Confound the egg!' cried Grantham irritably. 'You've got it on the brain.'

'I have,' agreed Ronald, unperturbed. 'But before we go any farther, let us examine the compartment thoroughly again.'

I watched them from the corridor for ten minutes, and at the end of that time the Inspector came out and joined me.

'Nothing of value; no trace of any weapon.'

'And no trace of any more eggs,' said Ronald. 'Now, don't get angry, Inspector. I'm not fooling. But when an extremely bizarre fact intrudes itself on one it is advisable not to overlook it. Now, have you ever heard of a man carrying one raw egg about with him? Frequently have I known people to take half a dozen or even three in a paper bag, but not one. There isn't even a paper bag. Was he, then, carrying this solitary egg in his hand or in his pocket? However, let us go on a little further. Assuming for the moment that he had got this one egg, why did he throw it at the door? It seems a strange pastime.'

'Your second point is easier to answer than your first,' said the Inspector. 'Goldberg was unarmed, and when he looked up and saw the murderer standing in the carriage he threw the first thing at him that came to hand.'

'This solitary egg.' Ronald stared at him thoughtfully. 'Was he holding it, studying its beauty? Or was it on the seat beside him? However, perhaps I am over-stressing the point. Where are you off to now?'

'To get on with the case, Mr Standish,' answered the Inspector tersely. 'I don't know how or why that egg got there, but I do know that that man was murdered. Almost certainly the murderer flung the weapon out of the window, but it is just possible he did not. So my first move will be to search the baggage of the four people I have detained.'

'Splendid,' said Ronald quietly. 'Have I your permission to wait here a little longer? There are one or two more points I would like to look into, and I will, of course, pass on anything I find to you.'

With a faint smile the Inspector departed and Ronald turned to me.

'There's something very rum, Bob—very rum indeed about this affair. Apart from the egg, who shut the window? Did Goldberg, after Carter had left him? Did the murderer, either before or after he'd done it? Or is Carter lying? I don't think he is.'

Ronald was talking half to himself.

'To place too much reliance on faces is dangerous, but I don't think he is. His evidence has the ring of truth. And I ask you—would he have left his gloves here if he'd done it?'

He went back into the compartment and stood staring round.

'The clergyman—what about him? And our military friend? As things are, the clergyman is the more likely, as the other had to pass the door to get to this compartment. Moreover, we only have the clergyman's word that he saw people beckoning to him from the other train. It's unlikely, of course, but it's conceivable that he, too, was in debt to Goldberg, and has staged a pretty piece of acting the innocent after killing him. Means his wife is in collusion with him, but stranger things have happened. But it's that damned egg that beats me.'

'Well, old boy,' I said, 'I admit it's very peculiar, as you say, but it seems to me we've got to accept it as a fact that Goldberg was in possession of one raw egg. I mean, it isn't likely the murderer came with an egg in one hand and a gun in the other.'

Ronald spun round and stared at me.

'Great Scott! Bob,' he cried, 'I believe—'

He broke off abruptly, and dashed into the next compartment, where he opened and shut the window several times, while I looked on in blank amazement. What on earth there was in my semi-jocular remark that had caused this activity was beyond me, but I knew better than to ask. And then he returned to the scene of the murder, and kneeling down on the floor by the door he examined the sticky mess of shell and yolk on the carpet.

'Hopeless,' he muttered, 'hopeless; but—ah!'

He was carefully picking out a piece of shell, which he placed on the seat. The search continued: two other pieces were selected, which, after a further scrutiny, he roughly joined together.

'Do you see, Bob?' he cried.

I did and I didn't. Stamped in violet ink on the fragments were some letters. On one piece was written 'atch'; on the other, 'ways.' Presumably part of the name of the firm where the egg had been bought, and I said so. But what further light that fact threw on the matter was beyond me, and I said that, too.

He put the bits of shell into an empty matchbox, as there came the sound of people getting into the carriage.

'Perhaps you're right, Bob; we'll see,' he said, slipping the box into his pocket.

Inspector Grantham was coming along the corridor, and with him was a man carrying a small black bag. A doctor obviously, but the thing that struck me at once was the expression of subdued triumph on the Inspector's face.

'Here you are, doctor,' he said. 'And as soon as you've made your preliminary examination I'll have the body moved to a waiting-room.'

Then, as the doctor entered the compartment, he joined us in the corridor.

'I've found the revolver, Mr Standish,' he remarked complacently.

'You have, have you?' said Ronald. 'Where?'

'In one of Carter's suit-cases.'

'Was it loaded?'

'No, but there was a half-open packet of ammunition. And that's better than your raw egg, I'm thinking.'

'How does he account for its being there?' demanded Ronald, ignoring the gibe.

'He doesn't. He simply says he was taking it down to the country with him.'

'Which,' said Ronald, 'is probably the truth.'

'Of course it is,' agreed the Inspector. 'I don't suppose for a moment that he brought it on the train to shoot Goldberg, but finding Goldberg in the same carriage with him he yielded to the temptation. Come, come, Mr Standish,' he went on good-humouredly, 'you're very smart and all that, but really there is no good trying to pretend that there is any mystery here. Goldberg was shot by someone in this carriage. Carter admits having had a bad quarrel with him; Carter is in possession of a revolver and ammunition. Moreover, no sign of arms can be found on the other three people concerned. The thing is as plain as a pikestaff.'

And I saw that Ronald looked worried.

'Too plain, Grantham,' he said. 'Altogether too plain. But if you're right there's only one place Carter ought to be sent to, and that's a lunatic asylum. The man must be crazy. Why on earth didn't he throw the gun out of the window?'

The Inspector shrugged his shoulders.

'Like your raw egg, Mr Standish, I can't tell you,' he remarked. 'Well, doctor?'

'Killed instantaneously, of course,' said the other, joining us. 'If you will have the body moved, Inspector, I will carry on at once.'

The Inspector bustled off, followed by the doctor, and Ronald turned to me.

'Bad, Bob; damned bad,' he said, and I have seldom seen him look so grave.

'You think Carter did it?' I asked.

'I am as certain as I can be of anything that he didn't,' he answered quietly. 'But on the face of it, Carter's position is about as serious as it could well be.'

And so Carter evidently realised. We found him in the custody of a policeman, and the instant he saw us he sprang to his feet.

'Look here, sir,' he cried to Ronald, 'I don't know who you gentlemen are, but I assume you're something to do with the police. Well, all I can tell you is that I swear before heaven I had no more to do with the death of Samuel Goldberg than you had. I often take a revolver with me when I go down to stay with my uncle. I'm a very keen shot, and potting at rabbits is marvellous practice.'

'I believe you, Carter,' said Ronald, holding out his hand. 'But there's no good blinding yourself to the fact that a combination of circumstances has put you in a very awkward corner.'

Carter's expression, which had cleared at Ronald's first words, clouded again.

'It's hideous,' he cried passionately. 'It's like a nightmare. I'm not a fool, and I see the gravity of the situation. Someone in the carriage must have shot him and I'm found with a gun. But if I'd done it should I have kept the revolver?'

'Exactly what I said to the Inspector,' said Ronald, with a grave smile. 'But you may depend on one thing—'

He broke off.

'Hallo! Grantham doesn't look too happy.'

The Inspector was coming along the platform with a puzzled frown.

'Well, Mr Carter,' he said, 'I must apologise.'

'What do you mean?' Carter almost shouted.

'The bullet doesn't fit your revolver.'

For a moment or two there was dead silence. Then Ronald stepped up to Carter and clapped him on the shoulder.

'Congratulations,' he said. 'Well out of a nasty position.'

'Thanks,' said Carter quietly. 'I don't want to go through another half-hour like that again. I don't blame you in the slightest degree, Inspector; it must have looked a cert to you. But you can imagine my feelings, knowing I hadn't done it.'

'I apologise again,' said the Inspector. 'But, damn it,' he burst out, 'who did? Well, it will be a question of searching the line till we find the revolver that that bullet does fit.'

'You never will,' remarked Ronald, lighting a cigarette.

'Why not?' demanded Grantham.

'Because it isn't there.'

'I suppose you're going to tell me next that Goldberg wasn't shot at all,' said the Inspector sarcastically.

'No, not that. But once again I am going to suggest to you that you consider in all its aspects the extraordinary phenomenon of the raw egg.'

'Any other points?' asked the Inspector, impressed in spite of himself.

'Two,' said Ronald. 'First—the strange fact that the window was open when Carter's interview with Goldberg finished, and was shut when the body was found. Second—that Carter is certainly not the only person in the world who owes Goldberg money.'

'Damn it!' exploded Grantham, 'I believe you know who did it.'

'No, I don't,' said Ronald emphatically. 'Moreover, it is quite possible I never shall. But we'll see. Once again congratulations, Carter, on a lucky escape. If that bullet had fitted your gun you would have been in the soup. Come on, Bob; here's our train coming. I've just got time to ask the guard of the express one question.'

And the only remark he made to me the whole way up to London added considerably to my mental confusion.

'Well done, Bob,' he said. 'You solved that in masterly fashion.'

'I solved it!' I spluttered.

'Of course you did, old boy. When you said the murderer had an egg in one hand and a revolver in the other.'

———————

For the next few days I did not see him at all. The newspapers, naturally, were full of the case, and interviews were published with all four of the other occupants of the carriage. In fact, 'Mystery of the Slip Coach' appealed immensely to the man in the street, owing to the strange circumstances of the crime.

And it certainly was a baffling affair. As far as the public was concerned, it was obvious that one of the four people in the coach was guilty, and in most clubs betting on the final result was frequent. And it was inevitable that Carter should prove the favourite in spite of the fact that the shot did not fit his revolver. The Vicar and his wife were a delightful old pair who had lived a blameless life for years at Meston; Major Blackton turned out to be an extremely wealthy man who had just returned to England after a prolonged absence abroad, and who had never heard of Goldberg in his life.

'You mark my words,' said a man one day to me, 'young Carter did it, and he's a mighty deep 'un. Shall I tell you how? He had a second revolver. D'you get me? The gun he shot Goldberg with he bunged out of the window, leaving the other one to be found.'

The trouble was that in spite of an army of searchers no trace of another gun could be found. A large reward was offered by the police, without producing any result, and another theory was started. Carter must have had a confederate who picked up the revolver when it was thrown from the train. And that held the field for quite a time, till it was conclusively proved that Goldberg had only decided to go by that train on the very morning in question, and that it was, therefore, utterly impossible for Carter to have known about it in time to make any such arrangements.

Another source of information from which the police had hoped to derive some help proved of no assistance. The people in the other train, who had first seen the body, could say nothing which threw any more light on matters. They were two young men, one of whom was standing up at the window watching the express as it gradually overtook them. He had seen the body sprawling on the seat and realising that something was amiss, he had, with his companion, attracted the Vicar's attention. But of one thing they were positive: the window of Goldberg's carriage was shut. And as time went on it began to look as if the mystery would prove insoluble, which would have been unpleasant for Carter. For there was no doubt that a large percentage of the public believed that in some way or other he had done it. And even though that belief was only due to the fact that it was most unlikely that any of the other three was guilty—that it was arrived at by a process of elimination, and was not the result of any positive evidence—it made things no better for him.

And then one morning I got a 'phone message from Ronald, asking me to go round to his rooms. He was not in when I got there, but, somewhat to my surprise, I found Inspector Grantham.

'Morning, Mr Miller,' he said gloomily. 'I hope Mr Standish has found out something, for this case isn't doing me any good.'

'I know he doesn't think it was Carter,' I said.

'Then who could it have been?' he cried. 'But I can't arrest him. We haven't a shred of evidence. If only we could find the gun it was done with.'

The door opened and Ronald entered.

'Come in, Mr Meredith,' he said, nodding to us. 'Here are the other two gentlemen who I know will be interested in our little venture.'

A morose-looking individual entered as he was speaking, who contemplated us suspiciously.

'You remember, Bob,' Ronald went on, 'our ideas about a chicken farm. Well—I've found the very spot, and Mr Meredith is quite willing to sell.'

'Give me my figure, and you can have it tomorrow,' said the new-comer. 'Not that it isn't a good proposition: it is. But I haven't the money to run it. I'll have a drop of Scotch, thank you.'

I glanced at the Inspector as Ronald filled a glass, but his face was impassive. Only the faintest of winks showed that he realised something was up, but I knew he was as much in the dark as I was.

'Here's how,' said Meredith, and drained his drink. 'Well, gentlemen, do we talk business?'

'No time like the present,' said Ronald cheerfully, ringing the bell. 'Take away that empty glass, will you, Sayers,' he told his man, 'and bring in some more clean ones. Now, Mr Meredith, I understand Hatchaways is for sale, and that the price you are asking is fifteen hundred pounds?'

'That is correct,' agreed the other, his eyes sparkling greedily.

'And it is not mortgaged nor encumbered in any way?'

'No; the property is quite clear.'

The door opened, and Sayers came in carrying some more glasses. And as he put them down I saw him nod to Ronald.

'Have you had to borrow any money on the place, Mr Meredith?' continued Ronald.

'You'll pardon me, Mr Standish, but I don't see that that has anything to do with you,' said Meredith truculently.

'You didn't borrow, for instance, from Samuel Goldberg, who has recently been murdered?'

Meredith gave one uncontrollable start. Then he pulled himself together.

'Never heard of the man till I saw his death in the paper.'

'Strange,' said Ronald quietly. 'He was a complete stranger to you, maybe?'

'Absolute.'

'Then why, Meredith, did you throw that egg through his open window in the Downwater express as his carriage came level with yours?'

Meredith lurched to his feet and tried to bluster. But there was sick fear in his face and Grantham moved towards the door.

'It's a cursed lie,' he said thickly.

'Oh, no, it isn't,' answered Ronald sternly. 'On the shell of the egg you threw are fingerprints: on the glass you've just drunk from are fingerprints. And those fingerprints are identical. There's your man, Grantham. He murdered Samuel Goldberg by shooting him through the head from the other train.'

For a moment there was silence, and then with a roar of rage Meredith whipped a revolver out of his pocket. But he was too late. Grantham was on him like a flash.

'And that is the gun, Inspector,' continued Ronald, calmly, 'that I told you you would not find on the permanent way.'

———

'I wish to heaven you'd elucidate, old boy,' I said a few minutes later, 'for it's the smartest thing I've ever known.'

Ronald filled his pipe thoughtfully.

'You may remember, Bob,' he said, 'that after your illuminating remark I went into the next compartment and started monkeying about with the window. Now, there are two main types of fitting in trains. The more common has a long strap, and with that sort, when the strap has been pulled to the full extent, an outward push on the bottom of the window is necessary to keep it shut. The other type has no strap, but a slot in the top sash which, when pulled up to the full extent, automatically remains there. And that was the type used in the slip coach.

'You may also remember how I harped on the raw egg. I could not place it, Bob; every instinct in me rebelled against the thought that Goldberg carried one raw egg with him. Then you made the remark about the murderer carrying it. Once again it was incredible if the murderer was in the carriage. He wouldn't come in, plaster an egg on the door, and then shoot Goldberg. But, supposing the murderer hadn't been in the carriage—what then? For a considerable time another train had been running parallel with the express, and at about the same speed. Supposing a man in that other train had seen Goldberg sitting in his compartment, and to attract his attention had thrown an egg through the open window, what would be Goldberg's reaction? He would get up to shut the window, to prevent more eggs following. Supposing that then the egg-thrower shot him through the brain. Now you and I have seen men killed instantaneously in France, and if you cast your mind back you will remember that quite a number threw up their arms and fell backwards. What would have happened if Goldberg's fingers had been in the notch of the window? Just what did happen in this case: he shut the window with his last convulsive jerk, thereby making it appear impossible for him to have been shot from anywhere except inside the carriage, which was, of course, an incredible piece of luck for the murderer.

'So on that hypothesis I started. You heard me say to Grantham that I might never find the man who did it, and but for luck which now turned against him I never should have. My starting point, naturally, was the other train and its occupants. Now the last station at which it had stopped, before the murder had been committed, was Pedlington, and so there I repaired. I made inquiries with the utmost caution, because it was essential that nothing should get into the papers if we weren't going to alarm our bird, whoever he was. And after talking to the stationmaster and getting in touch with the guard of the train, facts began to accumulate, though it was a slow business.

'The first thing I found out was that the train was comparatively empty—so empty that the guard was able to remember more or less accurately how the passengers were seated. And the important thing was to ascertain how many compartments had only one occupant. There were only three to his certain knowledge: one with a woman, two each with a man. More than that he could not say, except that the woman was very old.

'Now came the wearisome search. I eliminated the woman, and concentrated on the men. I went to every station after Pedlington at which the train stopped, and got in touch with the ticket collector. It was still an absolute toss-up if I could spot my man. If it was someone carrying a few eggs in a paper bag it was hopeless. And then came an astounding stroke of luck. The collector at Marlingham—four stations beyond Pedlington—remembered a man who got out there with a basket of eggs and who asked the way to some farm.

'Bob, I was getting warm. Off to the farm I went, and found that a man called Meredith, who owned a chicken farm called Hatchaways, not far from Pedlington itself, had been there. And now I knew I'd got him. You remember the letters on the broken shell—"atch" and "ways." He was my bird, but he was still a long way from the net.

'So back to Pedlington, where I posed as a man with a certain amount of money who was interested in chicken farming. And I soon met Master Meredith, who thought he had found a sucker. Further inquiries revealed the fact that he was in bad financial straits, and was only too ready to sell. Further inquiries also revealed the very significant and unusual fact that he always carried a Colt revolver in his pocket wherever he went—a habit, he said, he got into while out West. So I staged the little performance this morning. Marshall, from the Yard, the fingerprint expert, was outside, and when Sayers nodded to me I knew that there was no mistake.

'Just one of those strange crimes that nearly came off. It wasn't premeditated, of course. By a mere freak of fate the two trains ran side by side for some time, and Meredith saw the chance of getting rid of the man to whom he owed money in such a way that no suspicion could fall on him. And when Goldberg shut the window as he died, Meredith must have thought himself absolutely safe. Which,' he concluded, 'he would have been if he'd thrown a banana and not an egg.

The Level Crossing

Freeman Wills Crofts

Nobody, surely, was better qualified to write railway mysteries than Freeman Wills Crofts (1879–1957). His interest in railways dated from his childhood in Ireland; as a boy, he constructed a large model of the Forth Bridge for the railway in the garden of his family home. Beginning as a teenage apprentice on the Belfast Counties Railway, he rose to become Chief Assistant Engineer, working on the impressive and photogenic Bleach Green Viaduct among other projects. He retired to Surrey in 1929, by which time he was widely regarded as one of the leading detective novelists of the era.

Railways feature in many of his novels and short stories, starting with 'The Mystery of the Sleeping Car Express', first published in 1921. A recurrent element in his work is the apparently unbreakable alibi, often dependent on train times; a characteristic example is to be found in *Sir John Magill's Last Journey* (1930). The plot of *Death on the Way* (1932) involves a scheme to widen a railway on the south coast, while that of *Death of a Train* (1946), set during the Second World War and featuring a Nazi plot to sabotage a consignment of radio valves, brims with technical expertise. Crofts' short fiction tended to be less effective than his novels, but this story, which dates from 1933, is among the better examples of his work in the short form.

IN spite of himself Dunstan Thwaite shivered as he looked at the level crossing. For here was where he intended, this very night, to kill his enemy, John Dunn.

It was a place well suited to his purpose. A sharp curve and some belts of firs screened both sight and sound of approaching trains. Speeds were high and with only four or five seconds' warning the least carelessness or hesitation might well prove fatal. An accident here would raise no suspicions.

The crossing, moreover, was private; no signalman in charge, no gatehouse near. Nor in that lonely country was it overlooked. The nearest house was Thwaite's own, and even from it the view was masked by trees. The lane which here crossed the railway ran up into the country behind Thwaite's house and joined the main road at the opposite side of the line. But the crossing was seldom used. Because of the danger there was practically no wheeled traffic and the gates were kept locked. Wickets were provided, used mostly by foot-passengers seeking a short cut to the neighbouring station. But of these there were few and at the time Thwaite had in mind there would be none.

As he planned it there would be little difficulty in carrying out the crime. Nor was there the slightest chance of discovery.

The thing was safe, safe as houses. Only a little care, an ugly few minutes, and he would be once more a free man.

For five years now John Dunn had been his tormentor. For five years he had suffered because he had seen no way of escape. Even his health had become threatened and he was reduced to sleeping draughts to get a night's rest. Now he was shedding his burden. After tonight he would be free.

The trouble was of Thwaite's own making, though that did not make it any easier to bear. Thwaite was a climber and so far a successful climber. Left an orphan, he early had had to fend for himself. By a lucky chance he had got a job in the office of a large steel works. There he had worked with a single aim. It had borne fruit. At the age of thirty-five he was appointed accountant. Had it not been for his one act of suicidal mania, he would have felt his future assured.

His break had occurred five years earlier when he was assistant to his elderly and easy-going predecessor. Thwaite was about to be married 'above him,' as the silly phrase goes. The beautiful Miss Lorraine was not only one of the leaders of the local society but was reputed to have a well-lined pocket. Why she proposed to 'throw herself away' on a man in Thwaite's position, none of her friends could imagine. Some said it was a romance of pure love, others more cynically, that she believed that she had backed a winner. For Thwaite, at all events, it promised to be a brilliant match, but he found it was going to be expensive. In fact, the preparations pressed him so hard that he was faced with the choice either of obtaining more ready money or of losing Hilda Lorraine. Then suddenly the opportunity had presented itself and Thwaite had lost his head. A bit of casual slackness on the part of one of his directors, instantly seized and turned to his own advantage, a little extraordinarily skilful manipulation of the books under the nose of his infirm superior, and a cool thousand of the firm's money found its way into Thwaite's pockets. Needless to say, he had hoped to put it back after his marriage, but before he had time to do so the loss was discovered. Reason to suspect another clerk was discovered along with it. Nothing could actually be proved against the unfortunate man, but he was quietly got rid of.

Thwaite had sat tight and said nothing. He had got away with it—almost. No one knew, no one guessed, but his next in command, John Dunn. And Dunn wormed his way through the books till he got his proof.

But Dunn didn't use his knowledge, not in the way an honest clerk should. Instead he approached Thwaite secretly. A hundred pounds changed hands.

That hundred pounds, that and the knowledge of his power, satisfied Dunn for the first year. Then there had been a second interview. Thwaite had had a rise. Mrs Thwaite had brought money with her. Dunn went home with two hundred and fifty.

For five years it had gone on. Dunn's demands ever increasing and nothing to suggest they would ever cease. Nothing but the one thing, the remedy Thwaite was now going to take.

At first Thwaite had tried the obvious way of escape. 'I suppose, Dunn,' he had said, 'it hasn't occurred to you that you're in the same boat yourself? You've known this thing and you've kept silent; you're an accessory after the fact. If you send me to prison, you'll come with me.'

But Dunn had only laughed maliciously. 'Oh, come now, Mr Thwaite,' he had answered, 'you ain't 'ardly doin' me justice, you ain't.' As if it was yesterday, Thwaite remembered the mixture of mockery and cunning in the man's eyes. 'I'll only 'ave found it out the very day I make my report. See? I 'ad suspected it from the first, but I 'adn't been able to prove it. I'll tell 'em that that very day I was lookin' over the old ledger, an' there for the first time I'd seen the proof. No accessory about that, Mr Thwaite. Nothin' there but a poor clerk carryin' out a disagreeable dooty for the good of the firm.'

Thwaite had cursed; and paid. And now the fact was that after four years of married life he could no longer make ends meet. His wife indeed had brought money, but nothing like the sum with which rumour had credited her. Besides, she held that it was her husband's place to supply money. She demanded an expensive house, an expensive car, expensive servants, entertaining, suppers and theatres in town. Thwaite, moreover, had his own position to keep up. And he could not run to it, not with this continual drain to Dunn. With Dunn out of the way he could just manage.

'I went into Penborough yesterday and had a look at that Sirius saloon,' his wife had remarked a couple of nights before. 'It's a nice car, Dunstan. I don't see why we shouldn't have it now. If you're really so hard up as you pretend, we could get it on the hire-purchase system.'

'I don't want to begin that,' Thwaite answered. 'With it you never know what you own or where you are.'

'You don't want it perhaps,' his wife returned sharply, 'but what about me? What about my going about in a shabby old Austin years out-of-date and all my friends turning up in Singers and Daimlers and Lincolns? Look at Myra Turner with her new Rolls-Royce. I tell you I feel it. And I'm not going to stand it, what's more.'

'I know all about it, Hilda,' Thwaite said wearily. 'I know it's due to you and you shall have it in time. But we'll have to wait. Believe me, I haven't got the money.'

Her face took on the cold set look which he knew and dreaded. There had been many such discussions.

'I don't want to pry into your secrets,' she said in a hard cutting voice. 'Even if you're keeping up another establishment I don't ask about it. But I'll tell you this: if you don't order that car, I will. I don't see why your likes and dislikes should be considered but not mine. You can at least meet the first instalment, I presume?'

Thwaite sighed. His lips were sealed because he knew that she had reason on her side. It was not shortage of money nor the inability to buy expensive cars that had turned a loyal comrade into a suspicious stranger and their happy home life into a nightmare. It was her want of confidence in him. It was the knowledge that he had several hundred a year for which he would not account. She was no fool, Hilda Thwaite, and his early attempts to throw dust in her eyes had only confirmed her suspicions. Yet he believed that but for this money trouble their old happy relations might be resumed. But that was where John Dunn came in.

Lord, how he hated the man! The thought of the level crossing recurred to him. It was no new idea. Weeks ago he had thought out the ghastly details of what might happen there. His scheme had had its inception when the doctor had ordered him sleeping draughts. He had thought first of giving the man a concentrated dose. Then he had seen that this was too crude and a subtler way had suggested itself. With the level crossing at hand an innocuous dose only would be required.

Thwaite let his mind dwell on the completed scheme. With something not far from horror he felt himself being driven towards it by forces greater than himself. Like the man in Poe's sketch he seemed to see the walls of his chamber closing in on him.

The very next morning, while Thwaite was still hesitating,

Dunn himself had put the lid on the situation. The two men were in Thwaite's private room, discussing some business.

'Sorry to trouble you, Mr Thwaite,' Dunn began in his whining voice, when the firm's affair had been settled, 'but I'm in difficulty about my son. 'E's got into more trouble and 'e must produce five 'undred or 'e'll get run in. I was wonderin', Mr Thwaite, if maybe you could 'elp me?'

For a reason known only to himself, Dunn's demands always took the form of aid for a mythical son. On the first occasion when Thwaite had pointed out the flaw in this premise Dunn had cheerfully admitted it, but with cynical insolence his subsequent applications had been couched in the same terms.

'Damn your son!' Thwaite returned in low tones. Though the room was large he must be careful not to be overheard. 'Can you never say straight out what you want?'

'Straight as you like, Mr Thwaite,' the other agreed amicably. 'Just five 'undred quid. It ain't much from one gentleman to another.'

Thwaite felt a yearning to seize the creature and slowly to choke the life from his miserable body.

'Five hundred?' he repeated. 'You wouldn't like the moon by any chance? Because you're as likely to get the one as the other.'

Dunn washed his hands in air. 'Oh, come now, Mr Thwaite,' he whined. 'Come now, sir. That's a shockin' thing to say. To a gentleman like you five 'undred's a mere nothin'. Nothin'. You ain't surely goin' to make a difficulty about a trifle like that?'

'You needn't think you're going to get it from me,' Thwaite said firmly. 'And I'll tell you why. I haven't got it. A small sum I could manage, but not five hundred. You'll never see it in this world.'

Dunn smiled evilly. This was the stage that he really enjoyed.

'Five 'undred, Mr Thwaite,' he murmured. 'You wouldn't cheat a poor man out of his bit of money?'

Thwaite looked at him steadily. 'Don't you be a fool,' he advised. 'I've paid you something like three thousand in the last five years and I'm fed up. Don't push me too far.'

Dunn's face essayed the expression of injured innocence. 'Too far, Mr Thwaite? I wouldn't put you about, not for the world. I would never have mentioned this trifle if I didn't know you could oblige with ease. Sir, you 'urt my feelin's.'

'I could oblige, could I? Then since you know so much, just tell me how.'

Dunn grinned maliciously. 'I wouldn't 'ave presumed to suggest it, Mr Thwaite, but when you ask my opinion it's another thing. Since you ask me, sir, what about postponin' the Sirius? The Austin is still a good car. Many a man would give his ears for a five-year-old Austin.'

Thwaite swore. 'How the hell do you know about that?' he growled.

'Nothin' in it,' Dunn returned smoothly. 'Everyone knows that Mrs Thwaite 'as been tryin' out the new saloon an' it's not 'ard to guess why.'

It was then that Thwaite finally decided to carry out the plan. He pretended to think, then shifted impatiently in his chair.

'Well,' he said, 'we won't discuss it here. I'll do what I can. Come up tomorrow night and we'll go into it.' The following night Mrs Thwaite was going on a visit to town. 'And by the way,' he added, 'bring those quotations of Maxwell's also. No harm to have a reason for your call.'

So far, so good. Thwaite could see that Dunn suspected nothing. Of course, there was no reason why he should. It was not the first time he had been to Thwaite's house on a similar mission.

Next evening Thwaite made the few simple preparations necessary. He had already put notes for fifty pounds in his pocket and now he made sure that his bank-book, posted to date, was in his safe. Next he wrote a letter to his stockbroker, placed the carbon copy in his file and burned the original. Then he poured away the whisky in the decanter until only two moderate glasses remained, and into this he put half of one of his sleeping powders. He saw that an unopened bottle of whisky, a siphon, plain water, and glasses were available. In the right outside pocket of his overcoat, hanging in the passage outside his study door, he put a hammer and in the left an electric torch. Lastly, he put on both the clock and his wristwatch ten minutes. Then he sat down to wait.

It was necessary that he take the utmost care. There could not fail to be suspicion, and his scheme must be capable of withstanding a police investigation. Thwaite was aware that it was generally believed in the office that Dunn had some kind of hold over him. Things were overlooked in Dunn's case which would not be tolerated from any one else. But Thwaite would have a good alibi. He would be able to prove that he had never left the house.

The need for action over, Thwaite found that he could scarcely bear the weight of horror that was creeping down over him. Like most people, he had read about murders and had marvelled at the mistakes murderers made to their own undoing. Now, though the crime as yet existed only in his imagination, he understood those mistakes. Under the stress of such emotions a man could not think. He seemed as from a distance to see Dunn before him, alive and well, with not a thought of death in his mind. He seemed to see his own arm rise, to hear the sickening thud of the hammer on the man's skull, to watch the body relax and become motionless. Dunn's dead body! Dead all but the eyes. In Thwaite's imagination the eyes seemed to remain alive, staring at him reproachfully, following him about wherever he went. He shuddered. Heavens! If he did this thing would he ever know peace again?

He took out his flask, poured out a stiff tot and gulped it down almost neat. Immediately things once again took on their normal perspective. He had let his nerves run away with him. It was not his way to funk things, and he was not going to funk this one. A little courage, a nasty ten minutes, and then—safety, release from his present troubles, happiness in his home, assurance for the future! When half an hour later there came a ring at the door and Dunn was shown in, Thwaite was his own man again.

For the benefit of the servant he greeted his visitor cordially. 'It's those Maxwell quotations, I suppose? We'll do them at once.' Then, the door closed, he went on: 'Get them out, Dunn, and I'll initial them. No use in taking half a precaution. You came here to get them dealt with and we'll deal with them.'

They settled down to work, as if in Thwaite's room in the works. Fifteen minutes later the business was completed and Dunn pushed the papers back into his pocket. Thwaite leaned back in his chair.

'Now about the other matter,' he said slowly, while Dunn's eyes gleamed avariciously. 'By the way,' Thwaite rose to his feet as if for something he had forgotten, 'have a drink? No use in quarrelling even though we've got unpleasant business to do.'

Suspicion fought with desire in the man's shifty eyes. 'I'll not mind anything tonight,' he quavered.

'Don't be such an unholy fool,' Thwaite said roughly. 'What are you afraid of? Think I'm going to poison you? Here,' he shoved decanter and glasses across the table. 'Pour out the same for us both.' He dumped down the siphon. 'Add the soda yourself and don't be more of an ass than you can help.'

Desire conquered, as Thwaite knew it would. Thwaite drank his first, then Dunn, his suspicions dispelled by this ocular demonstration, followed suit. The dose was small, a quarter of the normal to each man, but it would fulfil its purpose. On Thwaite, because of its many predecessors, it would have no effect to speak of. Dunn it would make sleepy. Thwaite did not wish him put to sleep; he only wanted him to be stupid and off his guard.

With grim satisfaction Thwaite noted his first fence taken. He had now only to see that no inkling of his purpose penetrated the man's mind. He sat forward and became confidential.

'Now look here, Dunn,' he said in the tone of one man of the world to another, 'there's not a bit of use in your talking about five hundred pounds. I simply haven't got it and that's all there's to it. I told you that already. All the same I'm anxious to meet you. How would this do?'

He took the roll of notes from his pocket and threw it on the table. Then he went to his file and got the copy of the letter to the stockbroker. Dunn seized the notes then slowly, caressingly, as if taking a pleasure in their mere feel, he began to count.

'Fifty?' He cackled dryly. 'You always will have your little joke.'

'Read the letter,' Thwaite said impatiently.

Dunn did so, very deliberately. Then very deliberately he finished his whisky and equally deliberately he spoke.

'A sale of stocks for two 'undred an' fifty? You're very jokey tonight, Mr Thwaite.'

'Three hundred, Dunn! Three hundred pounds. Six times that roll of notes. Think of it, man! And I don't say,' Thwaite added, 'that it need necessarily be the last. Don't be a fool, Dunn. Take three hundred to go on with and be thankful.'

Dunn slowly smiled his evil smile.

'Five 'undred, Mr Thwaite,' he repeated. 'My son: I mentioned that—'

Thwaite sprang to his feet and began to pace the room. 'But confound it all, man, haven't I told you I can't do it? Damn it, do you not believe me? Look here.' He pulled out his keys, and going to the built-in safe in the corner of the room, unlocked it, swung the heavy door back, took out his bank-book and slapped it down dramatically on the table. 'Look for yourself. It's posted to this very afternoon.'

Again Dunn cackled thinly. 'A book, Mr Thwaite? You surprise me, sir. Surely a man of your skill with books wouldn't ask a friend like me to believe in a book?'

Thwaite felt a slight relief. The old fool was making his task easier for him. He ignored the gibe.

'Well, I've made you an offer,' he said. 'Fifty pounds now and two hundred and fifty more as soon as my stockbrokers can realise. Take it or leave it. But I tell you seriously that if you don't take it you'll get nothing. I'm at the end of my tether. I'm going to have done with all this.'

'An' may I ask 'ow?'

'You may. I'm going to let you put in your information. It's five years old and I've served the firm well since then. I've saved them a good deal more than that thousand. I'll sell this house and pay the money back with interest. I'll take my medicine, it won't be very much under the circumstances, and then I'll go abroad under a new name and start fresh.'

'Your wife, sir?'

Thwaite swung round. 'Damn you, it's none of your business,' he said angrily. Then more calmly: 'My wife will leave the country first, if you want to know. She'll be waiting for me under the new name when I get out; you'll not know where. She'll wait for me, two or three years; it can't be more. That's what'll happen. You can take your three hundred; I'll make it three hundred a year. Or you can do the other.'

Dunn sat staring at him, rather stupidly. The drug was acting already. Thwaite got a momentary panic that he had given him too much.

'Well,' he said sharply, glancing at the clock. Time was nearly up. 'What about it? Will you take it or leave it?'

'Five 'undred,' Dunn persisted in a slightly thick voice. 'Five 'undred I want. Not a penny less.'

'Right,' Thwaite returned promptly. 'That settles it. Now you can go and do your worst. I've done with you.'

Dunn gazed at him vacantly. Then he leered. 'No darned fear, you 'aven't, Mr Thwaite,' he muttered tipsily. 'Not you. Not such a fool, you ain't. Come, pay up.' He slowly held out a shaking hand. 'Five 'un'red.'

Thwaite glanced at him in real anxiety. 'Not feeling well, Dunn? Have a drop more whisky?' Without waiting for a reply he opened the fresh bottle and poured out a further tot. The clerk sipped it, and it seemed to pull him together.

'Strange, that, Mr Thwaite,' he remarked. 'I did feel a bit giddy for a time. But I'm better now. Indigestion, I expect.'

'I dare say. Well, if you're going on this train it's time you started. Sleep on this business and let me know your decision tomorrow. Take the fifty in any case.'

The man demurred, but he could not resist the notes and slowly put them in his pocket. Then he looked at his watch and from it to the clock.

'Your clock's fast,' he declared.

'I don't think so.' He looked at his own wristwatch. 'No, you must be slow. See here.'

Dunn seemed a trifle bemused. He stood up, swaying slightly. Thwaite congratulated himself. It was exactly the condition he had hoped for.

'Look here,' he said, 'you're not quite fit yet. I'll see you to the station. Wait till I get my coat.'

Now that the moment was upon him, Thwaite felt cool and efficient, master of himself and of the situation. He put on his coat, feeling the hammer in the pocket.

'Come along,' he said. 'We'll go out this way. Give me your arm.'

The study was entered from a passage leading from the main hall to a side door into the garden. This door Thwaite now opened, and when they had passed through, drew it noiselessly to behind him. Presently he would return, let himself in as noiselessly, alter the clock and his watch, make a noisy passage to the hall door, bid someone a cordial good night, and slam the door. At once he would ring, on the pretext that he was working late and wanted more coffee, and when the servant came he would draw her attention to the hour in explaining when to bring it. This would establish, first, that he, Thwaite, had not left the house, and second, that his victim had gone at the proper time to catch his train. These two admitted, his innocence would follow as a matter of course.

It was a fine night, but intensely dark. As they left the house a goods train clanked slowly by. Thwaite almost exulted. His ally! There were plenty of them at this hour. It was on one of them he was counting to blot out his crime. A blow on the head with the hammer; through the man's hat there would be no blood; then it would just be necessary to lay the body on the rails clear of the level crossing and the train would do the rest. There would be a few anxious minutes, then—safety!

Slowly the two men passed on, arm in arm. Now they were in the blackness of the shrubbery. Thwaite knew every step. He had brought the torch, only in case of emergency. A breeze met them, faint, but chill. It moaned dismally among the pines. Somewhere in the distance a dog barked. There was a little movement in the shrubs; a rabbit perhaps, or a cat. Thwaite's heart began to pump as he steered his unconscious victim towards his dreadful goal. Now they were going down the hide sidewalk to the gate. Now they were at the gate, were passing through, were in the lane. Not twenty yards away was the crossing.

It seemed to Thwaite that he had lost his personality as they walked that twenty yards. From a distance he, the real Thwaite, watched this automaton which bore his shape. His brain was numb. Something had to be done by this automaton, something nasty, and with detached interest he watched its performance. They reached the crossing and halted at the wicket. Save for the faint moan of the wind and the rumble of a car on the road all was still. Thwaite grasped the hammer. The moment was upon him.

Then he gave a sudden gasp as a thought flashed devastatingly into his mind. It hit him like a physical blow. He could not do it! He had made a mistake. He had given himself away. For that night at least, Dunn was as safe as if he were surrounded by a legion of angels with flaming swords.

His keys! He had left them in the safe. Without them he

could not get back into the house. He would have to ring. And if he had been out, no one would believe he had not gone at least as far as the crossing. It was too close to the house. Thwaite leaned against the wicket, grimly remembering his cocksure superiority as he had marvelled at the mistakes of murderers.

Then a rush of relief, almost painful in its intensity, swept over him. What if he had not remembered? Another minute and he would now be a murderer himself, fleeing from justice. The rope would be as good as about his neck. Nothing could have saved him.

The sudden revulsion of feeling unnerved him. For the moment he felt he could stand no more of Dunn. Unsteadily he murmured a good night and a safe home. Turning, he staggered back along the lane.

For ten minutes he paced up and down till he felt his manner had become normal. Then he rang at his door.

'Thank you, Jane,' he said automatically. He still felt in a dream. 'I went to see Mr Dunn over the crossing and forgot my keys.'

His relief at his escape had been instantaneous. Now to his surprise he found another and a deeper relief growing up within him. He was not a murderer! Now he began to see in its true proportions the hideousness of the crime. He felt that his vision had been the truth. If he had done what he intended he would never have got rid of Dunn's eyes. Peace, safety, happiness, assurance? He would never have known one of them! He would have changed his present thraldom for a slavery ten times as severe.

Light-heartedly and thankfully he went to bed. Light-heartedly and thankfully he got up next morning. He would be done with the whole horrid nightmare. That very day he would make a clean breast to the manager, take his medicine, and know peace once again.

And then at breakfast the blow fell. Jane, her eyes starting from her head, burst into the room.

'Have you heard the news, sir?' she cried. 'The milkman has just told me. Mr Dunn was killed last night; run over at the crossing! The platelayers found him this morning terribly cut up!'

Thwaite slowly turned a dead white. What had he told the girl last night? Already she was staring at him curiously. What could she be thinking?

With a superhuman effort, he pulled himself together. 'Bless my soul!' he exclaimed in shocked accents as he rose from the table. 'Dunn killed! Good Heavens, Jane, how terrible! I'll go down.'

He went down. Already the body had been removed to an adjoining platelayers' hut and the police were in charge. The sergeant saluted as Thwaite appeared.

'Sad affair this, Mr Thwaite,' he said cheerily. 'You knew the old gentleman, didn't you, sir?'

'Knew him?' Thwaite returned. 'Of course I knew him. He worked in my own office. Why, he was with me last night; going into some business, it must have been when he was leaving me that this happened. Awful! It's given me quite a shock.'

'Bound to,' the cheery sergeant sympathised. 'But, Lord, sir, accidents will happen.'

'I know, sergeant, but it's upset me, for I feel a bit responsible about it. He had had a drop too much. I offered him a very moderate drink, but he was evidently not accustomed to it. Of course, it only affected him slightly. All the same, I thought it wise to come out to see him safely to the station.'

The sergeant's expression altered. 'Oh, you came out with him, did you? And did you see him to the station?'

'No, the cold air seemed to make him all right. I turned before we reached the crossing.'

Was that the sergeant's ordinary look, or was he—already?

They came that day to make inquiries. They saw him at the office; presumably they saw the servants also. Thwaite told the truth; that he had gone as far as the wicket and then returned home. They took notes and went away.

Next day they came again.

At the trial the defence made much of the fact that Thwaite had gone openly to the crossing; he had not attempted to hide this action either from the servant or the police. But the defence could not explain the sleeping draught found in the dregs of the decanter and in the stomach of the deceased, nor the fact that the study clock had gone ten minutes fast since dinner-time, when Jane had noticed that it was correct. Nor could they hide the significance of a closely written sheet about ledger entries which was found in a sealed envelope in Dunn's lodgings. Nor yet of certain sums which on certain dates had vanished from Thwaite's bank account, and of similar sums which a few days later had appeared in Dunn's. Finally, the defence could offer no convincing explanation of two facts: the first, ascertained from dark stains on a certain engine, that the tragedy had taken place seven minutes before Thwaite returned to his house; the second, that the kitchen hammer, bearing Thwaite's finger-prints, should be in the pocket of the old coat he wore that night.

On the last dreadful morning Thwaite told the chaplain the exact truth. Then he showed the courage which was expected from him.

The Adventure of the First-Class Carriage

Ronald Knox

Ronald Arbuthnot Knox (1888–1957) was a member of a gifted family and himself a man of many parts: clergyman, broadcaster, translator, compiler of acrostics, and much else besides. In the field of detective fiction, he gained a curious kind of immortality as a result of producing the 'Detectives' Decalogue', ten mostly tongue-in-cheek 'commandments' supposed to promote the principle that whodunit writers should 'play fair' with their readers. He published six detective novels, and a handful of short stories, and was a founder member of the Detection Club.

Knox's love of the genre was fired by a passion for the Sherlock Holmes stories, which he shared with his brother 'Evoe', who later became editor of *Punch*. Their youthful writings about Holmes became the foundation for a paper, 'Studies in the Literature of Sherlock Holmes', which Ronald read to the Gryphon Club in Oxford in 1911, and which earned the approval of Arthur Conan Doyle himself. His other Sherlockian writings included 'Mycroft and Moriarty', an essay included in a book edited by H.W. Bell, *Baker Street Studies* (1934). This entertaining pastiche, Knox's last notable contribution to the crime genre, was published in the February 1947 issue of the *Strand*, and combines pleasing Holmesian touches with an 'impossible crime' scenario.

The general encouragement extended to my efforts by the public is my excuse, if excuse were needed, for continuing to act as chronicler of my friend Sherlock Holmes. But even if I confine myself to those cases in which I have had the honour of being personally associated with him, I find it difficult to make a selection among the large amount of matter at my disposal.

As I turn over my records, I find that some of them deal with events of national or even international importance; but the time has not yet come when it would be safe to disclose (for instance) the true facts about the recent change of government in Paraguay. Others (like the case of the Missing Omnibus) would do more to gratify the modern craving for sensation; but I am well aware that my friend himself is the first to deplore it when I indulge what is, in his own view, a weakness.

My preference is for recording incidents whose bizarre features gave special opportunity for the exercise of that analytical talent which he possessed in such a marked degree. Of these, the case of the Tattooed Nurseryman and that of the Luminous Cigar-Box naturally suggest themselves to the mind. But perhaps my friend's gifts were even more signally displayed when he had occasion to investigate the disappearance of Mr

Nathaniel Swithinbank, which provoked so much speculation in the early days of September, five years back.

Mr Sherlock Holmes was, of all men, the least influenced by what are called class distinctions. To him the rank was but the guinea stamp; a client was a client. And it did not surprise me one evening when I was sitting over the familiar fire in Baker Street—the days were sunny but the evenings were already falling chill—to be told that he was expecting a visit from a domestic servant, a woman who 'did' for a well-to-do, childless couple in the southern Midlands. 'My last visit,' he explained, 'was from a countess. Her mind was uninteresting, and she had no great regard for the truth; the problem she brought was quite elementary. I fancy Mrs John Hennessy will have something more important to communicate.'

'You have met her already, then?'

'No, I have not had the privilege. But anyone who is in the habit of receiving letters from strangers will tell you the same—handwriting is often a better form of introduction than hand-shaking. You will find Mrs Hennessy's letter on the mantelpiece; and if you care to look at her j's and her w's, in particular, I think you will agree that it is no ordinary woman we have to deal with. Dear me, there is the bell ringing already; in a moment or two, if I mistake not, we shall know what Mrs Hennessy, of the Cottage, Guiseborough St Martin, wants of Sherlock Holmes.'

There was nothing in the appearance of the old dame who was shown up, a few minutes later, by the faithful Mrs Hudson to justify Holmes's estimate. To the outward view she was a typical representative of her class; from the bugles on her bonnet to her elastic-sided boots everything suggested the old-fashioned caretaker such as you may see polishing the front doorsteps of a hundred office buildings any spring morning in the city of London. Her voice, when she spoke, was articulated with unnecessary care, as that of the respectable working-class woman is apt to be. But there was something precise and businesslike about the statement of her case which made you feel that this was a mind which could easily have profited by greater educational advantages.

'I have read of you, Mr Holmes,' she began, 'and when things began to go wrong up at the Hall it wasn't long before I thought to myself, if there's one man in England who will be able to see light here, it's Mr Sherlock Holmes. My husband was in good employment, till lately, on the railway at Chester; but the time came when the rheumatism got hold of him, and after that nothing seemed to go well with us until he had thrown up his job, and we went to live in a country village not far from Banbury, looking out for any odd work that might come our way.

'We had only been living there a week when a Mr Swithinbank and his wife took the old Hall, that had long been standing empty. They were newcomers to the district, and their needs were not great, having neither chick nor child to fend for; so they engaged me and Mr Hennessy to come and live in the lodge, close by the house, and do all the work of it for them. The pay was good and the duties light, so we were glad enough to get the billet.'

'One moment!' said Holmes. 'Did they advertise, or were you indebted to some private recommendation for the appointment?'

'They came at short notice, Mr Holmes, and were directed to us for temporary help. But they soon saw that our ways suited them, and they kept us on. They were people who kept very much to themselves, and perhaps they did not want a set of maids who would have followers, and spread gossip in the village.'

'That is suggestive. You state your case with admirable clearness. Pray proceed.'

'All this was no longer ago than last July. Since then they have once been away in London, but for the most part they have lived at Guiseborough, seeing very little of the folk round about. Parson called, but he is not a man to put his nose in where he is not wanted, and I think they must have made it clear they would sooner have his room than his company. So there was more guessing than gossiping about them in the countryside. But, sir, you can't be in domestic employment without finding out a good deal about how the land lies; and it wasn't long before my husband and I were certain of two things. One was that Mr and Mrs Swithinbank were deep in debt. And the other was that they got on badly together.'

'Debts have a way of reflecting themselves in a man's correspondence,' said Holmes, 'and whoever has the clearing of his waste-paper basket will necessarily be conscious of them. But the relations between man and wife? Surely they must have gone very wrong indeed before there is quarrelling in public.'

'That's as may be, Mr Holmes, but quarrel in public they did. Why, it was only last week I came in with the blancmange, and he was saying, *The fact is, no one would be better pleased than you to see me in my coffin.* To be sure, he held his tongue after that, and looked a bit confused; and she tried to put a brave face on it. But I've lived long enough, Mr Holmes, to know when a woman's been crying. Then last Monday, when I'd been in drawing the curtains, he burst out just before I'd closed the door behind me, *The world isn't big enough for both of us.* That was all I heard, and right glad I'd have been to hear less. But I've not come round here just to repeat servants'-hall gossip.

'Today, when I was cleaning out the waste-paper basket, I came across a scrap of a letter that tells the same story, in his own handwriting. Cast your eye over that, Mr Holmes, and tell me whether a Christian woman has the right to sit by and do nothing about it.'

She had dived her hand into a capacious reticule and brought out, with a triumphant flourish, her documentary evidence. Holmes knitted his brow over it, and then passed it on to me. It ran: 'Being of sound mind, whatever the num-skulls on the jury may say of it.'

'Can you identify the writing?' my friend said.

'It was my master's,' replied Mrs Hennessy. 'I know it well enough; the bank, I am sure, will tell you the same.'

'Mrs Hennessy, let us make no bones about it. Curiosity is a well-marked instinct of the human species. Your eye having lighted on this document, no doubt inadvertently, I will wager you took a look round the basket for any other fragments it might contain.'

'That I did, sir; my husband and I went through it carefully together, for who knew but the life of a fellow-creature might depend on it? But only one other piece could we find written by the same hand, and on the same note-paper. Here it is.' And she smoothed out on her knee a second fragment, to all appearances part of the same sheet, yet strangely different in its tenor. It seemed to have been torn away from the middle of a sentence; nothing survived but the words 'in the reeds by the lake, taking a bearing at the point where the old tower hides both the middle first-floor windows'.

'Come,' I said, 'this at least gives us something to go upon. Mrs Hennessy will surely be able to tell us whether there are any landmarks in Guiseborough answering to this description.'

'Indeed there are, sir; the directions are plain as a pike-staff. There is an old ruined building which juts out upon the little lake at the bottom of the garden, and it would be easy enough to hit on the place mentioned. I daresay you gentlemen are wondering why we haven't been down to the lake-side ourselves to see what we could find there. Well, the plain fact is, we were scared. My master is a quiet-spoken man enough at ordinary times, but there's a wild look in his eye when he's roused, and I for one should be sorry to cross him. So I thought I'd come to you, Mr Holmes, and put the whole thing in your hands.'

'I shall be interested to look into your little difficulty. To speak frankly, Mrs Hennessy, the story you have told me runs on such familiar lines that I should have been tempted to dismiss the whole case from my mind. Dr Watson here will tell you that I am a busy man, and the affairs of the Bank of Mauritius urgently require my presence in London. But this last detail about the reeds by the lake-side is piquant, decidedly piquant, and the whole matter shall be gone into. The only difficulty is a practical one. How are we to explain my presence at Guiseborough without betraying to your employers the fact that you and your husband have been intruding on their family affairs?'

'I have thought of that, sir,' replied the old dame, 'and I think we can find a way out. I slipped away today easily enough because my mistress is going abroad to visit her aunt, near Dieppe, and Mr Swithinbank has come up to Town with her to see her off. I must go back by the evening train, and had half thought of asking you to accompany me. But no, he would get to hear of it if a stranger visited the place in his absence. It would be better if you came down by the quarter-past ten train tomorrow, and passed yourself off for a stranger who was coming to look at the house. They have taken it on a short lease, and plenty of folks come to see it without troubling to obtain an order-to-view.'

'Will your employer be back so early?'

'That is the very train he means to take; and to speak truth, sir, I should be the better for knowing that he was being watched. This wicked talk of making away with himself is enough to make anyone anxious about him. You cannot mistake him, Mr Holmes,' she went on; 'what chiefly marks him out is a scar on the left-hand side of his chin, where a dog bit him when he was a youngster.'

'Excellent, Mrs Hennessy; you have thought of everything. Tomorrow, then, on the quarter-past ten for Banbury without fail. You will oblige me by ordering the station fly to be in readiness. Country walks may be good for health, but time is more precious. I will drive straight to your cottage, and you or your husband shall escort me on my visit to this desirable country residence and its mysterious tenant.' With a wave of his hand, he cut short her protestations of gratitude.

'Well, Watson, what did you make of her?' asked my companion when the door had closed on our visitor.

'She seemed typical of that noble army of women whose hard scrubbing makes life easy for the leisured classes. I could not see her well because she sat between us and the window, and her veil was lowered over her eyes. But her manner was enough to convince me that she was telling us the truth, and that she is sincere in her anxiety to avert what may be an appalling tragedy. As to its nature, I confess I am in the dark. Like yourself, I was particularly struck by the reference to the reeds by the lake-side. What can it mean? An assignation?'

'Hardly, my dear Watson. At this time of the year a man runs enough risk of cold without standing about in a reed-bed. A hiding-place, more probably, but for what? And why should a man take the trouble to hide something, and then obligingly litter his waste-paper basket with clues to its whereabouts? No, these are deep waters, Watson, and we must have more data before we begin to theorise. You will come with me?'

'Certainly, if I may. Shall I bring my revolver?'

'I do not apprehend any danger, but perhaps it is as well to be on the safe side. Mr Swithinbank seems to strike his neighbours as a formidable person. And now, if you will be good enough to hand me the more peaceful instrument which hangs beside you, I will try out that air of Scarlatti's, and leave the affairs of Guiseborough St Martin to look after themselves.'

I often had occasion to deprecate Sherlock Holmes's habit of catching trains with just half a minute to spare. But on the morning after our interview with Mrs Hennessy we arrived at Paddington station no later than ten o'clock—to find a stranger, with a pronounced scar on the left side of his chin, gazing out at us languidly from the window of a first-class carriage.

'Do you mean to travel with him?' I asked, when we were out of earshot.

'Scarcely feasible, I think. If he is the man I take him for, he has secured solitude all the way to Banbury by the simple process of slipping half a crown into the guard's hand.'

And, sure enough, a few minutes later we saw that functionary shepherd a fussy-looking gentleman, who had been vigorously assaulting the locked door, to a compartment farther on. For ourselves, we took up our post in the carriage next but one behind Mr Swithinbank. This, like the other first-class compartments, was duly locked when we had entered it; behind us the less fortunate passengers accommodated themselves in seconds.

'The case is not without its interest,' observed Holmes, laying down his paper as we steamed through Burnham Beeches. 'It presents features which recall the affairs of James Phillimore, whose disappearance (though your loyalty may tempt you to forget it) we investigated without success. But this Swithinbank mystery, if I mistake not, cuts even deeper. Why, for example, is the man so anxious to parade his intention of suicide, or fictitious suicide, in the presence of his domestic staff? It can hardly fail to strike you that he chose the moment when the good Mrs Hennessy was just entering the room, or just leaving it, to make those remarkable confidences to his wife. Not content with that, he must leave evidence of his intentions lying about in the waste-paper basket. And yet this involved the risk of having his plans foiled by good-natured interference. Time enough for his disappearance to become public when it became effective! And why, in the name of fortune, does he hide something only to tell us where he has hidden it?'

Amid a maze of railway-tracks, we came to a standstill at Reading. Holmes craned his neck out of the window, but reported that all the doors had been left locked. We were not destined to learn anything about our elusive travelling-companion until, just as we were passing the pretty hamlet of Tilehurst, a little shower of paper fragments fluttered past the window on the right-hand side of the compartment, and two of them actually sailed in through the space we had dedicated to ventilation on that bright morning of autumn. It may easily be guessed with what avidity we pounced on them.

The messages were in the same handwriting with which Mrs Hennessy's find had made us familiar; they ran, respectively,

'Mean to make an end of it all' and 'This is the only way out.' Holmes sat over them with knitted brows, till I fairly danced with impatience.

'Should we not pull the communication-cord?' I asked.

'Hardly,' answered my companion, 'unless five-pound notes are more plentiful with you than they used to be. I will even anticipate your next suggestion, which is that we should look out of the windows on either side of the carriage. Either we have a lunatic two doors off, in which case there is no use in trying to foresee his next move, or he intends suicide, in which case he will not be deterred by the presence of spectators, or he is a man with a scheming brain who is sending us these messages in order to make us behave in a particular way. Quite possibly, he wants to make us lean out of the windows, which seems to me an excellent reason for not leaning out of the windows. At Oxford we shall be able to read the guard a lesson on the danger of locking passengers in.'

So indeed it proved; for when the train stopped at Oxford there was no passenger to be found in Mr Swithinbank's carriage. His overcoat remained, and his wide-awake hat; his portmanteau was duly identified in the guard's van. The door on the right-hand side of the compartment, away from the platform, had swung open; nor did Holmes's lens bring to light any details about the way in which the elusive passenger had made his exit.

It was an impatient horse and an injured cabman that awaited us at Banbury, when we drove through golden woodlands to the little village of Guiseborough St Martin, nestling under the shadow of Edge Hill. Mrs Hennessy met us at the door of her cottage, dropping an old-fashioned curtsy; and it may easily be imagined what wringing of hands, what wiping of eyes with her apron, greeted the announcement of her master's disappearance. Mr Hennessy, it seemed, had gone off to a neighbouring farm upon some errand, and it was the old dame herself who escorted us up to the Hall.

'There's a gentleman there already, Mr Holmes,' she informed us. 'Arrived early this morning and would take no denial; and not a word to say what business he came on.'

'That is unfortunate,' said Holmes. 'I particularly wanted a free field to make some investigations. Let us hope that he will be good enough to clear off when he is told that there is no chance of an interview with Mr Swithinbank.'

Guiseborough Hall stands in its own grounds a little way outside the village, the residence of a squire unmistakably, but with no airs of baronial grandeur. The old, rough walls have been refaced with pointed stone, the mullioned windows exchanged for a generous expanse of plate-glass, to suit a more recent taste, and a portico has been thrown out from the front door to welcome the traveller with its shelter. The garden descends at a precipitous slope from the main terrace, and a little lake fringes it at the bottom, dominated by a ruined eminence that serves the modern owner for a gazebo.

Within the house, furniture was of the scantiest, the Swithinbanks having evidently rented it with what fittings it had, and introduced little of their own. As Mrs Hennessy ushered us into the drawing-room, we were not a little surprised to be greeted by the wiry figure and melancholy features of our old rival, Inspector Lestrade.

'I knew you were quick off the mark, Mr Holmes,' he said, 'but it beats me how you ever heard of Mr Swithinbank's little goings-on; let alone that I didn't think you took much stock in cases of common fraud like this.'

'Common fraud?' repeated my companion. 'Why, what has he been up to?'

'Drawing cheques, and big ones, Mr Holmes, when he knew that his bank wouldn't honour them; only little things of that sort. But if you're on his track I don't suppose he's far off, and I'll be grateful for any help you can give me to lay my hands on him.'

'My dear Lestrade, if you follow out your usual systematic methods, you will have to patrol the Great Western line all the way from Reading to Oxford. I trust you have brought a drag-net with you, for the line crossed the river no less than four times in the course of the journey.' And he regaled the astonished inspector with a brief summary of our investigations.

Our information worked like a charm on the little detective. He was off in a moment to find the nearest telegraph office and put himself in touch with Scotland Yard, with the Great Western Railway authorities, with the Thames Conservancy. He promised, however, a speedy return, and I fancy Holmes cursed himself for not having dismissed the jarvey who had brought us from the station, an undeserved windfall for our rival.

'Now, Watson!' he cried, as the sound of the wheels faded away into the distance.

'Our way lies to the lake-side, I presume.'

'How often am I to remind you that the place where the criminal tells you to look is the place not to look? No, the clue to the mystery lies, somehow, in the house, and we must hurry up if we are to find it.'

Quick as a thought, he began turning out shelves, cupboards, escritoires, while I, at his direction, went through the various rooms of the house to ascertain whether all was in order, and whether anything suggested the anticipation of a hasty flight. By the time I returned to him, having found nothing amiss, he was seated in the most comfortable of the drawing-room arm-chairs, reading a book he had picked out of the shelves—it dealt, if I remember right, with the aborigines of Borneo.

'The mystery, Holmes!' I cried.

'I have solved it. If you will look on the bureau yonder, you will find the household books which Mrs Swithinbank has obligingly left behind. Extraordinary how these people always make some elementary mistake. You are a man of the world, Watson; take a look at them and tell me what strikes you as curious.'

It was not long before the salient feature occurred to me. 'Why, Holmes,' I exclaimed, 'there is no record of the Hennessys being paid any wages at all!'

'Bravo, Watson! And if you will go into the figures a little more closely, you will find that the Hennessys apparently lived on air. So now the whole facts of the story are plain to you.'

'I confess,' I replied, somewhat crestfallen, 'that the whole case is as dark to me as ever.'

'Why, then, take a look at that newspaper I have left on the occasional table; I have marked the important paragraph in blue pencil.'

It was a copy of an Australian paper, issued some weeks previously. The paragraph to which Holmes had drawn my attention ran thus:

ROMANCE OF RICH MAN'S WILL

The recent lamented death of Mr John Macready, the well-known sheep-farming magnate, has had an unexpected sequel in the circumstance that the dead man, apparently, left no will. His son,

Mr Alexander Macready, left for England some years back, owing to a misunderstanding with his father—it was said—because he announced his intention of marrying a lady from the stage. The young man has completely disappeared, and energetic steps are being taken by the lawyers to trace his whereabouts. It is estimated that the fortunate heirs, whoever they be, will be the richer by not far short of a hundred thousand pounds sterling.

Horse-hoofs echoed under the archway, and in another minute Lestrade was again of our party. Seldom have I seen the little detective looking so baffled and ill at ease. 'They'll have the laugh of me at the Yard over this,' he said. 'We had word that Swithinbank was in London, but I made sure it was only a feint, and I came racing up here by the early train, instead of catching the quarter-past ten and my man in it. He's a slippery devil, and he may be half-way to the Continent by this time.'

'Don't be down-hearted about it, Lestrade. Come and interview Mr and Mrs Hennessy, at the lodge; we may get news of your man down there.'

A coarse-looking fellow in a bushy red beard sat sharing his tea with our friend of the evening before. His greasy waistcoat and corduroy trousers proclaimed him a manual worker. He rose to meet us with something of a defiant air; his wife was all affability.

'Have you heard any news of the poor gentleman?' she asked.

'We may have some before long,' answered Holmes. 'Lestrade, you might arrest John Hennessy for stealing that porter's cap you see on the dresser, the property of the

Great Western Railway Company. Or, if you prefer an alternative charge, you might arrest him as Alexander Macready, *alias* Nathaniel Swithinbank.' And while we stood there literally thunderstruck, he tore off the red beard from a chin marked with a scar on the left-hand side.

———

'The case was difficult,' he said to me afterwards, 'only because we had no clue to the motive. Swithinbank's debts would almost have swallowed up Macready's legacy; it was necessary for the couple to disappear, and take up the claim under a fresh *alias.* This meant a duplication of personalities, but it was not really difficult. She had been an actress; he had really been a railway porter in his hard-up days. When he got out at Reading, and passed along the six-foot way to take his place in a third-class carriage, nobody marked the circumstance, because on the way from London he had changed into a porter's clothes; he had the cap, no doubt, in his pocket. On the sill of the door he left open, he had made a little pile of suicide-messages, hoping that when it swung open these would be shaken out and flutter into the carriages behind.'

'But why the visit to London? And, above all, why the visit to Baker Street?'

'That is the most amusing part of the story; we should have seen through it at once. He wanted Nathaniel Swithinbank to disappear finally, beyond all hope of tracing him. And who would hope to trace him, when Mr Sherlock Holmes, who was travelling only two carriages behind, had given up the attempt? Their only fear was that I should find the case uninteresting; hence the random reference to a hiding-place

among the reeds, which so intrigued you. Come to think of
it, they nearly had Inspector Lestrade in the same train as
well. I hear he has won golden opinions with his superiors by
cornering his man so neatly. *Sic vos non vobis*, as Virgil said of
the bees; only they tell us nowadays the lines are not by Virgil.'

Murder on the 7.16

Michael Innes

The Edinburgh-born academic John Innes Mackintosh Stewart (1906–1994) chose the pen-name Michael Innes when he tried his hand at writing a detective novel set in Oxford, where he wrote *Death at the President's Lodgings* (1936; known as *Seven Suspects* in the United States), which introduced the likeable and learned policeman John Appleby and made an immediate impression. Innes' career as a crime writer lasted for half a century; Appleby earned a knighthood and, like Paul Beck senior and Dora Myrl, he had a son who followed in his footsteps. Under his own name, Innes also became a prolific author of mainstream novels, in addition to publishing non-fiction studies of authors as varied as James Joyce, Thomas Love Peacock, and Rudyard Kipling.

An enjoyable and interesting posthumous book, *Appleby Talks about Crime* (2010), gathered eighteen previously uncollected stories, included a memoir by the author's daughter, and reprinted an essay by Innes himself, in which he said of the stories, with characteristic modesty: 'The social scene may be embalmed, in that baronets abound in their libraries and butlers peer out of every pantry. But Appleby himself ages, and in some respects perhaps even matures. He ages along with his creator, and like his creator ends up as a retired man who still a little meddles with the concerns of his green unknowing youth.' Several of Innes' mysteries feature rail travel; this one was included in an earlier collection, *Appleby Talks Again* (1956).

———

Appleby looked at the railway carriage for a moment in silence. 'You couldn't call it rolling-stock,' he said.

This was true. The carriage stood not on wheels but on trestles. And it had other peculiarities. On the far side of the corridor all was in order; sliding doors, plenty of plate glass, and compartments with what appeared to be comfortably upholstered seats. But the corridor itself was simply a broad platform ending in air. Mechanically propelled contrivances could manoeuvre on it easily. That, of course, was the idea.

Appleby swung himself up and peered through one of the compartments at what lay beyond. He saw nothing but a large white concave surface. 'Monotonous view,' he murmured. 'Not for lovers of the picturesque.'

The Producer laughed shortly. 'You should see it when we're shooting the damned thing. The diorama, you know. Project whole landscapes on that, we do. They hurtle past. And rock gently. It's terrific.' Realising that his enthusiasm was unseemly, he checked himself and frowned. 'Well, you'd better view the body. Several of your people on the job already, I may say.'

Appleby nodded and moved along the hypertrophied corridor. 'What are you filming?' he asked.

'It's a thriller. I've no use for trains, if they're not in a thriller—or for thrillers, if there isn't a train.' The Producer didn't pause on this generalisation. 'Just cast your mind back a bit, Sir John. Cast it back to September, 1955.'

Appleby considered. 'The tail end of a hot, dry summer.'

'Quite so. But there was something else. Do you remember one of the evening papers running a series of short mystery stories, each called "Murder on the 7.16"?'

'Yes. Oddly enough, I think I do.'

'We're filming one of them.'

'In fact, this *is* the 7.16?' Appleby, although accustomed to bizarre occasions, was looking at the Producer in some astonishment. 'And perhaps you're going to tell me that the murdered man is the fellow who wrote the story?'

'Good lord, no!' The Producer was rather shocked. 'You don't imagine, Sir John, we'd insist on having you along to investigate the death of anyone like that. This corpse is important. Or was important, I suppose I should say. Our ace director. Lemuel Whale.'

'Fellow who does those utterly mad and freakish affairs?'

'That's him. Marvellous hand at putting across his own crazy vision of things. Brilliant—quite brilliant.'

———

It seemed that Whale was in the habit of letting himself into the studios at all hours, and wandering round the sets. He got his inspiration that way. Or he got part of it that way and part of it from a flask of brandy. If he was feeling sociable, and the brandy was holding out, he would pay a visit to Ferrett, the night-watchman, before he left. They would have a drink together, and then Whale would clear out in his car.

This time Ferrett hadn't seen Whale—or not alive. That, at least, was his story. He had been aware that Whale was about, because quite early on this winter night he had seen lights going on here and there. But he hadn't received a visit. And when there was still a light on in this studio at 4 a.m. he went to turn it off. He supposed Whale had just forgotten about it. Everything seemed quite in order—but nevertheless something had prompted him to climb up and take a look at the 7.16. He liked trains, anyway. Had done ever since he was a kid. Whale was in the end compartment, quite dead. He had been bludgeoned.

―――――

Ferrett's was an unsupported story—and at the best it must be said that he took his duties lightly. He might have to be questioned very closely. But at present Appleby wanted to ask him only one thing. 'Just what was it that made you climb up and look through this so-called 7.16?'

For a moment the man was silent. He looked stupid but not uneasy. 'I tell you, I always liked them. The sound of them. The smell of them. Excited me ever since I was a nipper.'

'But you've seen this affair in the studio often enough, haven't you? And, after all, it's *not* a train. There wasn't any sound or smell here?'

'There weren't no sound. But there was the smell, all right.'

'Rubbish, Ferrett. If there was any smell, it was of Whale's cursed brandy.' It was the Producer who broke in. 'This place makes talkies—not feelies or tasties or smellies. *This* train just doesn't smell of train. And it never did.'

Appleby shook his head. 'As a matter of fact, you're wrong.

I've got a very keen nose, as it happens. And that compartment—the one in which Whale died—does, very faintly, smell of trains. I'm going to have another look.' And Appleby returned to the compartment from which Whale's body had just been removed. When he reappeared he was frowning. 'At first one notices only the oceans of blood. Anything nasty happening to a scalp does that. But there's something else. That split-new upholstery on one side is slightly soiled. What it suggests to me is somebody in an oily boiler-suit.'

The Producer was impatient. 'Nobody like that comes here. It just doesn't make sense.'

'Unsolved mysteries seldom do.' Appleby turned back to Ferrett. 'What lights were on when you came in here?'

'Only the line of lights in the 7.16 itself, sir. Not bright, they weren't. But enough for me to—'

Ferrett was interrupted by a shout from the centre of the studio. A man in shirt-sleeves was hurrying forward, gesticulating wrathfully. The Producer turned on him. 'What the devil is wrong with you?'

'It's not merely Whale's flaming head that's suffering in this affair. It's my projector too. Somebody's taken a bleeding hammer to it. I call that beyond a joke.'

Appleby nodded gravely. 'This whole affair went beyond a joke, I agree. But I've a notion it certainly began in one.'

There was a moment's perplexed silence, and then another newcomer presented himself in the form of a uniformed sergeant of police. He walked straight up to Appleby. 'A fellow called Slack,' he murmured. 'Railway linesman. Turned up at the local station in a great state. Says he reckons he did something pretty bad somewhere round about here last night.'

Appleby nodded sombrely. 'I'm afraid, poor devil, he's right.'

'You didn't know,' Appleby asked next day, 'that there's a real 7.16 p.m. from your nearest railway station?'

The Producer shook his head. 'Never travel on trains.'

'Well, there is. And Slack was straying along the road, muttering that he'd missed it, when Whale stopped his car and picked him up. Whale was already a bit tight, and he supposed that Slack was very tight indeed. Actually Slack has queer fits—loses his memory, wanders off, and so on— and this was one of them. That was why he was still in his oil-soaked work-clothes, and still carrying the long-handled hammer-affair he goes about tapping things with. There just wasn't any liquor in Slack at all. But Whale, in his own fuddled state, had no notion of what he was dealing with. And so he thought up his funny joke.'

'He always was a damned freakish fool over such things.' The Producer spoke energetically. 'A funny joke with *our* 7.16?'

'Precisely. It was the coincidence that put it in his head. He promised Slack to get him to his train at the next station. And then he drove him here. It was already dark, of course, and he found it enormous fun kidding this drunk—as he still thought him—that they were making it by the skin of their teeth. That sort of thing. No doubt there was a certain professional vanity involved. When he'd got Slack into that compartment, and turned on your gadget for setting scenery hurtling by, it was too amusing for words. Then he overreached himself.'

'How do you mean?'

'If the doctors who've seen Slack have got it straight, it was like this. Whale suddenly took on the part of a homicidal maniac. His idea was to make Slack jump from what

Slack believed to be a fast-moving train. Only Slack didn't jump. He struck.' Appleby paused. 'And you can imagine him afterwards—wandering in utter bewilderment and panic through this fantastic place. He had another fit of destruction—I suppose your diorama-gadget makes a noise that attracted him—and then he found a way out. He came to his senses—or part of them—early yesterday, and went straight to the police.'

The Producer had brought out a handkerchief and was mopping his forehead. 'Slack won't be—?'

'No, no. Nothing like that. His story must be true, because he couldn't conceivably have invented it.'

'A plea of insanity?'

Appleby shook his head. 'You don't need to plead insanity if you defend yourself against a chap you have every reason to suppose insane. Whale's will be death by misadventure.'

The Producer drew a deep breath. 'A ghastly business. But I'm glad it wasn't a real murder.'

Appleby smiled. 'That's only appropriate, I suppose. It wasn't a real train.'

The Coulman Handicap

Michael Gilbert

Michael Francis Gilbert (1912–2006) achieved great distinction as a crime writer without ever becoming a household name. That was partly due to his personal reticence—he was a practising solicitor, and during his career, professional rules prevented any form of perceived 'advertising' by lawyers. It was also, perhaps, attributable to his unwillingness to stick to a single formula, far less keep writing about a *single* series character; in fact, he created more than half a dozen noteworthy series detectives, including Patrick Petrella, who features in this story, collected in *Young Petrella* (1988), but published in the 1950s.

Novels, plays, scripts, and non-fiction poured from Gilbert's pen (prior to his retirement from the law, he wrote on the morning train to his office in Lincoln's Inn), while there are few British crime writers of the last half-century who have written such accomplished short mysteries. Many of these first appeared in magazines that have long since vanished from the scene; happily, in recent years the critic and researcher John Cooper has gathered all Gilbert's uncollected stories, as well as other material, in four volumes which amount to a treasure trove in which the author's talent for the form is vividly displayed.

––––––––––

The door of No. 35 Bond Road opened and a thick-set, middle-aged woman came out. She wore a long grey coat with a collar of alpaca wool buttoned to the neck, a light grey hat well forward on her head, and mid-grey gloves on her hands. Her sensible shoes, her stockings, and the large, fabric-covered suitcase, which she carried in her right hand, were brown.

She paused for a moment on the step. Women of her age are often near-sighted, but there was nothing in her attitude to suggest this. She had bold, brown, somewhat protuberant eyes, set far apart in her strong face. They were not unlike the eyes of an intelligent horse.

She looked carefully to left and to right. Bond Road was never a bustling thoroughfare. At twelve o'clock on that bright morning of early April it was almost empty. A roadman, sweeping the gutter; a grocer's delivery boy, pushing his bicycle blindly, nose down in a comic; the postman, on his mid-morning round. All of them were well known to her. She waited to see if the postman had brought her anything, and then set off up the pavement.

In the front parlour of No. 34, a lace curtain parted one inch and closed again. The man sitting on a chair in the bow window reached for the telephone which stood by his hand and dialled.

He heard a click as the receiver was lifted at the other end and said, 'She's off. Going west.' Then he replaced the receiver and lit himself a cigarette. The stubs in the tray beside the telephone suggested that he had been waiting for some time.

At that moment no fewer than twenty-four people, in one way or another, were concentrating their attention on Bond Road and on Mrs Coulman, who lived at No. 35.

'It's a carrier service,' said Superintendent Palance of S Division, who was in charge of the joint operation, 'and it's got to be stopped.' Jimmy Palance was known throughout the Metropolitan Police Force as a fine organiser, a teetotaller, a man entirely lacking in any sense of humour, who worked with a Pawnbrokers' List and the Holy Bible side by side on his tidy desk.

'The first problem of a thief who steals valuable and identifiable jewellery is to get rid of it. What does he do with it?'

'Flogs it?' suggested Superintendent Haxtell of Q Division.

'No fence'll touch it,' said Superintendent Farmer of X Division. 'Not while the heat's on.'

'Then he hides it,' said Haxtell. 'In a safe deposit, or a bank. Crooks do have bank accounts, you know.'

'Or a cloakroom, or a left-luggage office.'

'Or with a friend, or at an accommodation address.'

'Or sealed up in a tin, under the third tree from the corner.'

'No doubt,' said Superintendent Palance, raising his heavy black eyebrows, 'there are a great number of possible hiding-places; I myself have listed twenty-seven distinct types. There may be more. The difficulty is that by the time the thief wishes to recover his loot, he is as often as not himself under observation.'

Neither Haxtell nor Farmer questioned this statement. They knew well enough that it was true. A complicated system of informers almost always gave them the name of the perpetrator of any big and successful burglary. 'All we then have to arrange is to watch the thief. If he goes near the stuff we will be able to lay hands on the man himself, and his cache, and his receiver.'

'True,' said Haxtell. 'So what does he do?'

'He gets in touch with Mrs Coulman. And informs her where he has placed the stuff. Gives her the key, or cloakroom ticket, and leaves the rest to her. It is not even necessary to give her the name of the receiver. She knows them all, and gets the best prices. She gets paid in cash, keeps a third, and hands over two-thirds to the author of the crime.'

'Just like a literary agent,' said Farmer, who had once written a short story.

'Sounds quite a woman,' said Haxtell.

'She has curious antecedents,' said Palance. 'She is German. And I believe, although I've not been able to check it, that she and her brothers were in the German Resistance.'

'The fact that she's alive proves she was clever,' agreed Haxtell. 'Now, I gather you want quite a few men for this. Tell us how you plan to tackle it.'

'It's going to be a complicated job,' said Palance. 'But here is the outline...'

At the end of the street, after turning into the main road, Mrs Coulman had a choice of transport. She could take a bus going south, or could cross the street and take a bus going north. Or she could walk two hundred yards down the hill to the Underground Station, or an equal distance up it to another. Or she could take a taxi. She was a thick woman of ample Teutonic build, and experience, gained in the last month of observation, had suggested that she would not walk very far.

Near each bus stop a man and girl were talking. Opposite the Underground a pair of workmen sat, drinking endless cups of tea. In a side street two taxis waited, a driving glove over the meter indicating that they were not for hire. A small tradesman's van, parked in a cul-de-sac, acted as mobile headquarters to this part of the operation. It was backed halfway into a private garage, chosen because it was on the telephone.

Mrs Coulman proceeded placidly to the far end of Bond Road, waited for a gap in the traffic, crossed the main road, and turned up a side road beyond it.

An outburst of intense activity followed.

'Still going west,' said the controller in the van. 'Making for Highside Park. Details one to eight, switch in that direction. Number one car straight up Loudon Road and stop. Number two car parallel. Details nine and ten, cover Highside Tube Station and the bus stops at the top of the hill.'

Mrs Coulman emerged, panting slightly, from the side road which gave onto the top of Highside Hill, paused, and caused consternation in the ranks of her pursuers by turning round and walking back the way she had come.

Control had just worked out the necessary orders to jerk the machine into reverse when it was seen that Mrs Coulman had retraced her steps to admire a flowering shrub in a front garden she had passed. Looking carefully about her to see that no one was watching, she nipped off a small spray and put it in her buttonhole. Then she turned back towards Highside Hill and made, without further check, for the Tube Station.

Details number nine and ten were Detective Sergeants Petrella and Wynne. They were waiting inside the station, at the head of the emergency stairs, and were already equipped with all-day tickets. When Mrs Coulman reached the station entrance, therefore, she found it deserted. She bought a ticket for Euston and took the lift. A young man in corduroys and a raincoat, and an older one in flannel trousers, a windcheater, and a club scarf were already on the platform, waiting for the train. They got into the coaches on either side of her.

Above their heads the machine jerked abruptly into top gear. A word was exchanged with the booking-office clerk and two taxis sped towards Euston.

Mrs Coulman, however, had disconcertingly changed her mind. Euston, Goodge Street, Tottenham Court Road— station after station came and went and still she sat on. Her seat had been chosen to command the exits of her own and the two neighbouring carriages. She seemed to take a close interest in the people who got on and off. But if she noticed that the men who had come from Highside were still with her, she gave no sign.

It was nearly half an hour later when she quitted the train at Clapham Common Station and made for the moving staircase, looking neither to right nor to left.

Petrella had time for a quick word with Wynne. 'It's my belief the old bitch has rumbled us,' he said. 'Get on the blower and bring the rest of the gang down here, as quickly as possible. Meanwhile, I'll do my best to keep on her tail.'

This proved easy. Mrs Coulman walked down the street without so much as a backward glance, and disappeared into the saloon bar of The Admiral Keppel public house. Petrella made a detour of the place to ensure that it had no back entrance, and settled down to watch. It could hardly have been better situated for his purpose. The doors of its saloon and public bar opened side by side onto the same strip of pavement. Opposite them stood a sandwich bar, with a telephone.

'I don't think we ought to crowd the old girl,' said Petrella into the telephone. 'It's my impression she's got eyes in the back of her head. If you could send someone—not Wynne, she seen too much of him already this morning—and put a man at either end of the street, so that *we* don't have to follow immediately she goes—'

The voice at the other end approved these arrangements. Time passed. Petrella saw Detective Constable Mote ambling down the pavement, and he flagged him in.

'She's been there a long time,' he said. 'It must be nearly closing time.'

'Sure she hasn't come out?' said Mote.

Petrella looked at his little book. 'Two business men,' he said. 'One youth with a girl-friend, aged about seventeen and skinny. One sailor with a kitbag. That's the score to date.'

The door of the public bar opened and three men came out and stood talking to the landlord, who seemed to know them. The men went off down the road together, the landlord disappeared inside, and they heard the sound of bolts being shut.

'Hey,' said Petrella. 'What's all this?'

'It's all right. There's still someone in the saloon bar,' said Mote. 'I can see the shadow on the glass. Seems to be knocking her drink back.'

'Slip across and have a look,' said Petrella.

Mote crossed the road lower down and strolled up past the ground-glass window of the saloon bar.

'It's a woman,' he reported. 'Sitting in the corner, drinking. I think the landlord's trying to turn her out.'

As he spoke the door was flung open and the last of the

customers appeared. She was the same shape as Mrs Coulman; but she seemed to have changed her hat and coat, and to have done something to her face, which was now a mottled red.

She stood on the pavement for a moment, while the landlord bolted the door behind her. Then she ploughed off, straight and strong up the street, dipping very slightly as she progressed.

A thin woman coming out of a shop with a basket full of groceries was nearly run down. She saved herself by a quick side step, and said, in reproof, 'Carnchew look where you're goin'?'

The massive woman halted, wheeled, and hit the thin woman in the eye. It was a beautiful, coordinated, unconscious movement, as full of grace and power as a backhand passing-shot by a tennis champion at the top of her form.

The thin woman went down, but was up again in a flash. She was no quitter. She kicked her opponent hard on the ankle. A uniformed policeman appeared, closely followed by Sergeant Gwilliam, who had been waiting round the corner and felt that it was time to intervene. The massive woman, thus beset, back-heeled at her first assailant, aimed a swinging blow with a carrier-bag full of bottles at the Constable, missed him, and hit Sergeant Gwilliam.

Some hours later Superintendent Palance said coldly, to Superintendent Haxtell, 'I take it that Sergeant Petrella is a reliable officer.'

'I have always found him so,' said Haxtell, equally coldly.

'This woman, to whom he seems, at some point, to have transferred his attention, is certainly not Mrs Coulman.'

'Apparently not,' said Haxtell. 'In fact she is a well-known local character called Big Bertha. She is also believed to hold the woman's drinking records for both draught and bottled beer south of the Thames.'

'Indeed?' Superintendent Palance considered the information carefully. 'There is no possibility, I suppose, that she and Mrs Coulman are leading a double life?'

'You mean,' said Haxtell, 'that the same woman is sometimes the respectable Mrs Coulman of Bond Road, Highside, and sometimes the alcoholic Bertha of Clapham? It's an attractive idea, but I'm afraid it won't wash. Bertha's prison record alone makes it an impossibility. During the month you've been watching Mrs Coulman, Bertha has, I'm afraid, appeared no less than four times in the Southwark Magistrates Court.'

'In that case,' said Palance reasonably, 'since the lady under observation was Mrs Coulman when she started, Sergeant Petrella must have slipped up at some point.'

'I agree,' said Haxtell. 'But where?'

'That is for him to explain.'

'It's a stark impossibility,' said Petrella, later that day. 'I *know* it was Mrs Coulman when she went into the pub. There's no back entrance. I mean that, literally. It's a sort of penthouse, built onto the front of the block. The landlord himself has to come out of one of the bar doors when he leaves. And our local people say he's perfectly reliable. They've got nothing against him at all.'

'Could she have done a quick-change act? Is there a ladies' lavatory, or some place like that?'

'Yes. There's a lavatory. And she could have gone into it, and changed into other clothes which she had ready in her suitcase. It's all right as a theory. It's when you try to turn it into fact that it gets difficult. I saw nine people coming out of that pub. The first two were business types from the saloon bar. The landlord didn't know them, but they seemed to know each other. And anyway they just dropped in for a whisky and out again. Then there was a boy and girl in the public bar.

They held hands most of the time and didn't weigh much more than nine stone nothing apiece.'

'None of them sounds very likely,' agreed Haxtell. 'And the three workmen were local characters, or so I gather. That leaves the woman and the sailor.'

'Right,' said Petrella. 'And since we know that the woman wasn't Mrs Coulman, it leaves the sailor. He was broadly the right size and shape and weight, and he was the only one carrying anything. Thinking it over, one can see that's significant. He had a kitbag over his shoulder.'

'Just how is a suitcase turned into a kitbag?'

'That part wouldn't be too difficult. The suitcase could easily be a sham. A fabric cover round a collapsible frame, which would fold up to almost nothing and go inside the kitbag with the wig and hat and coat and the rest of the stuff.'

'Where did the kitbag come from? Oh, I see. She would have had it inside the suitcase. One wave of the wand and a large woman with a large suitcase turns into a medium-sized sailor with a kitbag.'

'Right,' said Petrella. 'And there's only one drawback. The sailor was a man, not a woman at all.'

'You're sure?'

'Absolutely and completely sure,' said Petrella. 'He crossed the road and passed within a few feet of me. He was wearing bell-bottom trousers and a dark blue sweater. There are certain anatomical differences, you know. And Mrs Coulman was a very womanly woman.'

'A queenly figure,' agreed Haxtell. 'Yes, I see what you mean.'

'It's not only that,' said Petrella. 'A woman might get away with being dressed as a man on the stage. Or seen from a distance or from behind. But not in broad daylight, face to face in the street. A man's hair grows in quite a different way, and his ears are bigger, and—'

'All right,' said Haxtell. 'I'll take your word for it.' He paused and added, 'Palance thinks you fell asleep on the job, and Mrs Coulman slipped out when you weren't looking.'

'I know,' said Petrella. An awkward silence ensued.

Petrella said, 'Will they keep up the watch?'

'I should think they'd lay off her a bit,' said Haxtell. 'It's an expensive job, immobilising a couple of dozen men. And a dinosaur would be suspicious after yesterday's performance. I should think they'd let her run for a bit. There's no reason you shouldn't keep your eyes open, though—unofficially.'

Petrella devoted what time he could spare in the next six weeks to his self-appointed task. His landlady's married sister had a house in Bond Road, so he spent a lot of time in her front parlour and, after dark, prowling round No. 35, the end house on the other side of the road. He also made friends with the booking-clerks at Highside Station and Pond End Station; and spent an interesting afternoon in the German Section of the Foreign Office.

'One thing's clear enough,' he said to Haxtell. 'When she's on the job, she starts on the Underground. Taxis and buses are too easy to follow. If you go by Underground, the pursuit has got to come down with you. Or guard the exit of every Underground Station in London simultaneously, which is a stark impossibility. Anyway, I know that's what she does. She's been seen half a dozen times leaving Highside Station, carrying that trick suitcase. She books to any old station. She's only got to pay the difference at the other end. She's a bit more cautious, too, after that last fiasco. She won't get onto the train if there's any other passenger she can't account for on the platform. Sometimes she's let three or four trains go past.'

Haxtell reflected on all this, and said, 'It seems a pretty watertight system to me. How do you suggest we break in on it?'

'Well, I think we've got to take a chance,' said Petrella. 'In theory it'd be safer with a lot of people, but actually, I don't think it would work at all. That kind can always spot organised opposition. There's just a chance, if you'd let two or three of us try it, next time we get word that she's likely to be busy—'

'We'll see,' said Haxtell.

Three nights after these words were spoken, on a Saturday, the redoubtable twin brothers, Jack and Sidney Ponting, made entry into Messrs. Alfrey's West End establishment by forcing the skylight of an adjacent building, picking three separate locks, cutting their way through an eighteen-inch brick wall, and blowing the lock neatly out of the door of the new Alfrey strong room. When the staff arrived on Monday they found a mess of brickwork and twisted steel. The losses included sixty-four large rough diamonds deposited by a Greek ship-owner. They were to have formed the nuptial head-dress of his South American bride.

'It's a Ponting job,' said Superintendent Palance. 'It's got their registered trade mark all over it. Get after them quick. They're probably hiding up.'

But the Pontings were not hiding. They were at home, and in bed. They raised no objection to a search of their premises.

'It's irregular,' said Sidney. 'But what have we got to hide?'

'You boys have got your job to do,' said Jack. 'Get it finished, and we can get on with our breakfast.'

Palance came up to see Haxtell.

'They certainly did it. They most certainly did it. Equally certainly they've dumped the diamonds. And none of them has reached a receiver yet, I'm sure of that. And the Pontings use Mrs Coulman.'

'Yes,' said Haxtell. 'Well, we must hope to do better this time.'

'Are you set on trying it on your own?'

Palance held the same rank as Haxtell. But he was longer in service, and older in experience. Haxtell thought of these things and paused. He was well aware of the responsibility he was shouldering, and which he could so easily evade. Then he said,

'I really think the only way is to try it ourselves, quietly.'

'All right,' said Palance. He didn't add, 'And on your own head be it.' He was never a man to waste words.

Four days followed, during which Petrella attended to his other duties as well as he could by day, and prowled round the curtilage of No. 35 Bond Road by night. Four days in which Sergeant Gwilliam, Wilmot, and Mote were never out of reach of a telephone; and Superintendent Haxtell sweated.

On the fifth night Petrella gave the signal: Tomorrow's the day. And at eleven o'clock next morning, sure enough, the front door opened and Mrs Coulman peered forth. She was wearing her travelling coat and hat, and grasped in her muscular hand was the fabric-covered suitcase.

She walked ponderously down the road. However acute her suspicions may have been, there was nothing for them to feed on. For it is a fact that at that moment no one was watching her at all.

Ten minutes later she was purchasing a ticket at Highside Station. The entrance to the station was deserted. She waited placidly for the lift.

The lift and Sergeant Gwilliam arrived simultaneously. He was dressed as a workman, and he seemed to be in a hurry. He bought a ticket to the Elephant and Castle and got into the lift beside Mrs Coulman. In silence, and avoiding each other's eye, they descended to platform level. In silence they waited for the train.

When the train arrived, Sergeant Gwilliam hesitated. He seemed to have an eye on Mrs Coulman's movements. They approached the train simultaneously. At the very last moment Mrs Coulman stopped. Sergeant Gwilliam went on, the doors closed, and the train disappeared bearing the Sergeant with it.

Mrs Coulman returned to her seat on the platform and waited placidly. By the time the next train arrived, the only other occupants of the platform were three schoolgirls. Mrs Coulman got into the train, followed by the schoolgirls. Two stations later the schoolgirls got off. Mrs Coulman, from her customary seat beside the door, watched them go.

Thereafter, as the train ran south, she observed a succession of people getting on and off. There were three people she did not see. Petrella, with Mote and Wilmot, had entered the train at the station before her. Sergeant Gwilliam's planned diversion had given them plenty of time to get there. Petrella was in the first and the other two were in the last carriages of the train.

It was at Balham that Mrs Coulman finally emerged. Two women with shopping-bags, who had joined her carriage at Leicester Square, went with her. Also a commercial traveller with samples, whom she had watched join the next carriage at the Oval.

Petrella, Mote, and Wilmot all saw her go, but it was no part of their plan to follow her, so they sat tight.

At the next stop, all three of them raced for the moving stairs, hurled themselves into the street, and found a taxi.

'I'm off duty,' said the taxi-driver.

'Now you're on again,' said Petrella, and showed him his warrant card. 'Get us back to Balham Station, as quick as you can.'

The taxi-driver blinked, but complied. Petrella had his eye on his watch.

'She's had four minutes start,' he said, as they bundled out. 'You know what to do. Take every pub in your sector. And get a move on.'

The three men separated. There is no lack of public houses in that part of South London, but Petrella calculated that if they worked outwards from the station, taking a sector each, they could cover most of them quite quickly. It was the riskiest part of the scheme, but he could think of no way to avoid it.

He himself found her.

She was sitting quietly in the corner of the saloon bar of The Gatehouse, a big, newish establishment at the junction of the High Street and Trinity Road.

There was no convenient snack bar this time; there was very little cover at all. The best he could find was a trolley-bus shelter. If he stood behind it, it did at least screen him from the door.

The minutes passed, and added up to a quarter of an hour. Then to half an hour. During that time two people had gone in and three had come out, but none of them had aroused Petrella's interest. He knew, more or less, what he was looking for.

At last the door opened and a man emerged. He was a thick well set-up man, dressed in a close-fitting flannel suit which was tight enough across the shoulders and round the chest to exhibit his athletic frame. And he was carrying a small canvas bag of a type that athletes use to hold their sports gear.

He turned left, and swung off down the pavement with an unmistakable, aggressive masculine stride, a mature bull of the human herd, confident of his strength and purpose.

Petrella let him have the length of the street, and then trotted after him. This was where he had to be very careful. What he mostly needed was help. The chase swung back past the Underground and there he spotted Wilmot and signalled him across.

'In the grey flannel suit, carrying a bag,' he said. 'See him? Then get right after him, and remember, he's got eyes in the back of his head.'

Wilmot grinned all over his guttersnipe face. He was imaginatively dressed in a teddy-boy suit, and he fitted into the South London streets as easily as a rabbit into a warren.

'Doanchew worry,' he said, 'I won't lose him.'

Petrella fell back until he was a hundred yards behind Wilmot. He kept his eyes open for Mote. The more of them the merrier. There was a long, hard chase ahead.

He noticed Wilmot signalling.

'Gone in there,' said Wilmot.

'Where?'

'Small shop. Bit of the way up the side street.'

Petrella considered. 'Walk past,' he said. 'Take a note of the name and number on the shop. Go straight on, out of sight, to the other end. If he goes that way, you can pick him up. If he comes back I'll take him.'

Ten minutes went by. Petrella thought anxiously about back exits. But you couldn't guard against everything.

Then the man reappeared. He was carrying the same bag, yet it looked different. Less bulky but, by the swing of it, heavier.

He's dumped the hat and coat and the remains of the

suitcase at that accommodation address, thought Petrella. Even if we lose him, we know one of the Ponting hide-outs. But we mustn't lose him. That bag's got several thousand pounds' worth of stolen jewellery in it now.

Would it be best to arrest him, and give up any chance of tracing the receiver? The temptation was almost over-mastering. Only one thing stopped him. His quarry was moving with much greater freedom, as if convinced that there was no danger. Near the end of the run he would get cautious again. For the moment there was nothing to do but follow.

The man plunged back in the Underground; emerged at Waterloo; joined the queue at the Suburban Booking-Office. Petrella kept well clear for he owned a ticket which enabled him to travel anywhere on the railway.

Waterloo was a station whose layout he knew well. By positioning himself at the central bookstall, he could watch all three exits. His quarry had bought, and was eating, a meat pie. Petrella was quite unconscious of hunger. His eyes were riveted on the little bag, swinging heavily from the man's large fist. Once he put it down, but it was only to get out more money to buy an orange, which he peeled and ate neatly, depositing the remains in one of the refuse bins. Then he picked up the bag again and made for his train.

It was the electric line for Staines and Windsor. He went through the barrier and walked slowly up the train. There were very few passengers about, and it must have been near enough empty. He walked along the platform and climbed into a carriage at the far end.

Some instinct restrained Petrella. There were still five minutes before the train left. He waited. Three minutes later the man emerged from the carriage, walked very slowly back down the train, glancing into each carriage as he passed, and got into the carriage nearest to the barrier. The guard blew his whistle.

Two girls who had been sauntering towards the barrier broke into a run—Petrella ran with them. They pushed through the gate. The guard blew his whistle again; they jerked open the door of the nearest carriage and tumbled in together.

'We nearly left that too late,' said one of the girls. Her friend agreed with her. Petrella thought that they couldn't have timed it better. But he didn't say so. He was prepared to agree with everything they said. It was the quickest way he knew of getting on with people.

The girls were prepared to enjoy his company too. The dark vivacious one was called Beryl and the quieter mousy one was Doreen. They lived at Staines.

'Where are you getting out?' asked Beryl. 'Or is that a secret?'

'I haven't made my mind up yet,' said Petrella.

Beryl said he was a case. Doreen agreed.

The train ambled through dim-forgotten places like Feltham and Ashford. No one got out and no one got in. Petrella heard about a dance, and what had gone on afterwards in the car park. He said he was sorry he didn't live at Staines. It sounded quite a place.

'It's all right in summer,' said Doreen. 'It's a dump in winter. Here we are.'

The train drew up.

'Sure you won't change your mind?' said Beryl.

'Perhaps I will, at that,' said Petrella. Out of the corner of his eye he saw that his man had got out and was making his way along the platform.

'You'd better hurry up then. They'll take you on to Windsor.'

'That'd never do,' said Petrella. 'I forgot to warn her that I was coming.'

'Who?' said Doreen.

'The Queen.'

His man was safely past the ticket collector now.

'Come on,' said Beryl. They went past the collector together. 'Wouldn't you like some tea? There's a good place in the High Street.'

'There's nothing I'd like better, but I think I see my uncle waving to me.'

The girls stared at him. Petrella manœuvred himself across the open yard, keeping the girls between him and his quarry. The man had set off up the road without, apparently, so much as a backward glance, but Petrella knew that the most difficult part of the chase was at hand.

'I don't see your uncle,' said Beryl.

'There he is. Sitting in that taxi.'

'That's just the taxi-driver. I don't believe he's your uncle at all.'

'Certainly he is. How are you keeping, uncle?'

'Very fit, thank you,' said the taxi-driver, a middle-aged man with a brown bald head.

'There you are,' said Petrella. 'I'll have to say good-bye now. We've got a lot to talk about. Family business.'

The girls hesitated, and then withdrew, baffled.

'You a policeman?' said the taxi-driver. 'A detective something?'

'As a matter of fact, I am.'

'Following that man in the light suit? I thought as much. Very pretty, the way you got behind those girls. As good as a book.'

His quarry was now halfway up the long, straight empty

road, which leads from Staines Station to the riverside. He had stopped to light a cigarette, and in stopping he half turned.

'Keep behind my cab,' said the driver. 'That's right, well down. He's getting nervous. I'd say he's not far from wherever it is he's going to. Good as a book, isn't it? Do you read detective stories?'

The man was walking on again now. He was a full three hundred yards away.

'I don't want to lose him,' said Petrella. 'Not now. I've come a long way with him.'

'You leave it to me,' said the cab-driver. 'I've been driving round here for forty years. There isn't a footpath I don't know blindfold. Just watch which way he turns at the end.'

'Turning right,' said Petrella.

'All aboard.' The taxi shot out of the station yard, and the driver turned round in his seat to say, 'Might be making for the High Street, but if he wanted the High Street, why not take a bus from the other platform? Ten to one he's for the ferry.'

'I say, look out for that dog,' said Petrella.

The driver slewed back in his seat. Said, 'Effie Muggridge's poodle. Asking for trouble,' and accelerated. The dog shot to safety with a squeal of rage.

'Got to do this bit carefully,' said the driver as they reached the corner. 'Keep right down. Don't show so much as the tip of your nose, now.'

Petrella obeyed. The taxi rounded the corner, and over it, in a wave, flowed the unmistakable smell of the river on a hot day—weed and water and tar and boat varnish.

'He's in the ferry,' said the driver. 'Got his back to you. You can come up for air now.'

Petrella saw that a ferry punt ran from the steps beside a public house. There were three passengers on her, standing cheek by jowl, and the ferryman was untying and pushing out. He realised how hopeless he would have been on his own.

'What do we do?' he said.

'Over the road bridge, and back down the other side. Plenty of time, if we hurry.'

'What were we doing just now?'

The driver chuckled throatily. Petrella held his breath and counted ten, slowly. Then they were crossing Staines Bridge.

'Not much traffic just now,' said the driver. 'You ought to see it at weekends.' They did a skid turn to the left, and drew up in the yard of another riverside inn.

'There's two things he could do,' said the driver. 'Walk up the towpath to the bridge. There's no way off it. Or he could come down the path—you see the stile?—the one that comes out there. I'll watch the stile. You go through that gate and down the garden—I know the man who owns it. He won't mind. You can see the towpath from his summer-house. If you hear my horn, come back quick.'

With a feeling that some power much stronger than himself had taken charge, Petrella opened a gate and walked down a well-kept garden, full of pinks and roses and stone dwarfs with pointed hats. At the bottom was a summer-house. In the summer-house he found a small girl reading a book.

'Are you coming to tea?' she said.

'I'm not sure,' said Petrella. 'I might be going to the cinema.'

'You'll have to hurry then. The big film starts in five minutes.'

Behind him a hooter sounded off.

'I'll run then,' said Petrella. He scooted back up the garden. The girl never raised her eyes from her book.

'Just come out,' said the taxi-driver. 'Going nicely. We'll give him twenty yards. Can't afford too much leeway here. Tricky navigation.'

He drove slowly towards the turning, and stopped just short of it.

'Better hop out and look,' he said. 'But be careful. He's stopped twice already to blow his nose. We're getting pretty warm.'

Petrella inched up to the corner, and poked his head round the wall. The man was going away from him, walking along the pavement, but slowly. It was an area of bungalows, some on the road, some on the river bank, with a network of private ways between.

The taxi-driver had got out and was breathing down the back of his neck.

'Got to take a chance,' he said. 'If we follow him, he'll spot us for sure. I'll stay here. If he turns right, I'll mark it. If he turns left he's for Riverside Drive. You nip down that path, and you can cut him off.'

Petrella took the path. It ran between high hedges of dusty bramble and thorn; hot and sweet-smelling in the sun. It was the dead middle of the afternoon, with hardly a dog stirring. Petrella broke into a jog trot, then slowed for the road ahead.

As he reached the corner, he heard footsteps on the pavement. Their beat was unmistakable. It was his man, and he was walking straight towards him.

Petrella looked round for cover and saw none. He thought for a moment of diving into the shallow ditch, but realised that he would merely be attracting attention. The footsteps had stopped. Petrella held his breath. He heard the click of a latch. Feet on flagstones. The sudden purring of an electric bell.

The chase was over.

————

'I'm not saying,' said Palance, 'that it wasn't a success. It was a success. Yes.'

Haxtell said nothing. He knew just how Palance was feeling and sympathised with him.

'We've got back the Alfrey diamonds, and we've got our hands on that man at Staines. An insurance broker, of all things, and quite unsuspected. Judging from what we found in the false bottom of a punt in his boat-house he's been receiving stolen goods for years. And we've stopped up one of the Ponting middlemen at that tobacconist's in Balham. A little more pressure and we may shop the Pontings, too.'

'Quite,' said Haxtell sympathetically.

'All the same, it was a mad way to do it. You can't get over that, Haxtell. How long have you known that Coulman was a man?'

'We realised that as soon as we started to think about it,' said Haxtell. 'It was obviously impossible for a real, middle-aged buxom woman to turn into a convincing man. But, conversely, it was easy enough for a man dressed as a woman, padded and powdered and wigged, to whip it all off and turn back quickly into his own self.'

'Then do you mean to say,' said Palance, 'that the Mrs Coulman my men were watching for a month—doing her shopping, gossiping, hanging out her washing, having tea with the vicar—was really a man all the time?'

'Certainly not,' said Haxtell. Observing symptoms of apoplexy, he said, 'That was Mrs Coulman. She had a brother—two, actually. One was killed by the Nazis. The other one got over to England. Whenever she had a big job on hand, her brother would come along at night. The house she lived in was at the end of the row. There was a way in at the side. He could slip in late at night without anyone seeing him. Next day he'd dress up in his sister's coat and hat and go out and do the job. She stayed quietly at home.'

'When you realised this,' said Palance, 'wouldn't it have been better to do the job properly? You could have had a hundred men if necessary.'

'It wouldn't have worked. Not a chance. You can't beat a methodical man like Coulman by being more methodical. He'll outdo you every time. The Underground, the change of clothes, the careful train check before he started for Staines, the long straight road, and the ferry. What you want with a man like that is luck—and imagination.'

'Yes, but—' said Palance.

'Method, ingenuity, system,' said Superintendent Haxtell. 'You'll never beat a German at his own game. Look at the Gestapo. They tried for five years and even they couldn't pull it off. The one thing they lacked was imagination. Perhaps it was a good thing. A little imagination, and they might have caused a lot more bother.'